ALSO BY AUDREY STEVES

The Soul Collector Saga
The Soul Collector
The Dark Angel

The Anthologies
Out of the Cauldron: A Fall Fantasy Collection

THE DARK ANGEL

AUDREY STEVES

THE DARK ANGEL

AUDREY STEVES

For those who refuse to be consumed by the dark.

I see you.

God of Death's
Castle

Crossroads

The White
Tree

Aiden's
Castle

REALM OF

SOULS

PROLOGUE

Two Months Earlier
Aiden

His skin burned with her touch. Behind him, Esme's sobs were soft, like she was struggling to keep them silent. The sound followed Aiden as he quickly strode away from the tent where he left her.

Part of him wanted to storm back into the tent and hold her. To apologize and promise to keep her safe and happy. But he couldn't allow himself the luxury.

His friends sat near the fire with Esme's family, laughing and carefree as if the immortal he once thought of as a brother hadn't just shown up to kill them all and take Esme from him. He still couldn't comprehend the reasoning behind his old friend's actions. Aiden knew his father was skeptical about letting someone with Esme's power remain in the mortal realm. He'd considered having a Soul Collector brought to his realm for generations. Aiden just hadn't expected Esme to be the one he brought before his father.

The thought of Esme at his father's mercy threatened to weaken the warrior's knees. He stormed through the campground, eager to find

Hakan and order the guard to spar until they were both bloodied and limp with exhaustion.

The campground was otherwise silent, empty. The former festivities had dispersed with Ephraim's arrival, and the bloodshed his presence caused.

"Aiden!" Leander Ayres' voice called to him over his family's trilling laughter.

Reluctantly, Aiden turned toward the mortal. Again, it struck Aiden how drastically different this man was from his daughter. Where she hid her warmth behind fierce determination, Leander let the world see the tenderness he carried. Not to mention Leander's hair was golden brown and his skin pale, while Esme took after her mother with dark curls and bronze skin. He sauntered over to Aiden with a casual gait, though the stiff smile on his face was unusual for the man.

"Can I have a moment of your time?" he asked when he was close enough not to be overheard. Mousa, the eldest of the Loutari children, watched the conversation intently, though he remained seated beside the young blonde woman who'd joined their party.

Aiden nodded, electing to follow Esme's father toward their caravan. A form appeared in the shadows, catching his attention. Esme kept her eyes on her feet as she quietly made her way toward her siblings seated around the fire. He ached to go to her. He had never ached for another person in such a way, and he didn't know how to make it stop.

Seraphine wrapped her arm around Esme's shoulders, casting a glance in Aiden's direction. That gesture alone told him enough — his friend would look after Esme when he couldn't allow himself to get too close.

Frustration at his predicament rolled through him but he hid it well. He always did. The immortal prince learned long ago to hide his emotions behind a facade. If the world thought there was someone he cared about, then his enemies would stop at nothing to destroy them. And that was a fate he could not leave Esme to face. If anyone knew what she meant to him...it was a weakness he could not allow himself to show.

Tarsa appeared from the shadows of the surrounding trees. The warrior shook her head, an indication that Ephraim had truly disappeared.

That news disturbed him more than it should have. Ephraim had been one of his greatest friends for as long as Aiden could remember. He had cruel and malicious tendencies, yes. But, for most of Aiden's life, they had been the best of friends. It was only in recent decades they began to grow apart as Aiden was forced into the duties required of an heir, and Ephraim's position in Death's guard remained stagnant.

Leander ushered him into the caravan. Without the decorated fabrics which usually hung throughout the caravan, the space felt dim and empty.

The door closed and locked behind him. Had he been a mortal, his heartrate might have spiked at that notion. Instead, centuries of warrior training made him still. Aiden stood with his back to the wall as Leander moved to join his wife at the small table where Esme performed her duties.

"We have a favor to ask you," Leander began slowly. He kept his eyes trained on Aiden, studying him in a way that made him feel scrutinized.

Aiden nodded, silent permission to continue.

Elira, Esme's mother, took a steadying breath. "We need to make a deal with your father."

Aiden wasn't sure what he was expecting, but it wasn't that. Shock made the immortal's limbs grow cold as he studied the two humans before him.

"I'd advise against it," he said into the resounding silence.

Elira straightened her spine. "We need to protect Esme."

"Making a deal with my father is not the way to do that." Rumors of the God of Death's cruelty had spread far in this realm. He'd heard the tales mortals told each other of Death's love of violence and pain. But no one truly knew the conniving man behind the title like Aiden did.

"Well, the deal our ancestors made with you hasn't worked out well for our family either," Leander retorted.

Aiden flinched, the gesture small enough to go unnoticed by the mortals. Aiden was still a boy when he made that deal. No more than a young fool who wanted to get in his father's good graces and jumped at the opportunity. Ephraim had led him to it, had persuaded him this would be the best way to convince the God of Death that Aiden was ready for more responsibilities. That he wasn't still the immature child he once was. Instead, it caused a rift between Death and his son. A rift that had yet to be mended.

"Please," Elira whispered on a shaky breath.

Aiden couldn't look at her. Seeing Elira on the verge of tears reminded him of Esme, who he'd left only moments before shedding her own tears.

"We know Ephraim will come back for her," Leander interjected. "And we know the likelihood of our survival when he does."

"I promised to keep you safe," Aiden said firmly.

Leander smiled sadly. "This isn't an insult to your abilities, Aiden. Esme is what's important here. She needs to be protected; to live a long and happy life."

"She can't do that if she's worried for us," Elira added. "Esme has always looked after her family. Trying to keep us all safe will get her killed. We know this."

Aiden gritted his teeth so hard he wondered if they might break. "You know the risks of making a deal with my father." The mortals nodded, fiery determination stiffening their spines.

Leander held out an envelope. "Take this to him as soon as you can."

The prince stared at the envelope. He knew what it held. He knew the words would seal their fates as much as the words he had spoken with their ancestor did all those years ago. Esme's heart would shatter at the contents of this letter. This small envelope had the ability to tear her world apart.

"Please," Elira said again, reading the doubt in his eye.

Aiden stuffed the envelope into his pocket. "I cannot guarantee he will accept this, but he may take you up on your deal sooner than you'd expect. It would be best if you prepare Esme before he reads the letter. Once he accepts, no one will be able to speak of it. No one will be able to warn her. And no one will be able to physically interfere."

Leander looked at his wife, and that one glance contained so much pride and love Aiden wondered if there might be another way.

"We'll prepare them," he said to the demon prince. "Mousa and Cordelia will know. And when the time comes, I know you will help Esme through it."

"And if my father decides to twist your offer?" he asked. The two shared an uncertain look and his chest tightened. "If this letter isn't worded in the exact manner to restrict any loopholes my father may find, he will take advantage of that."

The mortal man nodded, gripping his wife's hand tightly in his own. "We were careful."

Aiden left the caravan, ignoring the questioning gazes from those by the fire. It wasn't until he was hidden in the shadows that the man's words finally sank in.

Hakan stepped forward, frowning at his prince. "What did the mortals want?"

Aiden's blood went cold as he watched the family from the shadows. Esme smiled, hiding the pain he could still see lingering in her eyes as her mother brushed a kiss along her brow.

Leander pulled Mousa aside, leading him toward the caravan and away from listening ears. Aiden glanced toward each member of Esme's family before settling on her and the smile she wore as she held onto her youngest sister.

"My prince?" Hakan asked, regaining Aiden's attention.

The demon prince pushed his emotions aside, stepping into his title role easily. "Deliver this to my father immediately. Be sure it is in his hands before you return."

His friend studied the envelope briefly before glancing at the family over his shoulder. "Does she know?"

Aiden frowned. "No."

Hakan didn't say anything more before turning to leave, but Aiden could hear the words he didn't say. The doubt Hakan exuded ignited the worry in his veins.

Aiden watched the fire dance across Esme's skin, filling her with the warmth she radiated toward everyone around her. That fire within her would be snuffed out as soon as this letter landed in his father's hands. And there was nothing he could do to protect her from the pain it would cause her.

ONE

I WAS GOING TO kill my husband.

Husband.

The word sounded like filth in my mind. In the days since my family's murder, I'd thought of many ways to kill the immortal I once thought I loved. Now, I was married to him.

I glanced toward the mark decorating the back of my hand. The vines and thorns twirled around my wrist and down the third finger on my left hand, a rose settled in the center of it all with stupid wings and a stupid crown. I buried the hand in my pocket, unable to look at it any longer without angry tears blurring my vision.

The ceremony had ended an hour ago, giving me time to collect my emotions in the privacy of the tent since Aiden's reveal of the mark's true meaning.

My stomach turned again as the skin beneath the marriage mark warmed. The connection I once had with Aiden felt deeper now that we shared this mark. I could feel him through the other end of our bond, pacing outside the tent while I sulked in private. My only hope for this grotesque marriage was that it would keep my remaining family safe.

The bodies of my slaughtered family were probably no more than ash on the wind by now. They deserved to be buried with Nonna, far in the deserted lands of wanderer territory. Instead, they were murdered by King Elroy in front of me. I could still feel their blood pooling beneath my knees, could still hear their pleas as their throats were cut. And every time I closed my eyes, I saw one of them die.

My family was with the stars now, where Kesson and Nonna were sure to welcome them.

I brushed a fallen tear from my cheek, my promise to Kesson fresh in my mind. I forced my pain away, burying it deep in my chest along with the ache caused by Aiden's betrayal and my family's deaths. Anger rose quickly, replacing the hollow spot where my heart once lived. A dark power fed into my thirst for vengeance. The two braided together in a content hum as I focused on my goal.

With a fortifying breath I pushed it all away. I pushed back against the pain and rage. Against the hurt and exhaustion that weighed down my bones. I pushed until the threat of tears was gone, until my breathing returned to normal and my pulse slowed.

I couldn't let Aiden win. To do what needed to be done to save my brother and sister, I had to feel nothing. I could feel no pain, no sorrow. I had to be empty – a shell. So that's what I became.

The flap to the tent opened, revealing Seraphine hovering nervously outside. Her freckled cheeks were rosy with shame as she stepped further into the space.

"How are you?" she asked gently.

I adopted Aiden's expression of indifference. Until I could find a way to kill the demon and protect my remaining family, I could pretend I wasn't breaking inside.

I made my voice sound cold and demanding. "What's taking so long?"

Seraphine stepped closer, gaze imploring. "We're packing everything now. This tent is next."

I stood from the small bed, thankful I wasn't expected to share it with Aiden tonight. "Fine. I'll wait outside."

The warrior stepped aside as I marched through the tent flap and into the chilly autumn air. We were farther north than I'd ever been. I wasn't even sure I'd ever seen a map that showed the location of the white tree.

The Angelwood Forest blocked any trace of sunlight from view, casting the ground in shadow. Trees stood tall, towering over the horses and the immortals that moved around them. A few trees were short and stout, but all had leaves in vibrant shades of russet and bronze.

I felt Killian watching me anxiously as I stepped away from the group. I wasn't sure where Aiden was, and I didn't particularly care. The less I had to see him before I found a way to kill him, the better.

Ignoring the glances I felt from the demons as they packed the tents, I followed the path toward the white tree. Its existence had always been thought of as no more than a legend. It was entirely different standing before it now, knowing its ties to my family, and now to my soul.

The tree stood taller than any of the others and wider than a boulder. Everything about it was white. The bark, the leaves, the branches, all white as snow and immovable in the breeze.

Light erupted from the tree, enveloping me in its warmth. Power danced across my skin in a thousand tiny pricks. It was mesmerizing.

I stepped closer, reaching a hand for the bark as the strange tree's power held me in its thrall.

"Careful," a low voice cautioned behind me. "You don't want to risk making the same mistake your ancestor did and enter into a debt you can't pay."

I fought against the sudden rise in my rage, turning to face the demon that stood half cloaked in shadow. His wings remained hidden with his dark magic, but the cool look in his eyes lingered as he gazed at the tree.

"This tree has been in existence for a millennium," Aiden said from where he casually leaned against a smaller tree. "Some say it has even grown sentient. You don't want to touch something so unpredictable."

His whiskey-colored hair was a deeper shade of chestnut in the faint light, the tied-back sides allowing me to truly see the guise of the Prince of Death.

"Why should I believe you?" I asked, taking a step closer to the tree. I was glad my voice sounded steady, unbothered. "How do I know the tree won't break this curse on my bloodline if I touch it?"

I watched as he collected himself. Whatever he'd been about to say vanished from his eyes the longer he studied me.

"It won't erase what has already come to pass." Though his expression remained blank, I could hear the note of sorrow in his voice.

My heart sank, the little hope that lingered vanishing entirely. I turned back to the tree, refusing to let him see the devastation his words brought me.

My hand fell to my side, resolute. Though I could feel power from this tree, I could also feel a similar power through the marriage bond that tied Aiden and I together.

"We'll be at my castle before daybreak," he said, still watching from the shadows.

"And then what?" A breeze filtered through the trees, touching every branch and leaf except those on the white tree. It made me wonder what sort of power this tree truly contained, and if there was one like it in the Wood of Rune where the secrets of the angels were kept.

I closed my eyes against that thought. Prince Elias and I had set out to venture to the Wood of Rune in search of the weapon that could kill a demon, rumored to be the only one in existence and hidden amongst the angels. Now my friend lay dying, possibly already dead.

Tears pricked my eyes again as I let that thought pull me deeper into the void. I pushed the emotion away, refusing to let it threaten the emptiness.

"Esme?" he asked, closer now. I hadn't heard him move. Sometimes it was easy to forget he wasn't the same boy I thought I knew. The boy I'd known half my life, and adored nearly as long, was no boy at all. He was the Prince of Death, the monster responsible for the death of my entire family and the curse upon my bloodline.

"How are you?" he asked, repeating Seraphine's earlier inquiry.

My jaw clenched painfully. I was angry. Sad. Broken. Dying..... Empty. "Fine." His gaze was full of pity as he watched me. "Don't you dare pity me. You killed my family—"

Aiden flinched ever so slightly. "I did no such thing." His jaw clamped shut with a snap.

"You did. You gave us all over to the king so you could whisk me away to your realm for your father's sake." Emotions I was fighting to keep hidden cracked through my shell, threatening to spill out. I wrapped my arms around my middle, fighting off the growing chill.

Aiden didn't respond. His jaw clenched again, strained.

"You have no right to pity me, or mourn my family when you are the reason they're dead," I repeated coolly.

A chilling laugh echoed through the trees, making my skin crawl. Aiden's hand shot out to pull me behind him, shielding me with his body as if protecting me was second nature to him.

"Is the happy couple fighting so soon after the wedding? What a shame." Ephraim stepped from the shadows, placing his back to the white tree so he was silhouetted in the dark. His horns curled from his hairline and cradled his skull in a deadly caress. Even his grey, feathered wings looked menacing as they stretched out wide behind him.

I felt, more than heard, Tarsa and Hakan in the trees as they positioned themselves not far from Ephraim's sides. Killian and Seraphine appeared on either side of Aiden and me, hands slack at their sides where knives hid beneath loose clothing.

Aiden's voice was cold as death. "Why are you here, Ephraim?"

The immortal chuckled again, sending a shiver down my spine. "Well, I was here for your bride, but it seems that isn't necessary anymore."

Confusion knotted in my gut. "What do you want with me? Aiden is already taking me to his father."

Ephraim's eyes briefly flashed to Aiden. The cold touch I felt a moment ago intensified as he locked me in his gaze. "I can give you what he can't."

"I don't want anything from either of you." My voice was surprisingly steady.

The immortal smiled at my retort. "You want revenge. That is something he cannot give you, but I can."

"Is that so?" I asked, not believing a word he said. The essence in my chest fluttered at his presence, eager to respond to my igniting anger, but almost hesitant to touch him.

His smile grew, more a flash of teeth than a grin. "It is."

"What gives you the right to offer her whatever she may seek?" Aiden's anger radiated from him as he stood at my shoulder, muscles tensed for a fight.

"Because," the immortal said, spreading his wings and stretching his arms in a welcoming gesture, "I am the Angel of Life. And only I can give her the revenge that lives in her heart."

TWO

EPHRAIM'S WORDS ECHOED THROUGH the forest. Behind me, Seraphine shifted uncertainly as she positioned herself closer to my shoulder, ready to pull me away should Ephraim attack. Aiden, however, remained frozen in place. I wasn't even certain he was breathing.

"You're lying," I said. Ephraim's gaze slid to me, causing a chill to dance along my skin.

"What do you feel when we are near each other, Soul Collector?" he asked casually.

Aiden's breath hitched in his throat, his hand twitching toward one of the many knives strapped at his waist. The warriors surrounding us sensed his unease as they too pulled their weapons free, awaiting bloodshed.

I swallowed, nerves tightening my throat. "Nothing unusual."

The angel shook his head, icy blue gaze unyielding. "You know that's not true."

Aiden's focus slid to me, a silent plea to contradict the immortal's claim. I'd nearly forgotten that Aiden mentioned he once considered Ephraim a brother. They'd probably known each other for centuries.

Part of me hoped this betrayal of his former friend hurt even half as bad as the betrayal I felt from him.

"A void," I said. Ephraim nodded, urging me to continue. "When you're near I feel a chill colder than any winter I've known. And when I look inside you, I see nothing. There is no soul within you."

I froze. Angels didn't have souls. Inside, Ephraim would only ever be a void; an empty, cavernous shell. The angel smiled maliciously as my thoughts finally caught up with everything the essence had been trying to tell me all along. Uncertain, I glanced toward Aiden.

The demon stared at me, dumbfounded. For just a moment I saw the shock play across his features as his shoulders slumped and his eyes went wide. But like usual with the demon, his emotions vanished between one breath and the next.

"So now you know," Ephraim said with a mocking bow. "I am the only person in existence who can give your bride the revenge her heart seeks, while you can only give her excuses and half-hearted apologies."

"Is that why you're here now? To twist her mind against us?" Hakan asked in his deep, steady voice.

Ephraim's eyes were only for me. "King Elroy made a deal with me long ago. One that promised you to me. But he was unable to keep you for more than a summer before your beloved took you from Elroy's castle and returned you to your family."

My stomach plummeted, filling the emptiness with a spark of pain. For months I'd wondered why the king tore me from my family. Why I, of all the wanderers, had been forced to endure his torment.

Aiden's hand clenched beside me, fighting off an emotion I couldn't read.

"You've appeared in Esme's life many times in the past year, and every time you have been unsuccessful in your attempts to take her,"

Aiden said, voice tight with anger. "Do not presume to think you will be successful this time either."

"Oh, I know I won't be taking her today." Ephraim shrugged. "But now there is no reason for me to hide in the shadows. You will be seeing me again. The fun is only beginning."

"She is my betrothed," Aiden said hotly. "My protection extends to her now, and to her family."

"Don't you mean what's left of her family?" The smile Ephraim flashed sent my pulse racing through my veins. "There are ways around that, my friend."

I blinked and he was gone, as if he'd never been there.

Tarsa and Hakan spun around, searching through the surrounding forest for any sign of the angel.

My eyes remained fixed on the spot where Ephraim previously stood. The one person Elias and I were after to aid in my revenge was *Ephraim*. He was the only person in existence with knowledge of a weapon that could kill a demon. And I needed that weapon if I planned to save my siblings and break this curse.

Slowly, the warriors began to relax; all but Aiden, who remained frozen. His posture was stiff, almost like he was forcing himself to remain here when he'd rather flee and hunt Ephraim to the ends of the realm. From the fury in his eyes, I knew he'd love to kill the angel.

"We need to keep moving," Tarsa finally said when Aiden still didn't move. "She'll be safer in the castle."

Aiden's gaze found mine. There was a battle in his eyes between giving in to his anger and his unexpected need to protect me that his cool exterior couldn't hide.

"Killian, Tarsa, grab the bags. Hakan and Sera, mind the horses. I'm taking Esme now. Before he comes back."

The others moved into action immediately, heeding their prince's words.

"Can he enter your realm?" I asked as I watched the warriors move through the trees with silent haste.

"Clearly," Aiden said curtly. "He's lived there right under my father's nose for nearly 300 years. I doubt he'll have any issue getting back in. Even now that he's revealed himself."

"But how he managed to get into our realm in the first place is the real question," Seraphine piped up as she wrangled the horses. "Angels shouldn't be able to use the white tree to enter Death's realm."

Aiden stilled, eyes narrowed in the direction of the white tree. "There should be no other way."

"And yet he's found one." Tarsa's voice was clipped and cold as she tossed a bag over her shoulder.

"What I don't get is why he'd bother revealing his identity when none of us suspected him," Killian said as he tossed bags over his shoulders.

Aiden considered his words. "He's planning something."

Tarsa snorted. "Obviously. But other than Esme, you have nothing he wants."

"That you know of," I muttered. I hadn't expected to say the words aloud, though as the others froze for a beat at my words, I could almost see their minds working through every possible answer.

"Why don't you just kill him?" I asked when they continued to stare around the forest uncertainly.

Tarsa scoffed. "Angels are not so easily killed. Or have you forgotten how quickly Ephraim heals?"

I bit my tongue against a retort. I'd seen all too clearly how fast Ephraim could heal. Not to mention he possessed enough magic to have his hand returned after Aiden cut it off. But I hadn't realized that made them truly immortal.

Aiden held his hand out to me. "Come. We must go now. We'll ride on horseback once we're in my realm."

I scowled at his outstretched hand. "Just lead the way. I'll follow."

"We have to go through together," he explained slowly. "You're not familiar with the magic in the tree."

"Then I'll follow closely."

Before anything more could be said, Aiden bent to toss me over his shoulder. I squealed as my face collided with the middle of his back.

"I hate this," I fumed.

Aiden merely grunted his response.

Unable to see, I cradled my chin in my palms as I hung there, once again reduced to the role of a limp doll for him to carry and protect. I was tired of being useless.

My gaze slid toward Killian, who walked a few paces away. I could see the extra weapons he carried strapped to one of the packs on his back. His chosen weapon, a bow and quiver of arrows, remained slung over his other shoulder.

I studied the knives he carried. An ordinary knife would not kill a demon, but it would do enough damage to keep me safe when I needed it.

The white tree lit the space around us as we neared. Killian stepped closer, just within arm's reach as he handed Aiden something I couldn't see.

While the others were distracted, I slipped a knife from his pack and shoved it up my sleeve, holding it there until I could conceal it within my boot.

Aiden's chest rumbled with softly spoken words. As soon as he fell silent, the tree brightened like the midday sun. I closed my eyes against the harsh white light. After only a brief moment, I was surrounded by darkness again.

A chill in the air raised the hair along my neck as Aiden gently set me on my feet. I stared around at the forest. I couldn't hear a single bird flitting through the branches, or any predators skulking across the forest floor. The only sounds were my short breaths and the nervous pounding of my heart. It was eerie.

We mounted the horses in silence, Aiden and I once again riding together. Tarsa and Killian moved ahead, leading the way while Seraphine and Hakan opted to take the rear as we advanced through the trees. Though it was early autumn in Cordovia, the air felt cooler here and the forest floor was already littered with fallen leaves.

The bare trees filled every corner of my vision as we wove through the overgrown path, close on Killian's heels.

"Scared, Princess?" Aiden said. Though his tone was mocking I could hear the undercurrent of another emotion he worked to keep hidden.

I glowered even though he couldn't see it from his place behind me. "No." He chuckled like he could sense the lie for what it was.

A breeze blew, sending a shiver along my skin. I wasn't sure how time changed between this realm and my own, but it felt closer to winter here, like several months had passed since my family's demise.

I forced the thought away and focused on my surroundings. Every tree looked the same. They were all too tall and too thin, but sturdy against the wind. Above, barely visible through the overgrown branches, the moon perched high in the sky. Its silver aura cast a faint light on our path.

We traveled like that for hours. The warriors remained silent and stoic while my breathing gradually grew ragged and harsh in the quiet night.

When the moon finally settled along the edge of the horizon, and the sky before us began to lighten with the beginnings of dawn, we stopped at the top of a hill. Below, a wide river split the valley in two.

"Where are we?" I asked as we remained perched at the top of the hill.

Aiden settled a hand at my waist, causing me to grow still. "This is the Realm of Souls," he said. "There," he pointed to my left, "is the Crossroads where souls go after death. Beyond that, deep in the northern mountains, is my father's castle."

"Is that where we're going?" My heart beat erratically at the thought.

Aiden shook his head. "We're going to my home. *Our* home now."

I followed his gaze due east. The beginnings of another forest could just be seen across the other hill's peak, and in the middle of it sat a large tower of stone. Its spires jutted far above the treetops and its vast width looked menacing even from this distance.

"That is not my home," I whispered. My heart ached to return to Cordovia, where Mousa and Cordelia were all that was left of my shattered family.

I felt Aiden's gaze on my face, scrutinizing my words. I forced myself to feel nothing. Empty.

"We need to keep moving," Hakan said from behind. "If your father's scouts see us out at this hour, he'll know what you've done. She needs to get inside."

Without a word, Aiden led the way through the valley, and we arrived at the gates of his castle all too soon.

Trees sprouted from the ground in an organized manner. A clear path led us through the small forest directly to large black gates. Spikes jutted from the top of the gate, nearly as tall as the trees, their message clear: do not enter.

A guard appeared out of nowhere and bowed at the sight of Aiden. "My Prince," he said in greeting.

The gate swung inward a minute later, revealing the yard beyond.

Tarsa took the horses from Seraphine, leading them around the castle where I assumed the stables were located. I could feel Seraphine's eyes on me, though she didn't speak. Her trepidation was nearly palpable as she strode at Killian's side.

"Welcome home, Princess," Aiden murmured in my ear.

I glared at the building before me. The guards patrolling the wall cast wary and curious glances my way, though they didn't dare question their prince's intentions.

The castle was built with varying shades of grey stone. Large windows were set every few feet, allowing the morning light to enter the rooms beyond the wall.

Aiden gripped my hand tightly, a silent urge to follow him. The warmth sparking in my chest threatened to melt the cool shield of emptiness. I quickly slipped the knife into my boot while our companions took in the castle, clearly glad to be home.

The closer I got to the castle doors, the more my hesitation grew. I knew what needed to be done, but what if the time came to kill Aiden and I couldn't do it?

Aiden paused in the large foyer. I could feel his growing discomfort as Killian, Seraphine, and Hakan filtered in after us. Servants and guards froze at the sight of me, their eyes drifting to our joined hands.

I watched the questions cross their expressions before they quickly bowed and scurried through different doors.

A staircase encased in the same white marble that covered the floor towered before us. I spun on my heel, staring at the height of the stairs as they gently curved around the tower above. There had to be nearly seven floors in this tower. I wondered how many rooms it held, and what they were used for.

Aiden pulled me down the hall to the right. Guards straightened at our approach, and servants ducked into rooms and hid behind doors. Whether they feared their prince or the presence of a stranger, I couldn't be sure.

My boots echoed off the white marbled floor as he led me through twists and turns in the hallway. Occasionally, I was able to see into an empty room and quickly take note of the space within. Some were empty, and some were so cluttered I wondered how anyone could walk through them.

Eventually, we came across another stairway, this one much smaller and more private than the one in the entry. Aiden quickly led us up three flights before coming to the top of the small tower.

My mind spun with what might come next. From the number of guards that patrolled this hall, I feared I would find myself in a cell, rather than an apartment.

We came to a stop at the very last door. The wood was dark, contrasting with the brilliance of the pale floors and bare walls.

Aiden paused for a breath, casting me a nervous glance before he opened the door and ushered me inside.

My breath left my lungs in a rush of air. This room was huge. A large fireplace was centered on the wall to my left, and a door to what I assumed was a closet was tucked beside it in the corner.

I stepped further into the room marveling at its decorum. Windows covered the back wall from floor to ceiling, revealing the last of the stars fading away as the light of day spread.

"This will be your room," Aiden said from his position in the doorway. I could feel him watching my every expression as I took in the room.

Soft sofas and cushioned chairs filled the space before the hearth. I ran my hand along the back of the settee, appreciating the soft, violet fabric.

I glanced toward the curtains tucked into the corner. They were the same shade as the furniture, only hemmed with gold in a pattern that resembled the night's stars.

My gaze sought out the large four poster bed to my right. The sheets were brilliant gold, the thick blanket laid across the bed a red so deep it looked like wine.

A crack split through the control on my emotions at my family's colors that filled every corner of the room.

"I thought you might like it better if it felt a little like home," Aiden said softly. I could hear the gentle vulnerability in his tone, and yet all I could focus on was my anger.

I turned to him, forcing the painful memory of my family away. The warmth in his eyes vanished into the cool, detached mask of the Prince of Death as he noted my expression.

"Anything else?" I asked, commanding my voice to remain as cold as his heart.

He glanced toward the door hidden in the corner near the hearth. "My room is just through there. A guard will be posted outside your door at all hours, but should you need anything please don't hesitate to ask."

I glowered at him. "Is the guard to keep me in my room unless you say otherwise?"

"No," he said slowly. "The guards are for your protection."

I turned away, dismissing him. "Fine."

Aiden was silent for a moment. I could feel him struggling over his next words before he left in silence, closing the door behind him. I could hear his quick footsteps as he retreated down the hall the way we'd come.

Left alone, I stood before the windows. The balcony beyond was wide and connected to Aiden's next to it.

I snorted, turning my back on the view. Instead, I ran my hands over the red fabric covering the bed. Everything in here reminded me of my family. The rich reds that we used to paint our lips, the deep purples that we wore on our skirts. Even the gold stars that we would sew onto our clothes. Everything felt like home, and yet I felt like a stranger here. It wasn't the warm, welcoming feeling I was used to when I saw my family's colors. It was a painful reminder of everything I'd lost, thanks to Aiden's betrayal.

A knock sounded at the door, pulling me from my pity.

Seraphine's head poked through, and Killian was quick to follow as they stood in the doorway.

Seraphine offered a tentative smile. "Are you settling in all right?"

I merely stared at her. Out of the group of immortals that claimed to want to protect me and my family, I had grown closest to these two. Apart from Aiden.

Seraphine's smile faltered. "Is there anything we can get you? Breakfast should be up shortly."

Again, I couldn't bring myself to respond. My heart fluttered angrily in my chest as I watched them study me.

"We're sorry," Killian piped up before Seraphine could silence him. "We didn't know what was going to happen. Honest."

"Is that so?" I asked, voice as cold as the breeze outside.

Killian nodded, his eyes pleading with me to understand, making him look no older than an adolescent. "We were sent away to deliver a message to this realm. When we returned, we found out what happened."

"We're sorry for your grief," Seraphine added.

I glanced between the two of them, noting the sorrow in their posture and the anguish on their faces. "You can leave now."

Seraphine hid her remorse better than Killian as they slowly left the room. With slow, exhausted movements I kicked off my boots and crawled onto the settee before the hearth. My body felt hollow and weightless as I slumped from exhaustion.

Finally, after the knock at my door signaling mealtime went ignored, and the sky brightened further with the day, I slipped into a restless sleep.

A stirring in my chest woke me hours later. Dried tears were crusted along my cheeks from a fitful sleep.

I glanced toward the windows, noting the starlit sky beyond. It looked to be well past midnight.

The fluttering in my chest drew my attention to the door near the hearth. Through it, I could feel Aiden's presence, just as I could subtly feel him at the end of the cord that bound us in marriage.

I sat for another hour, waiting for the presence of him to fade with sleep before I moved.

The steel knife in my boot slid free silently as I twisted the handle of the door that connected our rooms.

The door was unlocked and opened without a sound. I breathed a sigh of relief as I stepped through.

Like my room, his was large and dark with the night. Even his hearth remained unlit and his candles untouched. I didn't take time to study the space as I crept through on silent feet.

The knife in my hand wouldn't kill him, but I knew it could do enough damage to remind him of the pain he'd caused.

I stood at the foot of his bed, watching him sleep. The light of the moon painted him in its silver glow. In this state he looked young, possibly no older than Mousa. His reddish-brown hair fanned out around his head on the pillow, his scarred chest bare to the night.

My feet remained soundless on the carpeted floor as I moved to stand over him. Aiden shifted, rolling onto his back. His eyes stayed closed and his breath was deep with sleep.

Careful not to wake him, I cautiously knelt on the bed, needing a better angle.

I crouched there, leaning forward so the tip of my knife was pressed into his neck.

My eyes brushed over the scars that covered his bare skin, settling on the most recent one. The raised skin appeared like a dark bruise in the night; a permanent reminder of Ephraim's attack only two months prior.

My control wavered, threatening to betray my heart with the feelings that still remained for him.

Unwanted emotions pounded against the barrier I'd hid them behind, and tears blurred my vision as the memory of that night surged through me. I didn't want to remember the way he made me feel. To remember the love I thought I held for him, or that I thought he held for me. I wanted anger. I wanted fury and revenge. But all I felt was this crushing pain.

I needed to feel empty.

Aiden's eyes opened, staring at me as if he could read every thought.

My grip on the knife tightened, digging into the soft spot beneath his chin a little more. Aiden hissed as a small trickle of blood dripped down his neck.

The look on his face, the complete understanding and acceptance of what I felt I needed to do, was nearly my undoing.

"I promised I would kill you," I whispered hoarsely. Aiden only watched me silently as I forced the emotions away.

Digging the knife in deeper, I leaned forward, watching the way his eyes widened as I brought our faces closer together. "I am not the same girl you met all those years ago," I said firmly. "Do not think yourself safe because this knife will not end your life. I will end this heinous marriage, I will break this curse, and you will die."

Aiden swallowed, his expression revealing a fraction of the sorrow he hid. "Do what you feel you must."

Surprise flitted through me, enough so that when his hand shot out, I was defenseless against him. My knife landed on the rug with a dull thud.

Aiden watched me in the moonlight, not daring to speak. He let me see the anguish on his face for only a second before his jaw tightened and his sorrow retreated.

Slowly, I stood from my crouch on the edge of his bed. Aiden sat up, eyes never leaving mine.

"Do not think me so weak as to not be a threat," I warned, allowing venom to pierce my tone.

Aiden nodded. "You are anything but weak, Esme."

My heart nearly stopped. With burning eyes, I raced from his room.

The door slammed behind me as I collapsed to the floor of my apartment. I hated that I couldn't hurt him, that I still felt even a drop of love for him. He was too monstrous to deserve anything other than my disgust, my hate.

I moved away from my spot on the floor and onto the balcony. The cool wind dried my tears, whipping my hair around my shoulders as I stared at the starry sky.

With careful breaths I forced my mind into a blank state. The shaking in my hands ceased, and the pounding of my heart slowed. I would become what was needed to enact my vengeance.

The world is full of wicked monsters. The only way to survive is to become something just as wicked, just as dangerous. I only had to be willing to lose a part of myself along the way.

THREE

I WOKE AS DAWN was cresting over the horizon, erasing the stars. I'd tossed and turned for hours, and though I felt exhausted I didn't dare try to sleep again.

I'd spent the night dreaming of my family. Reliving their deaths over and over. Watching their blood pool on the marble floor and stain my hands, and no matter how much I wiped them dry, the blood remained. But their blood shouldn't be staining my hands; it should be staining Aiden's.

Between nightmare's of my family's deaths, my dreams drifted.

In the brief reprieve of my nightmare's, my thoughts were of Aiden—but worse, I *liked* it. The dream was a parade of memories. Memories of dancing in a campground full of people but feeling like we were the only two people in the realm. Memories of his touch, his lips. But no matter where the memory of him began, it always ended in death and bloodshed. I'd learned too late just how dark the monster beneath the mask truly was.

The lingering recollection of that evening's nightmare pulled me from my place on the sofa. My hearth remained unlit, but the chill of early winter didn't bother me.

I chased the unease away with a hot bath. Like the room I was provided, the bathing chamber was large for a single person. A giant-sized tub filled an entire wall beneath a window overlooking the surrounding forest and the mountains far to the north. I scrubbed the memory of the demon's touch off my skin as I watched the sun paint the sky in pastels.

A knock sounded at my door. I startled, splashing water over the side of the tub. I should've known someone would come for me eventually.

The door to my apartment opened and closed softly. I listened to the shuffle of footsteps on the other side of the bathing chamber door as I quickly wrapped a towel around my middle.

The person I found waiting near the hearth surprised me.

"Oh, hello dear," the woman said warmly. Her skin was dark, a shade darker than Tarsa's, and her silver-streaked hair was braided down her back.

I stared at the strange woman. "Who are you?"

She smiled, making the skin near her eyes crinkle even more. She looked to be a few years younger than Nonna. "You can call me Fen. I've heard quite a lot about you, Esme. I hope you don't mind my intrusion, but I could only remain curious for so long before I had to come see you myself."

The carpet felt oddly cool beneath my bare feet. "You're Fen?"

She nodded, still smiling. I studied her closely as I moved through the room. I'd briefly heard of Tarsa's sister, Seraphine's past love. But I hadn't expected her. I'd assumed she was immortal like the others.

"Come. Sit. You need to eat." Her voice was deep and scratchy, much like my Nonna's used to be.

I let her usher me to the chair closest to the window and watched as she placed a small tray on the table before me.

My stomach rumbled at the fragrances. Bacon, eggs, sausages, and biscuits were piled high on the tray. I could feel the heat emanating from the freshly cooked meal as the steam clouded around my face.

A fork was shoved into my hand before I could even consider refusing.

"Eat." Fen's command left no room for objection.

I shoveled food into my mouth as I watched the strange woman. She moved comfortably throughout my room, folding a blanket along the back of the couch, adjusting the untouched pillows on my bed, opening the door to the balcony so the fresh morning air could filter through the room.

"I hope you don't mind, dear," she said as she glanced my way, "but it smells a bit stale in here. You could use the fresh air."

My lips pursed at the minor insult. Fen moved to the closet near the bathing chamber. I scooped more eggs into my mouth as I listened to her sift through my wardrobe. When I discovered the closet the night before, I was surprised by the amount of clothes it already held. All of which were tailored to my size.

Fen returned with a simple dress and draped it over the foot of my bed. "I imagine you're ready to leave this room and explore the castle."

I shrugged, watching her return to the hearth. "I haven't thought much of it," I said dismissively.

The woman lit the hearth easily, the fire immediately filling the room with its warmth. "I was warned you were stubborn."

I chose to ignore her comment as I worked through my breakfast.

Fen took a seat across from me, close to the fire. "I was sorry to hear of your family," Fen said gently.

"Were you?" My throat felt suddenly thick as I forced more food into my mouth.

Fen pursed her lips, studying me. "The death of a loved one is never easy. No matter the circumstances or the reasons behind it. I know of the pain it brings you. And for that, I am sorry. You are too young to have experienced so much pain."

Emotion rattled the emptiness in me, threatening to shatter my control. I pushed back, forcing the void to protect against the pain.

Another knock at the door drew my attention. When I turned, Seraphine was standing in the doorway, uncertain.

"May I come in?" Her voice was oddly timid and unsure.

I opened my mouth to tell her to leave when Fen interrupted and said, "Of course. Come join us."

I glowered at my food. The gesture was childish, but I couldn't help the betrayal I felt for her hand in these latest events.

"I see you've met Fen," Seraphine said in an attempt to coax conversation from me.

Fen chuckled. "I sort of let myself in. Poor girl hasn't eaten since she arrived. She needed food."

Seraphine laughed with her. Their dynamic felt easy and warm. "Clearly the guards at her door are doing their job well then."

"Like they would tell an old woman no," Fen grumbled half-heartedly.

I studied the two of them as they laughed. The love between them was obvious. But so was the growing distance. I briefly wondered if Fen's returned mortality had caused the demise of their relationship, then I remembered I shouldn't care.

Fen caught my quizzical stare. "I was immortal when Sera and I first met," she said. "Tarsa and I served Aiden's mother briefly before he was born. Then we served him. And through him, I met Sera."

Seraphine grinned, but I could see the strain beneath it. "Fen gave up her immortality about 50 years ago."

There was a hint of pain in Seraphine's tone. Something that said this was a conversation they'd had many times before and she didn't like the outcome of it.

Fen waved her words away. "A conversation for a later time. But you, Princess, need to finish your meal. If you won't come to the dining hall for lunch or dinner, then I'll return with those as well."

I swallowed the last of my breakfast and shook my head. "That's not necessary."

She scoffed. "Either I bring your meals to you, or you eat with your husband in the dining hall. But I will not let you starve up here any longer. You're not a prisoner."

Seraphine offered a smile. "I can always ask Aiden to eat elsewhere so you can have the dining hall to yourself. He wouldn't mind."

I gritted my teeth. Their attempts to encourage me to leave my room and interact with Aiden angered me more than they probably should.

"And there's this." Seraphine set a knife on my lap when Fen took the empty tray. It was the same knife I stole from Killian and attempted to use on Aiden only hours ago.

I gripped the handle tightly, the metal cool beneath my skin. "What's this for?"

She shrugged. "He thought it would be good for you to have a
weapon. That it might make you feel safer. A blacksmith is standing by
should you be ready to have your measurements taken for a proper-fit-
ting weapon. Just say the word."

Seraphine and Fen made their exit without another word. I was left to
the deafening silence of my room and the void spreading within me.

My limbs were stiff as I stood, choosing instead to focus on the day
ahead. Fen was right about one thing; I couldn't hide in my room any
longer.

Braiding back my obsidian curls, I slipped into the simple black dress
Fen had pulled from the closet. It was a surprisingly thin fabric, hugging
my curves easily and pooling at my ankles. The sleeves were long enough
to hide the scars I still carried from King Elroy's chains but left the
markings on my left hand exposed for all to see.

I pulled on my boots, hiding the knife there again, and slipped from
the room. The guards didn't stop me. They didn't even move as I
marched through the hall. I expected them to trail me at the very least,
but they remained perched outside my door, their bodies still as statues
though their eyes followed my every movement.

The walls were completely bare, lifeless. I hadn't taken the time to
study much of the castle upon our arrival, but now I took in every detail.
I couldn't find a single painting; there were no signs of life in this castle
apart from the stiff guards perched at every corner.

The walls were a pale grey, only a shade darker than the white marble
of the floor. Almost every window was hung with black tapestry, fitted
to block out the day's sun.

I took the stairs to the lower level, eager now to explore the rest of the castle. Servants lowered their eyes in my presence and quickly stepped aside.

The stairs led me down an unfamiliar hall where hushed voices and soft footsteps revealed the presence of others. Careful to avoid any unwanted interactions, I turned in the opposite direction.

The hallway I wandered through was just as bare as the rest. But this time, not a single guard lined the walls.

I tried the first door I came to; locked. The second and third doors were locked as well. Disgruntled, I moved to the fourth. My curiosity at what lay beyond the locked doors had grown beyond control.

The fourth door swung open easily, but a quick glance inside showed the room to be empty. Only a single chair sat in the very middle of the room, with a black case on the floor nearby. The hearth along the far wall remained cold and unlit; the lack of ashes revealed the room to be unfrequented.

The final door opened for me as well. The hinges were silent as if this room was frequented often.

The room beyond was cluttered with books and paintings stacked against every wall. I felt as if I'd stumbled upon the castle's adornments, cast aside and hidden in this remote room.

The bookshelf in the corner was overflowing, and the shelves sagged beneath the weight. I ran my finger along the wood; no dust. The faint trace of cedar filled the air as I moved. My heart beat unevenly at the scent, so similar to another I knew all too well.

Every piece of furniture, apart from an elegant-looking stone bench, remained covered beneath white sheets. It was haunting.

A low chuckle drew me from my snooping.

I spun around, startled to find three strangers before me. A young woman and two men who each looked to be about my age stood in the doorway. They were dressed simply — dark tunics, dark pants, and scuffed boots. I swallowed nervously as I noted the weapons decorating their belts.

"What do we have here?" one of the young men leered.

The woman laughed shrilly, clutching her hands together in front of her. "Oh, please tell me this is the new princess. Please tell me it's her."

The singsong tone to her voice raised the hair at the nape of my neck. I stepped back, closer to the bookcase.

"What do you want?" I demanded in a cool tone. The knife in my boot was a steady beacon of courage, but I was no warrior. My only weapon was keeping the fear locked away, and the possible protection my title as Aiden's wife offered.

One of the men smiled, revealing a line of straight teeth. His golden hair was brushed back from his face. "We only wanted to meet our new princess."

"You can't blame us for being curious as to what the mortal girl might look like to prompt even our grim prince to marry," the other man said with a shrug. This one was the largest of the bunch. He towered over my short frame and looked nearly as wide, though I had little doubt his size was due to anything other than muscle.

My heart dared to hasten its pace. "You'd have to ask him."

The girl smiled wickedly. "You're just a simple thing, aren't you? What could you have possibly done for our prince that he would ignore the women at court and choose you? You won't even live long enough for him to remember you in a few centuries."

"Perhaps you're the one who turned him off of the demons here to begin with," I said, quick to let my anger control my tongue.

The pale haired boy chuckled at his friend's distraught expression. "She's feisty. Must be what drew Prince Aiden to her bed."

My cheeks heated at the insinuation. I dared another step away from them though there was nowhere for me to run.

"There you are, Princess." A familiar voice sounded from the doorway. A sliver of relief filled me as Aiden stepped into the room. His presence was enough of a threat to make the strangers step back. "I wondered where you ran off to."

I shoved the relief away, forcing the emptiness to fill me as I stepped between the strangers. When Aiden's hand brushed my cheek I froze, shocked by his touch.

"Your Highness," the woman cooed with an exaggerated bow. "We only wished to meet our new princess."

"Yes," her large friend added with his own debonair bow. "When we heard of your bride's arrival, we grew curious. It has been almost a whole day and there had been no sight of her. We merely wished to give her a warm welcome and offer to show her the grounds."

Aiden glowered at the warriors. "I see."

The girl stepped forward, twirling a strand of hair around her finger. "I'd be happy to personally see to her tour of the castle grounds, Your Highness."

Aiden glanced toward me. An emotion I couldn't name flitted across his face before disappearing behind the arrogance only a prince could carry.

"That won't be necessary, Drusilla. I am more than capable of escorting Esme through the castle if needed."

The girl, Drusilla, physically deflated at his rejection and I instantly wondered if she'd sought him out for other interests in the past.

I quickly forced that thought away. It didn't matter who Aiden was entangled with in the past. The only thing that mattered was that I found a way to break this curse and return to my siblings.

"Pardon my asking," the pale haired one spoke, "but who exactly is she?"

"I haven't heard of a noble woman in the mortal realm eligible to marry the Prince of Death," the thick man said.

Aiden took my hand in his, using his thumb to release the tension in my fist. "Esme was a wanderer in Cordovia. I've known her family for quite some time."

"A wanderer?" the round one said, brows scrunching in confusion as he studied me.

"Our princess is a wanderer?" the pale haired boy spoke with a mocking tone. "You mean a stage performer by day and a whore by ni—"

His words cut off on a gasp as Aiden's hand wrapped around the man's neck. The others cowered from Aiden's anger as he let the mask of the prince fall, his expression dark as his power flickered in his eyes.

"If you would like to keep your tongue, I suggest being careful with how you speak about my wife." Aiden's body shook with barely controlled rage as he dropped the man to the ground.

I remained frozen near the door as the three demons scurried from the room with muttered apologies.

My heart beat fiercely in my chest as I watched Aiden slowly collect himself. Again, his wings remained hidden with whatever sort of magic he possessed, making him appear as the mortal boy I once thought him to be.

"Who were they?" I asked when he didn't speak.

He kept his back to me, studying the room. "Why were you in here?"

My spine straightened at his brisk tone. "Fen told me to get out of my room for a while. So, I did."

Aiden turned to face me. His expression remained carefully closed off, but his eyes studied me with care. "You shouldn't wander alone. It's dangerous."

"I have a knife."

"That knife won't do you much good if you don't know how to use it."

I scoffed, spinning on my heel. "Then why bother returning it?"

His footsteps were silent on the marble floor, but I felt him trail me nonetheless. "I thought it might be nice to wake up to you in my bed again. The knife only made it more entertaining."

I shot him a disgusted look that he answered with an arrogant grin.

"You're despicable," I seethed.

His grin only grew, though it wasn't joyous. "And yet here we are. Husband and wife."

"Not by choice."

Aiden settled at my words, the grin disappearing from his face. I chose to ignore the emotion that flashed across his features, instead focusing on the path ahead. I hadn't paid much attention to how I'd gotten here after leaving my chambers.

After a few failed turns and retracing my steps, Aiden finally gave in to his annoyance.

"Lost?" I could hear the smile in his voice as he followed me, not bothering to tell me where I was heading.

I grunted my rebuttal which only made him chuckle.

"Why are you following me if you're not going to help?" The bare walls and white floors looked the same no matter how many halls I turned down.

He shrugged, pausing to lean against the wall as I turned another corner. It quickly became obvious I had once again taken a wrong turn. When I rejoined him, he watched me with an emotion I didn't care to examine.

"If you had a guard with you, you wouldn't be lost right now," he said casually.

I scowled and repeated my earlier question. "What good are you if you're not going to tell me where to go?"

He shrugged. "I find this entertaining."

"Of course you do. Was it entertaining for you to have my family slaughtered as well?"

As soon as the words left my mouth his demeanor changed. All emotion left his expression, and even his posture went rigid as he straightened from his perch against the wall.

The Prince of Death stared back at me now as his eyes scrutinized the emotion in mine. A muscle feathered in his cheek, like he was struggling to form words that he didn't speak. "Don't wander alone. Your guards are at your door for a reason."

And then he spun on his heel and left the way we'd come. As soon as he was out of sight, a nameless guard appeared to follow me as I wandered the halls of his castle alone.

FOUR

As soon as the sun disappeared beyond the skyline, I slipped from my room. I spent the better part of the day studying the stone along the side of the castle outside my balcony. It was just jagged enough that I could climb down. Though, now that I stood along the railing of my balcony, the three-story drop looked much more daunting than it had in daylight.

The wind was cool along my skin as it whipped my hair around my face. I dressed warmly in thick pants and a long sleeve shirt beneath a tunic. My knife was tucked inside my boot again should I need it. But as Aiden had pointed out, I still didn't know how to properly use it.

My grip tightened on the railing as I hoisted myself over the edge, toes scrambling for purchase. I had to be careful; Aiden's balcony was attached to mine. All I needed was for him to look out his window and see me hanging over the edge of the rail.

As soon as I found a reliable grip on the wall, I began my slow descent. I didn't really know what I planned to do once I left my room tonight. I just knew I couldn't spend another moment sitting in there alone when there were answers I needed. And I certainly couldn't find my answers with guards trailing me and reporting my every move to Aiden.

By the time my feet safely reached the grass, my limbs were shaking with exertion and sweat trailed down my neck. I could see guards stationed along the outer wall, and, thanks to the many hours I spent watching their patrol today, I knew when they would be distracted with the guard change.

Patches of light lit the ground in regular intervals through gaps in the curtains as I moved. I kept my shoulder against the stone of the castle, careful to duck beneath the windows as I passed by. I could hear the occasional muted voice in the rooms, but I didn't dare stay to listen to them whisper about my arrival.

A soft sound came from the room above. Not a voice, but music. Deep strumming flowed through the air in an eloquent hum.

Tears pricked my eyes as the familiar tune sang to my broken soul. The song of my family. A ballad written by a long-forgotten ancestor that was passed down to each generation. My mother and uncle performed this tune for years before teaching it to my cousins and siblings. It was a song that was meant to give hope and love.

Who played it now was a question I didn't want answered. No doubt it was merely a ploy to make me weak and naïve again. A tactic to keep me from getting the revenge I needed to erase the pain lingering behind my carefully constructed shield.

My boots were silent in the grass as I continued on my path. I stopped outside the window to the room I'd entered earlier. The space was dark as I pushed inside the unlocked window. Again, I got the impression this room was well cared for.

I moved silently through the cramped room, forcing my nervous breathing to remain even, though my pulse spiked with nerves.

Footsteps sounded softly in the hall beyond the door. I ducked behind a covered piece of furniture as the steps paused just outside the room.

My heart pounded in a frantic rhythm as I crouched in the dark. I'd hoped to study the books hidden away here, desperate for any hint of a way to break the curse on my bloodline. But if someone barged in now, my attempt would be forfeit.

"What do you think?" a familiar deep voice asked in a hushed tone.

An exasperated sigh sounded in answer. "It's her?"

I held my breath, awaiting the answer I knew would come.

"She's his bride now," Drusilla answered in her sing-song voice. "The young prince has married himself a Soul Collector."

"He won't be happy to hear of this news," the unfamiliar voice answered.

The deep voice of Drusilla's blond friend chuckled. "Maybe she won't be his bride for much longer. They haven't even shared a bed. They sleep in separate rooms."

My chest tightened, forcing the air from my lungs. They were watching me. Even when I remained alone in my room, I was being watched.

"Why bring her here at all then? What is he planning?" The unfamiliar voice shifted as the footsteps echoed through the empty hall; the sound of pacing.

"The women here have never been good enough for the prince," Drusilla whined.

"He keeps her under heavy guard," the blond man said. "But I've had no issue keeping an eye on her. She'll be easy to get to."

"And what of the prince? This marriage interrupts our plans for the girl, but the prince is not to be killed." The unfamiliar voice sounded faintly amused by that thought.

Drusilla giggled like a child. "He'll be punished. Punished. Punished." Her hands clapped softly between each word, articulating her threat.

Frightened, I stumbled out of the window and into the cool night air. Barely managing to keep my footsteps quiet, I raced away from the castle. The faint sound of my family's song and Drusilla's chants echoed in my mind, a braided taunt that promised pain and anguish.

My breath fogged the air as I raced along the stone wall. The castle was far from view now, my muscles aching from use. Small, groomed trees sprouted from the earth around me, bushes decorated with wilting wildflowers staggered between them.

In the moonlight, this corner of the grounds was bathed in silver. I imagined it might look beautiful during the day, so far from the darkness of the castle.

A gap in the stone wall caught my eye. I fell to my knees before it, exhausted from racing across the gardens. The fracture opened into a large hole — almost like a tunnel — through the thick barrier that had trapped me within the castle grounds.

I glanced back the way I'd come, half expecting Aiden or one of his guards to appear.

A tug from the essence in my chest urged me to return to the castle and the demon who waited for me. I ignored it.

The ground was cold beneath my hands and knees as I crawled through the narrow space. Stone scraped against my ribs and back until I finally found myself on the other side of the wall.

The air cooled further as I stood, turning the ground's lingering warmth into a thick fog around my ankles. My clothes stuck to the sweat that had formed on my chilled skin.

I glanced around the unfamiliar woods, suddenly uncertain. The trees were tall and wide, unkempt. The moon, though barely visible beneath the bare branches, provided just enough light to note I wasn't as alone as I thought.

Ephraim smiled coyly. "I wondered how long it would take for you to come to your senses and escape his clutches."

"I didn't escape," I said over my scrambled nerves.

"No? Then why are you out here while he is inside looking for you?"

I stilled. "How do you know he's looking for me?"

The angel's smile grew. "You're telling me after all those hours wallowing in your tears you still haven't decided to leave him? That's a little pathetic of you, don't you agree?"

A flash of anger warmed my veins, awakening the essence inside of me. "Why are you here?"

"For you, Soul Collector." I stepped back as he watched me with predatory focus. "Tell me, has Aiden told you what your power can do? What it *is*?"

From my silence, he got his answer. Since the moment I learned of my duty to my family, I was eager to learn of the darkness inside of me. Yet I couldn't bring myself to ask the question, afraid of the answer I would receive.

"Tell me, Esme," he said, hissing my name like a viper. "What do you want? What is your heart's greatest desire? Now that you don't have a family to protect, that is."

I scowled, forcing the hurt from my face as the memories flashed in my mind again. I could hear the slice of the knife through the air even now. I could hear Zaven's pleas and Kesson's screams as I watched them beg for mercy from the king. The king who only kept me prisoner because of what I could do as a result of the curse that had haunted my family for centuries. A curse that was given to us by Aiden.

Ephraim grinned, sensing the anger pulsing through me, raging against the betrayal haunting my heart as the empty void I'd created within myself filled with white-hot fire. "If it is truly revenge you want, I can help you get it."

I studied him, not trusting the gleam in his eye. "Why? How do I know you're not equally to blame for my family's slaughter?"

He chuckled. "Smart girl. But I had no part in your family's deaths."

My answering grin was as cold as the void where his soul should be. "You said you were behind my imprisonment in the first place. What did you mean?"

"Cordovia was falling apart," he started slowly. "Your king was greedy. Each generation of his family birthed a new heir raised to thirst for more and more power. Elroy was the worst of them.

"He sent his men to me at the first sign of spring," he continued. Ephraim paced the small space around us, the fog dancing around his wings. "His men claimed Cordovia was overrun by demons. That Death's reach had grown and taken more of their people. When I heard the tales they spoke about our war generations before, I laughed. Mortals are naive little things."

"You made a deal with Elroy," I prompted, bringing him back to the present.

He nodded. "He spoke of rumors that centered on a family. Rumors that to any mortal might sound like nonsense but to a fearful and suspicious king rang true."

"Rumors about my family?"

"The famous Loutari clan." He stopped his pacing to face me head on. The moonlight reflected off the dark scales of his horns and made his pale hair appear white in the night.

"I'd heard of your family for centuries," he said, stepping closer now. His wings shifted so the grey feathers brushed my arms. I shivered against the unwelcome sensation. "From the moment Aiden struck that deal with your ancestor we could all feel it. Every immortal in every realm could sense the power it would bring the God of Death."

"Because every soul I bring him is one less for you," I said, repeating Nonna's words from weeks ago.

Ephraim looked surprised before his expression cleared. "My need for revenge against Death goes back farther than the existence of your curse."

I studied him, scrutinizing the way his eyes lit with a thirst for bloodshed. "What did he do?"

The angel tilted his head, the gesture oddly birdlike. "How much do you know of the angels' war with Death and his demons?"

"Enough," I said, forcing my voice to remain certain.

His wings rustled, tightening behind his back. "My mother was The Angel before me. She ruled over my people for a millennium before Death stole her away. Not soon after, she birthed him a child. A dark angel."

The Angel of Light and the God of Death had a child? Nonna never mentioned this.

"It was in the days following that child's birth that my mother's immortal life ended," he continued in a stilted voice. "I felt her power fill me, claiming me as her heir immediately. I mourned her; all of my people did. And it was in those following days we began to plan our revenge.

"I knew it would take time," he continued softly, almost as if he were speaking to himself. "I knew the timing had to be just right for me to take something of equal importance from him. But when the time came to slay the child, I couldn't."

"Their child was your sibling," I whispered.

Ephraim nodded, eyes downcast like he couldn't meet my gaze. "A bundle of blankets and wide eyes, nothing more. It was while I stared into that infant's eyes that I decided on another means of revenge, something that would gain retribution for my people in the process."

"What happened to the baby? Did you take it?" The essence pulsed in my chest.

"No."

Oh stars, he did kill the baby. Of course he did. My pulse thundered in my ears as fear gripped me. "Why do you need me?"

"I need the power lingering inside you. I need you to awaken it. And I need you to be my eyes and ears inside Aiden's fortress."

As if in answer, the fluttering in my chest curled around my heart. I felt it pull me toward the castle, toward Aiden.

I shook my head, trying to free my mind of its uncertainty and confusion. "I'm not stealing another soul until I can save what's left of my family."

"It's not a soul I need you to steal," he said quickly. "There is a deadly strength to your power that can cause a rift in a place even as balanced as the Realm of Souls. Your arrival, and your marriage to the prince, will make even Death think twice about your existence. Your prince cannot protect you here."

"But you can," I guessed in a dry tone.

He smiled, chin dipping in a shallow nod though his eyes never left mine. "I can teach you how to call it. How to strengthen its raw power and mold it into something easily accessed. Others will wish you to keep it hidden. They'll fear your true strength and claim it's for your own safety that you reject it. But it will be your downfall if you do not strengthen it."

My mind whirled with the information he so willingly gave. If what he said was true, then Drusilla wasn't the only demon I would have to watch out for in this realm.

"You tried to kill me a year ago," I said, watching his carefully sculpted expression. "Why would you try to kill me only to wish to kidnap me a year later?"

He shook his head. "I didn't intend to kill you. The knife I carry is poisoned," he said, revealing a truth I already knew. "I needed to frighten your family, frighten Aiden. I'd hoped he would abandon his post as a guard and return to his father's realm, leaving you available for the taking."

My hand brushed the scar at my neck of its own accord. I could still feel the cool metal cutting through flesh and vein. The burn of the poison was a painful memory.

"I knew Aiden carried an antidote." His eyes tracked the movement as my hand brushed the scar. "I never believed you would die from my attack."

"But I am not a demon," I said, nodding toward the hilt of the knife he carried between his wings.

Ephraim nodded. "No, you are not. The knife I suspect you are referring to is only carried by the Angel of Life and only toxic to demons or those who have their souls bound to Death. Which you do."

My brows furrowed as I stepped toward the fissure in the wall. "Then what poison coats that knife?"

"It was a common poison," he said simply. "I needed something to shake Aiden's confidence without revealing who I truly was just yet."

I dared another step away, the essence practically lurching through my ribs to get back to the castle.

"Think about my offer," he said, watching my retreat. "I will help awaken that power, and in return we work together to get our revenge. Me, for my mother and my people, and you for your family."

I studied the angel before me, his hard features making his emotions difficult to read. When he didn't say anything more, my gaze slipped to the knife hidden between his wings.

"Think about it, Soul Collector," he said, stepping into the shadows. "Together, our revenge could bring enough chaos to rival a war."

"I don't want a war," I said honestly.

He smiled. "Maybe not yet, but my brother will gladly give you one if he learns of this conversation."

My heart stopped. "Your brother?"

"You didn't think I spoke of another offspring of Death's, did you?" he drawled. My eyes went wide which only made him laugh as he slipped into the shadows. "Think on it. I'll be here waiting when you come to your senses."

With that, he disappeared, leaving me alone with a racing heart.

FIVE

I SPENT THE NIGHT pacing through the castle gardens. My mind held a whirlwind of questions. Some I was almost certain I knew the answer to, but with others I remained lost.

Dawn crept over the horizon, melting the frost dusting the ground. I hadn't realized how cool the air had turned in the hours since I'd met Ephraim. My fingers were stiff as I fisted them at my sides, forcing warmth into them.

I collapsed beneath a large tree. My mind spun with the plan I'd made with Elias to seek the Angel of Life and ask for his help to kill Aiden and free my family from this curse. Now that I had the opportunity practically given to me, I wasn't sure I could follow through. And I hated to admit why.

The castle doors slammed open. I was near the stone wall at the edge of the gardens, but still the ground shook with the force from the blow, startling me.

Guards marched through the door, spreading throughout the grounds. Their eyes remained alert as if searching for something. Fear struck me as I began to wonder if they knew Ephraim had been here. That fear only grew when Aiden stormed after them, his strides quick and his expression dark.

My stomach tightened with nerves as I slowly got to my feet, toes frozen in my boots. If they knew I'd spoken with Ephraim, they would throw me into the dungeon without a second thought.

Aiden's penetrating stare landed on me instantly. The ferocity in his gaze morphed into something softer, warmer, for just a moment.

The guards stopped their searching, each going still as a statue as Aiden marched past them. His large frame was taut with tension, many years of warrior training possibly the only reason he hadn't begun to yell at me for meeting with his enemy.

His half brother.

The prince stopped just out of arm's reach, eyes scanning over every inch of me before returning to my face. His brows were furrowed as he studied whatever expression remained there.

I studied him too. I watched the way the storm in his eyes dimmed as he noted my lack of injuries. Or the way his hands fisted at his sides before he forced calm into his muscles.

"I see you're alive," he said stiffly.

"Disappointed?" I crossed my arms over my chest as the tension in my body eased, revealing just how cold I'd become.

He studied me a moment before speaking. "You weren't in your room."

I glanced around the garden. "I'm not? How strange."

Aiden returned my glower, a muscle ticking in his jaw as his patience wore thin.

"Are you all right?" His voice was tight, like he was speaking through his teeth.

"I'm alive."

He continued to study me as if trying to detect an underlying meaning to my words. "May I see you back to your rooms?"

The question brought me up short. My gaze flashed to his, confusion rocking through me as I waited for him to say more. Aiden continued to hold my gaze, unflinching. The prince was more disheveled than I'd ever seen. His hair hung around his face, ungroomed, and his clothes appeared to have been thrown on in haste.

"Am I to be locked away now?" I asked, studying his reaction carefully, waiting for any sign he knew who I'd spoken to in the hours before dawn.

Aiden sighed deeply. "You are not a prisoner here, Esme."

I arched a brow. "Then why am I to be escorted back to my room? Perhaps I merely sought a morning walk through the gardens."

He glanced at our surroundings. Bushes and vines had grown beyond control as they twisted up the stone wall, and trees bent at odd angles as they were forced to endure the elements without care. The only flowers that grew this far from the castle were wildflowers that bloomed in every color and looked an awful lot like weeds on the cusp of decay.

"There is a path through the gardens closer to the castle," he said. "It is well-guarded and well-kept so that it may be enjoyed. I suggest remaining there instead of in this deserted corner. You don't know what might be lurking beneath these bushes."

I turned toward the corner that housed the tunnel in the wall. "I don't mind the bushes. I like this corner far better than the rest of your gardens, anyway."

He considered this before turning toward the castle doors. "Come. Fen has probably brought your breakfast to your rooms already. If she is forced to wait much longer, she'll have my head for letting you miss breakfast."

"No thanks," I said, turning my back on him. "I think I'll stay here a while longer."

Aiden was quiet for a moment. "Esme, it is frigid. If you stay any longer you'll freeze."

"Doubtful."

He sighed. "Will you stop with the cold shoulder? It's beneath you."

I turned toward him, letting him see the rage simmering beneath my careful control. "You deserve far worse than a cold shoulder, Your Highness." I spat his title with disdain. "The pointy end of a knife through your heart might suffice."

"And yet, when you tried to kill me, you couldn't bring yourself to do it."

My jaw shut with an audible click. I watched his expression relax, like he'd won. It only infuriated me more. "Why is someone here playing my family's song?"

He blinked, his confusion evident. "What?"

"I heard it. Last night. Someone was playing the song my ancestors wrote for our performances," I said, crossing my arms against the cold. "How does someone in your court know that song?"

He shrugged, overly nonchalant. "Perhaps they heard it while venturing into your realm. Now come. It's cold, and you'll become ill if you stay out here much longer."

I scowled but opted to remain silent, instead working to fight the emotions pushing to the surface. He silently ushered me into the castle and through the corridors. Neither of us dared to speak a word as guards and servants stepped out of our path.

My mind continued to whirl with Ephraim's proposal as I caught sight of Drusilla and her blond friend whispering down a separate hall, grinning conspiratorially as I passed.

"Have they always been a part of your court?" I finally asked as Aiden led us up the staircase.

"Who?"

"Drusilla and her friends," I said. My voice cut off as his hand rested against my lower back, ushering me down the hall.

I forced my heart to calm, but the steady thrum of darkness enveloped every nerve in my body, eagerly responding to Aiden's proximity.

"No," he finally said as we stopped outside the door to my room. "They are fairly new to my court. Why do you ask?"

The door swung open before I could answer. Fen stood in the doorway, her tiny fists propped on her hips as she glanced between us.

"I understand a husband and wife need to spend time together, but it is rude to keep an old lady like myself waiting for so long."

I stepped into the room quickly, needing to put distance between Aiden and me. Seraphine smiled from her spot on the settee. The remembered betrayal sought its way into my heart again, but I couldn't erase the embarrassed flush from my cheeks as Fen ushered Aiden into my room.

"And you kept her outside without a cloak? Shame on you, Aiden Ozanne. You know better than to let a lady grow cold." She smacked him on his arm. There was little strength left in her mortal limbs, but Aiden looked surprised nonetheless.

"I didn't take her outside," Aiden said with a glance toward me. "I found her in the gardens."

Fen clicked her tongue, unaccepting of his response. Her hands were surprisingly firm as she pushed me into the chair closest to the flaming hearth. My mouth clamped shut as she wrapped a blanket over my shoulders. I hadn't realized just how cold I was until the fire's warmth melted the frost from my boots.

"You must be starving," Seraphine said, placing a tray of food before me.

"It's not as warm as it would've been had your husband returned you in time, but it's warm enough I suppose." Fen cast an annoyed glance in Aiden's direction, which he ignored.

Hearing Aiden being referred to as my husband still sent conflicting feelings through me. A year ago, I would've loved the sound of it. I would've basked in the way our names sounded together as husband and wife, and I would've taken every opportunity to marvel at the markings decorating the back of my left hand. Now I wasn't sure what to feel.

"I'll leave you to it then," Aiden said, starting for the door.

"Where do you think you're going?" Fen said in a tone that demanded attention. The way she spoke to him reminded me of how Nonna would speak to my siblings and I. Scornful with a hint of love buried beneath. "Sit. You should tend to your wife since she is obviously too cold from walking outside to venture to the dining hall."

I watched in muted horror as she pulled him to the seat across from me and took one of the plates from my tray, setting it in front of him. Seraphine watched with a coy smile on her mouth.

Aiden glowered at her. "I'm sure Esme would prefer I leave her to eat in peace, Fen."

"Nonsense," she said, waving away his concern. I scowled at my food, unable to meet their gazes as my face heated with a mixture of frustration and embarrassment. "She is new to this realm, Aiden. She shouldn't be left alone all the time. You'd do well to keep her company every once in a while."

"She's right," Seraphine chimed in with a teasing smile that Aiden answered with a scowl.

"Shouldn't you be patrolling with Killian?" he asked stiffly.

Seraphine shrugged, still smiling. "Tarsa's with him."

Aiden grunted noncommittally which only made her smile grow.

"Why do you need to patrol?" I asked, hoping they were still unaware of my meeting with Ephraim.

"Angels sneaking into this realm is no small matter," Fen said as she fretted about the room.

My brows furrowed, confusion settling in me. "So they really can't enter through the white tree?"

"No," Aiden said coolly. "The white tree is tied directly to my father. As soon as it is used to enter or leave this realm, he knows. He has put many protections around it, preventing it from being used by angels."

"Then how has Ephraim been able to enter this realm?" I asked. A tinge of fear began to beat against the shield around my emotions.

Seraphine sighed, brown eyes wide with worry. "We don't know."

"He shouldn't have been able to enter this realm at all," Fen added.

"Is there another way in?" I asked.

Aiden shook his head. "No. There shouldn't be." His agitation was easy to read as he toyed with the sword at his waist.

"We're looking for him now," Seraphine interjected calmly. "We're searching every corner of this realm for any sign of his entry point. You'll be safe here," she said, misreading my stress.

Fen sighed. "We'll leave you two to it then." Fen pulled her hand through Seraphine's arm, taking the immortal with her.

"Oh, don't look so glum, Aiden," Seraphine called over her shoulder. "It's not like you haven't been thinking of this since you brought her here."

My eyes shot to Aiden at the same time he dropped his gaze. Seraphine chuckled as she closed the door, casting us in silence.

I could feel my heart thunder away in my chest as I stared at my plate. Words I wanted to scream into the silence bubbled close to the surface. But what upset me the most was that I couldn't discern if my anger was directed at him or at myself for still wanting him here.

Aiden's gaze centered on me, mouth hanging open slightly like he was about to speak. His mouth clamped shut a moment later, so hard I heard his teeth snap together. Annoyed, I turned away, putting my back to him in a gesture so childish I nearly felt shame. The silence continued a heartbeat more before Aiden finally sighed.

"I should go," Aiden said into the silence.

I didn't look up as he carefully set his plate of untouched food aside. His gaze was warm across my face, but I refused to meet it.

After another moment, he finally retreated to his room.

My breath rushed out of me as I slumped in the chair. Melted frost dripped onto the floor from my boots as I stared into the flames. My emotions raged against the barrier I'd placed around them as they fought for dominance. One ready to throw me into Aiden's waiting arms, another begging to cry and scream for my family, and another desperate to cause as much pain as I felt in the hollows of my heart.

I couldn't begin to understand the war of emotions playing out within me. How any part of me could still love Aiden after what he did was astounding. But even more confusing was that he treated me with as much kindness as he could offer. He may have said I wasn't a prisoner in his realm, but I had little confidence in his words after his betrayal.

My tray of food remained untouched as I stared out the window, watching dawn become day and the hours fade. My mind was so full I hadn't even noticed that someone had entered until Fen pulled the tray from my lap, replacing it with a meal for midday.

"I can see you didn't waste any of your breakfast," she said in a chiding tone.

My stomach rumbled as I studied the steaming stew. "I wasn't hungry."

She snorted but didn't comment. I ignored her piercing gaze as I slowly spooned food into my mouth. My stomach immediately eased as I welcomed the vibrant taste of stew and potatoes. The fire in the hearth had grown cold, dimming over the course of the last few hours.

"You need to take better care of yourself." When I met her gaze I noticed the way lines around her mouth tightened with the pursing of her lips, and yet her eyes had a boisterous youth in them.

"I've survived in worse conditions," I said, thinking of the past months I'd endured. "This won't kill me. Whatever Aiden's plan for me is, I will survive it."

Fen scoffed, tossing her braid over a shoulder. "Aiden's only plan is to keep you safe. I assure you, he does not have some elaborate scheme like you think he does."

I spooned another bite of stew into my mouth, taking the time to ask my next question without raising suspicion. "Does his father know I'm here?"

Fen must've read the anxiety in my voice because her response was quick and firm. "No. If he was aware Aiden brought you here, he would have been at our doorstep in a wink. No one knows you're here beyond those who follow Aiden's rule."

I watched her closely. "And his mother?"

The slight narrowing of her eyes was the only sign of her unease. "We don't speak of her anymore."

"Why?" I asked, honestly surprised.

"His father has forbidden it. When Aiden was a boy, he would ask about his mother. Where was she? How did she die? Who was she? But his father refused to answer any of his questions. Eventually, Aiden would come to Tarsa or me as we served as her guards until her death. But when his father found out, we were forced into silence. After a while, the curious little boy turned into a silent adolescent. He stopped asking after her, stopped seeking to spend time with his father. He put all of his effort into training for the guard; it was a feat that went unnoticed by his father until Aiden formally sought entry into the guard."

My spine straightened, startled. "He wanted to serve under his father's guard?"

Fen nodded. "He'd made friends with Ephraim around that time. The two were inseparable. But Death refused."

"Because Aiden was his heir," I guessed.

"His only heir. When Death's reign ends, it will be up to Aiden to rule the demons and souls that are bound here."

"What happens to the souls that go to the angels?" I asked, genuinely curious as Nonna's story came to the forefront of my mind.

Fen sent me a quizzical look. "The angels? Dear, no souls ever go to the angels. The angels serve under the Angel of Life; they serve under Ephraim. They are meant to protect the souls as they arrive at the Crossroads for Death. Or they're supposed to."

Confusion filled me as I thought back to Nonna's story and Ephraim's words. None of what Fen told me matched with what I had been taught my entire life.

"You look concerned," she noted with a warm smile. "I'm sorry. I'm sure I'm boring you. You probably want to get back to your lonesome brooding."

I shifted uncomfortably under her scrutiny. "I don't brood."

Fen's laugh was warm and raspy. Something about it was oddly soothing as she slowly stood and moved toward the door, my untouched breakfast tray in her hands.

"If you don't brood then I must be the Queen of Cordovia," she said with a hint of laughter in her tone.

I shrugged off my irritation as another thought occurred to me. "Is there a library here?"

She didn't turn, but I could hear the smile in her voice. "A library? Of course."

"Where is it?"

She cast a glance over her shoulder and the wrinkles around her eyes deepened with her grin. "I'll let your husband know you asked. I'm sure he'd be more than happy to give you a proper tour." She closed the door as her words died on the air.

Exasperation filtered through my veins as I placed the tray on the table before me, ignoring the way the bowls clattered on their sides. I didn't need Aiden asking after my intentions with the books he may have hidden here.

I paced around the room, waiting for Aiden's inevitable arrival when that nosy woman would shove him at me, forcing us into close proximity.

When the knock sounded at the beginning signs of dusk, my heart nearly stopped. With sweaty palms I moved to the door, only for it to burst open.

I jumped out of the way as a scowling Tarsa marched into my room, a large black garment bag draped over her arm.

She took in the room with a single glance. "You need to bathe."

I grimaced. While her back was turned to drape the bag over the foot of my bed, I sniffed at my hair. It smelled fine. I'd washed it the day before.

"What's going on?" I asked, fearful that Fen might have led Aiden to believe that I wanted to dine with him tonight as well as have him tour me through the halls.

Tarsa barely spared me another glance before moving into the attached bathing chamber. "Aiden sent me to make sure you were prepared for dinner."

My stomach plummeted to my feet. "I'm not dining with him," I protested.

"Of course you are," Tarsa snapped, impatient. "You are madly in love with your new husband, and you cannot bear to spend any more time than necessary apart. That is why the God of Death will be joining you this evening. To meet his son's smitten new bride."

My heart throbbed at a breakneck pace against my ribs, forcing my breath to come in shallow gasps as panic rattled through me at my lack of control. "The God of Death is here? Now?"

"Yes. And as far as he is concerned, you and his son are madly in love."

I remained frozen in the doorway to the bathing chamber as Tarsa set about placing clean towels at the vanity and filling the tub. My palms began to sweat for an entirely different reason.

"Well don't just stand there like a fool," Tarsa snapped. "Quick, bathe. We have an hour to get you presentable before he arrives."

SIX

AN HOUR LATER I was brushed, groomed, and dressed in a simple yet elegant gown that swished when I walked. The candlelit sconces we passed revealed the gold stitched throughout the skirts, so the black fabric appeared to be lit up with stars directly from the night sky.

Tarsa walked in front of me, glowering at the other guards as they swiftly moved about the halls, anxiously awaiting Death's arrival. Beside me, Seraphine walked quietly, giving me the space I desired. Tarsa had asked for her aide in braiding my hair into a crown atop my head, but my former friend hadn't forced me into unwanted conversation.

Our steps echoed off the bare walls, the resounding beat an echo of my own thundering heart.

"Don't be nervous," Seraphine whispered as distant voices grew closer.

"I'm not nervous."

She smiled at the lie. "If you say so."

Guards positioned on either side of the double doors to the dining hall ushered us into the room.

I stood there, the large wooden doors open before me, with my feet rooted to the ground. Hakan and Killian stood facing me. The former remained impassive as he studied me, but Killian smiled in his usual warm manner.

Seraphine moved past me. I felt her hand brush mine in a silent moment of comfort, much like she had when these demons first took me from Elroy's castle many weeks before.

Aiden stood with his back to me. Whatever hushed conversation he'd been having with the other immortals had ceased as soon as I arrived; I watched as he slowly turned toward me.

His princely facade melted away as he took me in. I watched his eyes roam over the dress before landing on my face which I'd allowed Seraphine to paint with traces of cosmetics.

A sliver of pride curled in my chest as I took a tentative step into the room. Tonight, I wouldn't be the girl for them to pity–I'd be the Soul Collector they whispered about upon my arrival.

The power in my veins thrummed in response to Aiden as he moved toward me. I took the moment to study his attire, for we were once again dressed similarly. The demon prince wore clothes made entirely of black. His hair hung loose, floating around his face in a halo of reds and browns. There wasn't any sign of a weapon on him, but I had little doubt he carried them. Just as I carried the knife tucked into my boot.

"Princess," he said by way of greeting. The deep baritone of his voice sang to the darkness moving through my veins. "You look lovely as ever." His voice rang with truth, but I felt my eyes narrow anyway.

"When will your father be joining us?" I asked, moving past him in dismissal.

"The God of Death will be here shortly," Hakan said with a formal dip of his chin. His bronze skin contrasted handsomely with his dark tunic. Unlike me or their prince, no one else wore black. Killian wore grey breeches and a blue tunic that matched the blue of his eyes, Seraphine wore her usual creams, and Tarsa and Hakan wore varying shades of green and red. They were all dressed far more formally than normal.

"You'll sit here," Aiden said, pulling a chair out from the table. I glanced in his direction, noting the placement.

"Why there?" My nerves grew as the demons took their places around the table.

"You are our princess," Seraphine explained patiently. "It is expected that you sit beside your husband in a seat of power."

I scowled at the chair, offended by its size and artistry that matched only two others among the dozen surrounding the table, one to my right, the other directly across from me.

"And there's this," Aiden said. He turned away, taking a mysterious box from Hakan.

I watched with muted horror and panic as he opened the lid, revealing a small golden crown. My chest tightened painfully as he lifted it from the box, holding it aloft for me to see clearly.

It was a simple crown; no more than a gold band of twisted vines and roses. A mirror image of the marking that painted my hand. The vines embellishing the crown shifted, forming into a sharper peak along the front as the crown was placed on my head.

The metal was cool for a breath before quickly warming to the feel of my skin and tightening across my brow.

I gasped. "How did it do that?"

Aiden flashed a crooked grin that made my treacherous heart stutter. "Magic built this crown, and that same magic flows through my veins.

This is the crown's way of accepting you as my equal. It matches my own."

His crown appeared before my eyes, his power having kept it hidden in the same way it hid his wings. Part of me was a little surprised he had kept his wings cloaked in magic, but mostly I was grateful I didn't have to see them. It was only a reminder of what he really was. Of what he was capable of doing.

His crown was similar in many ways, but something about it seemed much more intimidating than the one sitting atop my head, framed by my braided hair.

"Your father has just arrived," Tarsa said from where she leaned casually against the wall. "He'll be escorted to the dining hall shortly."

My stomach twisted painfully as my nerves returned. A maelstrom of conflicting emotions rocked through me as I wrung my hands together, forcing calm into my body.

Aiden's hand gripped both of mine, forcing them into stillness. At my quizzical look, he sighed. "He needs to believe our marriage was born of love. Of the utmost desire to be together. If he sees it as anything else, he may feel threatened that I brought his Soul Collector to this realm and into my castle without his approval. We need to make him believe that we are here peacefully and nothing more."

"You want me to pretend?" Surprise made my statement a question.

He frowned slightly before his mask erased the emotions in his eyes. "If you need to. But I need you to hide your disdain for him and his power, and for me. Just for tonight," he added at my answering scowl.

"You ask a lot of me, Prince." I let his title roll off my tongue like an insult.

His answering smile was born of pure arrogance. "His reaction to your presence here could determine the survival of your family; of you."

"Will you be pretending too then?" I asked. The sound of rhythmic footsteps echoed down the hall. My pulse jumped in my veins as they neared.

His expression changed, shifting into an emotion resembling sorrow. The tension around his eyes warmed as he stared at me. The hand that entrapped both of mine softened, his thumb brushing over my knuckles where the marking of our marriage remained.

His answer came as the doors opened, his voice so soft I wasn't sure I'd heard him correctly. "No."

I didn't have time to process his response before a large man stepped into the room. He exuded power and arrogance with every step. Like Aiden, he had a sharp jaw and firm mouth that turned down in a frown as his gaze landed on me.

His attendants spread throughout the room. Some took positions along the wall, standing on either side of the large hearth behind me, while others stood just beyond the chairs on the other side of the large table.

The God of Death sauntered closer, comfortable in his position of power. His dark hair was cut short, barely hanging over his ears. His eyes were the same blue-grey as Aiden's. This similarity made something deep within my chest curl inward, away from his presence.

Everyone in the room bowed. I watched their heads dip in submission as he passed. Even Aiden offered a stiff dip of his chin toward his father.

"Will you not bow before the God of Death?" A female voice scolded from somewhere in the room.

My heart continued to race within my chest as the King of Demons kept me trapped in his gaze. As I opened my mouth to speak, I felt Aiden grow deathly still beside me.

"He is not my god." My voice rang out clearly in the following silence.

The room grew too still, too uneasy as tension rose. For a few moments, the only sound in the room was the crackling of the fire behind me. Then the demon king tipped his head back and laughed.

SEVEN

THE BLOOD FROZE IN my veins as I awaited the wrath that would follow his laughter. Seraphine stepped closer to my side, prepared to drag me away should Death decide to end my life here.

"You're as foolishly brave as I would expect of anyone who would dare marry my son without my permission," the God of Death said when his laughter died. Sweat formed along my palms as I watched the darkness swirl within his eyes, a limitless power visible within.

"Shall we sit?" Aiden asked, breaking the tension.

The demons that accompanied Death moved first, taking up the empty seats on either side of his chair. Death observed us carefully as Aiden pulled a chair out for me. Once I was settled, Aiden sat at my side, shifting his chair closer so his arm brushed mine.

Killian opened his mouth to speak but was interrupted by the arrival of our meal. Servants ushered in trays overflowing with various foods.

"I wasn't sure what you would like," Aiden whispered, his breath brushing against my cheek in a warm caress as a plate was placed before me. "The kitchen made a variety of things for you to try."

I nodded, studying the abundance of food. To my left, in front of Killian at the end of the table, sat a tray overflowing with fish and lobster. I made a mental note to steer clear of that tray; I hated seafood. In front of Seraphine was a basket filled with varying kinds of bread and jams. In front of Aiden was a giant roast pig, an apple settled in its snout. And far at the other end of the table was a stew that made my stomach rumble appreciatively. The smells were divine as they filled my senses; the warmth from the large fire at my back only enhanced the decadent aromas in the air.

"Would either of you like to tell me why my Soul Collector is in my realm? Or why you saw fit to bring her here without my knowledge or consent?" The clatter of knives and forks was the only sound for a beat.

Aiden carefully set his fork aside, watching his father closely. "I felt it was safest for her to join me in this realm."

"She's a mortal. Her realm is the safest place for her," Death countered with a scowl.

Aiden's expression was carefully blank. "Once, yes. But now, circumstances have changed."

"Ahh, of course. You sought to comfort her after her family's death," the god said stiffly. A muscle tightened across Aiden's cheek as he scowled at his father.

My gaze narrowed in Death's direction. "What do you know of my family's murder?"

He studied me a moment, noting the barely disguised anger in my gaze. My hands tightened on the arms of my chair.

"I am the God of Death, child. Why would I not know of their deaths?" His tone was laced with condescension.

"There's another issue at hand," Aiden said, drawing all eyes to him. "Ephraim is not who we thought he was."

Death's brows shot upward. "Is that so?" His tone remained disbelieving, arrogant. "Just who is he then? The best warrior I've ever had? The warrior who took the place in my guard you once thought of as yours? Don't tell me this is another jealous attempt to get me to doubt him."

Aiden's mouth snapped shut with an audible click. That familiar muscle feathered in his cheek as he glared at his father. I could just see the beginnings of a faint blush dusting his cheeks.

"Ephraim is the Angel of Life," I answered for him.

Shock cascaded through the room. Every demon froze mid-movement. Some halted their forks halfway to their mouths, others paused mid-step as they moved around the room to refill wine glasses. But in the end all eyes turned to me. I nearly smiled at the flash of disbelief in the demon's eyes.

"Ephraim is my most trusted warrior," he seethed.

Aiden's hand gripped his chair in a white-knuckled grasp. "Ephraim has lied to all of us. For centuries. What she says is true, Father. And he is planning something."

"What is he planning?" one of Death's demons asked, dark eyes watching me too closely.

"We don't know," Killian admitted.

The demon scoffed, but Hakan spoke first. "He made claims to take Esme. Whatever he is planning, she is a part of it. He must believe he can use her power against us, against our realm, and the mortals we guard."

"He will not take her." Aiden's voice reverbrated through the room with grim determination.

Death glanced between the two of us, brows furrowed. "So, you married her to protect her? Or to protect my realm? Am I really to believe this isn't a ploy to use her power for yourself?"

"I would never use her that way," Aiden protested.

"But you would. You are the one who offered that idiotic deal to her ancestor. You are the one charged with guarding whoever inherits the debt. You are the one who gains just as much power as I every time she takes a soul. Can you honestly sit there and tell me the thought of using her gift to your advantage hasn't crossed your mind?"

My lungs froze as I glanced toward the demon at my side. I watched the words he sought to speak play out in his eyes. The arms of his chair began to shake with the force of his grip.

"Once," he admitted, as if the word was torn from his throat. "I thought of it once. Years ago. But I have not even entertained the thought of using her power against her will since I've known her, really known her."

As his words faded his eyes found mine. A silent plea to believe the truth he spoke. I struggled to compose my expression as I turned away.

"Very well," Death said after a few silent moments. "I will send my most trusted spies into the mortal realm and search for any sign of him or his intentions."

Aiden inclined his head. "Thank you."

"I will also leave a few of my warriors with you should Ephraim decide to capture your bride from within your very walls. I think we can all agree, keeping her under our watchful eye is important."

"I am perfectly capable of protecting my wife." Aiden's posture turned uncomfortably stiff as he stared at his father.

The god shrugged, the hint of a mocking smile turning up the corners of his lips. "Let's just say I'm being extra cautious."

The room grew still as the two demons studied each other, measuring the other's intentions.

"Can't say I'm surprised about Ephraim." The demon that spoke shifted loudly, attempting to diffuse the tension.

"Why do you say that?" Seraphine asked as she placed another roll on my plate.

The demon shrugged, his dark hair falling in his eyes. "There have been rumors about him for centuries."

The white-haired demon at his side snorted. "Rumors don't determine facts, Daemon."

Daemon shrugged. "Most of them sounded true enough that now I don't think it matters much."

"What did these rumors say?" Killian asked before shoving an entire roll into his mouth.

"That he wanted power," the white-haired demon answered, sounding bored.

"Not just that," Daemon said over a mouthful of pork. "They say he would sneak into the libraries in the middle of the night and steal books about *Death*'s power."

Death appeared unbothered by this rumored revelation though he continued to scowl at his son.

"If he truly was after Death's power, then what would he want with me? What could I give him that he couldn't get from Death?" I asked when no one bothered to elaborate.

Daemon and the white-haired demon glanced at each other, almost surprised that I was bothering to listen to their conversation, let alone speak to them. Aiden's hand shifted to graze the back of my knuckles, sensing my distress. My heart matched the excited flutter of the essence at the contact.

The God of Death regarded me curiously. "You carry my essence, Soul Collector. The power you carry could be bent to his will, to allow him to steal souls that are mine and therein gain power."

Understanding filled me along with a hint of dread.

"Which is yet another reason why I continue to hate this damned tie to her bloodline," Death said to Aiden. "It is a weakness for my power, my reign. Though I cannot say it is any more of a weakness than what you've created for yourself."

Curiosity bloomed within me as Aiden went inhumanly still. His eyes and face were carefully blank as he stared at his father. The two remained trapped in a silent battle of wills.

I began to reach out a tentative hand, ready to comfort Aiden any way I could from his father's close scrutiny, but my hand quickly fell into my lap as I quelled that desire.

"Ofrin, you're too untrusting," one of the demons said as her hand rested upon Death's arm.

"I disagree," Ofrin said. It felt strange hearing the God of Death referred to by his birth name. Humanizing.

Aiden's expression was cold as he glowered at his father. "You don't trust that my feelings for her are genuine? Just that they're merely part of a plan I've concocted against you?"

Ofrin's frown deepened. "After everything that happened to her family, I find it hard to believe you two would choose to marry so soon."

"This marriage was for her protection as much as anything else."

"So you said." Ofrin's gaze was unwavering. "But you still had a hand in her family's demise. You stood by as they were slaughtered. You gave no warning. You felt their souls enter this realm as much as I did. I imagine that is not something that someone can easily forgive."

Anger quickly rose within, barreling through me until it stole my breath. But Ofrin expected this. The venomous gleam in his eye dared me to unleash my buried anger, waiting to use it as an excuse to disprove our claim.

I smiled, and it was as cold and wicked as his. "You seem to have given this a fair bit of thought."

"My Soul Collector married my son and entered my realm. I have great reason to think about such things." His chest puffed out as he glanced between Aiden and I.

I opened my mouth to retort, but Aiden placed a gentle hand on mine. He leaned forward in his chair, eyes like daggers.

"Your worries are misplaced. She is braver than you can imagine. And after everything she has been through, she has not even considered giving up. She would do anything for those she loves." His voice was thick with emotion. "Esme is admirable in every way. Of course I love her. For you to think otherwise, or to think I would use her power against her for my own selfishness, is an insult."

The room fell silent with his declaration. I could feel all eyes on me, burning along my skin as they waited for my reaction.

Aiden carefully avoided my gaze as he settled back into his chair. His sole acknowledgement of my presence came as he took my hand in his. I watched the light from the fire dance over the marking on the back of his hand as it held mine.

Those words. Stars, I would've loved to hear those words from his mouth a million times even a week ago. I would've prayed to any god that would listen for him to say those things to me.

Only now, I grappled with my emotions, forcing the emptiness to fill me. If he could remain emotionless while having my family murdered, I could do the same now. He even said we would need to pretend tonight, though the last words he admitted just before his father's arrival stirred in my thoughts.

"She's still a mortal," Ofrin said, watching the two of us closely. "Her lifetime will be only a blink compared to your existence."

A muscle ticked in Aiden's jaw as he stared at my hand in his. "I'm well aware."

"And yet you would waste these years of your life with her?" Daemon asked. His tone didn't carry an insult, but he was clearly trying to discern Aiden's decision.

"Yes," Aiden said, voice ringing with finality and truth. "Because any moment spent with her is not a waste."

I couldn't feel anything beyond the stupid skip in my heart. My body grew numb as I stared into his eyes, sensing the undying truth to every word he spoke. Only the brush of his thumb along my knuckles brought life back into my lungs. I remained trapped in his gaze until my pulse finally calmed, and I forced the threat of tears away.

When I'd forced myself back into my hollow shell, I dropped his gaze.

"And you, girl?" Ofrin demanded of me. "Do you claim to love my son as he claims to love you? Or have you created your own agenda to steal my crown?"

I frowned at him, trying to comprehend his belief that I could be powerful enough to undermine the God of Death. I knew how much power Aiden had, and I'd only seen a small fraction of it. I didn't even want to imagine the power that flowed through Ofrin's veins.

I remained conflicted. The easy answer was yes; a part of me loved Aiden. But I knew better than to acknowledge that part of my heart which remained scarred from his betrayal.

For this act of deception, though, I could let him see a glimpse. Even if it meant lying to myself.

"I do," I said. I forced emotion into my voice, hiding the emptiness from them. "Through the darkest parts of my life I've still loved him, even if I can't understand why."

"And I'm supposed to believe this? That you can so easily forget not only the death of your family, but that this man you claim to love stood by and didn't even lift a hand to interfere on their behalf?" His eyes scrutinized me closely as my hands fisted in my lap. Anger sparked within, but I couldn't let it ignite to anything more. "You've seen his strength. You know what sort of power comes with the title that you now have. Even now he hides his wings from you. I can't help but wonder if that small taste of power made you crave more and seek to kill me for it." His eyes hardened into dark pools of power as he spoke.

I met his gaze and let him see a glimpse of my own strength. "I wouldn't need your power to kill you."

Something like pride filled Aiden's eyes. My treacherous heart wanted to drown in it.

Ofrin chuckled. "Is that so?"

"I hear there is a very specific knife that would do the trick."

Tension grew, becoming nearly tangible on the air. Aiden's thumb continued to brush along my knuckles in a distractingly soothing manner, an offer of comfort. Ofrin's expression was closed off, hiding the thoughts whirling behind his eyes.

"It's nearly impossible to come by that knife," the white-haired demon said. "You'll die an old woman before you get your hands on it."

I shrugged, forcing the tension out of my shoulders as I returned to my food. My thoughts turned to Ephraim's offer. If I truly wanted that knife, I only had to agree to his proposed alliance.

Aiden's hand pulled me from that thought as he brought my knuckles to his lips. The chaste kiss contained all of the words he could not say aloud as his gaze rooted me to the spot. The smile that played at the corners of his mouth was not part of the ploy of the prince. It was entirely Aiden.

The look of pure, inexplicable love in his eyes was nearly my undoing as cracks formed along the barrier of my emotions.

I pulled my hand gently from his, choosing to rest it along his arm as I turned back to Ofrin.

"You think I am here to steal your throne." I spoke clearly. "You are the God of Death. If you truly think your claim to your throne is so fragile, then it's a wonder you've kept it this long and that a mortal wanderer would be any threat to you."

"Careful, girl," he warned in a deadly voice. "You are stepping onto thin ice."

I scowled, giving in to the anger boiling beneath the emptiness. "My family just died. I watched them slaughtered before me, their blood soaking my clothes. Everything was taken from me." I glanced to Aiden, recalling the words I once spoke to him in the quiet of a tent. "They were everything to me. And they were ripped away. Forgive me if I don't care for your insecurities."

"So, you admit this marriage is a ploy to steal my throne?" Ofrin leaned forward, eager to confirm his suspicions.

"No," I said slowly, recalling the ruse Aiden asked of me. "I meant what I said about your son. And I can say with absolute certainty that this marriage is not a plot against you."

Ofrin considered me. He turned his eyes on his son. "I do not believe you," he said firmly. "But consider it fulfilled."

I glanced between father and son. Aiden's shoulders visibly relaxed with his father's words, only adding to my confusion. The expression he turned on me was one of relief.

"But," Ofrin said, returning his gaze to mine, "your family died. It would be a shame for you to be killed trying to steal my throne. Then their deaths would mean as little as their pathetic lives."

I shoved back from the table before more could be said against my family.

My jaw ached as I gritted my teeth together, channeling my anger away to hide the hurt of Ofrin's insult. My steps were thunderous down the marble hall as I marched in the direction of my chambers.

Quick, near-silent footsteps trailed after me. My heart threatened to beat out of my chest as I spun around to face him, for I knew he would follow me.

Aiden paused a step away, closer than I would've liked. "Are you all right?"

His emotions were plain to see on his face. And they were devastating, raw. I turned away, unable to look any more.

"I've played my part for the night," I said, moving closer to the stairs. "I'm returning to my room."

"Esme," he pleaded. I felt his hand grip my arm gently, holding me in place. "About what was said..."

"It was a ploy. I know. I don't need you to explain it to me."

He shook his head, silently begging me to listen as his eyes softened even further. "No. None of what I said was a lie. But about your parents –"

"Don't." My voice was sharp as a blade. His mouth clamped shut with a snap. "Do not speak of them. You have no right."

Anguish tightened my chest, near suffocating as I struggled to return to the blank shell I needed. Only when I had my emotions buried deep within did I open my eyes.

Aiden's eyes narrowed as he noticed the change in my demeanor. I could see him register my anger and hatred as I used my hold on them to bury everything else that tried to overwhelm me.

"I cannot apologize enough for the anguish I've taken part in. But I can explain everything if you let me. Not a word I spoke tonight was a lie," he repeated, eyes scanning the blank expression I wore. "I do love you."

I took another step away. Beneath the desperation on his face lay an underlying current of hope that I would believe the words he spoke. I could not bear to see him look at me that way any longer.

I yanked my arm free. "Never say that to me again," I responded coldly.

He flinched, the gesture subtle enough that I might have imagined it.

I watched his mask return, erasing the emotion from his face entirely. I wasn't even certain he was breathing as he stepped back, hand still outstretched but no longer holding me.

Before he could utter another word, I spun on my heel and retreated to my room, where I would allow myself a brief respite to unleash the angry tears that still burned my eyes.

EIGHT

THE NEXT DAY DRAGGED on. I tried to explore the castle on my own, but every time I left my room a guard was close on my heels.

There had been no sign of Ephraim, and I still couldn't decide if I wanted his help. I knew if I had any hope of accomplishing my goal I needed him, but I couldn't trust that he wouldn't betray me as Aiden had.

A new set of footsteps sounded behind me. I'd been meandering through the halls, searching for the library Fen promised to tell me about. The guard that trailed me remained a few paces away, but close enough to interfere should someone decide to attack. The worst I got, though, were a few glares which came from Drusilla and her companions who I caught watching me through the halls.

Seraphine turned the corner. Her crimson hair was in its familiar twisted braids down her back, the color standing out against her pale clothing.

Her freckled cheeks warmed with a smile. "Esme," she called, waving me over.

I watched the warmth leave her brown eyes as she took in my scowl.

"Aiden sent me to escort you to his study," she said, the smile slipping from her face.

"Why?"

She frowned. "He's asked to speak with you. I don't know what about," she added when I opened my mouth to ask that very question.

Seraphine hesitated a moment more before turning to lead me through the halls.

I followed her up two flights of stairs. We turned down another long corridor with one wall made entirely of glass. Snow-capped mountains could be seen across the horizon to the north, their steepled peaks just touching the grey clouds looming over the realm. From the gloomy sky, dying leaves, and frozen ground, it was blatantly obvious this realm did not radiate the same warmth as the mortal world.

We made another turn into a small passageway that ended with a spiral staircase. I followed Seraphine silently up the stairs to a closed door. The dark wood stood nearly twice my height and almost as wide. I couldn't begin to imagine how thick it might be, but from the silence I guessed it would keep conversations private to any prying ears.

Seraphine didn't say anything before she pushed open the wide door. The room beyond was glorious. Two of the walls were filled with floor to ceiling bookshelves made of the most brilliant red cedar. The wood's strong aroma smelled as if it were freshly chopped from the forest. It smelled like....

Aiden sat behind a wide desk positioned in front of the back wall, made entirely of windows. This view looked out over the forest to the south and the sea in the distance. I wanted to bask in the view, to spend hours marveling at the beauty of the reds and yellows of the tree tops. But the demon prince quickly snagged my attention as he stood.

"You are to have two guards with you at all times during your stay," he said coolly. No hello. No nothing. Just business. I scrutinized his guarded expression, though he didn't meet my eyes.

Killian, Tarsa, and Hakan stood nearby, silent and stoic.

"Why?" I asked.

Again, he didn't glance toward me. Instead, he turned toward the window, putting his back to me. "My father left some of his demons behind. They're meant to offer you extra protection, and his spies are hunting for Ephraim. But we're certain he sent spies here as well. They'll be keeping a close eye on us, specifically our relationship and your whereabouts in this realm."

"He still thinks I'm plotting against him?" That thought seemed drastically foolish to me. I didn't care about the demon. I just wanted to rid myself of his son.

"We'll have to keep up our charade for a while longer." Aiden's posture had grown uncomfortably rigid as he glanced toward his friends. "He needs to believe this marriage wasn't a ploy to undermine him."

"It wasn't."

He sighed. "My father is a suspicious man. After the many centuries he's lived, he believes everyone wants his power."

I thought back to our dinner the night before. He seemed entirely disbelieving of the lies Aiden and I told. Or what I told myself were lies.

Realization dawned as Aiden's gaze finally crashed into mine, knocking the breath from my lungs.

Our charade from dinner must continue, indefinitely.

Anger ignited within me. "Why does it matter what your father thinks? We can continue as we are now, and it'll be clear enough that we're not trying to steal his crown."

The demon prince frowned. "If he doesn't believe this then there's nothing stopping him from taking you to his castle and holding you prisoner. He is too selfish and too skeptical to allow you back into the mortal realm now that he knows about Ephraim. He will lock you away and keep you hidden for the rest of your life until he can take back the power that lives in you."

My stomach tightened. The idea of returning to a life in chains made the scars marking my wrists and ankles burn with a phantom ache.

My hand gripped my wrist, pulling at the nearly too-short sleeves of my tunic. I could feel the air prick my scarred skin as if to taunt the memory I worked to keep hidden.

I felt Aiden's eyes on me like a bolt of lightning. He watched my hands fidget as I forced my gaze around the room, unable to meet anyone's eyes.

I looked over the books filling the shelves along the walls. The leather bindings of many of them looked so frail they might fall apart at the first touch, while others looked as if they'd never been opened and read.

Despair constricted my chest as I thought of Alfie, my younger brother. He'd always loved books and often lost hours in a day to a story. If he were here now, I don't think I'd be able to drag him from the room before he read every book housed on the shelves.

"Esme," Aiden said, exasperated.

I turned to him. "What?"

His brow lifted with something like wry amusement. "Did you hear me?"

"No, I've decided ignoring you better suits me."

Aiden frowned. "Don't be" - he waved his hand in my direction - "like this."

I stared at him blankly. "It's frustrating, isn't it? To talk to someone who feels nothing. Much like how I felt whenever I had to talk to you in Cordovia."

Killian sputtered, quickly attempting to cover the sound with a cough. Hakan frowned at him, patting him harshly on the back.

"It's not you," Aiden said, insistent.

"How would you know what I'm like after losing what I did?" I snapped, feeling the rumbling of anger in my bones. I pushed it down. "You took everything from me. Everything. I will not allow myself to feel that sort of pain again. I can't."

His face turned somber. "I would never wish to cause you pain."

"You already have."

A muscle feathered in his cheek. "Not again."

"You wouldn't get the chance." My voice rang with surety as his gaze met mine once more.

His eyes studied every inch of my face, searching with a growing desperation for any trace of emotion.

Tarsa sighed loudly, pulling us back to the present. I turned away from Aiden, opting to glower at the shelves instead.

"There is something I need to show you," he said, returning to our earlier conversation. "Do you think you are capable of containing your anger for a few moments?"

I scowled. "No, but show me this thing anyway."

He gave an exasperated sigh. Whether he was frustrated with me or the circumstance of our required charade, I wasn't sure.

Aiden pulled a large silver key from a drawer in his desk before approaching me, settling his hand at the small of my back. I opened my mouth for a retort only to be silenced by his scowl.

Already I hated this charade.

Tarsa and Killian exited the room ahead of us and took the stairs down, while Aiden took me up another floor. Hakan and Seraphine trailed closely behind us, eyes alert and watchful though the winding stairs were empty apart from us.

We stopped outside a single door.

Aiden pulled the key from his pocket, twisting it in the lock. My stomach swirled nervously as the lock clicked.

The door, an exact replica of Aiden's apart from the roses and vines carved in the wood, pushed inward silently. The room before me lay bare, containing no furniture whatsoever other than the empty shelves lining one of the walls. Windows that mirrored those in Aiden's study filled the entirety of the back wall, revealing a view of the forest and the half-hidden village it contained.

Aiden ushered me into the room, his hand still lingering on the small of my back. At my pointed scowl he only smirked.

"What is this?" I finally asked when no one bothered to speak. Hakan and Seraphine remained posted outside the door, guarding the empty staircase.

"A room." His voice dripped with sarcasm.

I fought the urge to roll my eyes. "I can see that. But what is it for?"

"It's for you," Aiden said. "This room will be for you to do with as you wish."

"There's nothing in it." I nodded toward the empty shelves.

"Fill it with whatever you like. Sera can take you to the village to visit the bookstore if none of the books here interest you. And she can take you to the carpenter's shop and they'll build you whatever you'd like."

I studied the space around us. It was large; not as large as Aiden's on the floor below, but still quite large for just me.

"Do I get the key to this room too, or will you be restricting my access here?" I asked, hiding my enthusiasm for this gift with an emotionless tone.

He held the key out to me. "This is your room. Only you will have access to it. But a guard will be posted outside whenever you are in here."

I sighed. "Of course. Can I expect your father's spies as well then?"

"I don't know who all of his spies are," he answered honestly. "They could be servants, guards, cooks in the kitchens, or even stable hands. But they'll be watching."

My shoulders sagged as I studied the room. When I turned to face the final wall, I froze. A map covered most of the space, the top standing an entire head higher than me and the bottom ending at my knees. I was almost certain it would be as wide as Aiden's wingspan, should he ever remove the magic that kept his wings hidden from view.

I lifted a tentative hand toward the map. The canvas was painted with the entirety of Cordovia. It even showed further into the lands of the Abandoned Desert in the west. Emotion rose in my chest, and tears blurred my eyes as I looked at my home.

"This is how I used to find you," Aiden admitted softly.

"It took you four months to find me in Elroy's castle through this map?"

"Not exactly," he said slowly. "Before, when I would travel into your realm every night to retrieve the souls you collected, this is what I used. When you were taken by Elroy, I had to remain in Cordovia and track you on foot."

"So, how does this work?" I asked, ignoring his proclamation.

Aiden pressed his palm in the center of the map and whispered my brother's name. My heart raced against my ribs as the map began to change.

The canvas darkened, fading to black. Then everything shifted. Cordovia was gone. Now in its place stood the vast lands of the Abandoned Desert. Aiden spoke another word I didn't hear, and the map shifted again. Oradea, a port city settled between the desert's two rivers, appeared now.

I marveled at the magic woven within the canvas. The tops of buildings and houses could be seen clearly through the map. Streets were marked and ships at the port bobbed as if in water. And through it all, small golden lights blinked into existence.

I didn't realize what I was truly seeing until the lights faded, softening into the canvas, leaving two behind. These two shone bright enough to resemble stars in the night sky. And they were together, side by side, on the outskirts of Oradea.

"Is that...?" My words trailed off with wonder.

Aiden's hand settled on my shoulder. "Mousa and Cordelia are safe. And they're together."

I nodded, blinking through the tears of relief that threatened to hide the map from view.

They'd really survived. Somehow, despite King Elroy's ploy, they made it out of the city. Even though Elias promised as much, I'd never really allowed myself to fully believe it before.

Aiden's hand shifted, moving to grip my hand. I forced the threat of tears away and stepped out of reach, letting emptiness replace the relief I felt a moment before.

"That's really how you tracked my family?" I asked.

He nodded, eyes solemn.

"Is that how you'll continue to track my brother and sister?" The thought of Aiden continuing to track my siblings unsettled me.

"This map is for your use now," he said. "You siblings will be protected, as promised, but this is for you to use as you see fit."

I considered this. "At least I'll be able to see if you betray me again."

The expression he wore now was unfamiliar as he studied me with guarded eyes.

He nodded toward the key I held. "Careful with that. You don't know what wicked monster might try to sneak in here if you're not careful." And then he left me in the empty room.

NINE

I SPENT THE REMAINDER of the day staring at the map, admiring the glowing orbs that signaled my siblings' location. At dusk, Fen brought my dinner to my bedchamber. For once she didn't bother to sit with me, claiming there was work she had to take care of instead.

I started a fire in the large hearth, hoping its warmth would chase away the chill in my bones. I was no closer to finding answers on ending this curse or guaranteeing my family's safety from the demons, or Ephraim. And knowing that only made my frustration grow.

Time moved swiftly as I stared into the fire. The sky outside darkened, the stars awakened, and the air cooled. My eyes grew tired, but my mind wouldn't sleep. The anger I directed at myself, at Aiden, at Ephraim, at everyone who had a part in my family's fate, refused to settle.

A knock at the door jolted me from my reverie. I glanced toward the small door in the corner that connected my room to Aiden's. My stomach tumbled as I straightened on the settee.

"What?" I called when the knock sounded again.

The door cracked open. "May I come in?" Aiden asked in a voice much gentler than I expected.

"If you must." I stood, moving so the settee lay between us as he stepped into the room. "What now?"

His eyes were ever watchful as he spoke. "I had something made; the witch in my employ was able to make this faster than expected." He held out a small vial of dark liquid.

I took it in my hands, grimacing at the smell it emitted. "What is it?"

"It will sever the marriage bond between us," he said, eyes somber. "Normally, the only way to break such a bond is through death, but I was able to find an alternative."

I frowned. "Why marry me in the first place if you're going to offer me this?"

"I am not asking you to take this and sever our marriage," Aiden clarified slowly, hesitant. "I meant it when I said I truly had your safety in mind when binding our souls. I've only ever wanted your safety and happiness, Esme. But it was my mistake in making that decision for you."

"Among others," I added stiffly.

He nodded. "It is true that the protection of my title extends to your siblings, and it is my hope to keep them safe. But the choices regarding your family's safety should be made by you. And if you feel this marriage is not the best way to keep them safe then that is a decision you should make. Not me."

I studied the small vial. "I drink this and our marriage ends? I am free to go?"

"You were always free to go, Esme," he said softly. "But I urge you to consider the repercussions of a decision like this. Do not make it lightly."

"When you trapped me in this marriage, did you make that decision in haste as well?"

Aiden was quiet for a moment. I could see thoughts swirling behind his eyes as he chose his next words carefully. "If you take this, my father may decide to trap you in his dungeons until he can siphon the essence from you. You would no longer be my wife, which would allow him to treat you as he sees fit. The same goes for Ephraim, though he may try to take you again anyway."

"And my family?"

His mouth tightened into a thin line. "I can offer to send Seraphine or Killian to look after them until you return to them, but my father may deem their lives forfeit anyway."

I scowled. "Then how are they protected now?"

"Now," he said, "they are shielded with the same magic I used to keep your family safe in Cordovia. Once our marriage ends, so does my power over their safety."

I tucked the vial into my pocket. It was true that I wanted out of this marriage, to be with my family. But I also knew the severity of the dangers lurking in the shadows. I wouldn't allow my family to suffer again because of this curse I was made to carry.

"Thank you," I said honestly.

Surprise flitted across his face for a breath before his expression cleared. With a stiff nod he turned to leave.

The light of the flames caught on a mark poking through the top of his tunic.

The memory of that scar's origin flashed through me. Ephraim, standing over Aiden's wounded form. A scream burning my throat. A poisoned knife protruding from Aiden's chest. And the moment after, in the tent when he pulled away from me.

A thought occurred to me as I studied the scar, much more prominent than the others I knew he carried.

"Why was Ephraim able to heal so much faster than you?" I asked as he reached the door to his room.

Aiden stilled. His eyes looked to the raised mark over his heart. "Ephraim is the Angel of Life. I am only the heir to Death."

"So, he's stronger than you," I said, letting my question come out as a statement.

His grimace held little heat. "I was spreading my protection to every member of your family for many weeks, Esme. My healing abilities, my strength, the protection of my name and connection to your family – over time that weakened me."

"So that's why you had them killed," I said, letting a touch of anger cool my voice. "To get your strength back."

He shook his head. When he took a step in my direction I backed away. The anger he must've seen plainly on my face made him pause. "No," he said through gritted teeth. "I spread my protection to all of them to keep you safe. To keep you all safe. It's what you wanted; for your family to be safe."

"And now they're dead," I said in a sepulchral tone.

A muscle feathered in his cheek. "Yes."

I looked away, hating the way my eyes filled with tears as my fury grew. I would not let him see me shed another tear over his betrayal.

"I cannot apologize enough for that," he said thickly. I studied the sadness on his face. Before, I would have believed the rawness of it. Now I could only see it as a deception, like every other interaction we'd had.

"No," I said shortly. "You can't. You are cruel, and selfish, and the worst of monsters."

"A monster?" he asked, scoffing with disbelief. "You do not know the truth of what you speak."

"You killed them!"

"It was not me," he yelled back. My mouth clamped shut, surprised by his outburst. His eyes turned pleading as he took a step toward me. "I did not kill your family. I can swear to the stars you love that I am not the cause of their deaths."

"Liar."

"I have not lied to you, neither now nor in the past," he said. "They knew what they were doing." His voice grew quiet, almost as if he wasn't sure he wanted to tell me.

"What?" My voice was soft with horror.

"They offered a deal to my father," he explained slowly. "I tried to convince them not to, that my father would have no trouble warping their offer to his will."

"My parents would never do such a thing," I raged. "They would never let Alfie, or Amara, or any of us die that way."

He didn't speak. He just watched me yell while he stood still, hands clenched tightly at his sides. I watched as he opened his mouth to speak, to lie again. But his mouth clamped shut, uncertainty settling over his features as he watched my fury burn brighter.

I grabbed the closest thing within reach and threw it at him. The pillow bounced softly off his chest. Frustrated tears filled my eyes, and the humming in my chest flowed through every nerve in my body as I reached for the fork on the table. I threw it at him, a cry of rage burning my throat as he dodged it effortlessly.

He looked too calm, too at ease as he watched the anger overwhelm me.

"Tell me the truth," I seethed as I threw the dinner knife at him. He batted it away.

There was a tenderness to Aiden's eyes that I hated. I despised the way that he could stand there so calmly and tell me my family chose death. That my parents would even consider agreeing to have their children murdered was an insult to their memory.

I buried my sadness beneath fury.

"I'm not lying to you," he pleaded. "Your parents did everything they could to protect you."

I shook my head, forcing the emotion away. "They wouldn't kill my siblings. They wouldn't. This is a cruel lie, even for you."

He didn't answer, and that only enraged me more.

"You're a coward to hide behind those foolish lies," I said scathingly. "Is this the fearsome Prince of Death I've heard tales about? A coward who hides behind false tales to protect his own power at the expense of a girl he convinced to love him?"

Aiden's gaze hardened. "Don't pretend you didn't feel it too."

"Feel what?" I snapped.

"The strength," he said, prowling closer. "The power that came with their deaths. I knew you felt it when Adine died. You said so yourself after watching your grandmother sacrifice herself to protect you. I felt it too. That's how I know you also felt it when your family died. Because I felt it when the king had them killed."

I backed away, not wanting to hear any more.

"I felt the strength of my power returned," he said, glowering at me. "I felt their souls leave their mortal bodies and join my father's domain. And it strengthened me, as his heir. Just as it did you, his Soul Collector. It was the very reason your brother and sister were able to survive. So do not pretend that strength didn't thrill you. That the power that flows through you now that their lives are no longer under my protection doesn't excite you."

I glowered at him. "You're wrong."

"Am I?" He took another step in my direction. "I am not the reason they were killed, Esme. But I don't deny that I was strengthened from it. Just as you were."

The truth to his words stung because I *did* feel their souls depart when they died, but unlike him I didn't bask in the high of it. I raged, and I used it to attack the king. While Aiden had stood by and done nothing.

When his icy gaze left mine, dipping to my mouth, I froze. I watched his fierce exterior melt into something warmer, tender. But I didn't want him to look at me like that anymore. I wanted him to hurt as much as I did.

"I hate you," I spat through my teeth. The warmth in his gaze evaporated in an instant. "You are as vile as the stories Nonna used to tell of the Prince of Death. I regret ever having met you."

My words seemed to hinder him as he dropped his chin, hiding his face beneath a curtain of hair. When his eyes found mine again there was a sadness to them that I didn't understand. I would've preferred his anger. I wanted him to rage at me as I raged at him. I wanted to yell and kick and scream and unleash every bit of anger I had held toward him since the day I learned his true name. I wanted an excuse to unleash the rage simmering inside me.

He wouldn't give that to me. But I knew who would.

"Leave," I said coldly. "I don't want you here anymore."

He flinched, casting his eyes down in an effort to hide it. I watched the impact of my words before his mask slid into place. The only sign he'd heard me at all was the stillness of his body. As if he wouldn't let himself feel the sting of my words.

He left without another word or a backward glance.

As soon as the door clicked shut behind him, I raced to the wardrobe. I slipped out of the casual clothes I'd been wearing and dressed warmly, prepared for the cold night ahead. I pulled on thick wool breeches, a shirt and a warm tunic, and a dark cloak.

After slipping my feet into heavy boots, I braided my hair down my back, careful to tuck it into the cloak to remain unseen.

I paused by the door leading to Aiden's room. The door was thick enough to block most noises, but I tucked a chair beneath the handle in a weak effort to prevent his return.

As quickly as I could manage, I slipped onto the balcony and climbed down the thick vines lining the stone wall of the castle. My fingers had grown numb from the cold by the time my boots hit the grass.

Guards continued their patrol as I took extra care to stick to the shadows. The music of my family did not tangle with the breeze this night; the gardens were soundless as I slipped through the shadows.

Before I knew it, I was on my hands and knees crawling through the hole in the garden wall. The forest beyond was deathly silent. There were no chirping birds, no soft footfalls of wildlife. Not even the wind made a sound as it brushed a loose strand of hair across my face.

It was silent as death. Fitting for the Realm of Souls.

"Took you long enough."

I spun around, finding Ephraim half hidden in shadow. His feathered wings pulled in tight across his back as he shifted closer. My breath clouded in the air before me, pushing away any feeling of discomfort or worry that my heart tried to make known.

"You said you could give me the revenge I want," I said, recalling his claim. He nodded slowly, the dawning of a smile lifting his mouth. "I'm ready to make him hurt, the way he hurt me. I want them all to pay."

His smile grew, shifting into something cold and wicked. Ephraim grabbed my hand and pressed his lips to my knuckles. I watched as he studied the marking decorating the hand he held — proof of my marriage to the demon prince.

"On one condition," I said before he could speak. One of his brows lifted in wry amusement. "My family cannot be harmed. By you, your angels, or any of the demons. When this curse is broken, we need to be free of it all."

Ephraim yanked on the hand he held, pulling me against his chest. The sun began to lighten the sky behind him, glistening off the frost dusting the tips of his feathered wings and the scales along his horns. I swallowed nervously against the brutality of the sight.

"Your family will not come to any harm by my hand. I will teach you just what sort of darkness lives within you," he pledged. "And through that darkness, we will both get our revenge. Of that, I can promise you. Your prince will hurt. Just as you do."

TEN

When I made my way back to the castle in the early hours of dawn, no one stopped me to ask where I'd been or how I'd escaped the confines of my room.

With no one to question me, I hurried through a hot bath and yanked a brush through my tangled curls. Choosing my attire was harder. With a new task from Ephraim, I had to pick something simple enough so as not to cause suspicion, but also elegant enough to draw the needed attention. I settled on a violet gown that hugged my middle and dangled loosely to my ankles. The thick velvet kept the winter chill at bay as I made my way to the dining hall for lunch. Daemon, one of Ofrin's demons, trailed behind me, along with Drusilla's blond friend who just happened to be the guard posted outside of my room. Their presence was almost easy to ignore, except unlike the other guards, Daemon talked too much.

"Do you make it a habit to strut about weaponless?" he asked as we passed a scowling Drusilla at the bottom of the stairs.

I ignored the crude demon's glower. "What makes you think I'm weaponless?" I still carried the knife Aiden had given me, keeping it hidden in my boot.

Daemon grinned, choosing to walk at my shoulder instead of trailing behind like the other guard. He was shorter than most men, only an inch or so taller than me. His skin was an olive shade that contrasted handsomely with the green flecks in his eyes. But he had a smile that elicited mischief, something that made me extra cautious around him.

"Something tells me that even with a weapon you'd be useless in a fight," he teased, bringing a scowl to my face.

The words he spoke were true. As Aiden told me the day before, just because I carried a knife didn't mean I knew how to protect myself. Luckily, Ephraim had promised to help me control the essence. Something that he explained was part of Death's power and strength, something born of this realm. Something to incite fear.

The catch was I had to allow myself to feel the emotions I had been working so hard to dampen. He claimed the essence was connected to my emotions. As long as I allowed myself to feel, I could control its power - a feat he seemed determined I accomplish with our partnership.

"Though Jadan was the same way," the demon said with a shrug, smile slipping from his mouth.

"Jadan?"

He nodded. "You met him at dinner."

"Your white-haired friend," I guessed.

"He was mortal once as well," he said. "Sacrificed his soul to Ofrin so he could protect his family. Fat lot of good it did him when the poor lad couldn't even wield a sword."

"So, is that what happened to all of you here?" I asked, eager to learn more about the demons that haunted this land. "You were mortal and gave up your soul, an eternity of promised peace, to serve the God of Death until he pardoned you?"

Daemon fell silent as we passed a group of servants. I watched the way their gazes scrutinized the demon at my side. It seemed most of Aiden's demons were wary of Ofrin's guards.

"Most of us were born," Daemon finally said as we entered the empty dining hall.

I blinked. "Born? Born a demon?"

Daemon nodded, his shaggy black hair falling over his forehead and into his eyes. "Making a deal with Ofrin isn't as common as you might think. There aren't many immortals left who struck a deal to serve him."

"Why not?" I asked, thinking back to Aiden's claim the night before. "I got the impression many make deals with Death. Most of the demons I've met sold their souls to him."

His face remained impassive. "Ofrin can be... Well, let's just say when you offer yourself to the God of Death, you must be extremely clear in your contingencies, or he may twist your offer to suit his needs."

"What needs does he have that would make him twist a deal?"

Daemon sighed, brow furrowing as he thought over his response. "Apart from protection or greed? Arrogance. Entitlement. The list truly goes on."

My brows rose in surprise. "Clearly you think highly of your king."

He smiled crookedly, shrugging like he had not a care in the realm. "He may be the God of Death, but that doesn't change what he's like at his core."

I considered his admission as we entered the dining hall. Daemon moved to stand in the far corner, leaning against the wall as if already bored.

"So," I said, taking my seat in front of the fire, "you were born a demon. You've always lived in the Realm of Souls, and you've always been immortal."

Again, the demon nodded. "Yes, Princess."

"How old are you?"

"I've lived for over five hundred years," he said, almost solemnly. "The entire purpose of my existence is to serve the God of Death, and his heir."

Unwavering sadness filled me as I studied him. His demeanor was calm, still. I couldn't detect any remorse for the life he had to live. But I couldn't imagine spending five hundred years in this realm, serving Death. After a while, I'm sure I would want to seek the sort of peace my friends had found, especially if they were mortals who'd had their souls returned.

I had agreed to attend lunch as Ephraim's eyes. I was to learn of Aiden's plans, if there were any, against the angel, and play the part of the loving wife. Not only because Ofrin's spies lingered in Aiden's court, but because in order to get close to Aiden again, he had to believe that I'd forgiven him.

"It's not as bad as you might think," Daemon said, noting my uncertain expression. "My parents were kind. They loved me endlessly. And I have had friends who spanned many centuries of my long life."

I raised a brow. "And the downside?"

Daemon smiled, flashing a chipped front tooth. He raised a hand to his head, pulling back the shaggy ends of his hair. I gasped as I caught sight of what was revealed.

Two small horns, barely larger than my thumb, stuck up from his hairline. They weren't like Ephraim's. These were deep red, the color of blood. And yet they seemed to brighten in the light of the fire behind me, letting the flames enhance their color.

"These are a bit painful when they first grow in," he said, letting his hair fall back over his forehead, obstructing the horns from view.

"Do all demons have those?" I asked.

He shook his head. "Not so much anymore. Even wings are a rarity in recent centuries."

Before more could be said, the doors swung open, cutting off our conversation.

Aiden stalked into the room, freezing mid-stride as his eyes found me. I watched the uncertainty filter through his face as he glanced toward his father's demon. Daemon grinned, waving in greeting.

I stood from my chair, running a hand down the front of my dress. "I thought I might join you for lunch. I hope that's all right."

He studied me a moment more. I could see the recollection of our last conversation play out in his eyes as he considered his response. It wasn't until the shuffle of boots sounded that he gathered his wits.

Aiden moved to my side, pulling my hand to his mouth where he placed a chaste kiss along the marriage mark painting my skin. I should've known he would slip into this charade easily.

"Of course." There was something hidden in his tone that I couldn't decipher. "I'd love nothing more than for you to be at my side."

Daemon snorted but was immediately silenced by Aiden's glower.

I placed a hand on Aiden's arm as he took his place in the seat next to mine. "Will the others be joining us?"

His body stilled beneath my touch. "Yes," he said, voice clipped. "They should be here shortly."

"Wonderful."

I felt his gaze focus on my face, his uncertainty and curiosity plain for me to read.

"What?" I asked when he continued to study me.

He shook his head, brows furrowed and mouth turned down in a frown. "I am continuously surprised by you." His voice was quiet so as not to be overheard.

"Is this not what you wanted?" I asked, allowing him to see some of the uncertainty I felt. He froze, watching me closely. "I thought you wanted me here to prove to your father's spies that our marriage is not a ploy."

"Yes," he said, leaning away though my hand remained on his arm. "But I trust my guards not to run to my father just because you are still adjusting to your new surroundings."

I rolled my eyes, forcing a coy smile. "They might not, but I can name at least one person who would run to your father."

Daemon raised his hand, flashing his chip-tooth grin. "I would."

Aiden glared at the demon. "It has only been a couple of days, Esme," he said quietly. "I understand if you need more time."

"Maybe she's stronger than you think," Daemon interjected, obviously listening though we spoke barely above a whisper.

"Maybe you should refrain from presuming to tell me about my own wife," Aiden snapped.

A shadow shuddered behind him. My chest tightened nervously as the hint of his wings flashed along his back. But as Aiden took a calming breath, the air cleared where his wings should be.

I scowled, his father's comment coming to mind. "Why do you continue to keep your wings hidden?"

"I thought, after everything, that maybe you needed time to adjust to our marriage before you were reminded of what I was." His voice was low as he spoke, practically between clenched teeth.

Hakan entered then, quickly followed by Tarsa, Killian, and Seraphine. They each glanced my way as they found their seats at the table. Only Tarsa looked unaffected by my presence. Her ever-present scowl remained in place as she took the seat directly across from me.

"Milady," Killian said with a dip of his chin. His usual smile was gone, replaced with trepidation as he took his seat beside Aiden.

Hakan merely nodded in my direction before he took the seat beside Tarsa. The tension in the room rose as they each glanced toward Aiden, questions in their eyes.

Seraphine offered me a tentative smile as she took her place in the chair a space away from Tarsa, leaving an empty seat between the two of them.

"It's good to have you, Esme," she said. The honesty of her words warmed something within me.

I nodded, not trusting my voice. The emotion filling me now was unfamiliar and untrustworthy.

A stout man entered before anyone could speak further. He had dark skin and dark hair braided down his back in a manner similar to Seraphine's usual style. He stood no taller than me and somehow managed to carry three trays of food in his arms.

"Here you are, Your Highness," he said in a gentle voice. "I hope everything is to your liking, and oh–"

His voice cut off so suddenly I jumped. His dark eyes were wide as he glanced in my direction, jaw slack.

"Pardon, Your Highness," he said, bowing low in my direction. "I hadn't known you would be here. I'm afraid I already sent your food with Miss Fen to your room."

I smiled, quick to ease the nerves I could practically feel radiating out of him. "It's not a problem. I'm sure Aiden would be more than happy to share with me."

The cook's cheeks reddened slightly as he bowed toward Aiden and quickly left the room.

Each tray carried several smaller plates filled with a different sandwich and soup pairing.

Aiden set his plate in the space between us. "This is Lurik's special recipe," he said, a hint of a smile in his voice. "He says it's so delicious because he cooks the pork in a secret sauce."

"What kind of sauce?" I asked, studying the sandwich as Aiden placed half of it in front of me.

He shrugged. "He'll never say."

"And believe me," Killian said around a mouthful of food, "we've tried to get an answer out of him. But the old demon is taking that secret to his grave."

I smiled, inhaling the mouthwatering scent. My stomach rumbled softly in response which brought the hint of a crooked smile to Aiden's lips.

"Try it," Seraphine said as she took a bite of her own sandwich, something containing leafy greens. "I promise it's good."

I could feel the eyes of the others as I bit into the sandwich. Rich juices flooded my mouth, flavors awakening every nerve on my tongue. I might've groaned because a moment later Killian laughed.

"Told you it was delicious," he said, taking another bite.

"I need to know what kind of sauce this is," I said over my mouthful of food.

Hakan huffed a laugh. "Good luck getting an answer out of him."

I sighed, taking the moment to bask in the glory of the succulent meat.

Aiden's thumb brushed along the corner of my mouth. Sauce I hadn't noticed escape my sandwich now covered the pad of his thumb.

I watched his eyes darken, mischief replacing the apprehension he may have felt at my presence. He placed his thumb in his mouth, licking the sauce from his finger.

Something burned deep within me; a fire I thought long burnt out erupted through my veins as my cheeks warmed considerably.

He held my gaze until he released his thumb from his mouth, dismissing me easily as he returned to his own food.

I blinked, forcing myself to remain focused by recalling his words from the night before. His idiotic claim that my parents were the ones behind their own murders.

The heat in my veins cooled immediately. I caught Seraphine's eye as she watched the interaction with Aiden. There was a softness to her that wasn't there before, like she saw something I missed.

But it was Tarsa's unyielding stare that made me pause. I was almost certain she could read every emotion and every thought playing out within me.

"There you are," Fen said as she stepped into the room, a tray held aloft. "I've been waiting in your room for a quarter of an hour."

I smiled apologetically but Aiden spoke before I could.

"Esme decided to eat with us today." He glanced at me as if still bewildered I was there.

Fen sat in the empty seat between Tarsa and Seraphine, smiling to herself. "I'm glad to see it," she said cheerily. "It's about time the young newlyweds spent some time together."

My cheeks warmed again as I returned to my food, avoiding everyone's gazes.

"I was thinking of heading into the village this afternoon," Killian said in the following silence. "The blacksmith has a new bow that he thought I might like to try. And a sword for you, Hakan."

Seraphine smiled, glancing toward Fen. "We'll go with you. Fen has some work to finish up at her shop and I wouldn't mind visiting the market."

"You have a shop?" I asked, looking to Fen. Now that she was seated beside Tarsa it was easy to see the familial resemblance.

"I do," she said, smiling toward Seraphine.

"She is the best seamstress in the realm," Seraphine said proudly.

The smile I wore now was entirely genuine. "So that explains why my wardrobe is filled with perfectly tailored clothes."

Out of the corner of my eye I saw Aiden glance in my direction, but I ignored him.

Fen blushed, bashful. "I couldn't help myself. When I heard you would be coming, I wanted to make sure you had enough clothes to last for however long you decided to stay."

My smile faded. She would've needed months to complete my entire wardrobe. When did Aiden decide I was coming here?

Sensing my growing agitation, Aiden turned to Hakan. "We have some time before meeting with more of my father's delegates this afternoon."

Hakan nodded. "I'll visit the witch's shop and bring it to your study." He left without another word.

"What is he getting?" I asked as Killian engaged Fen and Seraphine in conversation.

"You should go into the village with Sera and Fen," Aiden said instead. "Killian can show you the carpenter's shop and you can pick out a piece of furniture for your study."

I scowled but quickly erased it from my face before anyone could see. Instead, I forced a smile. "Maybe another time."

Killian stood as I did, smiling politely. "I'll be more than happy to take you, Esme. Just say the word."

"Of course," I said, returning his smile easily. "Once my shelves are filled with books I will send word to you."

The young immortal grinned before taking his seat again, returning to his meal.

Aiden only spared me a glance as I rose from the table. When I was certain he wasn't going to say anything more, I placed a chaste kiss on his cheek. His eyes speared me in place, and there was a question there beneath the surprise.

"I'll see you all later then," I said, smiling to myself as I left them in stunned silence.

Daemon didn't follow me right away like I expected. The other guard who trailed after us before lunch had disappeared too, leaving me to wander the halls alone as I began another search for the library.

I didn't make it far before arms wrapped around my middle like steel binds, yanking me from the empty corridor I had wandered into. I opened my mouth to call for Aiden, but a cold hand clamped over my mouth a moment later, muting my protests.

Before I could even think to reach for the knife in my boot, I was shoved into a dark room where the only sounds were my ragged breathing and the click of the lock in the door.

ELEVEN

I BLINKED INTO THE solid darkness that encroached on me. I spun around, searching for my attacker.

A soft chuckle sounded nearby. "Demon pet. Demon pet. What a lovely little demon pet." The airy voice made the hair at the back of my neck stand on end.

I spun again, turning blindly in the dark as the voice echoed around me. The only hint of light came from the gap in the drapes on the far wall. But it was such a small sliver that it did nothing to enhance my sight.

"Who are you?" I asked, fumbling for the knife in my boot.

My only answer was a soft scuffle of feet across the floor, closer than before. I yelped, lurching away.

"Such a pretty demon pet," the deep voice cooed.

Something brushed along my cheek, freezing the breath in my lungs. I leapt back, stumbling over the hem of the stupid dress I now regretted wearing.

"Who are you?" I asked again. I felt oddly safer holding the small knife aloft, though I knew it would do me little good in the dark.

"The same question. The demon pet only has one question." The voice sighed softly. "But I have many. I have questions for the demon pet."

Unease stirred within me as the essence shifted, warming my chest with its strength. I took a nervous step toward the curtains, hands shaking as I tightened my grip on the knife.

"No, no demon pet," the voice said, directly in front of me now. Cold hands folded around mine, quickly taking the knife from me. I gasped, trying to stumble away, but the hands found either side of my face, pulling me close.

White eyes blinked in the darkness. The eyes seemed to exude their own light as they glowed in the dark of the room, seeing what I could not.

"Tell me, demon pet," it crooned in its singsong voice. "What has teeth sharper than any knife yet soothes the heart's greatest strife?"

"What?" I asked, terror fogging my brain. I glanced toward the sliver in the curtains. It was still too far away for me to reach.

The demon tsk'd. "Poor demon pet. Doesn't know the answer. How about this one? What causes wars and bloodshed, but is breakable as a piece of thread and convinces many not to fear the dead?"

My throat tightened nervously as I stared into the demon's white eyes, my face trapped in its hands. There was a trace of the dark irises I imagined this creature once had, but now all I could see was the soft white glow.

Sharp pointy teeth flashed in my field of vision as the demon laughed under its breath. "It's the demon pet's last chance. It burns and devours; nourishes and grows; but when left to kings, may kill those you know."

"What?" I asked, trying to pull my face from the demon's cold hands. "I don't know what any of that means."

The demon sighed, digging its nails into my cheeks. "Demon pet must know. If it doesn't, then all will be ruined."

Fear rushed through me. Another release of breath sounded to my left, near the door that I was almost certain was still locked.

A chill whispered down my spine as I readied for a scream.

The demon clamped a hand over my mouth. "No no, demon pet. If it screams it will bleed."

Panic seized my lungs as the demon pulled me closer. My eyes widened as I saw the sharp points of its teeth.

"Reek," a deep voice said from the shadows. "Do not harm the human."

My mind whirled with the memory of that voice. I didn't know who it belonged to, or where I'd heard it before. But there was something eerily familiar about it.

Reek, the demon holding my face, groaned. I remained frozen as I felt him pull away in the dark, closing his eyes and taking their sinister glow with them.

"Know this, Soul Collector," that familiar deep voice said, closer now. "Whether you are a bride or a pet, your power will be brought to its full potential. Even if you try to avoid it."

I launched toward the drapes, panic making my limbs move more quickly than expected. I took my first real breath as the drapes fell to the floor, unleashing the yellow rays of the day's light.

I spun around, ready to run, only to find the room empty. My eyes landed on the door. It hung open, the hall beyond silent.

I was fairly certain I'd never seen the demon before. I couldn't put a face to either voice I heard, but the threat was real all the same.

Running a hand over my face, I moved toward the bookcase. A chill lingered along my skin in the aftereffects of the encounter. The knife the demon had taken from me lay on one of the shelves, placed carefully before the only stack of books.

I hid the knife in my boot, studying the titles. These books were old, far older than any of the ones I'd seen in Aiden's study. I pulled one from the shelf, gently cradling it in my hands. The leather felt as if it might crumble at the turn of a page. Dust covered the title, obstructing it from view.

Using the sleeve of my gown, I cleared the cover. It was a history book about the Realm of Souls.

My heart skipped. Warmth filtered into my limbs again as I stared at what I held. This could have the answers I needed, or at least some of them.

I reached for the others, eager to take them to my own study immediately.

My lingering panic was finally answered by the surging of the essence in my chest. In the demon's presence it had grown almost dormant. But now that my rattled emotions were free of the demon's proximity, the essence woke. I felt it trembling inside me, seeking a way out. There was no end to it as it forced its way into my mind, searching through my most painful memories as my terror grew, until finally, the power erupted.

I blinked into the light, surprised to find myself sprawled on my back. My limbs felt numb as I rose onto shaking knees. The room remained empty; no one had come to investigate the surge of power. No one seemed to have felt it as I had.

Scooping the books into my arms, I raced from the room before Reek could return.

I returned to find my apartment empty, which I was grateful for as I quickly tossed the books onto the bed and stripped for a bath.

The water was too hot against my skin, still chilled from the strange demon's touch. Fear churned in my gut as I scrubbed at my skin. I ached to be free of the feel of the creature's scaly hands that lingered on my skin.

Even the essence continued to react as if the danger remained. With every racing beat of my heart it pulsed through my veins, the dark power strengthening with every breath.

It seemed the longer I stayed in this realm the stronger it became. If I wanted to be free of it before it overtook me, I needed to break this curse, and soon.

"Esme?" a faint voice called from the sitting area.

I sighed. Of course I wouldn't be left alone for long. "Just a moment," I called.

Now that some semblance of warmth had returned to my body, I quickly dried and dressed in wool breeches and a fitted sweater. I was forced to braid my thick hair down my spine so it wouldn't completely soak the back of my sweater.

I grabbed a pair of thick socks, slipping them on to cover the scars at my ankles, before I noticed the scratch along my cheek. The air stung the sensitive area, thanks to the strange demon's too long nails.

The essence pulsed at a quickening pace as if sensing my unease. I forced calm into my body. I couldn't let anyone see me this way. It would stir up too many questions about the essence I carried.

When I stepped into the main room, Fen stood with her back to me, bent over the fireplace.

"Ah, there you are," she said as she spotted me. She took a seat on the armchair facing the fireplace, nodding to the one beside it. "Sit. I've brought some food for you."

My brow furrowed as I joined her near the growing fire. "We just had lunch. I thought you'd be in the village with Seraphine and Killian by now."

The look she gave me was one of surprise and confusion. "That was hours ago. Just how long have you been in that bath?"

I shrugged. Everything after my encounter with Reek had become a strange blur. Fen took my hands before I could say anything more. She turned my palms up, showing me the pruning of my fingers. She pursed her lips as she dropped my hands.

My gaze slid to the window, surprised to find the beginnings of night-fall darkening the horizon. "I guess I just didn't realize how much time had passed."

"Are you sure it has nothing to do with that mark on your face?"

Spine straightening, I lifted a tentative hand toward my cheek. The area was tender, sore from the demon's claws.

"Did someone try to hurt you?" she asked, voice laced with concern.

I shook my head. "I'm fine."

She scowled but said nothing more as she placed a tray of food in my lap. My stomach rumbled at the aroma of spices now coating the air.

"How was the village?" I asked, partly to distract her from her scrutiny and partly because I was curious, though I wouldn't dare admit it.

"You should come next time. I'm sure the people would love to meet their princess."

My throat tightened around a piece of food, making me cough uncontrollably. Fen only smiled, seeming pleased with herself as she watched me squirm.

"If you asked, I'm sure the prince would even take you himself. There isn't anything that boy wouldn't give you if you showed interest in anything."

I scowled. "I show interest," I argued, remembering my agreement with Ephraim. Convince Aiden I'd forgiven him, get close enough to learn his plans, and finally find a way to break this curse.

"You sulk in your room, child," she said with a raspy laugh. "Joining him for lunch once does not exactly prove your argument."

I sighed, letting my mind drift as I stared into the fire, food temporarily forgotten. Ephraim asked for me to play the part Aiden expected of me, and then some. But the problem was I just wasn't sure what Aiden expected of me and what he might find suspicious. How was one supposed to pretend to be in love with someone after that person killed their family?

"Eat. Before it gets cold." Fen's sharp voice pulled me from my thoughts.

I bit into the pork. The juicy flavor attacked my mouth just as the sandwich from lunch had.

"I need to know what Lurik puts in this sauce," I said over a mouthful of food.

"You're welcome to try and pry it out of him," she laughed. "But even my dear sister couldn't get that information."

"I keep forgetting Tarsa is your sister," I admitted. "You just seem so different."

Her brows went up. "Because she looks twenty and I look old?"

I choked on my food, face reddening. "No. No, that's not what I meant. I just meant you seem so nice, and Seraphine obviously loves you. But Tarsa is just so..."

Fen laughed, the deep sound reverberating off the bare stone walls. "Many people have voiced those exact thoughts."

"I just don't understand how you and your sister can be so different," I said with flushed cheeks.

"Are you and your sister not different?"

I shrugged. "A little. But even before I was taken, we weren't as different as you and Tarsa."

"Well, she's lived a much different life than I have," she said solemnly.

I studied her in silence. I wanted to ask about Tarsa, but I knew Fen wouldn't delve into the secrets of her sister's past. If those were answers I was desperate enough to get, I'd have to ask Tarsa myself. And I knew that would result in getting my tongue cut out.

Fen nodded toward the stack of dusty books on my bed. "Are those for your study?"

"Yes." I paused, unsure if I should reveal my latest encounter. "They looked interesting."

"I'll make sure Aiden carves out some time to take you to the palace's library soon," she said, smiling. "In the meantime, I'm sure he'd be more than happy to carry those to your study for you."

I shook my head. "That's not necessary. I can carry them myself."

She waved me away, standing to take my tray. "They are all eager to be your friends again, Esme. The only reason I keep bringing your food to your room is because they all fear you would let yourself starve before eating with them. Today gave them some hope, but not enough to feel confident in seeking you out."

I frowned, watching her move toward the door. "After what they took part in it's a wonder they don't understand that perhaps I just need time."

"Of course they do," she said gently. "But the threat to your life, to your brother and sister's lives, is still there. If you let yourself waste away in this room, it might be too late to save any of you by the time you reappear."

I watched her leave in silence.

They all thought I was remaining in my room, wallowing in my pain. But now, I had a purpose, a plan. And that plan didn't start with me hiding away as they expected.

On silent feet, I slipped into my warmer layers and shimmied down the vines along the wall. My new purpose was waiting for me in the forest.

TWELVE

THOUGH I'D DRESSED FOR the night air, I hadn't realized just how cold it would be. My fingers were frozen stiff as I paced the small clearing between the trees.

Ephraim had told me to meet him here at midnight, beneath the largest tree carved with three slashes down the trunk. At first glance I thought it was marked by some wild animal living in these woods, but upon closer inspection, I could see the beginnings of rot around the edges of the slashes. This tree had been marked by his poisoned blade.

Just like Aiden's wound, the scratches here were black. I didn't dare touch the markings, but I knew what I would feel. The frail bark would give way beneath my touch. Small lines filled with the poison trailed outward from the slashes as it slowly spread.

"Beautiful, isn't it?" Ephraim's voice echoed through the trees. I hadn't heard his approach in the silent forest. He moved as deftly as any predator.

His wings were tucked in along his back as he stepped out from the shadows. The air around him cooled as he joined me in front of the tree. "The poison. It's beautiful, the way it slowly kills."

I frowned, attempting to read his expression. "Do you have a lot of weapons with that poison?"

"That depends on what you consider *a lot*."

I turned away from the tree, unable to look at the deadly poison any longer. "If I'm not back before dawn they'll notice my absence."

Ephraim stepped closer. A break in the branches above allowed the faint trace of starlight to shine on his silver hair. "I assume they're still suspicious of your attachment to him?"

I nodded. "Most likely. I did threaten his life once or twice."

The angel smirked. "If only you were capable of such a thing."

"Why did you want to meet with me tonight?" I asked, pointedly ignoring his jest. "I thought you wanted me to remain in the castle to spy?"

"I do," he said, coming to stand a few paces before me. "You are to be my eyes and ears for conversations behind closed doors. Believe it or not there are certain places even my own spies cannot reach within your husband's castle."

I grimaced. "You have spies here too?"

"Of course," he said, aghast.

"Is Reek one of them?"

Even in the shadow of the forest I could see the way his face drained of color. "How do you know that name?"

I shrugged, confused by his trepidation. "I sort of met him earlier. Though I don't know who he is or what he really wants."

"Did he speak to you?"

I thought back to the encounter. "He spoke in riddles I didn't understand."

Ephraim remained silent for a beat. The wings across his back tucked in further along his spine. "That creature is not one of mine. Though my spies are large in number and very resourceful, there are still certain things they cannot learn without revealing themselves."

"Which is where I come in." The essence thumped unevenly alongside my own heartbeat. The closer Ephraim grew, the colder it became.

"Precisely," he said, grinning. "I was able to have a small box placed near your bed. Everything you learn you are to write down and place in there."

My brows furrowed as he stepped closer. I took an uncertain step back. "How will you get the letters then?"

"The chest is spelled, darling," he mocked. "Once you lock the letter in the chest, I will read it. No one beyond the two of us will be able to open it. Check the box every day, for I may have my own letters to send to you as well."

Ephraim's hard gaze flickered over my face. His frown deepened as he caught sight of the cut along my cheek.

He grazed his hand gently along the mark. "You were harmed, I see."

I stepped out of his reach. "It's nothing."

"Nonetheless," he said, scowling at me like I'd spoken out of turn, "you carry the essence of Death. It must be protected. Especially as you are a mortal in a realm full of beings stronger and more powerful than your weak body could imagine."

I snorted. "I appreciate your concern. But I'm fine."

"You should train," he said suddenly. His wings shook just enough that I noticed the bits of frost break off from the tips of his feathers and fall to the ground. "Have the guards teach you to protect yourself. Until the essence is awakened, you are the weakest prey here. Others will take notice of that."

"Who would try to kill me here? Besides the God of Death."

His gaze returned to the scratch along my cheek. "Clearly more people than you might think."

The essence swirled in my chest, squeezing my heart painfully as it recoiled from the frigidness seeping from the angel. His lack of a soul clearly unsettled the essence within me.

"When you were harmed, did the essence react?" Ephraim asked suddenly.

I stilled. "Yes."

He nodded, an excited smile turning up the corners of his mouth. "I suspected it might. The stronger your emotions, the stronger the essence becomes. This is good."

"Good how?"

"It will be easier to siphon from you if the essence is awakened," he said, slowly pacing the small clearing. "It won't awaken if you keep your emotions locked away, which is why I asked you to allow yourself to feel again."

"Well, when my emotions were heightened, it sort of burst out of me," I said dryly. "Is that what you anticipated?"

He chuckled. The sound was as wicked as the dark depths of his eyes. "Once you kill the prince there will be many who keep hunting you, and they will use your family to get to you," he said, changing the topic.

"Like you nearly did?"

He froze for a breath. When he turned to me there was an arrogant smirk on his mouth. "Exactly."

I watched in silence as he pulled the knife from its sheath along his spine. The scar along my throat burned with the memory of the poison it contained.

"How much do you know about the power you have?" he asked.

I shrugged. "Only that I can siphon souls for Ofrin."

"I see you met your new father-in-law," he teased, noting my sour tone. "Yes, you are able to collect souls, hence your title. But, there is much more to your gift than just that mundane power."

"Like what?" Nonna had told me little of what this curse was truly capable of. I hadn't had time to read through Alfie's notebook before my family's deaths. If anyone in our family had an answer, it would've been Alfie.

But Aiden took his notebook from Elias back in Cordovia. I wasn't even sure he hadn't destroyed it yet.

"I have had centuries to study your power, Esme," Ephraim said, pulling me from my thoughts. "I've read every book I could find. I've watched every one of your ancestors acknowledge this power within them and use it in many different ways. But never have I had the opportunity to work with a Soul Collector directly."

"If you've been studying it for so long, then why are you only now deciding to get your revenge?"

"Because there was never anything the demon prince cared about enough for me to try." His words sent an uneasy flutter through the essence, but he continued on, unperturbed. "Plus, Ofrin kept restrictions on his Soul Collectors and forced his son to tend to them every generation, so they were always heavily guarded. That left me with little room to make my move."

I scowled. "You didn't seem to have an issue cutting my throat," I retorted. "Or showing up again claiming I was needed here."

He grinned wickedly, a violent gleam in his pale eyes. "Yes. Well, I knew I wouldn't be able to take you. That was just some fun."

I glowered. "How were either of those moments fun? You nearly killed me and then you nearly killed Aiden."

"Which means I nearly saved you and your family a lot of pain and trouble, now didn't I?" he snapped. I clamped my mouth shut as the force of his remark sent my spine tingling with fear. "I just needed to get you to believe that you were summoned to the Realm of Souls. One of the many restrictive protections placed on a Soul Collector is they cannot be forcefully taken from the mortal realm. They must go willingly. It's probably why Aiden even bothered marrying you."

"So when you came for me two months ago, you weren't actually planning on taking me?"

"Of course I planned to." His eyes were scornful as he looked at me. "I just hoped to get you to believe that you wanted to come, or rather that coming with me would serve your duty and protect your family. It's called a loophole."

I snorted. "Right. So, you attacked me and my family for nothing then."

"No," he said slowly as if speaking to a child. "Again, it was a loophole. Had your damned prince not been so keen on keeping you safe, then it wouldn't have been an issue. Actually, had Elroy bothered to keep you like he promised, I would've gotten to you sooner."

My mouth clamped shut as I remembered his admission during his last visit. I wrapped my arms around my middle as the memories burned through the scars along my wrists and ankles.

The essence stirred suddenly, violently pulsing through my chest until my skin was afire with its presence.

I gasped. "Someone's nearby."

I wasn't sure how I knew that. Only that the essence lashed outward, brushing against the soul of the person only a mile away through the trees.

Ephraim smiled, like a child gifted a wonderful prize. "What do you feel?"

I shook my head. A cool breeze brushed along my cheeks, pulling at my hair and adding to the frigidness seeping from Ephraim's presence. "They're walking. Pacing. I don't know who they are."

He nodded, encouraging me to continue.

The essence shifted. I felt it the same way I might feel a blade between my fingers. Somehow, I was able to acknowledge that it was real, that I could understand it more than I ever had before. I didn't know what had changed; whether it was because I was now in the realm where it was created, or because I'd lived with it long enough now that I could decipher its reactions. But the essence definitely brushed against this stranger's soul.

I pushed all this new knowledge away, promising myself I'd worry about it later. Now, I followed the warmth in my chest as it curled around my heart. I felt it move through my veins, igniting a fire as it raised the hairs along my neck.

"Now, push it out of you," Ephraim said, startling me.

I frowned, gasping against the dark pull in my chest. "What does that mean?"

"Feel it," he said with exaggerated patience. "Feel it move through you and search for an outlet. It can sense the soul you feel. Let it wander beyond that. Let it encompass the rest of the forest around us."

I pushed outward, forcing the warmth in my chest to ignore the soul I already held, though I felt its reluctance. The forest around me was cold, contrasting with the warmth in my veins. I shivered as the chill threatened to seep into my body as I pushed the essence further.

My breath hitched in my lungs. "I feel something," I whispered. My breath fogged the air before me. The beginnings of winter masked the usual chill I felt around Ephraim.

"Tell me what you feel." His voice was tight with barely controlled excitement. I could feel it in the way he kept his body coiled tightly, forcing himself to remain still though his eyes were ever intent on my face.

I shook my head. "I'm not sure. There's someone further away. Through the trees to the north. They're standing still."

Ephraim tilted his head back and laughed. "Wonderful. Your range is magnificent."

"Do you know who that is?" I asked, confused as I let my power slowly return to its place near my heart.

The angel nodded, moonlight glinting off the dark horns cupping his head. "That is one of the guards at your castle, Princess."

"But we're miles from the wall. I could scream at the top of my lungs, and they still wouldn't be able to hear it."

His smile turned wicked. "Exactly. And yet you could feel them. That is the power that lives in you. That is how strong it truly is."

I looked to the hilt barely visible between his wings. The promise of the death it held sent my pulse racing.

"There is more to your gift than just collecting souls." A mischievous gleam lit his eyes. "And there is much more power to it than you can imagine."

I shivered in as the warmth left me, being replaced by the chill of the night air.

"Come," Ephraim said, turning toward a path nearly hidden in the trees. "We'll do it again, farther this time. The essence needs to be strengthened. Then you'll return to your husband and pretend you're the same weak girl they brought here only days ago."

THIRTEEN

A SOFT KNOCKING PULLED me from sleep. I huddled further in the blankets, cursing whoever decided to disturb me so early.

The knock echoed through my room again, dragging a groan from my lips. I sat up, blinking into the bright light of early morning. I'd forgotten to close the drapes when I returned from training with Ephraim only an hour ago.

Another knock sounded, firmer this time. I scowled as I realized it wasn't coming from the door where guards stood silently outside. The knocking came from the door connected to Aiden's room.

I stumbled from the bed, quickly reaching for the nearest pair of pants I could find as the door opened.

Aiden carried a tray in one hand as he kicked the door closed. "Esme?"

My feet tangled in the breeches as I attempted to pull them on, sending me crashing to the floor with a yelp. My hip throbbed as I slowly got to my feet. As I caught Aiden's eye over the bed, I felt my cheeks burn with embarrassment. Apart from the brief lunch, I'd hardly spoken to him since he gave me the potion that could end our marriage bond.

"I wasn't aware you had a habit of falling out of bed." His eyes glinted with mirth.

I scowled, fastening the buttons of my breeches as I got to my feet. "I don't."

He set the tray of food he carried on the small table before the hearth. While his back was turned, I moved the box Ephraim had spoken of and hid it beneath my bed and out of sight. It was just large enough to hold a small stack of paper. It would be easy to conceal and pass letters to the angel as I received new information to give him.

I pushed my tangled curls back from my face as I moved to join him.

My gaze fell on the door to the hallway. "Is Fen all right?"

"Yes," he said slowly, uncertain. "She thought it would be a good idea for us to spend some time together, alone."

My heart stuttered in my chest. "Oh."

"I thought it would be best for the two of us to be seen together as well. For my father's spies to believe our ploy," he added. He was careful to keep his posture relaxed, though I could see the tension that made his spine stand unnaturally straight.

I removed the breakfast tray's cover and sighed. "This smells amazing," I said as I plopped one of Lurik's freshly baked biscuits into my mouth.

I glanced up to find Aiden staring at me, anger hardening every line of his form. His fists hung stiffly at his sides, shaking with his dissolving control.

"Aiden?" I asked, keeping my voice carefully calm.

His hands reached for my face, causing me to grow still. The warm feel of his hands was tender on my cheeks, gentle. I watched him closely as all sense of warmth left his gaze. Power, unattainable and violent, shook the walls. But there was nothing dangerous about his touch. It was intimate, delicate, like he was afraid I might shatter.

"Who did this?" His voice was guttural.

My brows furrowed. "What?"

I winced as his finger gently pressed to the sensitive spot along my face. The memory of Reek's claws flashed through my mind as I pulled away.

"It's nothing," I said, hastily pulling my hair over the scratch.

Aiden tucked the curls behind my ear, putting the mark on display. "That is not nothing, Esme," he said firmly. "Who harmed you?"

"It doesn't matter. It's just a scratch."

A muscle feathered in his jaw. "Esme," he started slowly.

"Aiden," I snapped.

He scowled. "You were harmed in my own court. That is not acceptable. I will have the head of anyone who harms you. Of that, I can promise you."

Warmth spread through my chest that had little to do with the essence. I rejected the emotion, pulling free from his grasp.

"That's a little overdramatic," I mumbled under my breath.

His hand came up under my chin, forcing me to make eye contact. "You are my wife, Esme," he proclaimed, voice tight. "There is not a single person in any realm that deserves to live after they raise a hand against you. Now," he said, speaking over the beginnings of my protest, "who hurt you?"

I swallowed, trapped in his gaze. "I don't think I've met him before," I muttered reluctantly. "He found me yesterday after lunch. But, I think it's the essence that frightened me more."

Concern etched every line in his face as he continued to study me. "What do you mean?"

I shrugged. "After he left, something just happened," I said slowly, remembering my panic with the overwhelming memories from home. "The essence, it sort of lashed out. Like it needed an outlet and it just burst from me."

Aiden frowned, dropping his hands. His movements were stiff with exaggerated slowness as he sat on the sofa. When I sat beside him, he didn't acknowledge me, instead remaining deep in thought.

My mind returned to the attack, and the moments before. "I did learn his name though, the demon that pulled me into that room."

"Yes?" he said, encouraging me to continue.

"Reek." His body went taut beside mine. "The room I was pulled into was dark, so I couldn't see, but the demon was called Reek. That's all I know."

I watched this information settle in his mind. Whoever this demon was, Aiden knew of him. And he wasn't happy about the encounter. Ephraim had reacted much in the same way at the mention of this mysterious intruder.

"What did he say?" he asked when I didn't continue. "What, *exactly*, did he say?"

I shrugged. "I don't remember. Something about teeth and bloodshed? He spun a couple of riddles for me, but I didn't understand any of them. That's when another man took him away. But I didn't see his face."

Aiden was up and pacing before I could track his movements. Every muscle in his warrior's build was tight with unease.

"Who is he?" I asked.

He didn't answer for a while. His pacing persisted to the point where I worried for the rug beneath his boots. I continued to eat the breakfast he'd brought, relishing in the new flavors Lurik was introducing me to with his brilliant cooking.

"Reek is a menace," Aiden finally said. "He is vile and brings trouble everywhere he goes. But he is not a fighter." His eyes shot to the mark on my cheek. "I would normally assume he wouldn't cause you any physical harm himself, but that's not to say he wouldn't trick you into danger. That's why he has a handler."

"A handler? You mean the other voice I heard?"

He nodded. "He used to be a valuable warrior in my father's guard. But when Reek began to lose his mind to madness, the warrior left. Took Reek and disappeared. Hardly anyone has seen him in centuries. There were rumors that he brought Reek to the mountains and threw him over the edge of a cliff before jumping himself."

I thought back to the man's familiar voice. "What was his name? His handler?"

"Only my father remembers, and he's too superstitious to say it aloud for fear that if he lived, he would return." Aiden's jaw clenched, showing his frustration.

"Is he dangerous?" I asked, fear uncurling in my stomach.

Aiden shrugged. "You are a mortal in a realm full of demons. Everyone is a danger to you."

"Even you?"

My question brought him up short. Aiden's gaze found mine, the familiar emotion I refused to put a name to glistening in his gaze.

"No," he said, voice a delicate promise. "I would never harm you, Esme."

Emotions barreled through me. I didn't want to feel the anguish of everything my life had consisted of these last months. Even the small moments of joy felt like a betrayal to my family if I allowed myself to feel them.

I closed myself off from them, welcoming the cool emptiness. A loose tear trailed down my cheek before I could wipe it away. Aiden was on his knees before me in an instant.

"What is it?" His voice was unusually soft. Much like how he used to speak to me before my family's deaths.

"I'd like to train to protect myself," I said in as casual a voice as I could muster.

His brows furrowed as he studied me a moment longer. I knew he was trying to understand my drastic change in emotion.

Finally, he stood, opting to sit in the chair across from me. "I think that's a great idea. I can arrange for Sera to train you."

I stared at him, almost surprised by his quick approval.

"Esme, I want nothing more than for you to be safe," he said, concerned. "I think the best thing for your safety is for you to learn to take care of yourself. I would never expect you to rely solely on me for protection."

I blinked, gaining control of my bewildered expression. "Oh, all right then."

A small smile pulled at one corner of his mouth, though he didn't say anything more. I ate in silence. Aiden sat across from me, his presence both a welcome comfort and ill-favored all at once. The duty I owed my family battled the betrayal of my heart as I studied him in the morning light.

"What are you thinking?" he asked after a while.

I placed the lid over the now-empty tray. "What?"

"I can see thoughts swarming behind your eyes," he said, leaning forward so his elbows rested on his knees and his face stopped just inches from mine. "What is it that has you so distracted?"

I frowned. "Nothing."

Aiden chuckled, and it was warm and open. This was my husband now sitting before me. The same boy I'd secretly loved for years.

Who'd also killed my family.

"I want Tarsa to train me," I said, speaking the words as soon as they came to mind.

His brows rose, surprised. "Okay, I can arrange that. Why her?"

"Because I asked nicely."

Understanding softened his features. He knew better than anyone the friendship I'd made with Seraphine and Killian. And he also knew how hurt I was by what happened.

"I'll make sure she sets aside time to train you as soon as you wish to begin."

I offered him a shy smile. "Today?"

Aiden's smile grew, warming. "As you wish."

We fell into a deafening silence. Sleep still clouded my mind though the sun outside signaled late morning. Already I could see the uncertainty leaving his eyes as he studied my hesitant smile.

He glanced at something over my shoulder. "I'm assuming those are for your study, and not simply because you've decided to hoard all of my books in your room."

I followed his gaze to the books stacked in the corner. "I'd hoped to put them in the study."

"Fen did demand I show you the library."

I chuckled apprehensively. "I figured she'd make you do that."

Aiden's soft laughter followed mine, sending a warm caress through me. "Fen is...motherly, to say the least."

"I noticed," I said, smiling. This soft side of him contrasted so greatly with the cool, bare tones of his palace. Yet it fit perfectly with the cluttered, dark room I had first discovered.

"That room you found me in last week..." I started slowly, "What is it?"

Sorrow replaced his smile. "It's the last of my mother's things."

"What happened to the rest of it?" I asked. My chest ached knowing the truth of his bloodline. A truth I couldn't allow myself to reveal. Not before my family's safety was guaranteed and this curse was broken.

"My father destroyed everything that reminded him of her," he said slowly. "That was all I could find that he hadn't had a chance to get rid of. So, I keep it here, hidden away. You're the first person who's been in that room other than me."

"I'm sorry," I said quickly, worried I may have crossed some sort of line. "I didn't mean to overstep. I just found the room by accident."

A sad smile pulled at the corners of his mouth. "You are welcome to anything here. There is not a corner of this realm that I wouldn't give to you if I could."

My cheeks flushed as I tore my gaze from his. The truth of his words pulled at something deep inside me.

"Am I allowed to decorate?" I asked, forcing myself into a calm state. "Since your decorating skills are sorely lacking."

His brows rose, noting the teasing tone to my words. "There's never been any reason for me to decorate," he said casually. "It would just be more things for me to replace should any part of the castle fall under siege and be destroyed."

"So, if I can't decorate the rest of the palace, am I allowed to decorate my rooms as I see fit? Or are there restrictions?"

"Decorate as your heart desires," he said with a smile.

Tentative excitement filled me at his approval. "Good. I'll need to fill my study with as many books as it can fit. I'm sure I'll go through this selection quickly."

"Is it safe to presume your brother got his love of books from watching you read?" Though his words were gentle, they still stung.

Alfie had loved books since he first began to read. Out of the group of us, it was always he who begged to go into town to visit the bookstore. Mousa would often lend him money for a new book if our parents couldn't spare the coin. But now, he was gone. Just as all of his favorite books were gone. Even the notebooks he would scribble in with every thought that passed through his head. Every one except...

"Do you still have Alfie's notebook?" I asked, remembering Aiden stuffing it into his pack when he took me from Elias.

Aiden nodded slowly. "I do."

My throat burned as I wrung my hands together. He still had it, and he hadn't bothered to offer it to me. Though it was my brother's, Aiden kept it for reasons unbeknownst to me.

I thought back to everything I'd learned since marrying him. Every interaction, every conversation. And there were still parts of him I didn't understand.

"Could we have dinner sometime? Alone?" I asked, hesitant for his answer.

I watched his brows shoot up as his breath hitched with surprise. Whatever he was expecting me to say, it wasn't that. His gaze was so focused, so intent, that I nearly flushed from it. I could practically feel him trying to decipher the reasoning behind my request.

"If you don't want to, I understand," I said, mind racing to think of another way to get the information Ephraim needed.

He leaned forward, the corners of his mouth turning up. "I would love nothing more."

Warmth spread through me. It was almost enough to make me forget everything that had transpired between us these last weeks. Almost.

He stood. "It'll be good for my father's spies and the members of my court to see us together more."

"Of course," I said, hiding the disappointment I felt at his mention of our charade. "Have you any word on Ephraim's movements?"

Aiden paused. His expression was quizzical as he stood near the door. "No. Tarsa has been patrolling the realm with other guards but there has been no sign of him."

Nerves tightened my chest. At the moment no one knew of my deceit, but it was only a matter of time before they discovered I conspired with their enemy and locked me away. There would be no protecting Mousa and Cordelia then.

"We're still searching for him," Aiden vowed, misreading my expression.

I nodded. "Am I allowed to be with you when Tarsa brings news of Ephraim's whereabouts? Or any updates on their searches?"

"Of course," he said. "As soon as someone brings news I will send word to you. You'll be kept up to date on all planning concerning Ephraim."

"Just what are you planning?" I asked, noting the way he cut himself off from saying more.

"Nothing beyond preventive measures." A muscle tightened in his cheek, revealing there was still more he wasn't saying.

The door to my room opened then. Daemon strode through the entryway, taking in our sudden silence. The demon grinned wickedly. "Do you make it a habit to sneak into your wife's bed chamber?"

Aiden scowled, all manner of casualness evaporating. "Shouldn't you knock before entering your Princess's room?"

"She doesn't seem to mind," Daemon said, shooting me a wink.

It was my turn to scowl. "Don't be so sure."

The demon chuckled as he lounged on the edge of the armchair near the hearth. His black hair hung into his eyes as he looked up at Aiden, a taunting challenge written in every line of his posture.

"Don't get your swords stuck in places where they don't belong, Prince," Daemon said as he sprawled across the armchair. "I'm just doing my duty to your father."

Aiden's expression darkened. "I don't think my father ordered you to sit in her room with her."

Daemon shrugged. "What better way to keep an eye on her than when I'm sitting directly in front of her?"

I studied the casual posture of the horned demon. There was something elusive beneath the smile he wore that unsettled me. "And where were you when Reek pulled me into a room yesterday?" I snapped.

The demon stilled, sparing a glance toward Aiden. All pretense of play was put aside. "Reek was here?" he asked, more serious than I'd ever seen him.

"Had you been following her as you should have, then he wouldn't have gotten to her," Aiden snarled.

Daemon nodded toward the mark on my face. "He did that to you?" I nodded, fingers tracing the sensitive skin. "You should learn to defend yourself, Princess. Wouldn't want someone sneaking in here to whisk you away or anything," Daemon said, shooting a pointed look in Aiden's direction. "Although if Reek was able to waltz through the palace undetected then there probably isn't anyone that can't just run up and grab you."

"No one touches her." Aiden kept his eyes on me as he spoke with the command worthy of a king. "If anyone touches her, they die."

Daemon stared at him as if he were utterly bored. "I'm well aware, Your Highness," he drawled. "Though your threats are misplaced when directed at me. I have no intention of harming your mortal."

"You'd likely die trying," I mumbled under my breath. I hadn't expected either one to pay any attention to me, but they both sent me incredulous looks. Daemon looked almost pleased by my response, while Aiden looked proud as he stood over me.

His knuckles brushed along the length of my cheek, cautious of the mark. I leaned into his touch, placing a chaste kiss in the center of his palm. I told myself I was only playing the part Ephraim required of me, ignoring the emotions rattling inside me at Aiden's touch. The gesture surprised him; Aiden's eyes widened before he briskly turned away and left through the open door to the hall.

When I turned to Daemon I scowled at the too-wide grin on his face.

"What?" I snapped.

He shrugged. "You are possibly the most stubborn woman I've ever met."

I stood, placing him at my back as I retrieved my boots. "Then your knowledge of women is lacking as much as to be expected of an arrogant man."

The demon laughed, waiting for me at the door. "Whatever you say, Your Highness."

FOURTEEN

SWEAT DRIPPED DOWN MY spine as Tarsa threw me onto my back with a loud smack. The wind left my lungs in a rush as I lay there, struggling for breath.

"Again," she said tersely.

I'd been training with her for over an hour now. Shortly after Aiden left my room, she found me wandering the halls with Daemon and brought me to the training room. Now, my body felt sluggish and bruised.

I struggled to my feet, my muscles shaking with the effort. I couldn't remember the last time I felt this physically incapable of anything.

Tarsa crouched before me, eyes intent on my center. I put my hands up, blocking my face from her blow just as her leg swept out and hooked under my ankle. My back hit the floor with another smack.

"Again."

I got to my feet slower this time. Tarsa had made me spend the first thirty minutes of our session just running around the large training room and doing various stretches and exercises. By the time she finally deemed me ready to begin basic defensive maneuvers, I was already fatigued.

Daemon sat silently through it all. He took up a place in the corner of the room and watched Tarsa with keen interest. Jadan appeared once, silently and seemingly out of the shadows. But the two only whispered for a moment before the white-haired demon left once more.

The muscles in my legs shook uncontrollably as I dropped into the stance Tarsa had showed me an hour before.

The fearsome warrior scowled. "No," she said, stepping closer. Tarsa's foot gently kicked my heel, shifting my foot forward an inch. Her hands poked in various places along my middle to get me to stand just the way she wanted.

"This is exactly how I was standing," I grumbled. My patience was beginning to wear thin as the lack of sleep from the night before only increased my growing exhaustion.

Tarsa glowered at me. "If that were true, then I wouldn't need to fix your form."

"Come now, she's not so bad for a beginner," Daemon called, coming to my defense.

Tarsa considered me coolly. "She is as weak as a bird and uncoordinated as a toddler learning to walk."

I grimaced, offended. I may have been unaccustomed to combat, but I wouldn't say I was as bad as she described.

Daemon stood, moving to join us. He ignored me completely, focusing solely on the immortal warrior.

Tarsa's spine went straight as he stopped just within arm's reach. "You have no business being in the training room," she said curtly. "The girl is not in any danger while I am here."

"I am here to monitor her," he said with a shrug. "That includes sitting in during your teachings. However poorly they may be going."

My cheeks warmed with annoyance as his gaze turned my way. Had I been able to breathe properly without gasping for air, I might've argued with his statement.

"Go back to your corner, Daemon." Tarsa's voice held the lilt of annoyance that I had always assumed was reserved just for me.

The demon smirked, tilting his head so his hair fell into his eyes. I caught a glimpse of one of his horns before he moved again, hiding it from view. "Why don't we give it a go?"

Tarsa snorted. "I wouldn't waste the time on you."

"Perhaps it would be beneficial for her to see two skilled warriors spar," Daemon said with a shrug. "At the very least it will give her a moment to catch her breath."

I watched the decision settle over Tarsa's features. "Fine. Esme, sit over there."

Without a word, I sat along the wall where she'd pointed, keen to take a moment to rest. Even propped against the wall, my muscles continued to shake uncontrollably.

Daemon smiled, strutting around the warrior as if he were all too eager to spar with her. Tarsa, however, looked bored.

I watched the two circle each other, their moves carefully calculated. Daemon's lips moved with softly spoken words reserved only for Tarsa. Whatever he said made her lips peel back from her teeth in a snarl.

The lithe warrior struck. Her moves were a blur of speed as she stumbled into the space Daemon once occupied. I hadn't even seen him move.

Daemon stood a few paces away, watching her with raised brows. Tarsa said something unintelligible that made him laugh.

With his head tipped back, Tarsa struck again, landing a solid kick to his knee. The demon went down with a thud that made me cringe. Tarsa didn't wait for him to find his footing before she grabbed a fistful of his hair, pulling his face down atop her knee as she thrust her leg upward.

I shuddered as the sound of his nose cracking echoed through the empty room.

Blood dripped down his face as the demon laughed from where he knelt. Just as Tarsa wound up for another blow, he was up and moving. He was faster than I expected. Every time she struck, he ended up a few steps away. And every time she spun, preparing for his attack, he was already out of reach.

The demon was impressive. I watched, wide-eyed, as he managed to evade her attacks. Tarsa's lips tightened into a thin line as her frustration grew.

Daemon appeared behind her again, wrapping his arm around her throat and holding her against his chest. His shorter stature didn't hinder his attack.

Her elbow thrust back, smacking against his gut hard enough that I heard his grunt as the air left his lungs. Daemon drove his foot into the back of her knee, forcing her to the ground.

When he had her on her stomach, he bent down and whispered something in her ear. Tarsa reacted quickly. In a flash, she had him on his back, straddling him. A blade I didn't know she carried was held against his throat.

My heart rate spiked as I watched the events unfold. I struggled to my feet, using the wall for support as my legs wobbled.

Daemon laughed again, his voice carrying through the room as I moved closer. "How did I know you'd want to finish on top?"

Tarsa snarled, pressing the blade in so a drop of blood ran down the side of his neck. "This lesson is over," she said, quickly getting to her feet.

She stormed from the room without another word. As the door slammed shut behind her, I turned toward the demon.

At my scowl he only laughed harder, utterly unconcerned about his broken nose.

"She's brilliant," he said before spitting a mouthful of blood onto the floor.

I cringed away from the gesture. "You do realize she's going to be even more pissed during my next lesson. And she won't bother taking it out on you when she can use me as her punching bag."

Daemon smiled, teeth coated in blood. "Can't wait to watch."

I spent the rest of the afternoon in my study. Daemon disappeared as soon as guards arrived to stand outside my door, mumbling something about finding Jadan to fix his nose. Like most immortals, Daemon healed quickly, but this accelerated healing was causing his nose to heal crooked.

My muscles continued to ache and grow stiff as I sat on the floor in the middle of the room. Daemon had helped me carry my small stack of books across the castle to the study immediately after my failed training session with Tarsa, and I hadn't moved from my spot on the floor since.

After Tarsa had left the training area, I'd allowed myself a small amount of time to practice my parents' famed performance. Now, not only did my lower body throb painfully, but my arms shook with strain after only half an hour of throwing knives.

My study had fallen dark, the only light coming from the glow of the magical map decorating the wall behind me. I glanced toward it, pleased to see Mousa and Cordelia's glowing orbs still safely together in the Abandoned Desert. I had even checked on Elias earlier and was relieved to see he was back in the castle in Cordovia.

I could stare at that map every hour of the day and never cease to feel relieved as I reaffirmed that my brother and sister were together. Safe.

Forcing myself to turn away, I reached for another book. The four that I'd found after my encounter with Reek were basic history books. One told the histories of the realm, another contained children's stories, and one contained recipes for what looked like concoctions of some kind. If there truly was a witch here, I wondered if this book was meant for her.

The last book was the one that originally caught my eye. I flipped through it, waiting for something to pop out and give the answers I desperately wanted.

Each page was filled with minuscule script so small I had to squint to read it in the fading light. The pages were rough beneath my fingers, paper thin and worn like they'd been read thousands of times before.

A passage caught my eye, the words "siphon" and "soul" written plainly in the middle of the page surrounded by mostly faded ink. Between the scrawl were cramped drawings of various weapons. Bows, daggers, swords, and even a crown.

The hairs along the back of my neck stood on end. An unconscious shift in the essence told me someone was nearby. I straightened, glancing around the empty room.

Light fell over me a moment later as the door swung inward. A large silhouette filled the doorway, and I stilled as I felt his gaze focus on me in the dark. Steam rose from the plate he carried, bringing with it an aroma that made my mouth water.

"I figured you might be hungry," Aiden said casually. I watched him set the plate of food on the floor in front of me.

"Thank you," I answered as warmly as I could allow myself. My stomach growled as I pulled the plate closer.

Aiden remained standing, uncertain, in the middle of the room. "Daemon mentioned you would be hungry after your lesson with Tarsa."

"He was right," I said around a mouthful of food. My lack of manners brought an amused tilt to his mouth.

I swallowed, embarrassed. The flush of my cheeks only made his hesitant smile grow.

"Are these the books you found yesterday?" he asked, nodding toward the open pages spread around me.

"They are." I'd read through most of their contents and still I had been unable to find a way to break this curse beyond killing Aiden. So far, I'd only found mention of a small knife Death created centuries ago, a children's tale about a hollowed mountain, and a recipe for what sounded like a remedy for food poisoning.

"I don't think I've read any of these," he said, squinting at the title on the nearest one. "Have you found anything interesting?"

I shook my head. "Nothing terribly exciting. I was hoping this one would be, but so far it's as boring as the others."

He smiled again and it nearly made my heart stop. This was Aiden with me now. The boy I'd known half my life and admired from the shadows. The one who protected me from mobs of people and desperate bounty hunters and who had wrapped my wounds caused by months in King Elroy's castle.

As if he felt me staring, Aiden cast a wary glance through the strands of hair that had fallen into his eyes. "What?"

I shook my head, forcing the emotion away again. "Nothing. I think I'm just tired."

"I can imagine. Tarsa did say you had a tough time during your training."

I scowled. "I don't think I was that bad."

Aiden chuckled at the childish refusal in my tone. His hair hung loose around his face, appearing a darker shade of brown in the faint light. There was a softness to his features that I hadn't seen since the night he kissed me. Seeing it again now caused my chest to warm against my better judgment.

"Can I see the library tomorrow?" I asked, distracting myself from his proximity as he settled himself on the floor amidst the books scattered around me.

"I told Jester, my Keeper of Books, that you would like to visit the library, and he has taken it upon himself to have every shelf dusted and all the books reorganized so it is ready for you." There was a sense of exasperation in his tone that revealed how ridiculous he considered the notion.

I smiled. "I don't mind reading dusty books."

"That's what I tried to tell him," he said, shaking his head.

"Has Jester always been your Keeper of Books?" I asked.

Aiden nodded. "He, like Fen and Tarsa, served my mother before coming into my court. He's known me my entire existence."

I thought back to the room filled with covered furniture and paintings and books. "Is he how you got those items from her?"

"He is. Jester tends to collect things other people may wish to throw away." Again, there was a hint of emotion I couldn't quite name, but I suspected this Jester was probably more family to him than his father may have ever been.

"I see you've been enjoying the map," he added, nodding toward the large tapestry.

I glanced at its glow over my shoulder, relief filling me once again.

"I love having it here," I admitted quietly. "It's nice to know they're safe and together."

Aiden stood, offering me a hand to help me to my feet. I stared at it for a beat. When I placed my hand in his, a jolt went through me that sent my heart racing against my ribs as I followed him to the map.

"It can do more than simply show you where they are," he said. I watched him place his free hand on the map, fingers splayed wide. "What do you wish to see?"

I shrugged. "What can it show me?"

"Anything," he answered with a gleam to his eye.

I stared at the map, forgetting my secret ploy against Aiden, forgetting my revenge, even forgetting the duty I owed my family to break this curse on my bloodline. The essence hummed inside me as a memory came to mind.

"There's a small clearing near the River of Fates, just below the mountains in the north," I said, excitement filling me as I pictured the area. "In autumn, the leaves don't just turn auburn and fall. They're bright red, like rich wine. And at dawn they paint the forest floor with their color, making it appear as though the ground is bleeding."

My family often traveled to the small forest near the Howling Mountains in autumn simply because the trees were so beautiful. If there happened to be snow on the ground, it was mesmerizing.

Aiden whispered something I couldn't discern before the map began to shift. I watched, wide-eyed and filled with awe, as the map disappeared altogether. In its place now sat a landscape of the scene I just described.

Tall, thin trees filled the canvas. The river traveled through one side of the forest floor while the rest of the ground was painted with the red from the leaves. The golden dawn bled through the sky, erasing the last traces of night. Everything shone in vibrant shades of gold and red. Warm. It was home.

My heart sped up as my throat burned with the threat of tears. I could even see the traces of the mountains through the trees, and could easily imagine the Sea of Wings beyond.

"It's exactly how I remembered," I whispered, awestruck. "Though we haven't been in years. Not since Amara was just a babe and Aunt Kiva was still pregnant with Jac."

Aiden's hand squeezed mine gently, reminding me of the contact. "Beautiful."

I nodded. "It is."

The image faded, returning to the map. I glanced toward Aiden, ready to ask him to pull up the image again when I caught him watching me.

The emotion was raw in his eyes, looking at me as if I were as treasured to him as those memories were to me. The essence in my chest warmed, burning through my veins and centering around the feel of Aiden's hand in mine.

My emotions were at war with each other as his free hand brushed a loose strand of hair from my face, resting against my cheek. I wanted this — needed this closeness to make him believe the charade — and yet the feel of his skin on mine only made the memory of my family's deaths stronger.

I was beginning to doubt I was even capable of fulfilling what Ephraim asked of me, what I'd demanded of myself.

Aiden pulled away first, seeing the uncertainty on my face. I took an extra step away from him, forcing myself to get control of my emotions.

"There's one more thing," he said slowly, trepidation written plainly across his face.

Before I could ask, he pulled an old notebook from his waistband. The breath rushed from my lungs as my mind seized.

Aiden held the notebook out to me, but I couldn't feel my body. A cold numbness took over my senses as I stared at the familiar notebook. My chest ached as Alfie's memory washed over me.

"I'd hoped to return it to you sooner," Aiden said gently. "But it took longer than I expected to get it cleaned."

I nodded, remembering the way my brother's blood once soaked through the pages, making his careful scrawl illegible.

My fingers trembled as I reached for it. The binding was worn enough that I feared I might tear it apart with my violent shaking. I ran a hand over the cover where my brother's name was written in his familiar handwriting.

"How?" My voice croaked with the strength of my emotions.

Aiden seemed to follow my thoughts as he wrapped my hands around the notebook. "The witch who created that potion for you, the one to end our marriage bond. I asked her if there was anything to be done to save your brother's notebook." The potion he spoke of remained in my pocket. I hadn't been able to bring myself to take it after making my bargain with Ephraim. "When we returned to this realm, I had Hakan visit her shop at the far wing of the palace. I showed her your brother's notebook and asked her to create something to clean it for you. So you could have a piece of them here, with you."

My throat tightened painfully as I cradled the notebook to my chest. "You did that as soon as we arrived?" His gaze was answer enough. "Thank you."

Aiden nodded, erasing emotion from his face as he continued. "There's more. In the last few pages of the notebook, you'll find letters."

"Letters?" I asked, confusion replacing the sentimentality.

"From your family before they—" he averted his gaze, gritting his teeth— "well, before Elroy."

Icy resolve froze my veins as I met his gaze. I hadn't forgotten his attempt at placing blame on my parents for the death of my entire family. His half-hearted claim that they made a deal to sacrifice themselves for me.

"You mean, before *you*?" The calm I felt moments ago was now forgotten.

Aiden flinched slightly. "I understand your anger and your pain. But my father is watching us closely, Esme. He must think us to be madly in love. That we are too absorbed with one another to even consider stealing his throne."

"And what if I don't care what your father thinks of my opinion of you?"

Aiden's expression darkened, turning to one I knew would make any other tremble. But not me. There was nothing about him that I feared. "I think you do care. I think you care more than you would like to admit. Not only about what my father may do if he hears you speak so ill of me, but also of the true feelings you force yourself to fight."

"You're delusional."

His princely demeanor turned arrogant. "And you're lying."

I scowled, knuckles going white as my grip tightened on Alfie's notebook. "No more than you have lied to me."

"I did what I thought was best. As did your parents."

I snorted. "See, I was right. You are delusional," I snapped, elbowing my way past him.

Aiden moved, blocking my path as I backed against the wall. The breath left my lungs as he towered over me, close enough that we shared breath. One hand gripped my chin with a featherlight touch so I was forced to look into his eyes.

Aiden's thumb brushed over my lower lip. My breath was ragged, too shallow, like I couldn't get enough air into my lungs no matter how hard I tried.

The demon prince's gaze burned across my face as he watched my emotions closely. "You have every right to hate me," he whispered into the narrow space between us. "But I can see the emotions you fight to contain. I see it in your eyes, and yet as soon as you recognize it for what it is, you destroy it. Pluck it away and hide it beneath forced hatred. Why do you fight what you feel?"

I swallowed, forcing my breathing to slow, though another brush of his thumb on my lip sent my pulse racing.

"You hate yourself for what you still feel for me," he said when I didn't speak. "So, you tell yourself to hate me instead, because it would be easier than admitting the truth."

"You think too much of yourself," I seethed.

His eyes were sad. "If you say so, but it does not make my words any less true."

I glowered at him, ignoring the sensations pulsing beneath my skin at his touch. "You have done nothing to deserve anything other than hatred from me," I said in a broken whisper. "Tell me why I should even consider believing what you say is true."

Aiden pulled away slowly, reluctantly.

"You're right," he said. "From where you stand, I have yet to do anything deserving of the truth you keep hidden. But I hope someday you can find it within yourself to see your feelings for what they are."

I forced a deep breath into my lungs as he stepped away. "And what is that?"

"The truth," he whispered, eyes dancing across my face. "You deserve a lifetime's worth of peace, Esme. Do not keep yourself from it by convincing yourself to feel something you don't."

He turned and left without a response. It was only long after I regained control of my pulse that I fled to my bedchamber.

FIFTEEN

I slammed the door shut behind me. The colors of my family that decorated my bed chamber no longer held their familiar comfort. With Alfie's notebook in hand, my room felt cold, unfamiliar.

Jadan and the large demon that I often saw with Drusilla stood guard outside my door, Daemon having yet to return. Neither demon acknowledged me beyond a casual glance when I stormed into my room, a courtesy I relished at the moment.

I sat on the foot of my bed, staring at the notebook I clutched tightly. Alfie's final words came back to me in a haze. My desperation to seek answers battled with the choking pain I knew would come from reliving those final days with my family.

Blinking harshly, I turned to the first page. My brother's crooked scrawl reopened the broken part of my heart I'd poorly patched. The pain lanced through me as I stared at his barely legible scribbles.

I couldn't focus on his words, on the stories he captured. I could only flip through the pages, letting the memories of seeing him bent over this notebook for hours on end fill me with warmth. Drawings were made in the margins. Drawings of swords, axes, and bows — the weapons carried by Aiden and his friends. There were lists of tales told by Nonna, her version of our ancestors' curse, and even tales given to him by Seraphine and Killian.

My hands shook as I turned the pages, stilling again when I found one name written across the top of a page. This was Aiden's story. I flipped past it quickly, unable to make myself read the lies he may have told my brother. Instead, all I found was more of his story. And again on the next page. And again.

My heart pounded against my ribs as I flipped through several more pages, eager to get away from this affront to my senses. I couldn't deny that a part of my heart fluttered excitedly at knowing he'd taken the time to sit with my brother and tell him these stories, but I also knew the likelihood that many of these tales were probably false. Regardless, my foolish heart seemed to care little for the truth in the memories it held of the demon prince.

I turned the page again, forcing myself to move on, and stopped cold.

My mother's handwriting appeared. Her elegant scrawl was written in clean lines across the entirety of the page.

Tears blocked her words from view as my vision blurred further. I closed the notebook, pushing it away. I couldn't bear to read the letter she'd written. The letter that began with the words "I'm sorry".

Questions poured through my mind as I pulled a pillow to my face, screaming into it as an agony so hot it lit a fire in my veins poured through me.

I felt hollow beneath the strangling force. The sadness twisting the remains of my heart pulled at me, demanding I sink further into its depths until I couldn't move, couldn't breathe.

But I would not allow this. The sadness, the pain and despair, would not win. I couldn't let them, for even beyond the depths of my agony lingered the smallest trace of hope. A trace of joy in the memories I held. It was because of those memories that I couldn't give in to the darkness. For Mousa and Cordelia.

The hollowness I once felt beneath the strangling force of the pain finally began to fill. Not with anger, but with a newfound determination to seek the truth.

I didn't want to believe that what Aiden had said about my parents was true. I couldn't even let myself think the words. I refused to believe they'd be willing to enter into any sort of deal with Ofrin. They would protect my siblings and I at all costs, but deals with Death were too malicious.

I had too many questions and not enough answers. Beyond the need to break this curse, I just wanted information. I wanted to know the truth of why my family was torn apart.

Beyond the curtains, the night sky glistened with the twinkle of a thousand stars. "What am I to do?" I begged to the souls of my family. "Why did you leave me behind?" I got no answer except the wind whistling through the forest below.

When Kesson's soul had appeared, I promised I'd fight back. I promised to stay strong. But all I could think about was the pain I felt.

I didn't want to hurt anymore. I didn't want to feel the pain from my family's secrecy or Aiden's betrayal. Hurting was so tiring. I just wanted to rest.

The vines and thorns twisting around my left hand snagged my attention as the light from the moon illuminated them in the dark. I glowered at the tattoo, hating what it symbolized; that I was trapped here, away from my family, and forced to live among those who would see me dead to use the essence for their own gain.

The urge to curse it all and let Ephraim burn the realm to ash was strong, but my brother and sister remained. Out there, far from where I sat, the last of my family fought to stay alive in a world that would see us dead. I failed my family once, but I wouldn't do it again.

The box under my bed rattled. Wiping the tears from my cheeks, I knelt beside the bed, carefully pulling it free. It was unlocked, yet not empty. Inside sat a single letter. Unfamiliar, sharp scrawl filled the page.

"At the moon's peak, come to the tree."

Ephraim was summoning me to the forest.

An hour later I was on my hands and knees crawling through the fissure in the outer wall of the castle grounds. Winter was getting closer, and the air remained cool with its arrival. My breath fogged on the air before me, reminding me of the chill Ephraim always brought with him.

A shadow loomed over the frosted patch of grass by the time I made it through the wall. Ephraim stood there, towering over me with a prominent scowl on his face.

"You're late," he said curtly.

I pulled myself to my feet. "I was busy."

"Crying in your room again?" His condescending tone set my teeth on edge.

I bit back on my frustration. "Are you still watching me?"

Ephraim turned on his heel, walking through the narrow trees. His wings were tucked in against his back, feathers bristling in the faint breeze. I trailed after him. Something about the anger he radiated tonight sent my stomach churning nervously.

"I've always had eyes on you," he finally responded when we were farther from the wall. "The essence you carry is important to my plan. I need to make sure it's safe."

I rolled my eyes at his back. "That was the same excuse Ofrin used when he left some of his guards and spies in Aiden's court."

The angel spun around so fast I nearly slammed into his chest. "Never compare me to that monster again. Or it will be the last thing you ever do."

The essence hummed dangerously in my chest. "You can't hurt me," I said with more confidence than I felt. "You need me alive to fulfill whatever revenge you seek."

"Alive, yes." A smirk tilted the corners of his mouth. "But that doesn't mean unharmed."

I swallowed back the sudden nervousness I felt as I watched his gaze harden with resolve. I reminded myself that we were not friends, barely even allies. He was no more than a means to an end, the same as I was for him. I couldn't allow myself to forget that.

"Now," he said, turning away again to continue through the trees, "how has your power felt?"

I shrugged, trailing after him hesitantly. "Fine."

The look he sent me was not amused. "That's helpful."

"I don't know. It hasn't changed much I guess."

"Then that's something we need to work on, and something you should continue to practice when I'm not around."

"How is it that you're able to come into this realm, unseen, when Ofrin and Aiden have so many of their people looking for you?" I asked, voicing the question that had been nagging at me.

"Because he is stronger than they realize," a feminine voice called.

I froze in place as an unfamiliar female appeared from the shadows. Her crimson hair hung to her shoulders in straight lines, making her sharp, pointed features stand out. The woman's dark eyes flew to Ephraim.

"This is the vessel?" Her voice was emotionless, cold.

Ephraim nodded. "Esme, this is Viema. She'll be helping you train today."

"How is an angel going to train Death's essence?" I asked. I still hadn't voiced my recent revelation. Though I craved the destruction of this curse, I needed answers. And I was no longer sure if Ephraim was the way to get the answers I needed.

The angel, Viema, studied me intently. "Angels have changed since their creation by Ofrin's grandsire. We are stronger, our powers more potent. They are foolish to not realize this."

"Aiden's great grandsire created angels? That doesn't make any sense," I said, confused.

Viema stepped closer, brushing a cold hand along the mark on my cheek. "Many centuries ago, Death needed an army, so he created the angels. Only they lived by a different name then. They were soldiers, hunters of the lost souls who feared what came beyond the Crossroads. Until they wanted more."

My brows furrowed. "So, you were created by Death?"

"No," she said, voice still vacant of emotion. "I was chosen by Ephraim to serve in his court. That is why I am here."

"You were human?"

She nodded. "Once. Many decades ago. I surrendered my soul to serve the Angel, and now I am here to study the essence you carry."

As my uncertainty grew, the essence awakened, flitting around my heart in a nervous buzz. "What does that mean?"

"It means," Ephraim said, pulling the angel away from me, "she is here to help train you to strengthen the essence of Death you carry."

Viema's dark eyes narrowed slightly but she otherwise appeared unperturbed by his words. The essence he spoke of twirled in my chest in response.

I hesitated, studying the two angels as I thought through everything I desired and what they could offer me.

Immediately, my family came to mind.

"Can you tell me anything about why my family died?" I asked.

Viema sent Ephraim an exasperated look, but he didn't see it. His eyes were quizzical as he studied me in the faint light. "Your husband is selfish and cruel. Is that enough of an answer?"

"I need to know what really happened," I said. "I need to know why they died."

Viema snorted. "You were right. She does whine a lot."

Ephraim stepped closer. Gone was the placating look in his eye. His anger made my confidence waver. "What lies has he been telling you?"

"He hasn't told me anything." And that was true enough.

"Clearly something has been said to you," Ephraim said, prowling closer. "Don't tell me the stories he's been spinning for you have made you change your mind about our deal."

"She's human," Viema drawled. "She's not thinking of what great things can be accomplished with her power. She's only thinking of herself."

"I've been nothing but clear about my desire to keep my family safe," I said firmly. "That has not changed."

"So, sit down and let's start training that power," Ephraim said. I remained standing, uncertainty and stubbornness giving me a false sense of bravery. "During our last encounter we focused on extending the reach of your gift. To see how far you could sense another soul," he said. He sat at the base of a tree, pointing to the spot across from him. His wings relaxed around him so his feathers brushed the cold ground. "Tonight, I need you to attempt to call those souls."

My brows furrowed as I glanced toward Viema, still as a tree herself. "How am I supposed to call them?"

"The essence you carry came from Death," Viema said curtly. "It was your prince who gave it to your ancestor, but it is a part of Death all the same. You can wield it to do the same things Death can."

"And you want me to call a soul? As in tear it from its body? Why?" I asked incredulously.

"If the essence is awakened, it can be easier to siphon from its carrier. If you continue to reject its power then it will only make taking it from you that much more challenging," Viema said. Her gaze was full of judgment as she studied me.

Ephraim sighed, exasperated by my lingering confusion. "Don't siphon the souls completely. Just call the person whom the soul belongs to."

"How do you know I would even be able to do that?" I asked, essence already thrumming through me.

"Because your husband can and he is only Death's heir," Viema said.

"Ofrin can call a soul with a single thought," Ephraim said, slipping his poisoned knife from its sheath as he began to clean it idly in front of me. "Aiden can do so with the aid of a siphon. Both can claim a soul with something as small as a touch."

"I don't want to claim a soul," I argued. "I just need to get this power out of me so I can return to my family."

Ephraim sighed. "The stronger your gift, the easier it will be to get rid of."

"That doesn't make sense," I said, ignoring the feeble excuses I was being offered.

"Do you trust me?" he asked harshly, irritation plain in the stiffness with which he held his jaw.

I thought about that. Did I trust him? He could help me break this curse, an offer no one else made. Yet doing so would cause chaos throughout the realm. He would destroy everything weaker than him, and I would be aiding him.

My once-overwhelming desire for revenge had settled into something softer. The pain and anguish molded together in mourning that no longer demanded I make others experience the same destruction.

What I really craved now was the truth. I wanted this curse extinguished from my family, and I wanted to know why I had been lied to by everyone I trusted.

I shook my head. "I don't want the same thing you do anymore."

Viema moved faster than my eyes could track. She was suddenly crouched before me. "I told you she was weak," she spat, gripping my chin tightly.

"Viema," Ephraim chided. "Let the girl go. She's only confused."

The angel jerked away, turning toward him. "This is a waste of time that we do not have. We cannot sit around and marvel at these flimsy human emotions. She needs to be stronger than this. Her power needs to be stronger."

I studied the two of them as Ephraim gently pulled her away. Their heads bent toward each other, speaking softly so I couldn't hear.

Unease made the hair on the back of my neck stand on end as I glanced between them. My pulse quickened as I got to my feet on shaking legs.

Ephraim's wings blocked Viema's glower; when they tucked back against his spine, she had composed herself.

Ephraim sent me a chilling grin. "Fine, I'll sever this bargain with you. I can see it is not something you can be forced into."

Viema stiffened significantly at his words. I watched the way her eyes widened in surprise, and her jaw hardened with barely leashed rage. Whatever she wanted him to say, it wasn't that.

"But there is something else I must ask of you," he said slowly. "Since you're the one going back on your word, it is the least you could do for me."

"What?" My unease continued to grow.

He stepped toward me. "There is a witch that lives in Aiden's court. She is said to have a...potion of sorts that I need."

"I haven't met a witch," I said. The witch who'd cleaned Alfie's notebook and provided me with the vial of liquid to end my marriage remained unknown to me.

Viema snorted but Ephraim spoke over her. "Meet her. She has vials of a dark potion, blue in color and smelling like lavender. Find this potion and deliver it to me in two week's time."

"That's too long," Viema snapped.

Ephraim cut her off with a look. "It will be fine."

"Why? What kind of potion is it?" I asked as I mustered my courage.

"It's important that I have it. It will help keep your family safe," he said when I opened my mouth to ask for clarification. "I need you to bring me whatever prepared vials the witch has. It's important. Not only for our agreement, but for your family's survival. Do this and I will consider our bargain moot. You will not have to kill your husband and his friends who betrayed you so cruelly."

As I studied the angel, questions I was ashamed I hadn't thought of before came to mind. Whatever this potion was, he claimed it would protect Mousa and Cordelia. And at the end of the day, that was what I wanted.

Eventually, I nodded. "Fine. I'll find it. But that's it. After I bring you those vials, I'm done. I need to focus on finding the truth of my family's deaths."

"Of course," he said with a nod of understanding.

I took a deep breath, convincing myself I could do this one last thing. "How am I to get the vials to you? I don't think they'll fit in the box."

He shook his head. "Viema will remain behind to keep an eye on you. Once you have the potion, tell her and she will summon me. I will come."

I opened my mouth to ask another question, but the two angels disappeared into the shadows without a trace.

SIXTEEN

Tarsa's fist collided with my gut, again. She had arrived in my room at the break of dawn and dragged me from the warmth of my bed to begin training. My body once again lagged with exhaustion from the little sleep I'd received the previous night.

"Again," Tarsa demanded as she stepped back from my bent-over form.

I gasped air into my lungs as I righted myself. Daemon sat with Jadan in the far corner. If it weren't for Daemon's chipped-tooth grin, or Jadan's white hair standing out against the stone, I would have forgotten their presence altogether.

Though midday was approaching, the day was dark and gloomy. Storm clouds filled the sky and blocked out the sun, casting the world in shadow. The temperature hadn't warmed with the dawn like I'd expected, so the halls throughout the castle were just as cold as the outdoors.

"Fix your feet," Tarsa ordered with her usual scowl.

I glanced at my feet, frowning. "This is where you told me to— oof."

My words cut off with a grunt as Tarsa took my distraction as an opportunity to sweep my feet out from under me and slam my back onto the floor.

"Never take your eyes off your opponent." The deadly warrior turned her back, effectively dismissing me.

Daemon's soft chuckle echoed through the room. I sent a glare over my shoulder, wincing as my muscles strained. The demon only laughed harder in response.

"When I said I wanted to start training, this isn't exactly what I had in mind," I said as I got to my feet. The muscles in my legs protested with each movement.

Tarsa spun around to face me, a smirk on her mouth. "What did you expect then, Princess?" The way she spoke the title was filled with mockery.

"That you would at least be fair and neutral in your training," I snapped. My hands tightened into fists at my sides, making the growing blisters along my palms screech in agony.

The immortal's eyes widened momentarily with surprise at my tone. "I am nothing but fair with you."

I didn't know whether it was my frustration or my growing exhaustion, but the leash on my anger snapped.

"Being unnecessarily cold is fair? Brutalizing me for your own enjoyment is fair? Refusing to fairly train me to protect my family, to protect Aiden, is fair? If that is true, then your sense of fairness is warped. You are taking your anger out on me because you think you can."

Tarsa snorted. "If you think the world, or I, owe you an ounce of fairness, then you're even more naive than I first thought."

"You don't owe me anything. The world doesn't owe me anything," I said hotly. "But that doesn't mean you can decide to refuse to properly train me to defend myself. I will not be reliant on you, or Aiden, or anyone else for my safety any longer. The last time I did that my family ended up dead."

A soft whistle sounded from the far corner of the room though neither of us turned toward the source. I watched Tarsa's features change; the stiffness in her shoulders relaxed, and the tightness around her eyes diminished as she scrutinized every emotion that played out on my face.

"So, is no one going to acknowledge that she just admitted to wanting to protect Aiden?" Daemon called from his perch in the shadows.

My frustration evaporated. Had I really said that? I'd convinced myself the feelings that lingered for him were a mockery of my pain. Nothing more.

"I'm glad I wasn't the only one who heard that." The familiar voice sent my heart racing for an entirely different reason as I spun toward the door.

Aiden leaned casually against the doorframe, his hair pulled back from his face. Daemon snickered behind me as he and Jadan moved closer.

"Bet you wish you paid more attention to your surroundings right about now, don't you?" Daemon whispered.

I spared him a scowl as Aiden pushed away from the doorframe. He came to a stop just before me, his gaze unwavering. There was something in his expression I didn't understand, something akin to relief.

"Tarsa," Aiden said, finally releasing me from his gaze. "Will you kindly gather the others and wait in my study? I'll have Esme up there shortly. And pass this along to Hakan." He handed her a folded slip of paper.

Tarsa nodded, her expression once again cool and collected. "Of course. Anything to worry about?"

Aiden's gaze swept over the demons from his father's court. "Not at the moment."

The warrior nodded, spinning on her heel without a word and disappearing from the room.

Daemon stepped up to my shoulder, gazing toward the door. "She's always been glorious, but there's just something about watching her throw you around a room that I find wildly appealing."

I scowled. "Just me? Or would you find that appealing if she were throwing you around as well?"

The demon's smile turned as wicked as the thoughts I was sure raced through his mind. "Depends on where she's throwing me."

"I'm beginning to wonder if those horns haven't impacted your sense of survival," Jadan said seriously.

"From my recollection, Daemon has never had a sense of survival," Aiden mused.

I glanced between the three demons, noting their shared looks of amusement. "Are you *friends*?" I asked, surprise erasing the embarrassment I previously felt.

All eyes turned to me, each wearing expressions ranging from incredulous to wry amusement.

"Do you think I would allow just anyone into my court?" Aiden asked.

I shrugged. "I figured you didn't have a choice. That your father just made you accept whoever he chose to send."

"And why do you think he sent us?" Daemon asked, wiggling his dark bushy brows.

Surprised filled me. "You offered?"

Jadan sighed, exasperated. "Of course we did."

"I don't understand," I said, glancing to Aiden for clarity.

The demon prince smiled. "Daemon and Jadan are here at my behest. Not only to ease my father's suspicions, but also to aid in your protection."

"Among other things," Jadan added. Aiden sent him a cool look which the demon ignored. "If that'll be all, I'll see myself out. Maybe tomorrow you can finally throw Tarsa on her ass for once."

I scowled. "Why don't you just train me instead?"

The white-haired demon chuckled as he moved to the door. "I can't even pretend to entertain that idea. There's so much else I'd rather do than train a mortal in the basics of combat."

My frown deepened as he disappeared into the hall.

Daemon patted my shoulder. "It's okay, Esme. You'll get the hang of it eventually."

I snorted. "Let's hope that happens before someone else tries to kill me." The slowly fading scratch along my cheek throbbed in remembrance.

"Speaking of Reek," Daemon's steps paused at the door, "has he sent another riddle?"

Aiden shook his head. "No."

Daemon mulled over this. "I'll send word to a few others that can be trusted. Did he speak in riddles before?"

Both looked at me. "Yes, but I don't know what he meant by them," I said, thinking back to the strange demon's words.

I watched the widening of Daemon's eyes as his gaze met Aiden's. A silent conversation passed between the two of them before Daemon gave a stiff nod and left the room without so much as a word.

"Why is everyone so afraid of Reek?" I asked when we were alone.

Aiden moved, slowly pacing the room. "It's not who he is so much as what he's capable of, or what his little riddles might mean."

"What do they mean?" I turned, reaching for two throwing daggers carefully splayed along the wall.

"Depending on what he said, his words could mean anything from a mischievous trick to insights into things that have yet to come to pass."

I threw the first dagger at the distant target, landing just off center. "What is he doing here then?"

Aiden shrugged. "No one knows. He no longer serves a purpose in my father's realm apart from causing unnecessary mayhem."

I shivered, remembering his cool touch. "What does he want?"

Aiden paused as I threw the next dagger. I loosed a sigh of relief as it landed with a dull thud on the center of the target. The blisters on my palms ached from the constant practice, but I enjoyed practicing my family's trait too much to stop.

"The answer to that can only be found in what he told you." He stopped his pacing to stand beside me, his expression thoughtful.

I ran a hand over my face, suddenly far more exhausted than I was a moment ago. Between worrying over my siblings, my new bargain with Ephraim, and searching for a way to break this curse, I was spent.

Warm hands wrapped around my wrists, gently pulling them from my face. I met Aiden's steely gaze reluctantly, heat spread through my cheeks as I recalled what I'd said upon his arrival.

"Reek is a worry for another day," he said. "For now, there's something else we need to worry about."

My stomach plummeted. "What now?"

The annoyance in my tone made a corner of his mouth quirk up. "Come. They'll be waiting for us by now."

"Who?" I asked, trailing him.

I received no response beyond a wry smile as he led me from the room.

Everyone was waiting in his study when we arrived. Tarsa and Hakan were bent over Aiden's desk studying a rolled out map while Killian sprawled in Aiden's chair, his scuffed boots propped up on the edge of the desk.

Killian jumped up as we entered, his round cheeks flushing pink as he moved to stand at Seraphine's side along the wall. The young demon smiled at me as I trailed Aiden into the room.

"Why did you call us here?" Seraphine asked as she studied the map.

Aiden sighed, sharing a serious look with Hakan before moving to stand behind the wide desk. The day's light shining through the large windows gave him a fascinating silhouette. "There's been news of Ephraim."

Tarsa glanced in my direction. "Should she be here?"

I frowned but Aiden quickly came to my defense. "This concerns her too. No decision is to be made about her safety or her family's without her consent or knowledge."

"Well, that's a new tactic for you," Seraphine muttered dryly.

"What's happened?" I asked, eager for any new information in my quest for the truth.

Hakan nodded to the map on the desk. "Sources confirm the white tree has not been used by anyone other than us in recent weeks. But we are still unable to pinpoint Ephraim's exact point of entry into this realm."

"How is that news?" I glanced at the demons around the room.

Aiden's expression turned sorrowful. "The guards I'd sent out to search for Ephraim have either not returned or returned on the brink of death. We've been unable to get any sort of lead."

My heart skipped in my chest as I studied the map. It was a plainly drawn map of the Realm of Souls. Unlike the canvas hanging in my own study, this did not glow with the presence of my siblings. But it was marked with small ink blots to pinpoint where Aiden's spies had gone missing.

"What do you plan to do next?" Guilt threatened to loosen my tongue and spill secrets of my own. But I forced it away. I couldn't tell them of my bargain with Ephraim just yet. Not until I had more answers and a means to protect my family.

"We keep looking," Hakan answered simply. "We'll send out more guards and hopefully find an answer soon."

"Is no one else worried about how he was able to create a new way into this realm?" Killian piped up.

Seraphine crossed her arms over her chest, gaze thoughtful. "I suspect he found a loophole of some kind. Maybe even a witch."

"Not likely," Aiden added. "Witches are not as easy to find in the mortal realm as they used to be. He'd be hard-pressed to find one that would be willing to admit what she is."

"Still, breaking past your father's barriers into this realm would require great strength," Hakan said.

My mind raced with thoughts of Ephraim and Viema. They seemed certain that they held the power to siphon this curse from me so long as I allowed it to awaken within. If they could do that, then I found it easy to believe they could also find a way into this realm. Which I knew they had succeeded in doing. I just wasn't sure how.

A knock silenced the menial conversation around me.

At Aiden's behest, a young guard entered the study. Her face was watchful as she glanced toward the demons filling the room. When her eyes landed on me, my breath caught in my throat.

Viema smiled pleasantly. "This was just delivered for you, Your Highness," she said in the cool voice of a dedicated guard.

Aiden took the white envelope she held out to him. "My father?" he asked, reading the scrawl across the front.

The angel nodded. "Sent by way of a messenger."

With only a brief glance in my direction, the angel left. My pulse pounded nervously in my ears as I studied the others in the room. I waited for any sign of recognition from them, any hint that they knew who she truly was. But none came. To them, she was only a guard. Little did they know...

"What is it?" Seraphine asked as Aiden stood, smiling coyly.

"Here." He handed the envelope to me. "This is for you."

The elegant wording across the front was unfamiliar to me. Frowning, I opened it and read the invitation it held.

"Your father is inviting us to a ball?" I asked, perplexed. This was not what I was expecting.

"It's the invitation to your formal coronation," Aiden clarified. "It'll be held over winter solstice. I'd say we have until then to prove our marriage wasn't a ploy against him. If he doesn't believe us by then, then I suspect your coronation will actually be a trial that will end in bloodshed."

I shuddered. "And Ephraim? Does the king not care about your claim of Ephraim being the Angel of Life?"

Aiden's gaze flitted over my features again, studying whatever he sensed in my tone that I wouldn't acknowledge. "Knowing my father's suspicious tendencies, I suspect he hasn't even bothered to look for him, let alone prepare a plan of defense or attack against him."

"Do you have a plan of defense?" I asked, curious.

Killian grinned. "Of course."

"Why do you think there are so many guards roaming the halls?" Seraphine added.

"We're still organizing a plan of attack," Aiden said with an unreadable glance toward his friends.

"But until then, guarding you is our priority," Killian said, puffing out his chest proudly.

I raised a brow, amused by his confidence. "Oh?"

"You know, in case Ephraim comes to take you, or sends an army of angels to steal you away." Killian's eyes widened with the excitement of battle as he wrapped his hands around the bow hanging off his shoulder.

"I thought the protections Ofrin placed on the Soul Collector would keep me from being taken from this realm?" I asked. The essence thrummed in my chest as I considered what would happen if Ephraim decided to whisk me away to his realm once my part of the bargain was fulfilled.

Aiden nodded. "They would've protected against your unwilling removal from the mortal realm. But here they do not matter."

Seraphine waved away his concerned tone. "We can worry about that later. We have something bigger to deal with at the moment."

The essence opened up within me as my nervousness grew. "What?" Aiden's lips twitched toward a smile at the fear in my tone.

"You need a dress," Seraphine said excitedly. Her arm looped through mine, leading me toward the door. "And I know just where to get one."

SEVENTEEN

SERAPHINE AND I RODE on horseback through the forest. Though I was freshly bathed and in clean clothes, I still found horsehair to pick off of my cloak as we dismounted outside a small cottage.

"Don't worry about keeping clean," Seraphine said, tying the horses to a post nearby.

I sighed. "It's just these clothes are brand new," I complained. "I'd hoped to keep them clean for as long as possible before ruining them."

Seraphine laughed, her brown eyes softening. "They're riding clothes, Esme. You are allowed to get them dirty between washes."

I offered her an uncertain smile. "I can still wish to avoid dirt until then."

Seraphine shook her head, twisted braids moving over her shoulder as she led us to the door.

The cottage was small. There were two windows on the front of the house and a smaller one at the peak, just below the shingled roof. The exterior looked to be made of clay, pale from endless hours in the sunlight. The yard surrounding the cottage was small, most of it covered in shadow from the forest beyond.

The noise and bustle of the village nestled in the trees echoed along the dirt path splitting the forest. Laughter and shouts could be heard clearly. It sounded...peaceful.

"We can head there next, if you'd like," Seraphine said, sensing the direction of my mind.

"That's not necessary." I buried my curiosity.

I felt Seraphine's gaze along my back as she held the door open for me.

"There you are," Fen called from within the cottage.

The room I stepped into was a small kitchen. Cabinets lined one wall and a small cooking area was laid out beside the sink. The window above welcomed the faint light drifting through the looming clouds.

I followed Seraphine through the kitchen and into what appeared to be a sitting area. Tarsa sat rigidly in an armchair beneath the second window while Fen kept busy at the hearth, shifting the wood to keep the fire going.

"Let me help you with that," Seraphine said, quickly stepping into action.

"Let her do it," Tarsa said, her voice having lost some of its usual annoyance when I was around. "Stubborn old woman refused my help, determined to do it herself."

"That's because your version of help, Tarsa, is to simply ignore it until the fire goes out completely, and then complain when you get cold," Fen said, straightening slowly. "And I am not old. Not yet."

The barest hint of a smile pulled at my lips. Somehow, in this small cottage far from the castle where reminders of the darkest parts of my life remained, it became easier to forget. Or at least pretend the hurt didn't linger.

Tarsa rolled her eyes, standing far more gracefully than a mere mortal could manage. "I'll be back later," she said, moving past me and through the door before Fen could reply.

Fen shook her head, sighing. "Sometimes it's a wonder how she and our father ever managed to survive together. They are both too stubborn for their own good."

Seraphine smiled, wrapping an arm around Fen's shoulders. "I do believe she just called you stubborn as well. So, which is it? You or her?"

The mortal woman scowled, though it held little heat. "I am not stubborn."

"Of course not." Seraphine winked in my direction. There was no fighting the amusement that made me grin.

"Esme," Fen said warmly, reaching to pull me into a hug. "Tarsa mentioned you would be coming by. Aiden's letter said you have an official coronation coming up and you need a dress. Do you have anything in mind that you might want to wear?"

Fen took my hand, pulling me through the small hallway and to the cramped staircase leading to the attic. Though she moved at a slow, mortal pace, Fen's movements still managed to contain the deadly prowess that came with centuries of battle.

"I've never attended a coronation before," I said honestly. "I'm not even sure what sort of dress I should wear."

Seraphine remained just a step behind. "You're the princess. It's your coronation. You can probably get away with wearing whatever you want."

"Although a formal ball gown is usually recommended," Fen added as we reached the attic space.

I glanced around the small room. The ceiling came to a peak down the middle of the room and the walls were painted a pale shade of blue, much like the sky with the midday sun.

Reams of fabric sat on every surface. Some were stacked against the wall, clear to the ceiling above my head, and others were settled along chairs and the small desk beneath the window. Every color I could put a name to, and some that I couldn't, were on display before me.

"I think a ball gown would be nice," I admitted softly. I'd never imagined wearing something that would be deemed important enough to be made from fabric of the quality I saw here. Most of my clothes were Mousa's hand-me-downs or plain breeches and tunics from shops in the villages back home.

"Wonderful," Fen said, parading through the room with newfound energy. The smile on her face was infectious. "Let's start with your measurements while you decide on a color."

Fen ushered me to a small pedestal in the far corner. The mirror before it was practically overcome with swaths of fabrics draped across it. Seraphine shook her head, a smile on her mouth, as she carefully folded the fabrics and set them aside.

While Fen set out a notebook and her measuring tape, I glanced toward Seraphine, watching her struggle to find a place to sit.

"How do you manage to find the fabric you want?" I asked, glancing around the space as Fen began measuring me.

Seraphine chuckled. "She doesn't."

"Now that's not entirely true," Fen argued half-heartedly. She ran the measuring tape along the outside of my leg. "I find the right fabrics just when I need them. If I can't find them when I'm looking for them, then that just means they weren't meant to be used for that design."

Seraphine laughed as she finally cleared an armchair. "That sounds like a fool's excuse."

Fen turned to scowl at the warrior. "I'm sorry dear, I didn't quite hear you. What was that?"

"I said, I thought this fabric looked great for Esme," Seraphine teased, holding a ream of brilliant gold satin.

My breath caught as I stared at it. Warmth spread through my chest. A coronation was something I never imagined being a part of. And of course, now that it was happening, my mother wouldn't be here to see it. She wouldn't be here to help me pick the colors for my gown. Nor would Amara, who would've been content to live in this room, surrounded by the brilliant colors.

Fen harrumphed and nodded to the desk beneath the window. "Set it aside then, and we'll consider it later."

I remained silent and still as Fen measured my other leg, and then both arms, and every part of my body she deemed necessary for the gown. By the time she had an entire page full of my measurements, my feet were growing sore from standing.

"What style of dress were you thinking?" Fen asked as she sifted through a stack of fabric.

"I'm not really sure," I said, following her reflection in the mirror.

I watched Fen toss another ream of fabric onto a growing pile in the center of the room. Seraphine moved to fix the stack before it fell over and caused an even bigger mess.

"What will Aiden wear?" I asked when I saw a bright pink ream of fabric fly through the air. Seraphine ducked just in time to avoid a blow to her head.

Fen sighed. "Oh, the prince will likely try to wear something I've already made for him."

"Meaning black and plain," Seraphine added with a wry grin.

I returned her smile easily, picturing the usual garb Aiden wore. Her smile widened with mine.

"But he won't get off that easily," Fen called from wherever her hunched figure was hidden amongst the stacks of fabrics.

"You'll be making him something new then?" I asked.

"Of course. There hasn't been a coronation in the Realm of Souls since His Highness' own nearly two centuries ago. I think that calls for new attire, don't you?" Fen asked, poking her head above the wall of fabrics.

The sight made my chest lighten even more. "Yes. I do."

"Good. Now that that's settled, let's pick a color." She nodded toward the crooked tower in the center of the room.

Seraphine and I shared a smile as Fen moved into view, carrying what might possibly be the world's ugliest shade of yellow.

"Not that one," I practically begged.

Fen raised a brow as Seraphine turned to hide her amusement. "I thought you weren't sure what you wanted?"

I shook my head at the hideous fabric. "Well, I know I don't want that one."

Fen rolled her eyes, tossing the ream over her shoulder. Beside me, Seraphine sighed, though her mouth still tilted up in a grin.

Standing there, surrounded by chaotic stacks of fabrics, it was easy to momentarily forget what had plagued my mind these past weeks. The pain that haunted my heart grew lesser as a long-forgotten sense of joy warmed my chest. The bloodshed and destruction that had become my life made its way to the recesses of my mind as I laughed among friends.

EIGHTEEN

SERAPHINE AND I SPENT the better part of the afternoon at Fen's cottage. Despite the hours there, we never decided on a color for the gown. Instead, I watched the two of them bicker over how Fen should organize her reams of fabric.

We left at the first hint of dusk. Seraphine escorted me back to the castle only to return to Fen's cottage immediately upon seeing me safely inside.

As I walked through the castle halls, I couldn't help but notice the serenity flowing through me. After only a few hours away from the overwhelming thoughts of Ephraim, this curse, and mourning my family, some of the darkness had lifted from my chest. I felt lighter, breathing easier.

This acknowledgement felt monumental as I turned toward my study. The change I felt today, at my being here, was something I wasn't entirely ready to address yet. But I knew I couldn't ignore it for much longer.

I came to Aiden's realm with the purpose of killing him and breaking the curse. Now, I was partnered with the angel who had tried to kill me more than once and who now sought a way to take the curse from me. Something that I was all too happy to give up, especially if it meant I didn't have to kill Aiden in the process.

I didn't allow myself to think too closely about why keeping Aiden alive mattered to me.

The essence in my chest warmed as I made my way up the winding staircase leading toward my study. The door to Aiden's study was closed. No guards stood by, so I assumed that meant he was off elsewhere, doing whatever it was he did at night.

Curiosity bloomed as I stood outside his door. Aiden had kept his distance during most of my stay, and yet, after all we'd been through, I couldn't help but wonder where he went to find joy and pleasure in his world.

Suddenly my thoughts were bombarded with images of him enjoying the company of other women. Perhaps somewhere in the village beyond the trees, where surely there would be more than enough women to entertain him.

Emotion burned through my veins as I lost all manner of sense and shoved the door aside.

I came to a stop as soon as the door smacked against the interior wall. Aiden sat behind his desk, silhouetted by the setting sun shining through the large windows behind him.

He looked up as the door swung back toward me, the momentum from its collision with the wall startling me with the strength of my anger.

My lungs seized as I stared at him. I quickly closed my mouth as his brow quirked up in question.

"Sorry," I mumbled, shifting uncomfortably. The strange emotion vanished as quickly as it had appeared. "I didn't realize you'd be in here. There wasn't a guard at the door."

He set the book he was reading on his desk with exaggerated slowness. "Do you make it a habit to barge into my study when you think I'm not here?"

My cheeks heated. "Everyone else is out. I assumed you would be with them."

The corner of his lips twitched to hide a smile. I swallowed, embarrassed, as he got to his feet with a warrior's grace. His eyes remained on me as he moved around the large desk, crossing his arms over his chest as he leaned against it, his posture the picture of ease.

"Everyone else has the night off," he said calmly.

"And you don't?"

He shook his head, a small upturn to his mouth. "Hakan and Killian went to a pub in the village. Tarsa is doing whatever it is she does when she's not guarding the realm. And Sera and Fen are spending the evening at Fen's cottage." He shrugged. "I opted to stay here."

I frowned. "Why? Is there something else happening that I don't know about?" His smile widened, amused. "What are you smiling at?"

"You. Your confusion at finding me here, but also the anger with which you entered." His crooked grin remained as he continued to study me. "I can't help but wonder what upset you so strongly that you kicked in my door."

"I can think of many things about you that would upset me," I said coolly.

Aiden's expression sobered. "Yes, I suspect you can."

"I didn't kick in your door," I said in a poor effort to tear the sorrow from his eyes. "I just hadn't expected it to open so easily."

"Ah, yes. Because you assumed I would be gone and the door would be locked." Despite his guarded expression, amusement lit his eyes. "So again I ask, what were you thinking when you decided to break down my door?"

The warmth in my chest spread to my cheeks. "I was curious."

"About what?" The tilt of his head caused a loose strand of hair to fall over his cheek. The sudden urge to brush it aside shocked me.

I shrugged. "You."

He stayed silent for a moment, just watching me. I could feel his eyes roaming over my face like a brand along my skin. That acknowledgment brought fresh heat to my face as I forced my gaze away from his.

The words he'd last spoken to me in my own study came to mind as I glared at the books lining his walls. I forced the feeling away, instead turning my mind to more important things than whatever I might feel for the demon prince.

I needed to find this witch's potion. A difficult thing to come by within the next two weeks, but an important factor in freeing myself from this curse so I could return to my family.

With my thoughts muddled over Ephraim's demand, I turned to go, only to be stopped by a gentle hand on my arm.

The look on Aiden's face, his eyes unusually wide and nervous, gave me pause. He dropped his arm immediately, flexing his hand, as if stung by my touch.

"There's something I'd like to show you." His tone drew my eyes back to his. "I was going to wait another day, but I don't think Jester will mind if I show you now."

Hesitant excitement replaced the swarm of mixed emotions I'd felt a moment before. "The library?"

Aiden's sheepish grin returned. "Jester finished arranging everything this morning. I planned to show you tomorrow. I knew you would be at Fen's all afternoon, and I figured you would be tired upon your return."

I shook my head, turning back toward the stairwell. "I'm ready now."

His soft chuckle followed me down the winding stairs until we reached the main floor of the castle. Excitement buzzed through my veins as Aiden walked beside me, leading the way through halls I'd yet to see.

Like the rest of his home, the walls remained bare apart from the dark drapes bordering every window, and the white marbled floors were without rugs.

My mind drifted back to the abandoned room overflowing with what little remained of his mother's belongings. I remembered seeing paintings in there, and rugs rolled up in a corner. Surely they could be used to bring some life into this vast space.

Briefly, I wondered how Ephraim would feel knowing that only a small room's worth of trinkets remained of his mother's memory.

But Aiden's reluctance to bring warmth and welcome to his abode returned to the forefront of my mind. Did he truly care about the possibility of an attack and the prospect of replacing what was lost, or could he simply not find it within himself to care at all? Something about that thought made my chest squeeze with sadness.

The hall he turned down now was much larger than the others. The ceiling stood two stories tall and large windows covered the walls on either side, letting the fading light filter through the corridor.

Aiden paused outside a dark set of doors. The design carved into the wood was similar to what could be found on the door to Aiden's study. Vines and thorns swirled together across their length.

He turned, flashing a quicksilver grin. "Welcome to your library."

The doors slid back across the wall to reveal a vast, brightly lit space.

I stared at the hundreds of books lining the walls and breathed in the warm scent of discovery. I could feel Aiden's gaze studying my reaction, but I couldn't drag my eyes away from the room as I stepped through the door.

"There's more," Aiden whispered, leaning close enough that I felt his mouth brush the shell of my ear.

He reached his hand out, pausing for a beat as he waited for my inevitable rejection. I placed my hand in his, letting him gently pull me further into the space. A large design of the white tree was painted into the marble flooring, nearly taking up the entire entryway. Aiden stopped as we stood in the center of the painting.

His eyes were alight with joy as he leaned close. "Look up," he whispered.

I did, and the smile that overtook me was entirely genuine. The library soared five stories high and had bookshelves lining every wall, expanding in twisting rows toward the center of the room. A large staircase wound loosely around the middle of the room, starting at the roots of the painted white tree along the floor.

"This is amazing," I whispered, awestruck.

Aiden's smile was so brilliant that my cheeks flushed upon looking at it. The windows remained open to the night sky between each shelf, but his smile shone brighter than any star in the sky.

"Your Highness," an aged voice said from behind, making me jump. When I turned, I caught sight of the librarian shuffling into view.

"Jester," Aiden said politely. His hand moved to my lower back as he spoke. "This is my wife, Esme."

My heart fluttered at his words, but my mind told me to banish the tentative excitement. To hold onto the cold anger and determination that first pushed me to bargain with Ephraim.

I grappled with my conflicting thoughts and emotions as Aiden stared at me like I was the moon and stars lighting the realm.

I pushed the overwhelming emotions aside, smiling. "Nice to meet you."

Jester, the Keeper of Books, smiled crookedly. His wrinkled face was half hidden behind a thick beard the same shade of silver as his hair. "Your Highness," he said with a deep bow. "It is an honor to have you in my small corner of the castle."

"I think your library is far from small," I noted with a glance toward the ceiling towering above our heads.

Jester's grin widened, crinkling the corners of his eyes. "I hope it is to your liking."

"I told her you needed a few days to organize," Aiden said, glancing toward the hundreds of shelves. "Though how you manage to keep so many books organized is beyond my imagination."

"That is because you spend most of your time ruining my shelves," Jester scolded playfully. "Is there anything in particular you were looking for, milady?" he asked me.

I thought over all the answers I still needed. "I was mostly curious about the history of my family's tie to this realm," I admitted. Aiden stiffened ever so slightly at my side.

The Keeper of Books smiled, turning toward the foot of the stairs. "I have just the texts."

Aiden trailed behind me as I followed the elderly man. I wondered about his immortality, as he's known Aiden for a long time, but the only other person I met here who didn't live with everlasting youth was Fen and she was no longer immortal.

"I hope you've enjoyed your time in our realm, Princess," Jester probed as he led me down a row of books on the second level. "I've heard a great many things about you since your arrival."

I started, daring a questioning glance at Aiden. "You have? I hope they've been relatively kind things."

The bookkeeper sent me a bewildered look as he came to a stop at the end of the row. "Well of course they have, Your Highness. We are nothing but pleased to have you here. We've been waiting a great many years for this one to bring a bride into our home."

"I don't think she needs to hear about that," Aiden cut in with a frown, though a warm glint remained in his eyes.

Jester shrugged, unbothered. "As you wish, Prince."

He turned to me. "These books contain everything I have in relation to your family's debt and the contingencies of bindings between the Realm of Souls and the mortal realm. Is this what you were looking for?"

"Yes," I said, relieved. "That's it exactly."

"Wonderful," the bookkeeper said with another eye-crinkling grin. "Shall I have my assistant bring these to your chambers in the morning?"

"Actually, would it be possible to have them brought to my study?" I asked.

"Certainly, Your Highness. Whatever you wish."

A canvas along the back wall caught my eye. It shimmered in the faint glimpse of moonlight, sitting beyond the reach of the candles' glow.

I moved toward it, heart pounding. The same glow of whatever demon magic powered the map in my study seemed to fill this map. Only this particular canvas wasn't a map like my own.

"What is this?" I asked, stopping before it.

The pad of the bookkeeper's boots on the marble floor echoed through the shelves as he moved closer. Aiden's footsteps were silent, though I felt the warmth of his presence as he stopped at my shoulder.

"This is how we manage the souls that pass through our realm." Jester's voice was monotone, making me think this was a question he answered frequently.

I thought back to Nonna's tales. "The wicked souls?"

"Every soul that departs the mortal realm comes through the Crossroads," Jester said, pointing to a bright spot in the middle of the map. "They wait at the Crossroads until Death can welcome them into the afterlife. For some that is peace, for others it is not. But every soul comes to this realm. The angels no longer have any connection to the souls of the departed."

"But they did at one time," I noted, turning away from the map.

"They were created many centuries ago to hunt the souls that attempted to return to the mortal realm," Aiden said; Ephraim had told me this bit of knowledge only days ago.

"Now they are nothing more than an arrogant nuisance of a species," Jester muttered under his breath.

"So, who hunts those souls if not the angels?" I asked.

Jester shrugged, running a hand through his beard absentmindedly. "Your husband has a rotation of guards that serve at the Crossroads."

I looked to Aiden. "Really? Is that how you knew what happened to the souls I would siphon?" I remembered his tales of souls finding peace when reunited after my siphoning.

He nodded. "It is."

"Of course this was all discovered after the Dark War many ages ago," Jester said with a sigh. His eyes remained focused on the map. "After the angels rebelled and threatened every mortal life in your realm, Ofrin had no choice but to expel them from our realm and add protections for the mortals."

"I thought the Dark War started because the demons wanted control," I said, recounting the history we were taught in Cordovia.

Both demons stared at me with varying looks of astonishment.

"No, my dear," Jester said, aghast. "The angels were created to keep order among the dead awaiting Death's welcome into their new realm. Some grew greedy and wanted the same power and control over souls the God of Death possesses. And when denied that power, they rebelled. That action started a decades-long war that ravaged the human lands."

"What stopped it?" I asked.

Jester's eyes shot toward Aiden for a moment, which went unnoticed by the demon prince. At his steadily growing unease, I recalled the secret which Ephraim imparted to me. And from that I could deduce what actually stopped the war.

"Our prince was born," Jester answered. My gaze collided with Aiden's. "His birth brought a stalemate to the war. Though it seems that the Angel himself actually decided to spend the next two and a half centuries plotting against him. Against us."

I nodded, letting my gaze return to the map. "So now Ephraim is working toward his revenge and aiming to steal the essence to get it."

Aiden nodded slowly. "We think he believes that if he can somehow take the power from you then he will hold the same power over souls as my father."

Unease filtered through me as I thought of the bargain I'd made. "And what could he do with that power, exactly?"

Jester sighed. "Start another war? Take every soul from every mortal in the realm and use them as his own army? A great many things could be possible."

I frowned. "But what would he get out of accomplishing that? It doesn't make sense to kill every mortal in existence."

"He wouldn't just be killing them," Aiden explained. "He would siphon their souls as you would. Only he would keep them trapped so they would be forced to bend to his will. It is possible for someone with my power, or my father's, or even yours, to bind another soul to their own so they would be forced to obey."

I shuddered against the chill crawling down my spine. "So why is it that we're taught the opposite? That angels are to be praised and adored while demons are cruel, selfish creatures?"

Again, Jester sighed. "The mortal mind remains a mystery to us all. They are stubborn beings who are determined to survive no matter what fiction they choose to write into their histories."

I turned back to the map. There were so many bright spots lighting the entirety of the realm. Most congregated in the middle where the Crossroads was located. The white tree stood out as well, a bright spot in the center of surrounding darkness.

"Can you see Ephraim on this map?" I asked as another idea came to mind, making my pulse spike.

"No," Aiden said, voice a growl of pent-up frustration.

"Angels cannot be detected on this map," Jester interjected calmly. "They have no soul for this map to find."

"And me? Can I be found?" I asked.

He shrugged and pointed to what I guessed was the castle. "We are here in the castle's library, but as you can see, there are only two beacons."

Somehow that unsettled me more. "Do I not have a soul?"

"You do," Aiden reassured me. "But you are a mortal in a realm full of demons with souls bound to my father, or myself. To most, you would remain unseen on this map."

A darker splotch caught my attention, not too far from the bright spots Jester indicated were he and Aiden. "What's this?" I asked, pointing to the faded orb of light.

A knowing smile turned up the corners of Aiden's mouth. "That is Ridha. She is the witch who made the ointment I used to treat your wounds this summer."

"And made the potion that would end our marriage," I added. Aiden nodded solemnly while the vial I spoke of burned a hole through my pocket in recognition. I frowned at the faded light. "Why does she appear differently?"

"Magic is a strange and twisted thing," Jester said cryptically.

"Is that where she lives?" I asked, recalling Ephraim's orders to retrieve the mysterious potion from her.

"It is her shop where she makes her antidotes and ointments," Jester said. "She rarely leaves. Much like me, she has grown a bit too much in love with her work."

I twisted my fingers together nervously as I studied the map. Agitating the blisters I'd formed during this morning's training.

Aiden's hands caught mine in his grasp. "You're hurt?" There was a hint of accusation in his voice as if I'd hidden the injury from him.

I shook my head. "It's just blisters from training. Nothing important."

His mouth turned down in a scolding frown. "If you don't tend to them now they will only grow more troublesome."

"Maybe I'll have to pay this witch of yours a visit then," I said as a plan unfolded in my mind.

He continued to hold my hands delicately. His touch made my skin burn with longing and my heart trip over itself as he stared at me, ever watchful. Then his gaze landed on the map behind me, and his entire demeanor changed.

His hands cooled on mine, and he stepped closer as if unwilling to be more than an arm's reach away. "We need to get you to your room."

"What? Why?" I asked, trying to turn toward the map again.

Aiden pulled me away with a quick nod toward Jester who was already scurrying out of sight. My heart raced against my ribs in growing panic.

"What's going on?" I asked as Aiden led me out of the library.

"There's a cluster of souls coming this way. It appears they've escaped the Crossroads and have wandered too close."

I frowned as we turned down an unfamiliar corridor. "Why would that be a problem? They can't do anything here, can they? They're already dead."

"Exactly," he said between clenched teeth. "They are already dead. Which means they cannot be killed again. However, what they can do is destroy everything or everyone in their path if one is not properly trained to fight against them."

"But can't you just control them? Send them back to the Crossroads?"

We came to a sudden halt in a bare hall. The guards were slumped on the floor, unconscious. I couldn't even be certain they were still breathing as I stared, dumbfounded, at their forms.

I opened my mouth to speak when the essence in my chest spread through me. The power unleashed itself, opening to me more than it ever had before. My knees grew weak at its strength, causing me to lean heavily into Aiden's grip.

The essence hummed along my body like a second skin as I caught sight of what really filled the hall before us.

A moment earlier, the hall was bare apart from the two slumped guards. Now that the essence pulsed through my veins, I could see every soul that blocked our path to my chambers.

They were dark shadows, faceless and indiscernible from one another. The air around us grew sweltering as the essence rose. I felt it from the tips of my fingers to the center of my bones. There was no end to the power I possessed.

As one, the shadows turned toward us, and the essence recognized them for what they were. They watched us, waiting.

The essence pulsed through me again, stronger. Each soul hissed as the reach of my power touched them.

"What do we do?" I asked, nerves stealing my breath.

Aiden pulled me closer, body shielding me from the shadows of souls as they crept closer. As the souls unleashed a ragged cry, Aiden's own power erupted.

NINETEEN

MY HEART WAS IN my throat as Aiden pulled me through the hall. Unyielding, shrill cries echoed around us. My skin tingled with the over-whelming power that sought to tear itself from me and attach to the souls that stalked us.

Aiden pushed me into a doorway. "Here. This will lead you to your chambers. Bar the doors and do not open them for anyone. Do you hear me? No one."

His eyes were filled with worry for me as he brushed a hand over my cheek. I could feel his power radiating through the air with a darkness that called to my own. In the distance the souls still howled with frus-tration.

He turned back the way we'd come. "Where are you going?" I asked, panicked.

"Go, Esme," he ordered. He moved to close the door, blocking the souls' paths. "They've sensed your power, and my own will not deter them forever. This palace was not built to contain souls like the Cross-roads was. They will get free again, and they will come for you."

His gaze met mine for one last moment before he slammed the doors closed, leaving me alone in the hall.

My breath came in panicked gasps as I stood frozen. The cries of the dead could still be heard through the thick cedar door, and it made the essence respond in kind.

Power warmed my chest, burning through my veins as I finally spun and raced through the hall. Aiden was right. I barely knew how to fight with a sword. There was certainly no way I would be able to fight off the dead. But surely I could find someone who would help him.

My boots echoed on the marble floors as I raced, desperate for another guard to pop into view. Of course the one time I actually needed them, they were gone.

"Your Highness?" The sound of the unfamiliar voice eased some of my panic as I spun toward it.

"Aiden needs help," I said breathlessly. The guard's eyes widened as he studied the hall behind me, searching for the prince. "There are souls here. He...He needs help. There are too many."

Reading the panic on my face for what it was, the guard nodded and moved past me. "You must find somewhere to hide until it is safe, Princess. His Highness would be most upset if you were harmed."

I let his words pass over me, ignoring the truth to them.

Before I could respond, the essence burned along my skin. I gasped and fell to the floor just as a soul launched through the air right where I'd been standing.

Like Kesson's soul, it was nearly translucent. It appeared no more than a shadow, a wraith in the hall as it loomed over me. The essence burned at the soul's proximity, allowing me to see it more clearly. There was no sense of self to it that I could perceive. Where eyes would normally be, there was only a vast emptiness. The essence shuddered in recognition as I stared at it.

The guard launched himself at the soul before it could attack again. I scuttled backward, out of the way. I had a brief moment of panic where I wondered if a soul had already gotten past Aiden's defenses, but I pushed it away as I stood on unsteady feet.

When the soul cried again, I was forced to cover my ears. Its shrill screech shook the walls and made blood drip from my ears.

The guard howled in pain as the soul reached its hand into his chest and pulled. I gasped as the guard's soul was ripped from him. The essence shuddered at the sight.

Two souls stood before me now. And like the one that first attacked, the soul of the guard seemed incapable of any form of reason. The guard's mind was lost along with his crumpled body. And like the first soul, emptiness also filled his gaze.

I pressed my back against the wall, trying desperately to put space between us. The hall around us remained empty. There were no guards. Aiden was fighting off the other souls. And I was alone.

The essence burned again, tingling through my veins as the first soul attacked with impossible speed.

I ducked as its hand crashed into the marble, the sound loud enough to compete with a clap of thunder.

Again, I leaped out of reach. Both souls were closing in. Their heads tilted curiously as the essence grew stronger, bolder.

When the first soul attacked again, I didn't move. The essence wrapped around my panic-filled heart and calmed it, taking over. My vision brightened like a fog had been lifted and now a veil of power hung over my eyes.

Both souls halted. I saw the fight leave their forms as they watched me eagerly. My feet felt frozen to the floor as I stood there, staring in mild fear. The essence echoed my pulse as it filled me, warmth seeping to the very tips of my fingers.

Through the veil of power filling my sight, I noticed a single rope, made entirely of shadow, gradually forming from the souls' chests and reaching toward my outstretched hand.

Uncertainty forced me to hesitate for only a moment, and that was all I needed.

Shouts I hadn't noticed before grew nearer, breaking my focus. I turned, momentarily forgetting the lost souls. Jadan and Daemon skidded to a halt as they stared at me. Their eyes widened with matching expressions of horror and confusion before they noticed the souls.

"Esme, get down!" Daemon yelled at the same time Jadan launched toward me.

I crashed to my knees, wincing as they collided with the marble floor. My vision returned to normal as the veil of power disappeared.

Strong hands gripped my elbow, dragging me across the floor. I could hear Jadan's sword sing through the air as he fought, but I didn't dare look. Something about what nearly happened sent a shiver of unease through me.

"Are you okay? What happened? Where's Aiden?" Daemon's voice was clipped and focused as he pulled me to my feet.

I looked around the corridor. "He made me leave him. There were too many souls, and I was sent to hide."

He nodded. "Where did they come from?"

"I don't know. We were just in the library, and when I saw the map...that's when we ran into the souls."

The demon nodded, glancing over my head toward the fight. The tips of his horns stuck out from his inky black.

"Can you get to your chambers on your own?" he asked.

I nodded. "I can. But Aiden needs help."

"I know. We'll find him, Esme."

I swallowed back a wave of nervousness before he yanked roughly on my arm. I was flying through the air a moment later. The breath rushed from my lungs as I crashed into the opposite wall.

A soul had gotten past Jadan and now fought Daemon. My eyes widened as I glanced between the two souls and the demons they fought. Both souls fought like unhinged, bloodthirsty savages. There was no reason to their movements. They appeared desperate to get to me.

"Get out of here!" Jadan yelled.

My legs felt weak beneath me as I got to my feet. I could feel the pull of my power stretching outward, toward the lost souls. This felt different from what I'd practiced with Ephraim. There was something darker, stronger, to whatever the essence was doing now.

The veil returned over my eyes, casting the world in rippling shadows. My chest warmed with the power of the essence as it filled me entirely. Calm radiated at its presence within me, erasing the panic I felt a moment before.

"Release them," I ordered in a voice unfamiliar to me.

Both demons continued to fight, ignoring me. But the souls froze. A familiar presence neared—Tarsa. I found I could now recognize her soul as she stopped at my shoulder.

"Release them," I repeated in that same, powerful voice.

This time both demons paused, confused. Jadan went still in the way only an immortal could. It was unnatural, like he wasn't even breathing. Daemon's eyes widened as he studied me.

"Esme, what are you doing?" he asked. If I didn't know any better, I'd think he was afraid.

Power erupted from me, blinding us all with its darkness. The souls screeched loud enough to shake the walls as the essence claimed them.

Something cold and heavy was pushed into my hands. The essence strengthened its hold on the souls, pulling them toward the siphon I held. They wailed and cried incoherently, but they didn't fight it. The cold siphon warmed to an unbearable heat as the essence took over, easily controlling its own strength.

I could feel the demons watching me, but I couldn't allow myself the distraction of looking at them. Their concern was practically tangible on the air.

The siphon began to glow in the familiar way it had when I'd collected souls for my family. The smoke inside of it spun erratically, welcoming the new souls. I blinked through the sudden blinding light of the power that this siphon contained. It was unlike any I'd felt before. My palms nearly burned from holding it.

The white light finally faded, forcing us all to blink in the sudden darkness. I watched the light in the siphon dim to a pale shade of blue.

"Esme?" a familiar voice asked warily.

I looked up, catching sight of Aiden standing at the end of the hall. There was something in his expression I couldn't quite decipher.

Jadan stepped forward silently, taking the siphon from me and placing it into a sack he carried over his shoulder.

"I'll take them back to the Crossroads," he said to Aiden.

The demon prince only nodded, eyes not leaving mine. Exhaustion settled deep in my bones as the essence returned to its resting place near my heart. I felt it curl around itself in a relaxed state. The veil lifted from my eyes a moment later, letting my vision return to normal once again.

I forced air into my lungs, unaware I'd been holding my breath. I stumbled back a step, legs growing weak again.

Tarsa caught hold of me, wrapping her arms around my waist with little effort.

My gaze found Aiden's once more, noting the worry that filled his eyes, just before everything went black.

TWENTY

I awoke in Aiden's study. Tarsa stood, scowling, in the corner of the room while Seraphine dabbed a damp cloth on my forehead.

"You're awake," she said, smiling. "How are you feeling?"

My pulse pounded in my ears in time with the throbbing in my temples. "What happened?"

"He's coming," Tarsa said, cutting me off.

The door burst open a moment later. Aiden stood in the doorway, backed by Killian and Hakan. The harsh expression on his face settled into something gentler as he caught sight of me.

I sat up tenderly, fully aware of the pounding ache in my skull. "What happened?" I repeated.

Aiden moved swiftly. Kneeling before me, he cradled my head gently in his hands. The gesture was soft, like he feared I might shatter. "How are you feeling?"

I stared into his eyes, unable to look away or move as the full force of his concern for me pulled at a long buried emotion. "My head hurts."

"You need to rest," Seraphine interjected kindly.

"What about the souls?" I asked, pulse skipping nervously.

Aiden's jaw tensed for a moment. "The problem has been resolved."

"They're back at the Crossroads?" I asked, curious about the look Hakan and Tarsa shared.

"Daemon and Jadan are taking them there now," he said.

Killian smiled, stepping forward. "You were badass. I didn't know you could do that."

I frowned. "Do what?"

"Do you remember what happened? Right before you collapsed?" Aiden asked gently. His thumb brushed along my cheek as he spoke.

I tried to shake my head, but he still held onto my face, keeping me still. "I remember Tarsa arriving. And the souls fighting Daemon and Jadan."

Seraphine knelt beside Aiden. "You used your power," she explained calmly. "The essence inside you pulled the souls into the siphon Tarsa gave you."

"But one of them belonged to the guard. Couldn't it be returned to his body?" I asked, already sensing the answer that would come.

She shook her head. "That's not how it works. Both had to be brought to the Crossroads with the rest."

I glanced toward Aiden. "How did you get the rest to the Crossroads? Did you use a siphon too?"

"No, Esme." There was something in his tone, in the way he spoke the words that made my stomach tumble. "You did. You captured every loose soul and bound them into the siphon."

"It was badass," Killian repeated with a shy grin.

Hakan stepped forward, frowning slightly. "Your power is far stronger than it should be. No one apart from Ofrin should be able to wield that much control over the lost souls. Not even Aiden holds that much power."

I pulled my face gently from Aiden's grip, suddenly needing space. My thoughts raced with the guilt of working with Ephraim. And worse, that they might suspect something of me. But I forced all that away. Instead, I only focused on the sedate calm that hummed through me now.

"How?" I asked. I was surprised my voice sounded steady, hiding my nerves.

Aiden shrugged, a storm brewing in his eyes. "We're figuring that out."

"Maybe it's because you're in this realm now," Seraphine added. "There has never been a Soul Collector here before. It's possible your proximity to Ofrin or even to the Crossroads could be what is strengthening your power."

I nodded, choosing to believe that for the excuse it was. "How did they manage to escape the Crossroads in the first place?"

They all shared an uncertain glance.

"We don't know," Seraphine said.

"The guards on duty were found dead, but their souls were missing," Killian added.

"Missing? How can they be missing?" I asked, confused.

Aiden ran a hand through his hair. "We suspect Ephraim was involved."

My confusion only grew. That didn't make any sense. Ephraim wouldn't have wanted me attacked in such a way when he needed me alive in order to break this curse.

Except I did just sever our bargain under the pretense of collecting the mysterious potion for him.

"Have you figured out how he got into the realm?" I asked.

"The only way he could've gotten past our spies is if he had someone helping him," Tarsa noted. Her piercing gaze made my palms break out in a nervous sweat.

"We'll figure this out," Aiden offered comfortingly, once again misreading my nerves.

I could only nod. The exhaustion I felt now reminded me too much of the aftereffects of siphoning souls before Nonna's death. The essence I carried felt elated and strong, but my mortal body felt drained.

"For now, you need to rest," Seraphine said.

"See that she gets to her rooms safely," Aiden said quietly. Worry lined his face as he helped me to my feet. "I'll send word to Fen to bring her food when she's ready."

I felt Aiden's lingering gaze as Seraphine led me from the room. Her arm remained firmly wrapped through mine as we walked in silence toward my chambers.

Many more guards than usual were positioned throughout the halls. Each remained focused and poised for another attack, though the thought seemed unlikely. Even Drusilla and her friends, stationed in the halls as guards, appeared far more attentive to their surroundings than of me for once.

By the time we reached my rooms, I was dead on my feet. Seraphine practically carried me to my bed where I fell unconscious as soon as I collapsed on the blankets.

When I awoke next, it was from the cool brush of a hand along my cheek. A familiar, warm scent of cedar wrapped around me as a blanket settled over my shoulders. I fell asleep so quickly again I was almost certain I dreamed it.

TWENTY-ONE

A FEATHER-LIGHT TOUCH ALONG my brow woke me. The soft light of dawn crept across the sky through the opening in the drapes.

As the rest of the room slowly came into focus, I caught sight of the person kneeling at my bedside. His red-brown hair hung loose, framing his face handsomely as he studied me.

"Are you well?" His voice was gentle as he watched me pull myself upright.

I groaned, mind still heavy with sleep. "Why did you wake me?"

"I apologize," he said with a hint of a smile. I rubbed the sleep from my eyes as he stood gracefully. "But you are needed in my study."

"It's barely dawn," I said, pouting.

He nodded. "I know. If it were up to me, you would not be bothered."

Something in his voice made the remnants of sleep evaporate. I tossed the blankets aside, slipping into the boots at the foot of my bed. My eyes caught on the small box hidden just beneath my bed, remembering the half-witted bargain I'd trapped myself in.

"What now?" I asked, quickly running my fingers through my tangled curls.

The annoyance in my tone made a corner of his mouth quirk up, but his eyes remained grave. "My father has honored us with a visit."

I frowned at the bitterness in his tone. "He's here?"

"He is," he said, leading us toward the door. "And he has asked to speak with you."

With every step we took toward Aiden's study, my throat tightened a little more and my heart sputtered nervously in my chest. Drusilla and her friends stood in the shadows of the corridor. Their heads were bowed as they whispered, watching me with thoughtful expressions. My stomach turned again as we passed Viema on the stairs, her guise of being a guard still intact.

Hakan stood outside the door to Aiden's study, and another demon I didn't recognize stood across the stairs from him, scowling.

"He's been waiting," the unfamiliar demon said scornfully.

Aiden didn't spare him a glance. "That happens when you show up uninvited and unannounced."

The demon grunted something unintelligible as Aiden opened the door. I stood in the doorway, uncertain. Ofrin had his back to me, arms clasped behind him as he studied the books filling Aiden's shelves.

"Father," Aiden said by way of greeting. "You asked for Esme?"

As the God of Death turned, slowly and dramatically, to face me, I felt myself sink into the blankness I'd adopted in my early days here. The essence awakened just enough to snuff out my remaining trepidation as I met the demon's eyes.

"A while ago, I do believe," Ofrin said with inflated self-importance. "I'd like to speak to the girl alone, Aiden."

Aiden scowled at his father. "Whatever you have to say to her, you can say in front of me."

Ofrin studied his son, eyes scrutinizing every inch of him as if he were just now bothering to take notice of him. "You think I would harm her? You are that untrusting of your father?"

A muscle tightened in Aiden's jaw. "You yourself have deemed her a threat to your throne. If you're so concerned about that, what's to stop you from removing that threat right now?"

"She still has the essence, boy." Ofrin's voice was sharp as a blade. "I am not so foolish as to wipe that from existence just yet."

My gaze flicked between the two demons. "Why am I here?"

Both looked at me as if just remembering I was there. Ofrin took in my sleep-tousled hair and blistered hands with a look of disdain.

"Out, Aiden," Ofrin demanded. "I will not ask again."

Aiden and his father continued to glower at each other, holding some silent conversation I wasn't a part of. Finally, Aiden relented.

He dropped Ofrin's gaze, turning to me. "I will be just outside with Hakan should you need anything."

I nodded, watching him leave. As soon as the door closed behind him, I felt my pulse quicken.

Ofrin was watching me curiously when I turned to face him. "He puts on a good show, doesn't he?"

"I don't know what you mean."

The God of Death scoffed, moving to sit at Aiden's desk as if it were his own. "It does not matter. That is not why I am here."

"Why are you here?" I asked, remaining by the door.

He leaned back in Aiden's chair, the portrait of confidence. Even sitting, he somehow managed to look down his nose at me. "I came to speak with the witch, but I figured speaking with the carrier of Death's essence was within my right as its rightful owner. Especially after the stunt you pulled last night."

The essence in question stirred, warming my veins with its fiery touch. "Have you come to take it back?"

Anger flashed across his expression. "No," he grumbled. "Not yet anyway."

I hid my surprise behind stillness. Ephraim's mention of the protections around the essence came to mind as I studied the demon before me.

"From your casual coolness toward my son, I expect he hasn't spoken to you yet," Ofrin said, changing the topic.

My brows furrowed, confused. "Spoken to me about what?"

"Your parents of course," he said as if it were obvious. Ofrin watched me closely as he continued. "He's been relieved of his part in that bargain, so he is able to speak of it again."

I shook my head, still not understanding. "I've no idea what you mean."

Surprise sent the God of Death into a burst of harsh laughter. "He hasn't? Well, isn't that a surprise. As soon as he was pardoned, I assumed he would've swept in with the truth of it to spare himself the pain of your anger toward him."

I studied the amused demon in silence. My thoughts whirled with possible explanations for his words, yet I came up empty.

"What bargain?" I asked, heart racing against my ribs.

The demon's eyes narrowed. "Interesting," he muttered to himself. "Though I can't say I'm surprised. It is like Aiden to allow you to keep hating him. I'm sure he feels he deserves it."

I frowned, mind racing.

"You wish to know the truth of your parents' deaths, yes?" His lips twitched into a wicked smile at the pain I had little doubt appeared in my eyes the moment he recalled their murders.

"I know the truth of their deaths." Even I heard the bitter edge to my voice.

Death stood, chuckling. "I see you're as stubborn as your parents. It wasn't charming on them, and I don't find it charming on you either."

My heart stuttered in my chest as he moved closer. The essence tightened its hold around my heart, forcing it to slow.

"It was a pitiful offer they made," he said, coming to stand before me. His cold eyes were devoid of emotion as he watched me, waiting for his words to sink in. "Their lives in exchange for the safety of you and your siblings. What a waste. As if I would consider the two of them to be of equal measure against the vessel carrying my essence."

Blood pounded in my ears as my breath shortened, horror breaking through the calm illusion offered by the essence. "What are you saying?"

"Your parents forgot who holds the real power in this realm; in every realm." His voice was cutting as he glowered at me like I was to blame. "They dared bargain with me. They got what was coming to them, to all of them."

Horror and anger melded together, rising inside of me, and with it quickly came the strength of the essence. I felt it swell, stretching outward like a bird stretches its wings before taking flight.

Aiden had spoken the truth. He hadn't lied about my parents' deal with Ofrin.

"If it weren't for my damned son they would all be dead," he continued, unaware of the storm brewing within me. "He was not to interfere, and yet his strength had grown to allow him to defy me and save your siblings. Now do you understand why I am so wary of this marriage farce?"

"No." My mind refused to settle after this onslaught of revelations.

Ofrin scowled. "No one should have been able to stop that weak king from slaughtering your family. Their souls were mine; I claimed them as such. And now the one person who has ever been able to put a stop to my power and the very person who carries an essence of that same power have bound their souls in marriage. You expect me to believe you are not here for my crown?"

I returned his glower with one of my own, essence rising with my anger. "I do not want your crown."

"I am not a power to be trifled with, girl." His voice boomed through the room. "You best remember that before you dare to deem yourself strong enough to go against me."

"I haven't deemed myself anything," I argued.

He raised a quizzical brow. "No? Did you not siphon hundreds of souls only hours ago? Did you not use my own power out of turn? One might see that as an outright attack on my authority."

"Then one would be a fool."

The door opened before the words disappeared on the air. "That's enough," Aiden said calmly. I could see the tension in his posture as he came to stand at my side. Something stirred inside me as I studied his expression. He'd told the truth. I struggled to grapple with that revelation.

My mind opened up to new questions I needed answered.

"If you have another moment to spare, Father, I'd like to brief you on our newest findings regarding Ephraim," Aiden said, cutting off the previous conversation.

Ofrin grunted. "You need to leave that matter alone, boy. The angels cannot get into this realm."

"Clearly, they can," Aiden said. "Ephraim has been coming and going as he pleases for centuries."

"They will not attack," Ofrin said with animated arrogance.

I frowned at him. "How can you be so certain?"

Ofrin waved away my question, moving past us to leave.

"We've put plans in place to draw him out," Aiden explained quickly. Ofrin continued toward the door, all but ignoring his son. "We will have Ephraim in your dungeons as early as next week."

Ofrin spun on his heel. "You will do no such thing," he snapped. "In order to capture the foolish angel, you would need an army. Raising an army in your favor would only further prove that you plan to take my crown by force. No, you will not attack the angels."

I stared, dumbfounded, at the demon.

"This matter cannot wait," Aiden argued.

"It can and it will," Ofrin said. The demon scowled at my unmasked surprise. "Do not forget your invitation."

"We haven't," Aiden replied stiffly.

"The coronation will be held on winter solstice," Ofrin reminded us, moving again toward the door. "Only after you've proven your marriage to be of nothing but desperate love, and swear loyalty to me, will we discuss the angel. But I will not have you going out and starting a war by capturing their king."

"So, you are demanding we sit by and do nothing while Ephraim plots against us." Aiden's voice was as cold as I'd ever heard it.

Ofrin turned, glowering at his son. "I am telling you, you have larger issues at hand."

"Like what? Telling you time and again that we are not after your crown?" I asked, baffled.

"Yes," he seethed. "Exactly that. Your very life is in my hands, *Princess*. Do not make the mistake of ignoring that."

He stormed out without another word, leaving Aiden and I in stunned silence.

TWENTY-TWO

A WEEK WENT BY with no word on how the souls had been released. Aiden sent another guard to Ofrin's castle, seeking any answers he would give. But none came. Not even Ephraim bothered to respond to the letter I placed in the box immediately after Ofrin's departure.

I hadn't dared speak to Aiden about what his father revealed to me just yet. Part of me remained reluctant to accept it. But the other part of me swelled with relief knowing he didn't kill them.

Even if it did leave me with a growing mountain of questions.

Daemon and Jadan had been following me more closely as of late as well, though they tended to remain in the background. Seraphine and Killian returned to their places at my side too. Though our friendship was not as warm as it once had been, I couldn't bear to remain cold toward them any longer.

Both stood on the far side of the training room now. They sparred together while Tarsa threw me around the room like a sack of grain. The blisters on my fingers bled from the sword fighting, and my arms shook as if they were ready to fall from my body.

Tarsa kicked my shaking legs out from under me. I grunted as my back slammed against the floor, the air forcibly yanked from my lungs.

"Don't plant your feet," she ordered. I watched her walk away to place her practice sword with the others along the wall. I'd only ever seen her fight with her twin axes, but she was just as formidable with a sword.

I sucked in air as I remained sprawled on the stone. "If I didn't plant them, I would've fallen. I already can't feel my legs," I complained.

"Then you're still too weak," she said simply.

The door opened as Daemon sauntered into the room. His face lit up with a devilish grin as he spotted first me on the floor, then Tarsa standing above me.

"You just love putting people on their backs, don't you?" he drawled with a crooked smile.

Killian dipped his chin to hide his amusement as he continued sparring with Seraphine.

Tarsa grimaced. "You again."

"It's me," Daemon said with a flourish of his hands. "I only came to relieve these two," he nodded toward Killian and Seraphine, "and look after our princess."

I rolled my eyes as I slowly sat upright. Every muscle in my body protested painfully. "I don't need to be watched like a child."

"You're the realm's princess," Seraphine said, moving closer with Killian. "You require protection from any number of people who might wish you harm."

"If only she could protect herself and save us the trouble," Tarsa muttered under her breath.

Seraphine shot her a scathing look which went ignored by the warrior. Daemon's smile only grew.

"Aren't you needed elsewhere?" Tarsa snapped at the demon-born. "To muck the stables perhaps?"

Daemon shrugged, unbothered. "I would never deny myself the opportunity to watch you fight, milady."

Killian coughed to hide his laugh. The scowl Tarsa sent his way was enough to make me grow nervous.

"You're a menace," she cursed, storming from the room.

"And you are a goddess," Daemon called after her. The light in his eyes was enough to make me worry for his sanity as he turned back to face us.

"I think I liked you better when you clung to the shadows and didn't speak," Seraphine noted.

"Like Jadan," Killian added, still grinning.

Daemon shrugged before pulling me to my feet. "Jadan speaks, but he's not as pleasant as I am."

"You consider yourself pleasant?" Seraphine teased.

Daemon scowled, though it held little heat. "I consider myself enjoyable company, yes."

Killian snorted and tossed his practice weapon toward the wall. The clatter of the wooden sword on the stone echoed. "Well, if you're here, then I'm off to bathe before I have to find Hakan."

"I'll go with you," Seraphine added, trailing after the young immortal. "I'll see you at lunch, Esme."

I waved as they disappeared into the hall. Daemon turned to follow.

"Where are you going? I thought you came here to follow me around?" I asked. My legs shook slightly as I moved. I'd planned to practice knife throwing again even though the blisters on my fingers bled lightly.

"You need to bathe," he said, glancing at me over his shoulder. "You smell."

I scrunched my nose, glancing at my sweat-soaked shirt. "I think I would've preferred you lie instead of insult me."

Daemon chuckled. "Would you rather I ask about your husband?" The flush in my cheeks changed from that of overexertion to embarrassment. "Or perhaps about the feelings you have for him that you work so hard to ignore?"

"I don't know what you're talking about," I said as we walked through the empty halls.

His ink-black hair fell into his eyes with his dramatic sigh. "Whatever you say."

"Is there an update about the souls from the Crossroads?" I asked, desperate for a change in topic.

"Not yet," he said. His droll tone suggested he was unhappy with that acknowledgment. "Jadan has been interrogating the guards at the Crossroads and searching the realm for any insight into Ephraim's location though."

"So, you still think he had something to do with it?" I thought through every interaction I'd had with the angel. No matter what angle I took, I couldn't find a plausible answer to his reasoning for letting the souls loose. He must've known what would've happened if they found me, and though he despised me, he wouldn't put the essence at such risk.

Daemon shrugged. "I don't know who else would."

I sighed, mind racing with the likelihood of Ephraim's secret agenda. "What about Reek?"

Daemon considered this as we came to a stop outside my bed chambers. "I suppose it's possible. Only Reek isn't one to make plans or plot against anyone in any way. He doesn't have enough sense for it. Though he does like to play games."

"What about the man who was with him? Aiden said there was someone who looks after him?"

"Again, it's possible. But there just aren't enough answers about how the souls were released to come to any sort of conclusion yet." Seeing my frown, he continued. "I will let you know as soon as I have answers to give. Now take your bath and get rid of that salty smell. I'll send word to have Lurik bring you a snack once you're done."

I frowned. "Why? Lunch isn't that far off."

He sent me a coy look as he moved down the hall. "You get mean when you're hungry, and you'll be starved as soon as your adrenaline wears off. I've seen you target your anger toward Aiden, and I have no wish to be on the receiving end of your wrath, Princess."

He departed without another word, leaving me alone outside my chambers. A guard stood on either side of my door, each still as a statue. Unfortunately, Drusilla's large friend was one of them. His sly smile sent a shiver down my spine as I slipped past him.

I entered my room alone, finding solace in the silence. My body ached as I moved toward the closet in the corner. My skin felt sticky and hot with sweat after training, and my hands stung with half-healed and freshly created blisters. The idea of a warm bath before lunch with Aiden and the others was nearly enough to make my knees weak.

Just as I moved to slip my tunic over my head, the essence awakened. Power burned through me as I spun around and scanned the room.

A form stepped from the shadows near the unlit hearth. "It's about time you returned." Drusilla's snide voice startled me. "We've been waiting a long time for you, Princess."

"We?" The word barely left my lips before strong hands wrapped around me and tossed me onto the sofa. My body was too weak and strained to fight against his unwavering strength.

The blond man stepped around the sofa. His sneer was arrogant as he stared down his nose at me. "You've been an even bigger thorn in my side than I expected."

My brows furrowed, confused and angry. "I have no idea what you're talking about." All I wanted was to take a hot, relaxing bath and stuff my face with Lurik's amazing food. I was too tired to deal with these fools.

Drusilla laughed, the sound as shrill and sing-songy as her voice. "We've been trying to get close to you for weeks. Alvize had to rearrange Delvin's guard shifts for this."

"Again, I don't understand what you mean," I answered honestly, temper rising.

Delvin, the large brute of the group, stormed into the room. I had just enough time to catch sight of the other guard outside falling to the ground, unconscious, before his hand fisted in my hair. I was yanked back against the sofa so I was forced to look at him.

"You have something we need," Delvin said. "You're going to give it to us now."

My frustration morphed into anger. The essence in my chest responded in kind as I glowered at the three of them. "I have nothing of yours."

Drusilla's hand shot out in a blur and smacked me hard across the face, stinging my cheek. The mark left from Reek's claws had finally turned to a faded pink line, its tenderness only just fading.

"Of course you do, stupid mortal," she sang. "It shouldn't have been yours to begin with."

I'd left the dagger I usually kept in my boot by the bed this morning, figuring I wouldn't need it during training. Now I cursed myself for believing that I would be safe, even in my own chambers.

"The essence? Are you really here because you think you deserve it?" I snapped. "If you've come here to torture me for it then you're out of luck. You can't have it."

The three of them laughed, not at all worried by my claim. Power burned through my veins, strengthening with my anger.

Alvize took my chin in his hands, forcing me to meet his gaze. "You are quite pathetic, aren't you? The only thing interesting about you is the power you hold. You're just a vessel until the prince can gain your power upon his ascension to his father's throne."

Drusilla crouched down, bringing her face level with mine. Her nose was as pointed as her chin, making her features appear harsher beneath the curtain of her dark hair. "Did you think he liked you for anything other than what he can use you for?"

My throat closed up. In Cordovia, I never thought about what Aiden wanted from me. He was just a boy I'd grown to love. Then everything changed and I believed him responsible for my family's deaths. Yet even after I'd learned the truth, I couldn't be sure just what Aiden wanted from me. I hadn't dared to ask, afraid the truth would be just as Drusilla said. That I was no more than a source of power for him.

The hands pinning me to the sofa released me suddenly. I slouched forward before catching myself. Drusilla backed away quickly, eyes wide as they looked over my head.

I turned around, tensing when I saw who stood there.

Daemon held Delvin, a knife pressed to his throat. I'd never considered Daemon to be large, yet somehow, he managed to appear far more menacing than the larger demon he held pinned against his chest.

"Someone want to explain to me why you're here threatening the princess? In her private chambers?" he snapped. The anger in his face made my sore muscles tense, preparing for a fight.

Alvize stepped forward, smiling as he brushed his golden hair back from his face. "We were only having fun. Esme is a friend of ours." Drusilla nodded along enthusiastically at his side, though the sanity seemed to have left her eyes.

"Is that so?" Daemon drawled, clearly disbelieving. "Is that why the guard outside is unconscious and slumped on the floor? Were you not meant to protect her as well?"

Drusilla giggled. A shiver trickled down my spine at the eerie sound. "Perhaps he fell asleep?"

Daemon released Delvin, shoving him toward the door. "Out. All of you. Aiden will be sure to hear of this."

Alvize's sneer remained, seeming unbothered by the vague threat. Drusilla, however, looked like she'd been struck. Her eyes were uncharacteristically wide before she dropped her gaze to the floor.

"We only wanted to play with our friend," she said softly. Her words made my skin crawl with revulsion.

I stood, placing more room between me and the trio. "I am not your friend."

The trembling from moments ago had vanished. Her entire body went unnaturally still. Slowly, her gaze lifted to meet mine and the complete void I saw there made my chest tighten; there was no humanity left in her eyes.

"The princess speaks as if the power can protect her. It cannot and she will die because of it. He says it is so," she said in her singsong way.

Daemon scowled. "Out."

Alvize wrapped an arm around Drusilla's shoulder and ushered her from the room, Delvin on their heels.

Daemon slammed the door closed before running a hand over his face. "Did they hurt you?"

I shook my head. "I'm fine."

The demon turned to look at me, an apology plain on his face. "I shouldn't have left you. I'd assumed the two guards outside your door would be sufficient while you bathed. I should have checked that the room was safe before leaving. I'm sorry."

I waved away his concern, wincing at the tension in my muscles. "It's not your fault. They were guards themselves, and two stood outside my door when we arrived so there was no reason for either of us to be concerned."

"I will tell Aiden about this," he declared. "He will put a stop to their games."

My body's exhaustion weighed on me as I moved toward the bathing chamber. "They're no more than a nuisance. No more than immature children. I may not like them, but I don't think they need to be imprisoned for their taunts."

"Whatever they intended to do, it was beyond childish taunts. They won't be chained, Esme," he said seriously. "He'll likely just kill them for hurting you."

I rolled my eyes. "That's a bit overdramatic."

"Not when it protects the one you love." When I turned to ask him what he meant, he swiftly left the room. I spent the next hour sitting in the bathtub with his words haunting my thoughts.

TWENTY-THREE

THE DOOR TO MY chambers burst open just as I pulled a tunic over my head. My damp hair dripped onto the floor as I hurried into the main room.

Fen and Seraphine stood near the hearth, watching warily as Aiden stormed across the room, eyes blazing.

"What is going on?" I asked.

Aiden's touch was feather-light as he took my chin in his hands, turning my face side to side. "Are you hurt?"

"No," I said, pulling my face free.

"You'll have to eat lunch in your chambers today," Seraphine said apologetically. Aiden collected himself as she spoke, eyes ever watchful.

I glanced between my guests uncertainly. "Why? Has something else happened?"

Fen snorted, turning from the tray of food she placed on the table. Seraphine sent her a pointed look before turning toward me.

"Aiden has decided to formally introduce you to his court this evening," Seraphine said. "The preparations have already begun, and members of the court will begin to arrive at the palace in the next few hours. In the meantime, we are here to help get you ready."

I glanced toward Aiden. "Why do I feel like I won't be able to wear something from my wardrobe?" Aiden's lips twitched toward a grin, some of the hardness in his eyes melting away.

"I've already designed a gown for your formal introduction to court," Fen said with a wave of her hand. I stood to the side as she rushed past me. Her small form vanished into the large closet only to appear a moment later with a red gown draped over her arm.

"You'll wear this." Her voice left little room for argument.

I didn't have time to study the fabric too closely before she laid it across the foot of the bed.

"Are you sure you're all right?" Aiden asked, leaning in as Fen and Seraphine began discussing ways to style my hair.

My cheek still stung from Drusilla's blow, but I was almost certain it wouldn't bruise. "I'm fine," I said, offering a tentative smile. As I stood before him now, Ofrin's words about my parents came to mind. While some of the darkness that had been directed toward Aiden had fled my heart, I still had many more questions. Not to mention I still had to deal with my bargain with Ephraim.

"Out with you," Fen ordered, nearly shoving Aiden toward the door. "We'll have her downstairs on time."

Aiden rolled his eyes as Fen slammed the door in his face. She turned back with a proud grin.

"Come," Seraphine said from her spot on the sofa. "Eat quickly so we can get started."

Fen looked me up and down as she walked past again. "It seems we have a lot of work ahead of us."

I spent the afternoon being brushed and dusted with powders. I'd asked once if I could go to my study to retrieve the books Jester had delivered to me, but Fen immediately shut the idea down and told me to stay put. They'd placed me on a stool before the bathing chamber's vanity and I hadn't been able to move since.

"Ouch," I grunted, wincing as Seraphine pinned another curl to my head and out of my face.

"I'm almost finished," she promised for what might've been the hundredth time.

Fen shook her head, grinning. "You fidget too much, Esme. If you'd hold still this would all go a lot faster."

I snorted. "I doubt it." Seraphine smiled at the bitterness in my tone.

"Do you have any questions about tonight?" she asked.

I shrugged and instantly regretted it as the movement pulled at a piece of my hair she was working to pin out of the way. "Is there anything I need to know?" I asked. "I assumed I would just have to sit beside him and try not to look like I'd rather be anywhere else."

"That is most of it," Fen said. The lines near her eyes deepened with a grin.

"You will be formally introduced as the Princess of the Realm," Seraphine added, pinning another curl in place. "You will be given your crown before the court and then there will be a dinner where guests can introduce themselves to you and pledge their loyalty to you and Aiden."

I watched her reflection in the mirror before me. "Will Ofrin be there?"

A crease appeared between her brows. "No. He has decided to remain at his castle in the north."

"The God of Death has claimed his absence to be related to the mysterious release of souls and early preparations for the solstice ball he is holding in your honor," Fen said in a sour tone.

A cool sweat broke out over my palms. Ofrin's threat had been nearly forgotten with the truths he'd spilled so easily.

"Finished," Seraphine proclaimed, stepping away to admire her work.

Fen groaned dramatically. "It's about time. I've been waiting for you to finish her hair for ages."

The two women shared a teasing, but no less loving, look. Seraphine stepped back, letting Fen take her place in front of me while she perched atop the vanity counter, out of the way.

"Daemon told us what happened earlier," she said with false casualness while Fen began dusting powders along my eyes.

"What?" I asked, confused.

"With Drusilla and her minions." Her voice was cool as she spoke of them.

I sighed, thinking back to the way Aiden had barged into my room in a panic. "It was nothing."

"That girl is senseless," Fen said, hovering too close to my face. "She should have been put down decades ago."

I watched as Fen began to dust powder along my cheeks. "How old is she?" I asked.

"Too old," Fen muttered coolly.

Seraphine's brows furrowed, looking thoughtful. "Drusilla is probably about as old as Hakan."

"Which is old," Fen added.

Seraphine sighed. "Sometimes the humanity leaves us if we remain tied to the God of Death too long. And with our humanity goes our sanity in most cases."

"So, she's just losing her mind because she's ancient?" I asked. "I assumed it was because she wanted Aiden for herself."

"I'm sure that's part of it," Fen said, painting my lips a deep rouge. "But not everyone was meant to serve Death for eternity. Even those who sell their souls into his debt."

I considered this as she stepped back, smiling at me. "Did that play a part in why you asked for your mortality back?"

Seraphine grew still. I couldn't imagine spending decades with someone only to watch them suddenly begin to age and grow closer to death while I remained unchanged.

"That is for another time perhaps," Fen said quickly. "For now, you need to focus on your presentation to the court. We have a few minutes to spare before you are needed."

I glanced toward the window above the giant tub. The sky had already begun to fade to dusk. My nerves made my heart beat faster in my chest.

It took both of them to carefully work me into the dress Fen had created. The fabric glided over my skin easily, soft as silk. The skirts fell to the floor in a pool as still as water, covering the plain shoes Seraphine helped me into.

The dress was nearly too tight across the bodice, providing just enough coverage that I wouldn't tear it with shallow breaths. That thought only aided my nervous, quick inhalations.

"There," Seraphine said, stepping back with a satisfied look on her face. Fen stood at her shoulder, smiling proudly.

"Is it all right?' I asked, growing nervous when neither spoke.

Fen's eyes nearly burst from her face as she spun me toward the mirror. "Is it all right...it is far better than that."

The girl in the reflection was nearly unrecognizable. My skin held the same rich golden tones it once did, long before the heartbreak of my family's deaths stole the life from me. My dark curls were pinned back from my face, twisting down my spine. The powders Fen dusted across my face were simple, but dazzling. Just a touch of rouge on my cheeks, shadows and gold dusted across my eyes, and rouge on my lips.

The only flaw remained in the red scar across my neck. A deadly reminder of the bargain I was trapped in.

The dress itself was a work of art. The fabric was luminescent, smooth beneath my fingers as I trailed a hand down the skirts. The cascading sleeves that hung off my shoulders and fell around my wrists effectively hid my scars.

Gold was threaded masterfully through the seams. As I shifted in the light, I could see it sparkle like starlight. The skirts pooled loosely around my legs to graze the marble beneath my feet. Every inch was covered in what looked like hundreds of minuscule gold stars.

"This is beautiful," I said, admiring Fen's work with genuine awe.

She smiled sheepishly. "Aiden thought you would like it."

My brows furrowed. "Aiden chose this?"

"Of course," she said as if surprised I didn't already know. "He thought you would like to have some of your family with you."

My confusion only grew until she held up a portion of the skirt so the tiny stars were more visible.

"You were taught that souls go to the stars, were you not?" Her voice was thoughtful as she shifted the fabric, allowing the stars to twinkle in the light.

Emotion poured through me as I studied the gown. The anger and betrayal I once felt for him vanished entirely as I ran a hand over the gold stars.

Suddenly, I felt the need to speak to Aiden as soon as possible. I needed to know if the feelings I still harbored for him were not misplaced.

"It's time," Seraphine said softly, sensing the storm of emotions within me.

I nodded, forcing it all away. Later. I would make time to speak with Aiden later. And when Aiden finally confirmed the truth, I had to tell him the secrets I kept as well. He deserved to know who Ephraim truly was to him.

Fen left us as she went to join the other guests in the great hall. Two guards trailed behind Seraphine and I while Daemon led the way, his usual crooked grin in place, showing off his chipped front tooth.

He bowed deeply to me when he first arrived, an act that I was not expecting and only made me more nervous for what was about to follow.

More guards than I'd ever seen lined every corridor. Though the majority of the castle appeared as silent and empty as usual, the faint hum of voices could still be heard in the distance.

My heart began to pound against my ribs the closer we got to the sound. Daemon and Seraphine led me down an unfamiliar corridor. I caught a glimpse of the hall that led to the room of Aiden's mother's things, but our entourage walked in the opposite direction.

An abnormally large vase of flowers sat atop a table in the very middle of this corridor. This hall was nearly as wide as it was long, and as I moved past the first vase of flowers, I noticed another. And another after that. Every few feet sat a table decorated with an enormous vase of flowers.

My chest warmed as I recognized the flowers as the beautiful wild-flowers sprinkled over the far corner of the gardens where Aiden had found me that first morning. Their wild, untamed beauty illuminated the otherwise plain corridor, lifting some of the strain on my nerves.

A wide set of double doors signaled the end of the corridor. The wood was dark oak, embellished with carvings of a war I could only guess was the rebellion of the angels. Warriors could be seen battling with swords and creatures with wings and horns flew above as bloodshed ensued. It was a deadly masterpiece.

"Are you ready?" Seraphine asked under her breath, pulling my mind away from the intricate carvings.

I forced as deep a breath as the dress would allow into my lungs as the sounds of the crowd grew.

Before I could respond, Daemon nodded to the doormen and the large doors swung outward, revealing the room beyond.

Daemon immediately stepped to the side, and Seraphine copied his movement to my right. My nervous pulse pounded in my ears as the conversations silenced, and all eyes turned to me.

The crowd split down the middle, creating a path directly to the dais along the far wall. Members of the court filled every space in the grand hall. Some wore finery far beyond anything I'd seen in Cordovia, and some opted for simpler gowns and tunics that appeared to blend in more with what I saw Aiden wear on a normal day.

Hakan stepped forward on the dais ahead. "All welcome Princess Esme Loutari-Ayres, wife to Prince Aiden Ozanne, our realm's Soul Collector, and protector of the dead."

Seraphine's hand gently pushed against the small of my back. My gaze shot to hers, nerves rising as the hall remained silent.

"Go," she mouthed silently.

Somehow my feet began to move though I wasn't sure I could feel them. I forced the calm I felt moments before into my body as my legs carried me forward. Gazes slipped over me as I passed. Some looked on dismissively, and others looked in complete awe of the bride their prince had brought to the realm.

I forced my gaze away from the crowd as their mixed emotions collided with my own. My gaze landed on the large dais at the end of the room.

Aiden sat atop a dark throne, an omen of my future. A gold crown sat atop his brow. This one was far more spectacular than the simple crown he wore during Ofrin's first visit weeks ago. His reddish-brown hair was groomed as it hung loosely around his face, and he'd traded his usual attire for a much finer jacket and pants. Each item of clothing was as dark as the wings he still kept hidden.

I watched the way his jaw went slack and his eyes widened at my approach. Standing from his throne, a private smirk pulled at the corner of his lips. The look in his eyes, the raw pride and overwhelming love, was nearly enough to make my knees give way. Heat poured through me as he stared, smiling softly as I moved toward him. My heart pounded away in my chest as I reached the dais steps.

Aiden reached out a hand, eyes keeping me enraptured. His hand was a warm, steady presence as I placed mine into it. I felt his touch clear to the bone, burning with the emotion barreling through me as he ushered me to the center of the dais.

He bent down so his lips brushed my ear. "Breathe, Princess."

I forced air into my too-tight lungs, turning to face the crowd. Aiden kept his hand in mine as he stood at my shoulder, grinning at me like I was something to worship.

I could feel the weight of the throne behind me, but I couldn't pull my gaze away from the watchful crowd.

I leaned against Aiden. "Am I supposed to say something?" I whispered.

The prince smiled. "Not if you don't want to."

"I don't know what I'm supposed to say," I admitted under my breath.

Aiden's crooked smile grew. The gentle heat in his eyes made my heart pause, a familiar warmth spreading through my chest as I remained trapped in his gaze.

He hadn't looked at me this way since the night he kissed me.

Someone cleared their throat, making me jump. Aiden's deep chuckle rumbled through his chest as he straightened and faced the crowd.

"My friends," he announced in a voice that carried easily over the gathered crowd. "It is my greatest pleasure to introduce my wife to you all. I know many of you have been eagerly awaiting this moment."

His words were erased by the thunderous roar from the crowd; their attention brought a flush to my cheeks. But it was the silent few that made worry fill my chest. Drusilla and her two minions were among that small crowd, half-hidden in shadow.

"My father has announced he will be holding a ball in Esme's honor over winter solstice," Aiden continued. "But given recent events, I thought it best to have some issues resolved before then."

I sent a quizzical look in his direction, which he ignored. Aiden strode down the steps, his movements slow but certain. Every eye was centered on him as he glared toward the shadowed corner of the room where Drusilla and her friends resided.

Aiden's small, sudden movement was hardly perceptible, yet Killian and Tarsa snapped into action. Jadan stepped forward as Drusilla and her friends were dragged to the center of the room. The white-haired demon remained half in front of me while Hakan shifted closer, prepared to pull me away from any threat of danger.

Drusilla remained slack in Killian's arms while Tarsa shoved Alvize and Delvin to their knees. The three of them faced me from the floor below. Aiden stood with his back to them, focusing on the emotions playing out on my face. My throat tightened with unexpected panic as the scene disappeared before me only to be replaced by that of my family, chained and on their knees before they bled out onto the ground.

Aiden's soft features hardened as he turned to face the crowd. Most faces were unsurprised to see the three kneeling before me. But my gaze caught on the few remaining in shadow who looked outraged by the display.

"It seems," Aiden began in an authoritative voice, "that not everyone was as welcoming toward my wife as I would've hoped."

I blinked, and my family knelt before me in the dark memory. I blinked again, and Drusilla and her friends returned. Overwhelming panic constricted my chest as my breathing turned shallow. As if sensing the path of my thoughts, Aiden turned to catch my eye. Understanding rested on his face as he stepped toward me.

"I have never allowed disloyalty amongst my trusted attendants. Nor have I allowed any member of my court to be disrespected." Aiden turned to face the crowd. "But you didn't disrespect just anyone in my court. You disrespected *my wife*. You raised a hand against *my wife*. Your Princess. That is unforgivable."

Drusilla sputtered, clearly nervous at Aiden's accusations. "We didn't mean anything by it, Your Highness."

"It was just some fun," Alvize added half-heartedly. I could see the regret in his eyes as he glanced toward Drusilla.

Aiden scoffed. "You left a mark on her face. You assaulted her guards and hid in her private chambers, intending to harm her."

"She attacked us first," Drusilla cried desperately. "She used your father's power to hurt us, Your Highness. We were just protecting ourselves."

I scowled at her poor attempt to place the blame for her stupidity on me. The essence she spoke of reared its head, spreading through me until my vision shifted, the veil of power returning.

"You failed to protect yourself from me," Aiden snapped. "Did you really think I would ignore an attack on my wife? No matter how pathetic your attempt at harming her might've been, you should have bothered to give a second thought to the outcome of your mistake."

Before the immortal could speak again, a blur of movement flashed across my vision. In the next breath, she fell to the ground. I blinked into the aftermath of his words. Drusilla lay on her side, eyes open yet unseeing. Blood pooled from a hole in her chest.

The veil remained over my eyes as I let my gaze slide to Aiden. The prince turned to face me, slowly, so everyone in the room had a chance to glimpse what he held before him.

I gasped. Aiden held a dark, bloody object in his hand. Her heart. He held her heart.

A deafening silence fell over the room as he dropped the heart to the floor. My stomach churned as the blood spattered outward.

"Esme," Aiden whispered, pulling my attention from the death. "The others?"

I glanced toward Alvize and Delvin. They glared daggers at Aiden's back, though neither dared to move. Tarsa stood over them, Killian at her side as they each kept their hands near their weapons.

"No," I said, surprised my voice sounded sure and clear in the vast room.

Surprise flitted across Aiden's face briefly before his blank mask returned. "As you wish."

Tarsa and Killian dragged the two immortals to their feet before escorting them from the hall.

Slowly, the veil lifted from my eyes. The essence I carried burrowed in on itself as my anger at the immortals calmed. Aiden smiled, sensing the change in my power.

Seraphine appeared at my side, holding a wooden box out to him. Aiden sent me a crooked grin before turning his back, hiding the box from view. The crowd gasped in unison, followed by sighs of admiration as they got a glimpse of what it held.

I tried to lean around Aiden only for him to pivot again so whatever he now held was entirely blocked by his form.

"I hope you will all join me in giving a warm and proper welcome to your new princess," Aiden said into the silence.

When he turned, my breath caught in my throat. The crown he held was not the same dainty crown I wore for his father's visit. This was a crown fit for a queen. Or a god.

The gold band was embellished with wings standing into points around the entirety of the crown. Roses and vines and thorns were delicately etched into the precious metal, reflective of the marriage mark on my hand. Dozens of small rubies filled the spaces between the pairs of wings, making it appear as if it was painted with the blood still staining Aiden's fingers.

Aiden held the crown aloft, silently asking for permission; his eyes smoldered as I nodded. His smile warmed my heart, and I returned the expression tenfold as he placed the breathtaking ornament on my head.

As soon as the crown settled, it warmed, forming to my head perfectly.

Aiden stepped off the dais, smiling at me like I was the sun and stars in the sky.

"All welcome Esme Loutari-Ayres Ozanne." His voice was triumphant as he tacked his last name onto mine. "Princess of the Realm of Souls." His voice rang into the silence only a moment before a chorus of voices echoed his words.

Aiden kept me trapped in his gaze as the room fell silent again. With a pounding heart, I watched as he slowly knelt for all to see. One hand curled into a fist over his heart as he dipped his chin, a sign of respect among wanderers in Cordovia.

The breath left my lungs in a rush as every person in the room quickly followed after their prince.

One by one they all knelt until I was the only person left standing.

TWENTY-FOUR

THE DROLL TONE OF the clock chiming midnight echoed through the hall. What I assumed would be no more than a quick show of power on Aiden's part had officially lasted through the night.

After he'd placed the crown on my head and knelt before me, every member of his court lined up to greet me and formally welcome me into their realm. I hadn't even had a chance to eat the delicious meal Lurik prepared. A meal that Viema, still in her disguise as a member of Aiden's court, brought to me.

I could feel my eyes beginning to droop as another young man stepped forward and bowed. Aiden brushed his hand softly along my arm to keep me awake, and while the gesture served its intended purpose, it also brought the reminder of him ripping Drusilla's heart from her chest. There were so many questions I still needed to ask him.

"Are you all right?" Aiden whispered as the man finally moved away. I hadn't heard a word the man had said.

I nodded. "Just tired."

His hand moved along my arm again. "You've tolerated this long enough," he said as another couple moved forward. "I think it would be acceptable if you were to excuse yourself now and return to your chambers if you wish."

I shook my head, smiling at the couple as they stood from their bows. "I don't mind staying a little longer."

Aiden didn't respond, instead settling for tightening his arm around my shoulders. We sat side by side, me on his throne, and him in a simple chair next to me. When I'd tried to take the plain chair, Aiden would have none of it. He placed me on this throne for all to see.

"Your Majesties," the gentleman said, smiling. "It is an honor and a pleasure to join you in your palace tonight and to welcome our new princess to the realm."

His wife sent me an odd look I couldn't decipher before fixing a smile on her face. "Yes. We are very pleased and flattered to have been invited."

I glanced toward Aiden at her careful wording. His princely mask was in place again as he dipped his chin. "Of course. I appreciate your kind welcome of my wife."

Again, my cheeks flushed at the ease with which he used the term. His wife.

As the couple moved away, Aiden turned toward me. He leaned down so his lips nearly brushed my cheek. I heard a few members of the crowd voice quiet approval at what they assumed was a display of affection.

I took a bite of cold stew to keep the flush of his proximity from my cheeks. The sour taste made my stomach turn.

"What is bothering you?" he asked under his breath.

I studied him through my lashes, hiding the way his closeness sent my heart into a frenzy. "I don't know what you mean."

He sighed softly so as not to be overheard. "Since the dinner began you have been uncharacteristically quiet."

I shifted to face him and stopped immediately. The slight movement brought us nose to nose. One more inch and our lips would touch.

My skin heated for an entirely different reason as we stared at each other. The memory of his lips on mine was enough to make my heart race in my chest. His eyes darkened as they fell to my mouth, seeming to follow the same path my own thoughts took.

"Nothing is the matter," I said, swallowing past the growing unease in my stomach.

The corner of his mouth turned up. "Liar."

I fought the urge to roll my eyes, finally looking away. "Perhaps I am merely disgusted by your display of bloodshed at my official welcome."

"No," he said with an amused chuckle. "That's not it. I saw the way your power called to the souls."

"That had nothing to do with me," I snapped. At a few questioning stares, I quickly schooled my expression into one of false calm. "Like you said, it was the power I carry. The essence of the Soul Collector. Not me."

Aiden sighed. "It responds to your emotions, Esme. It is a part of you, as it has always been. It's no longer something foreign that lives within you. It's as much a part of you as your own thoughts are."

His words only sent my thoughts tumbling even more, spiraling beyond reasonable control. My stomach turned again, forcefully.

I stood too quickly, nearly tripping over the hem of my gown. Aiden's hand shot out to catch my elbow.

"Where are you going?" he asked, concern now lacing his tone.

I brushed him away casually, sensing all eyes turning toward me. "I just need a moment."

His hand left my arm with some reluctance and I moved swiftly through the room. Guests made to block my way, offering smiles and words of greeting, but Tarsa or Killian were always there to help me escape the overfilled grand hall.

Only when I was out of sight of the crowd did I break into a run. The churning in my stomach grew as I raced to my rooms.

I didn't dare stop as I sprinted through the halls and barged into my bed chambers. My knees smacked against the marble floor as I collapsed before the pail in my bathing chamber, promptly hurling the meager contents of my stomach.

It took a while for my body to settle. Sweat dripped down my brow and there was an ashen sheen to my skin when I caught a glimpse in the mirror.

My stomach felt truly empty now, leaving my limbs weak and shaky as I pulled myself to my feet.

A scoff sounded from the doorway. I spun, immediately regretting the movement as the room began to spin. Viema stood there, her arms crossed over her chest as she sneered at me, displeasure palpable.

"What are you doing here?" I hissed, worried someone might come looking for me and find me with Ephraim's closest confidant.

She lifted a shoulder in a shrug. "I was sent to see if you have Ephraim's potion yet. But I can see you are too busy partying with your new friends to do what you promised."

I scowled. "I'm looking for it. I've just gotten a little sidetracked."

"Clearly," she said with a look of disdain. "Don't forget you are not their princess. I shouldn't have to drug your stew for you to remember that."

I racked my brain for an excuse, but she continued before my sluggish mind could catch up to her words.

"Stop playing dress up and get that potion. You're running out of time." Her dark eyes were repulsed as she sneered at my dress.

"I need more time," I argued.

I didn't think it was possible, but somehow her scowl deepened. "Circumstances have changed. Ephraim needs that potion now."

"There was an attack," I explained, mindful of the temper growing in her eyes. "I wasn't able to move freely around the castle."

"You are the prince's prisoner. Of course you won't be able to move freely around the castle. That is why you must go when they think you are otherwise occupied."

It was my turn to scowl. "Just ask Ephraim for more time."

She shook her head. "There is no more time. You've already gone back on your word once. I suggest you don't do it again. Get that potion, Esme."

"And if I say no?" I dared to ask. Ofrin's reveal had made me question every decision I'd made since my arrival. Especially the bargain I'd foolishly trapped myself in.

Viema stepped closer, her posture threatening. "Are you saying no?" I stepped back nervously. "If you were, that would cause quite a problem."

I swallowed the bile threatening to rise. "No." She raised a brow. "No, I'm not saying no," I clarified, though the words tasted foul.

Viema studied me a moment before she spun on her heel to disappear into my bedroom. I trailed after her as a thought occurred to me.

"Was it Ephraim who let the souls loose?" I asked.

She paused at the balcony doors. "What?"

"The souls from the Crossroads. When they got loose and attacked the castle. It was you and Ephraim, wasn't it?"

Viema slowly turned to face me with narrowed eyes.

"I have no idea what you're talking about." Then she took one step onto the balcony and leapt to the ground below.

I waited for the sound of her feet hitting the ground three floors below, but it never came.

My stomach churned again. Many days had passed since I'd last seen Ephraim. Yet so many secrets had come to light in that time that showed me just how warped my perception of events had been.

A knock sounded at my door, pulling me from my thoughts.

"Are you all right?" Seraphine asked as she stepped into the room. She was still dressed in her pale cream and taupe gown. The light tones made the freckles along her cheeks pop.

"Is it over?" I asked.

She sat on the edge of my bed. "Mostly. Tarsa and Killian will stay to look after the remaining court members who've decided to stay and drink a while longer. Hakan is with Aiden now."

I nodded. "And Daemon and Jadan?"

"They're wandering about," she responded. "Jadan sent word to Hakan that one of Ofrin's spies contacted him for an update while you were being paraded before the court."

My chest tightened. "An update on what?"

"On you." I stopped my pacing at the seriousness of her tone. "Ofrin is still uncertain of your intentions here, especially of your marriage to his son. I doubt he is likely to remove his spies from Aiden's court any time soon."

"Does he not suspect Daemon and Jadan of being friends with Aiden?" I asked.

She shook her head. "Not that we know of. Those two have always been good at keeping their secrets...secret."

I sighed. My thoughts remained bombarded with concern for my brother and sister, but also with the determination to remove this curse so I could return to them. Yet I wasn't sure I could do that until I found the witch and got Ephraim his potion. And the very idea of letting him destroy this realm for his own revenge over his mother–Aiden's mother–sent an odd feeling through me. I was undeniably concerned for Aiden.

"Are you sure you're all right?" Seraphine asked again. "You left in a rush, and you look a little green."

I waved away her concern. "Just bad stew is all."

Confusion furrowed her brows. "Lurik has never made a bad meal in his life."

"Then I don't know what sort of an answer you're looking for." The conflicting thoughts rallying in my mind and my growing exhaustion were shortening my temper. I felt nearly ready to burst.

"The truth, Esme," she said gently. "Honesty."

I continued my pacing. "I could ask the same from you."

"What do you mean?" she asked, affronted.

I stormed to the nightstand, yanking Alfie's notebook from its hiding place in the drawer. I'd refused to let myself read any of the letters I found in the back. I had accepted the truth of Aiden's claims, but there were some goodbyes I wasn't ready to have.

"This," I said, tossing the notebook at her. "Alfie wrote down everything you and your friends told him. And yet there is no mention of the truth of the bargain they made with Ofrin. You kept that from me; you all did. I have not lied to you as you have to me."

Seraphine stared at the notebook in silence for a short while. I began to wonder if she was even going to respond when she finally set it aside and met my gaze.

"It is clear you have not read the entirety of the contents in this notebook, otherwise we would not be having this conversation." Her tone was cooler than usual, guarded. "I was not even aware they were going to be killed until after it happened."

"But Aiden was?" I asked, uncertain if I was ready to know the answer.

She stood, gently taking my face in her hands so I was forced to look at her. "Aiden had no choice once the deal was struck. Ofrin may seem like a worrisome fool, but he still has power beyond your imagination."

I frowned. "If he knew about it, then why didn't he say anything? None of you did, not even my parents." My voice broke as I spoke of them.

"No one can speak of a deal made with Death," Seraphine said softly. "When a deal is struck, it cannot be spoken of, nor can anyone physically interfere until Ofrin relieves them of their part in the deal. That is why he could not tell you. It's why you remained in the dark until after Ofrin relieved Aiden."

I thought back to Ofrin's strange command at the dinner following my arrival. "He tried to tell me," I said breathlessly. "He tried to tell me, and I wouldn't let him. Stars, I hated him, Seraphine."

"I know."

"And he let me." I stepped away. "He let me hate him and believe the worst of him."

Seraphine sighed, expression somber. "Aiden believes he deserves it. When Killian and I returned after your family's deaths, he was furious. I'd never seen him so angry. It took every ounce of power he had to penetrate Elroy's mind and stop him from killing Mousa and Cordelia."

"What?" Shock rippled through me at this revelation.

"He tried to save the others," she continued. "He used so much of his power that it nearly killed him. Ofrin was furious with him, of course. He even sent some of his men to capture Aiden and send him to the dungeons in the mountains."

I shook my head, overwhelmed with these new revelations. My heart raced against my ribs, each pulse sending a cascade of emotions through me.

"You don't need to fight it anymore, Esme," Seraphine said, taking my hands in hers. "I can see the light in your eyes when you talk with Fen, train with Tarsa, or even when you're with Aiden. And yet the second you realize you are enjoying a moment of your time here, you close yourself off again. You don't need to do that any longer. It's okay to be happy here."

"You're imagining things," I insisted, turning away.

Her hand shot out to grip my arm in a firm but gentle grasp. When I spun around to face her, I was surprised to see the ferocity in her expression.

"I am not," she said. "I can see the love you have for Aiden. We all can."

Tears threatened to blur my vision, but I quickly blinked them away. Pulling my arm from her grip, I stepped back. "I do not love him. Not anymore."

"But you do. That is why you can let yourself forget to be angry in those moments." Her voice was nearly pleading as she spoke. "And it's okay that you do love him. There is nothing wrong with that. Especially because he loves you too," she added, seemingly as an afterthought.

My thoughts returned to the night of Ofrin's first visit those weeks ago. I'd refused to let my mind dwell on anything Aiden had spoken that night.

Guilt soured my mood even further. Even when Aiden tried to tell me the truth, I hadn't let him. And now I was caught in a half-witted bargain with someone far more deadly.

"No," I said, shaking my head, forcing the strong emotions away. Being angry was easier than being hurt. "It does not matter."

Seraphine snatched the notebook off the bed and practically shoved it into my hands. "Read this," she said. "If you feel the same way after you read it, then fine. I will let you go on being angry at everyone here. But you need to have all the facts before you commit yourself to a life of misery and anger."

I turned away. "I cannot love him, Seraphine. I cannot live my life here, in this castle, enjoying even a second of my time while my family lies buried somewhere in Cordovia beneath unmarked graves."

She stepped into my path, demanding my attention. "No one would blame you for letting yourself be happy here, Esme," she said, her own eyes glistening with tears. "I promise, your family would want you to be happy. Do not keep yourself from loving Aiden, from loving any of us, just because you feel guilty."

"It's not fair," I whispered, voice breaking.

"It never is," she said honestly. "But that doesn't mean you must live your life in fear of being happy. Your family would not fault you for it."

"I cannot love him," I said as I shook free of her grip. "My only goal has always been to keep my family safe. And that will never change." I ignored the voice in my head that considered those words to be more for me than her.

Seraphine offered me a sad smile, seeing the cool resolve settle over my features. "Should you change your mind, just know that you have a friend in me, Esme."

She left without another word. A moment after the door closed behind her, I heard the soft sound of a second door closing. The door that joined my room to Aiden's.

TWENTY-FIVE

As soon as I was alone, I stripped out of the elegant gown and climbed into bed. I stared at Alfie's notebook in the dark of my room. Seraphine's words echoed through my mind as I stared at the creases in the spine. Not a trace of my brother's blood remained behind thanks to Aiden's witch, but the memory of it still lingered.

Unable to ignore the temptation any longer, I pulled the notebook into my lap with trembling hands. My room was dark, the only light coming from the single candle I kept lit at my bedside, making my brother's scrawl barely legible.

I skipped through the majority of the notebook. Alfie's drawings and notes from Seraphine and Killian's stories blended together, page after page. But it was not what I searched for now.

As soon as my mother's handwriting appeared on the last page, my heart stopped. My throat tightened with the threat of tears I'd long ago promised myself I would stop shedding.

"My dearest Esme,

I'm so sorry. If you are reading this, then it means the God of Death has accepted our offer and you are safe. That is all I ever wanted for you, though

I do hope you are not alone. It is my greatest wish that you are surrounded by your siblings where you can mourn your father and I together. Even if we are not truly lost to this world.

The Soul Collector has always played an important role in the survival of the Loutari family, and now that torch must be carried by you. It is a burden I never wished for you to bear but one you must carry all the same. And there is no one else strong enough to brave the destruction this curse brings except you, my dear. As much as I loathe the thought of you serving Death for the entirety of your life, it could not have passed down to a stronger soul.

Your father and I searched long and hard for a way for us all to remain together, where we could look after you and your siblings and aid you in serving Death. But it seems that dream was impossible.

At this very moment, you are sitting beside the fire with your siblings. And you are happy. I managed to wrestle Alfie's notebook from his careful grasp to write this, but he remains the ever-quizzical audience while Killian and Mousa twist tales for him. I do worry for Cordelia though. She hasn't taken her eyes off of Killian the entire time they've been seated at the fire."

I laughed, remembering exactly the night she spoke of. Ephraim had just attacked, and we all sat outside the large fire in the middle of the campground. It was only a few months ago and yet it felt like an eternity.

"It saddens my heart to think we won't be here to watch you all grow. After you went to Aiden's tent to treat his wounds, your father and I came

to a decision. One that will affect all of our children, but will hopefully keep you all together. And most importantly, safe.

A parent's wish is to keep their child safe. To be the thing that keeps them happy and alive and among friends or loved ones. But it has become clear to your father and I that we are not strong enough to keep you safe from the demons that will continue to hunt you. Nor will we be strong enough to protect your siblings when one undoubtedly comes for them in an attempt to get to you. That is why I must write this letter.

Your father and I have offered ourselves to Death. Not to serve as one of his immortals as Seraphine and Killian do, but to serve you in after-death.

The Soul Collector is a dangerous title to hold. Not only for the one who carries it, but for her enemies as well. It is for that reason your father and I wish for nothing more than to protect you. But due to events unforeseen by Death, we can only do that after our mortal lives have ended.

Aiden has fought against this. He's determined to run to you now and tell you of the deal if only to convince us to change our minds. But once this deal is struck, he cannot speak a word. None of us can. Aiden, more than anyone, understands what this deal means. He's promised to look after you once it is struck. And I believe that he will. You may not see it right away. You may not even want to believe it. But he does love you, my dear. There is not a doubt in my mind that he will do whatever he can to keep you safe, just as your father and I will.

The deal we made will secure your safety in Cordovia. Your father is speaking to Mousa now to tell them of this deal before Death prevents our tongues from speaking of it. But the sacrifice of our lives will force Death's hand to protect yours. Not only from King Elroy, but from anyone who seeks your destruction. Aiden is sure of it.

This will not be easy for you, for any of you, but just know that we have not left you. We will never leave you. You are the only person in existence who can reach us now. And if you ask, we will always find you.

Be happy, my dear. For all you must do is look to the stars, and I am there.

> *All my love,*
> *Mother*

A tear dripped from my cheek onto my mother's letter, smearing some of the words.

"Why, Mother?" My whispered question was met with silence.

The secrecy stung as I confirmed the truth from her writing. Their choice to leave me alone in this, to think that their sacrifice would be enough to keep me safe, created a painful bind around my heart. Now, thanks to their deaths, I was stuck in the Realm of Souls with a husband who was adept at keeping secrets and an angel who was prepared to turn this realm to ash because of the pain that had been inflicted on his mother centuries before.

A mother he shared with Aiden.

My gaze landed on the door connecting to Aiden's room. I knew it was time I told him the truth. Not only were there still holes in this story I'd been told, but I knew I had information about Ephraim that could save innocents from his wrath.

I ran a hand over my mother's scrawl, wondering if she could see me now.

She must be at the Crossroads. Both my parents, as well as my youngest siblings, must all be there waiting for me.

I studied the few words she'd written describing the deal she made with Ofrin. She struck a deal to serve me in after-death. Me. Not Ofrin. Did that mean her soul was still at the Crossroads with the others? Or was her soul being kept elsewhere, away from peace until I could find her?

These thoughts haunted my mind through the night. It wasn't until the dark sky became painted with orange that I realized how long I'd sat studying my mother's letter, scrutinizing every word and every phrase for an answer I desperately needed yet could never grasp.

TWENTY-SIX

I WAITED UNTIL AN hour after dawn before knocking on Aiden's door.
I'd spent the entirety of the night combing through my brother's notebook, searching for an answer as to where my mother's soul remained,
and came up empty. There was only one person who could give me the
answers I needed now.

The door swung open before my fist fell to my side, revealing a disheveled Aiden in the doorway. His hair hung ungroomed around his
face and his chest was bare to the cool morning air.

I blinked several times before I was able to pull my gaze away from his
bare skin.

"Yes?" he said, smirking obnoxiously at my ogling.

I cleared my throat. "Will you train with me today?"

That brought him up short. The smirk fell from his face only to be
replaced by a nervous scowl.

"Is Tarsa not training you well?" All pretense of amusement forgotten.

I shrugged. "She's fine. But I'd like to train with you today if you're up
for it."

Aiden remained frozen for a beat while he considered every possible
meaning behind my proposal.

"If that is what you wish, then of course." His eyes searched my face.

"And, here's this," I said, forcing the small bottle of potion into his hands.

Aiden's eyes narrowed as he studied the concoction he had his witch make so I could end our marriage bond.

"This was made for you," he said, holding it out to me again. "I don't want it back."

I shook my head. "Then give it back to the witch. I've decided not to take it."

He studied me for a moment, emotions flitting across his face too quickly for me to decipher. "Very well. If you're certain."

I nodded, promptly slamming the door in his face as soon as the corners of his mouth began to turn up. Even as I strode toward my closet I could hear his soft chuckle through the closed door.

I wiped a bead of sweat from my brow. "Can I actually pick up a sword now?" I begged. Aiden and I had been training for roughly two hours, and the majority of that time was spent doing various exercises he claimed would help strengthen the muscles I needed to fight. This was essentially what Tarsa made me do for thirty minutes at the beginning of every session.

Aiden snorted. "You're not ready to wield a sword yet."

I scowled at the arrogant grin he wore as he lounged nearby. Seraphine, Killian, Hakan, and Tarsa trained together on the far side of the room. The four of them offered us what little privacy they could while remaining close by as dutiful guards.

"Tarsa lets me spar with a practice sword," I argued.

He sent me a doubtful look. "And how well has that worked out for you?"

"I do all right," I said with a shrug.

Aiden shook his head, loose strands of his hair falling into his face. "Try again. And then we'll discuss your use of a sword."

"I've been training with swords for weeks," I argued. My limbs shook with exertion. "I could wield one now if you'd let me."

Aiden came to stand before me, leaning forward just slightly so his posture was almost imposing. "I don't *let* you do anything. You are not my prisoner, Esme. If you want to wield a sword, then do so. I will never get in your way."

I studied the smug look on his face for only a moment before shouldering past him to the collection of practice swords. Some were small enough for me to carry easily and others were as large as Hakan's broadsword that he kept strapped across his back.

I reached for the smaller sword I practiced with and turned to face Aiden. The prince dipped his chin in acknowledgement before reaching around me to grab another; his shoulder brushed mine, sending tingles along my skin.

Stepping away, I held the sword aloft, pointing it at his chest. Aiden smiled, noticing the distance I placed between us.

"Are you sure you're up for this, Princess?" The small grin he wore made my heart stutter.

I raised a brow. "Are you?"

Aiden's smile widened, ever amused with my temper. "Oh, absolutely."

He attacked as soon as the words left his mouth. In two swift movements Aiden had my sword on the ground and my back pinned against his chest. I felt the rough wood of his sword against my throat.

"That was easier than I expected," he teased. His breath made the loose strands of my hair stick to the sweat on my face.

I struggled in his grasp, twisting until we were face to face. His grip shifted so his hands settled at my waist, holding me against him. "Sorry to disappoint you," I said, going slack in his arms.

"You just need more practice," he said, gentler now. He loosened his grip, and I didn't hesitate.

I slammed my fist into his gut, relishing in his surprised grunt, and slipped free of his grip. I jammed my knee into the back of his leg just as I reached down to retrieve my sword. The pointed end of my sword was at his throat a moment later.

"Was that better?" I asked, feeling myself smile.

The playful joy he'd had in his eyes a moment before changed, darkening to a hunger I felt deep in my chest.

"Much," he said in a hoarse voice.

I stepped back, letting him rise from his knees. "I would've thought you'd be used to kneeling for me by now," I teased.

"I will always kneel to you," he said, standing with a warrior's grace. "I just prefer not to kneel with a sword at my throat."

I made a show of looking at the dull wooden blade. "I think if I tried to cut through anything with this, my arms would grow tired before I made a scratch."

The air shifted, and I felt a quick brush against my cheek as something whizzed past my face. A loud crash sounded a second later, shaking the walls.

"The key is to learn how to wield every weapon accurately. No two knives will cut the same, but they'll both do the job if you know how to use them." Aiden stood with his hands behind his back – the portrait of casual arrogance of a boy raised under a crown.

I stared open-mouthed at the handle of his practice sword protruding from the door. "Show off."

Killian chuckled from across the room. "Now you know why we don't let him use practice swords."

"Or practice with real swords," Hakan added between blows with the blond immortal. "Princes can be quite temperamental when allowed to handle sharp objects."

Aiden scowled. "Says the man who is banned from every pub in the realm because he can't control his anger enough to avoid a brawl."

Hakan disarmed Killian before turning to face Aiden. "It's not my fault the drunken fools can't take a joke every now and then."

"From what I hear, it was more of an insult than a joke," Aiden said, grabbing another practice sword from the collection. "I believe you compared a man's daughter to a troll?"

Hakan spun on Killian. "You told him."

The young immortal sputtered defensively, shielding his face with his hands in a sign of surrender. "He asked. What, did you expect me to lie to him?"

Hakan snorted, crossing his arms over his chest. "You gossip more than the barmaids who get paid to spill others' secrets."

Seraphine laughed at Killian's expression. "Don't fret, Killian. It's why Fen adores you so much." She kissed his cheek sweetly.

"I don't gossip," Killian muttered under his breath.

I smiled. "Is that not what you did with Mousa practically every day?"

Out of the corner of my eye I could just see the smirk Aiden fought to keep hidden. Killian shrugged, round cheeks flushing slightly.

"Killian listening to your brother's exploits hardly counts as gossip," Tarsa said. She picked an invisible piece of lint from her tunic. "From what I recall, it was your brother who gossiped. Perhaps that is why it was practically impossible to keep your family hidden from the public eye."

My blood cooled drastically. "What are you saying?"

Aiden's hand came down on my shoulder. "Tarsa, leave her be." I shrugged out from under his grip, glaring at the warrior who wouldn't even look in my direction. The familiar veil of power slipped over my eyes, responding to my surging anger.

"Are you saying it's his fault?" I asked, voice cold.

Tarsa sighed, finally turning to look at me. "It would've just been easier to follow orders had he bothered to think beyond the women he took to his bed."

A tremor shook the walls as I took one step toward her before Aiden blocked my path. "Move."

"No," he said, all pretense of humor gone. "Not until you get control of yourself."

I glowered in Tarsa's direction. "I do have control of myself."

His hand pulled at my chin gently, forcing me to meet his gaze. Aiden's expression was blank, carefully neutral apart from the concern he tried to hide. "You're angry. And the essence knows it. It's responding to your anger, and if you're not careful you could level this entire building."

"I can't do that," I argued.

"You can," he said with a soft smirk. "You could also harbor her soul for yourself. And that would make my father very unhappy."

I frowned, confused. "I'm fine."

Aiden waited until my vision cleared before he released me. "You're getting stronger."

"Not strong enough," I muttered under my breath. Pulling a knife from my boot, I spun, sending it flying through the air to land in the splintered wood beside Aiden's practice sword. Seeing it settle into the wood calmed some of the stirring anger.

"Come. Let's keep training." Aiden eyed the knife appreciatively before moving so my back was to the others.

I held up my small practice sword once again. The blisters I'd developed began to ache from the rough hilt of the sword. The pain centered me, diminishing the anger.

He struck without a word. I could tell his movements were slower, careful, like he was moving for my benefit rather than training for his own. He moved like a sluggish, weak mortal. The thought allowed me to focus, reminding me why exactly I asked him to train with me today.

"I read the letter," I said between blows. His brows contracted slightly but he didn't respond. "From my mother; about the deal she made with Ofrin to protect me."

"I see," he said with exaggerated calm. The breath left my lungs as his new sword jabbed me in the ribs. He stepped back. "You're dead. Let's try again."

I scowled as he returned to his starting stance. "Some of what she said doesn't add up."

He dodged my blow far too easily. "Oh?"

"She claimed the deal was just for her life and my father's." Seraphine's reveal the evening before lingered in my mind as I watched Aiden's carefully blank expression.

"That is true." His sword stopped at the side of my neck. "You're dead. Again."

I stepped back. "If that were the case then why did my siblings, aunt and uncle, and cousins have to die?"

Aiden considered his answer carefully as we began to spar again. I forced my mind away from the aching pains in my limbs as he moved about easily.

"I cannot claim to know the ins and outs of my father's mind," he finally said. "But I do know that he would only take as many lives as he thought were worth the trouble of protecting yours."

I winced as his sword came down hard on my wrist. My own sword clattered to the ground. "I thought his Soul Collector was supposed to be important to him?"

"You are," he said, bending to pick up my sword. "But my father also enjoys manipulating situations in his favor. Every soul that leaves the mortal realm passes through the Crossroads. But my father has found a way to harness the souls that bargain with him. They're bound to him in a way, and that makes him stronger."

"So, he decided to take all of their souls to gain more power for himself?" Aiden's sword poked me in the ribs again. "Don't say it," I grumbled, rubbing at the sensitive place where a bruise was sure to form.

A small grin pulled at the corners of his mouth. "I wouldn't dare."

I tucked the practice sword beneath my arm, forcing breath into my tired lungs. "Is your father always this manipulative? I'm fairly certain my parents wouldn't have made that bargain had they known they'd be sacrificing more than themselves."

"As I've said before, he has grown more distrustful in his long life," Aiden explained carefully. "I can guess that he saw an opportunity to make you more indebted to him, and he took it."

"So, he took my siblings' lives in an attempt to make me fear his power? How did he even go about having them killed?"

"Fear is a very powerful weapon. Some might say it is the most powerful of all." He brushed a loose hair from my face. "I believe he used one of his spies to make Elroy's fear of your family turn him to desperate measures."

"And what of my family's souls?"

Aiden hesitated. "They're in waiting."

"What does that mean?" My pulse sped at the thought of my parents trapped somewhere.

A low whistle sounded through the room. We turned to see Jadan and Daemon striding toward us, each admiring the shattered door.

"I can't decide if I want to know what happened, or if I'm afraid to ask," Daemon laughed. He stopped to pull the broken sword from the door, pocketing my knife.

"I don't want to know," Jadan said in his usual serious manner.

"It's not as exciting as it looks," Killian said, casting a sly look in Aiden's direction.

Aiden ignored Killian's remark. "Any news?"

Jadan shook his head, white hair shifting around his face. "None."

"News of what?" I asked.

"Ephraim," Daemon said. He winked in Tarsa's direction which only hastened her pace as she left the room.

"After Ofrin forbade us from truly capturing him, we decided we should at least continue to look for his point of entry into this realm. Only there is no sign of him," Seraphine said.

My chest tightened. "How is there no sign of him?"

Daemon shrugged. "He's the Angel of Life. He probably has hiding places in every realm. It won't be long before we find him."

Guilt and shame settled in my bones. "Is it possible he is just remaining in his own realm, wherever that is?"

"The realm of the angels is hidden to anyone who has a soul," Jadan said.

I turned to Aiden, understanding. "Angels don't have souls. You do. Mortals do. That's why my ancestor couldn't find the angels when he went to the Wood of Rune."

He gave a shallow nod. "Among other things."

"Like angels being selfish, murderous monsters," Killian added quietly.

"What about in the mortal realm?" I asked, panic growing. "Could he have sent angels after my brother and sister?"

"Your family is safe," Hakan assured me. "They are not without protection."

I nodded, making a mental note to check the map in my study again. Just to be sure.

"We still don't know what he wants," Seraphine argued. "He's made no move to attack us apart from letting the souls loose from the Crossroads. And there's been no sign of him or any angels. It's very unlike him."

"Perhaps he is making moves against us, and we are just unable to see it," Jadan suggested.

My guilt tasted sour on my tongue. I took a fortifying breath, readying myself to spill the truth I'd been hiding for far too long. But fear kept the words at bay. How would they react when I told them what I'd agreed to do for Ephraim?

Killian smirked, swinging his practice sword around playfully. No one seemed to notice the shame stirring within me. "It doesn't matter what he's planning. As soon as the solstice ball is done, we'll go find him."

"I thought Ofrin forbade us from going after Ephraim?" I asked.

Aiden shrugged, running a hand through his sweaty hair. "He only said we couldn't hunt Ephraim before your ball. So we've decided to postpone our plan to draw Ephraim out and capture him until after the event."

Daemon grinned foolishly. "It may not have been our original plan, but at least now we can spend the extra time searching for his entry point. Then, when we draw him out, we will be waiting for him."

Knowing what I did about Ephraim, I couldn't help but imagine his reaction at being caught, and how he would retaliate.

"I have to go," I said suddenly, moving toward the door.

"I thought you wanted to train," Aiden teased half-heartedly.

I nodded. "I need to check something. On the map."

His expression smoothed to one of understanding. "I will see you for lunch then."

I could only nod, unable to find my voice as I fled from the room. My nerves had grown in the span of a few minutes. Before, I'd let myself fall into a sense of safety knowing my family was not here. But now that I bothered to remember Ephraim had a plan of his own, and my family was still out there waiting for me to protect them, my panic returned tenfold.

"For someone who got kicked around the training room all morning, you move pretty quickly," Daemon said, jogging to catch up.

I suppressed a sigh. "Why are you following me?"

"Oh, I'm sorry, is it a shock to you that I, your guard and spy, am following you through the halls as I've done for weeks now?" He snorted at my annoyed expression. "Just because we don't know where Ephraim is doesn't mean it's safe for you to wander around alone."

"This castle is under heavy guard," I said, pointing to the several guards standing nearby. "I'd hoped by now that you would realize I don't need a shadow with every step I make through the castle."

Daemon shrugged. "Tell that to your husband. I'm following his orders. Besides, we can't forget that Drusilla and her friends were also guards in this castle. Not everyone can be trusted."

The truth of his words rattled me. What would they do when they learned of the secrets I'd been keeping as well?

The demon glanced at me, smirking mischievously. "You kiss him yet?"

I balked. "What?"

"Well, I imagine the yearning looks you send each other's way when the other isn't looking have continued. And that the sword in the door was your doing. So, you can't blame a man for wondering."

I glowered at him. "No. And I don't plan to."

The demon smiled, showing his chipped tooth. "You're still doing that thing then, huh?"

"What thing?" I grumbled, frustrated.

"The thing where you pretend to hate him. It's okay, we understand."

"I'm not pretending to hate him," I snapped. "And who is we?"

Daemon shrugged. "All of us? There's a bet to see how long you can last before giving in and just kissing him again."

"I thought you were supposed to be here under the pretense of serving Ofrin. Shouldn't you refrain from participating in childish bets like that?"

His smile grew, clearly pleased to have struck a nerve. "I should. But I didn't."

I pulled the key to my study from its hiding place sewn into my pocket. "You can wait out here," I said curtly.

The demon bowed dramatically. "Of course, Princess."

I slammed the door in his face as soon as I stepped into my study. The room remained bare of furniture as I'd yet to venture into the village to purchase anything. Instead, the shelves were slowly filling with books from Jester's library.

The only light, apart from the grey sky beyond the window, came from the glowing map hanging on the far wall. Mousa and Cordelia's orbs remained bright as ever. Only now they were not together. Mousa remained deep in the Abandoned Desert while Cordelia had ventured farther north.

My heart sped up as I considered the reasoning behind their separation. I knew it wouldn't have been a decision made lightly on either of their parts.

I quickly altered the map to include Elias. As expected, the prince was still safe in the castle in Cordovia.

A deep longing filled me as I stared at the three glowing orbs, so far from each other on the map. What I wouldn't give to return to them.

I silently cursed the essence within me. It was once gifted to save my family, and now it only caused us pain and damnation.

My mind flashed to the promise I'd made Ephraim. One last promise to him before I would hopefully be done with that heinous bargain I'd rushed into. I sped from the room, newfound determination and acceptance guiding my feet.

"Where are you running off to?" Daemon called as he struggled to keep up.

"The library," I called over my shoulder.

"Why? Don't you have enough books to keep you busy?"

I sped down the corridor. "That's not why I'm going."

Daemon groaned. "What else is there besides dusty books and haunting silence?"

"You don't have to come with me."

"Of course I do," he grumbled.

I smiled. "Then keep the whining to a minimum, if you don't mind."

Daemon mumbled something unintelligible under his breath that I chose to ignore.

The library was empty, just as I hoped. Daemon continued to linger throughout the entirety of the afternoon, even long after Aiden came to check on me and Seraphine offered to relieve him of his guard duty. And all I did, in that entire time, was study the map hanging in the library. By the time night fell and I snuck from my room, I had the path to the witch's shop memorized.

Trying to find a path through the castle without a guard noticing me was trickier than I expected. Aiden had always taken my safety more seriously than I thought necessary, but since the attack from the loose souls he'd added far more guards than before.

Luckily, after spending hours staring at an enchanted map of Aiden's castle, I knew the exact path to take that would bring me into contact with the fewest guards.

Like the previous nights when I'd snuck from the castle to meet with Ephraim, I climbed from my window. The air was much cooler now as winter had finally arrived. My fingers began to numb almost immediately as my feet hit the dirt below, making it easier to ignore the painful blisters I still harbored from training.

My boots were near-silent on the frozen ground as I sped past the side of the castle. The familiar string music could be heard from an open window on the first floor, but I pushed past.

Blood pounded in my ears as my nerves spiked. This was no different than sneaking from my room to train with Ephraim, but somehow it felt more deceptive.

But it would be the last thing I did for the angel.

The witch's shop was located on the eastern corner of the castle grounds; a small cupboard of a room that could only be accessed from the outside.

Guards laughed amongst themselves along the wall, paying me no mind. I slipped easily from the shadows and toward the door of the witch's room. The handle turned easily beneath my hand, a small relief. I quickly slipped into the room before the guards noticed.

The space was cramped, dark, and small. Shelves lined the far wall, each overflowing with jars of unknown substances in varying colors. A table sat to my right. Just like the shelves above, the table was also full of supplies. Books with strange titles in various languages towered over me. And the smell... it was atrocious. Strange scents came from the jars nearby, mixing unpleasantly with the herbs and plants sitting along the wall.

As I turned to study the space, a small cabinet caught my eye. It was about waist high, and the wood was worn enough that it looked heavily used. There was nothing extraordinary about it, but it held a lock. The cabinet door was cracked open as if someone left in a hurry, but the lock itself was scarred and scratched like it'd been turned often.

I stepped toward the cabinet, ignoring the foul smell that came from the vials within. My heart began to race as I recognized the tiny vials filled with deep blue liquid. This had to be the potion Ephraim demanded I steal for him.

"Excuse me?" An unfamiliar voice came from behind me, causing me to jump.

When I spun around, I froze at what I saw in the doorway. I wasn't sure what I'd expected when it came to the witch, but there was no mistaking her for what she was.

Fierce hazel eyes met mine, and I knew she would have my head if I didn't think of an excuse. And fast.

TWENTY-SEVEN

THE WITCH WAS ONLY a few inches taller than me. Dark hair hung loose to her chin, curling at the ends. Her face was pointed — pointed nose, pointed chin. She was more striking than beautiful. And possibly no older than twenty, though for all I knew she'd given up her mortality decades ago and was far older.

"Well? Do you need something?" she snapped when I didn't respond.

I closed my mouth, not realizing it had been hanging open in shock. "Sorry. I'm Esme. I was just looking for something."

The witch's expression relaxed ever so slightly, but her suspicion remained. "So, you're the new princess. I've heard a great many things about you."

I swallowed, backing away from the cabinet. "I can't imagine anything you've heard is interesting to you."

She raised a quizzical brow. "No? Are you not Ofrin's Soul Collector? Married off to his only son? And now here you are, in my shop. Snooping."

Her frown only made my heart rate pick up again. It was beating so loudly now, I was almost certain she could hear it in the overwhelming silence of the room.

"I just needed some things," I explained, searching quickly for an adequate excuse.

She turned away, closing the door and trapping me in the room with her. I stayed silent as she waved her hand in the general direction of a candle I hadn't noticed before. The flame lit instantly, filling the small space with light.

"And what is it you felt you needed in the middle of the night?" she asked.

My hands wrung together as I struggled to come up with something believable. Sneaking around was more Cordelia's game. She would be better at this than me.

I winced as my blisters reopened. Cursing under my breath, I quickly released the tight grip on my hands.

The witch caught the movement. "Here. Sit," she said, pulling a stool from beneath the table. I sat as instructed. "I take it Tarsa has been holding you to a strict training schedule?"

I nodded. "For the most part."

The witch smiled, though it didn't soften her features. "She's a tough one, that warrior. Most of my patients used to come from her training classes."

She returned to me with a handful of herbs and a paste that smelled oddly familiar.

"Do you treat everyone at the castle?" I asked, desperate for anything to fill the silence and cover the sound of my nervous heart.

"Mostly," she answered.

"You're Ridha. Right?"

Ridha nodded, sending her short dark hair into her eyes. "I am."

We fell silent as she began to massage the pungent ointment into my open blisters. A small smile crossed her lips as I winced from the sharp sting.

"Hold still," she commanded. "It's not so bad."

"Have you applied this on your own wounds?" I asked, frustration blocking the painful sting.

She shrugged. "Once or twice."

I scowled as she continued to work. This felt much different than the ointment Aiden had once used on my wounds. The smell was nearly the same, but the medicine he applied was soothing against what were now scars. This just ached.

"I've treated many wounds and ailments in my long life," she said unexpectedly. "But nothing seems as menacing as a warrior's blister."

I couldn't be certain, but something about her tone suggested she was mocking me.

Once she finished applying the paste into the open wounds, I watched her break apart the plant she carried and tear off the leaves into a separate bowl.

"What is that for?" I asked.

Ridha didn't glance at me as she reached for another plant. "This will help seal the wound faster so your hands won't ache as much."

I nodded. "Is that what Aiden used for my wounds in Cordovia?"

The witch cast me a quick, indiscernible glance. "I'm not certain what the prince used. He carries many of my remedies with him during his travels."

My mind returned to Ephraim's attack over a year ago. The burning of the poison in my neck and the numbing of the antidote Aiden used.

"You make the antidote to the angels' poison, yes?" I asked while she mashed the plant mixture together.

Her hands paused in their task for a fraction of a moment. "I do," she said hesitantly. "I make antidotes for every poison, remedies for every illness, and ointments for every injury."

"And you are the only witch here who can make those things?" If Ephraim knew this, then she would certainly be a target of his if she wasn't already.

Her sharp eyes shot to mine. "Yes."

"What about your family?"

Ridha returned to her work. Her movements were rougher than before. "I do not know what they are capable of anymore. Last I heard they were still in Cordovia."

"Your family did not come here with you?" I asked, working to hide my surprise.

"Are you always this quizzical of people you've just met?" Her tone was as sharp as her glare as she turned to face me, the mixture forgotten in her hands.

I shrugged. "I've never met a witch before."

That nearly made her smile. "I doubt that. We are much better at going unnoticed than you might think."

Ridha took one of my hands in hers and began to add the herbal mixture into the open blisters. The steady ache dulled to a numbing tingle within moments.

I sighed. "Thank you."

"I suggest wrapping your hands in cloth the next time you train. I hear it helps."

I nodded. "I'll keep that in mind."

As soon as she finished with one hand she moved on to the next. Though she was careful to avoid the scars that showed beneath my sleeves, I could feel her eyes lingering on the marks. "I hear you were King Elroy's prisoner for a time," she said. Ridha reached for a clean strip of cloth and began wrapping it around the palm of my hand as she spoke.

I nodded. My cheeks heated with shame as I fought the urge to pull at my sleeves.

"I was once his prisoner too," she added. My spine straightened with surprise. "Many years ago. It was long before his son was born and tamed him."

My brows furrowed. "Elias tamed the king? I find that hard to believe."

"King Elroy was...." Her voice drifted off as she moved to my other hand and began wrapping it in another strip of cloth. "Let's just say he has always been one to blame others for his wrongdoings."

I snorted. "That's not surprising."

"I also heard he killed your family." Her voice was cool, not exactly harsh, but certainly not warm enough to imply empathy.

"He did."

Her features softened, though it didn't suit her. She looked to be someone who always carried a fierceness about her, not someone who was generally kind and warm.

"I am sorry to hear that. The death of a loved one is never easy." The warmth in her eyes vanished in a blink. "But I suppose that is something mortals must become accustomed to in their short lives. Friends leave and family dies."

I scowled. "Did your family die?" Ridha stiffened significantly. "Or did they choose to leave you?"

The witch turned her back, making herself busy with work. "I left them. That is why I am here."

"To make ointments and remedies for Aiden," I said, voicing my question as a statement.

"To protect the realms. Mortal and immortal alike." Her tone was sharp once again though she didn't turn to face me.

I studied her stiff posture, fully aware that I had no idea how powerful this witch was and that I was currently in a room alone with her with no one else the wiser. "Are you the only one who can make the antidote?"

She turned to face me again, suddenly apprehensive with my line of questioning. "I am. It is a difficult mixture to perfect and it takes weeks to make even the smallest dose correctly. It is a very valuable skill to have."

"And no one else in your family knows how to make such a thing?"

Her scowl deepened. "Not to my knowledge. Why do you ask?"

I stood from the stool, taking an uneasy step toward the door if only to place some distance between us. "Because that seems like something many would kill for. Whether they wanted the knowledge of how to make the antidote or to destroy any knowledge of its existence."

The smile Ridha gave me was anything but warm. "Don't tell me you're concerned for my safety now."

"No," I admitted nervously. "I was merely admiring how valuable you must be to Aiden's court."

She snorted. "Hardly. Ephraim is the only one who may consider my knowledge valuable. Yet he knows better than to come after me."

That brought many questions to mind that I didn't dare voice. "And your family? Does he know not to come after them?"

"They hold little interest for him."

"Because they can't make the antidote to his poison, and you can," I clarified.

She shrugged. "That's part of it. The witch clan I come from certainly poses their own threat to the angels. But I doubt he'd be able to find them. Witches these days excel at hiding in plain sight."

"Have I met any of your family?" I asked, genuinely curious.

"How would I know that?" she snapped. "Besides, even if you had, I doubt you would know."

I shrugged. "Possibly."

Ridha studied me a moment longer before turning her back again. "Is that all you came here for? Or was there another reason you were snooping through my things in the middle of the night?"

I stayed silent a beat, glancing toward the cabinet along the wall.

"Then out with you," she said without turning to face me. "I have work to do."

I pointed toward the cabinet with the lock, my curiosity getting the better of me. "Work on that?"

Ridha froze as her gaze followed where I pointed. "That is none of your concern."

"Very well," I sighed, struggling to find any reason to prolong my stay. I was almost certain the potion hidden in the cabinet was exactly what Ephraim asked me to retrieve.

No sooner had my hand gripped the door handle than Ridha spoke again.

"Take this," she said, shoving a small sack into my arms. "Use this again after your next training lesson. But wait to apply it until after you've cleaned your hands. Your wounds must be thoroughly washed before reapplying the mixture."

I gripped the bag tightly. "Thank you."

She waved away the nicety. "Don't let me find you sneaking through my storage again. It's rude. I don't care if you're the beloved princess. I'll still feed you enough poison to make you vomit your guts out if I find you snooping again."

Surprise at her blunt threat nearly made me smile. "Of course. I wouldn't want that."

Ridha grunted something noncommittal before I escaped through the door. I hugged the herbal mixture to my chest as I raced through the gardens and back toward the towering vines that led to my balcony.

The same symphony of music that I'd heard the first night I ventured from my rooms echoed through the gardens as I grew closer to the room of Aiden's mother's belongings.

It was the song of my people. One my family often performed during festivals. The familiarity of it nearly brought tears to my eyes as I paused outside the window. The room beyond was dark.

I could spare a quick glance, certainly.

On careful feet, I reached up to peer inside the window. The room was nearly pitch-black. The only light came from a wilted candle placed on the floor behind whoever played the stringed instrument.

The man was broad of shoulder and slim in the waist. Much like a warrior would be. The instrument he held sat on the ground between his feet and ended near his face, which was turned away. I watched as he slid a bow across the strings, pulling the song from its depths.

The sound was unlike any I'd ever heard. The instruments often used during a wanderer's performance were small and easy to travel with. This was the opposite. I couldn't imagine my family finding a place to pack away this stringed beast in our caravan every night.

As the song came to a close, I held still.

The man sighed and it was an eerily familiar sound. My breath caught in my throat as he slowly stood, placing the large instrument in a box at his feet.

I had to clamp a hand over my mouth to keep my surprised gasp concealed.

It was Aiden. Aiden played my family's song on that instrument.

I watched as he slowly turned, bending to pick up the candle. As the light reached the window, I was already gone. My feet carried me hurriedly back to my room while my mind raced with questions about what I'd just witnessed, and my heart warmed with a tenderness I hadn't expected to feel for him ever again.

TWENTY-EIGHT

THE FOLLOWING DAY WENT by in a blur. Aiden trained with me again. He didn't mention the bandages and ointment I kept with me, and I didn't ask about the song.

Even lunch with Seraphine, Killian, Fen, and Hakan was relatively normal. Tarsa opted to patrol the village instead of joining us for lunch. Daemon trailed after her as he'd begun to do.

Apart from the new secrets between us, things with Aiden were beginning to feel strangely comfortable again. I wasn't sure how to feel about that, so like all my other problems, I ignored it.

Now, long after nightfall, I crept through the castle. The steady drum of boots on the marble floor echoed through every hall as guards patrolled.

Thanks to the training I'd had with Ephraim, I was able to harness the power of the essence to guide my expedition. I let it expand, filling every fiber of my being until its veil of power awakened my muted mortal senses.

I could feel the souls of the guards nearby like a brush of warmth across my mind. Their steady pacing as they patrolled the wall passed through my awareness like a subconscious thought; a faint awareness of what lay just out of sight.

I could feel the essence wavering, attempting to take more of their souls. The strange sense of greed from the essence unnerved me. There was no denying that its strength continued to grow the longer I remained in this realm.

A chill rose along my skin as I stepped into the night. Winter had officially arrived and with it came the frost that signaled a coming snowfall.

Ridha's shop finally came into view, no more than a dark door surrounded by stone. It appeared lifeless, the window dark. The essence seeped from me, searching for a soul beyond the door, and found none.

A new awareness in my mind told me someone was nearby. Quickly, I turned the handle, surprised it was unlocked, and moved into the room. As soon as the door closed behind me, I was cloaked in shadow.

It took a few moments before my eyes adjusted to the darkness. The only light was the faint trace of moonlight from the crack in the window.

Ridha's shop was just as I remembered. Books and strange plants remained cast aside as if forgotten and left to fend for themselves while bottles and vials of foul-smelling pastes and mixtures filled every shelf and cabinet.

With a racing heart, I knelt before the locked cabinet that contained the vials of potion I was to give to Ephraim. The lock was secured, because of course it was.

I cursed, sitting back on my heels as I decided how to proceed. I needed to find a way into the cabinet without leaving evidence of my intrusion.

"Oh my. Oh my. A tricksy thing, a lock is. To break is to be known, but to open she cannot. What is the demon pet to do?" The voice came from the shadows, making me choke on a surprised yelp.

Something moved through the darkness in the corner of the small room. The only sign of another presence was the lanky shape forming from within the shadows themselves.

"Is it stuck?" Reek's voice sounded again, closer this time.

A shiver trailed down my spine. The essence hadn't sensed his arrival, or his proximity. "What do you want?"

Reek chuckled. The shrill sound grated my teeth. "Demon pet is afraid of Reek. It's not nice to be afraid of a friend."

I sighed. "Can you help me with this lock or not?"

Reek tsk'd, much like he had the first night we met. "Does it know the answers to Reek's riddles? The game is only fun if both parties play."

I scowled. "I'm not playing a game with you."

I felt Reek kneel beside me though he remained invisible in the dark. "But games show us what we refuse to see. Demon pet knows the answers to Reek's riddles, but it doesn't say so."

"Reek, can you help me with this lock or not?" The essence began to warm again as another soul neared the door. I didn't have to look outside to know it was Ridha.

Something brushed my hands in the dark, making me jump back. Reek sighed, leaning closer so the heat of his breath brushed my cheek.

"What, once given—."

"I don't have time for your riddles," I snapped quietly. The essence warmed further as Ridha drew closer to her door. "Please, if you can open the lock, then do it."

The strange demon sighed but I heard the click of the lock a moment later. I shoved the cabinet door aside, hastily grabbing every vial of the potion I could manage.

"Demon pet must hurry if it wants to go unseen," Reek cooed.

With every vial I could find shoved into every pocket of my clothes, I grabbed a handful of other vials off the counter, shoved them in the cabinet and replaced the lock. Ridha was nearly at the door. If I wanted to leave, I had to go now.

I took a step toward the door and froze as a vial slipped from my fingers and rolled beneath the table. I cursed, kneeling to search for it.

Reek chuckled again. "Demon pet must hurry. If it is caught, then it is not as smart as Reek first thought."

I cursed as I quickly got to my feet. Ridha was on the other side of the door; I could feel her soul. I racked my brain for another way out of the room, but the door was the only one I could see in the dark.

A cold hand closed over my wrist. "This way, Demon pet. Reek will help his friend."

I stumbled through the dark after Reek. His hand was the only thing I could feel as he pulled me along. Behind, I could hear the door to Ridha's office open and close, but when I dared a glance over my shoulder, I couldn't see anything beyond the tip of my nose. It was black as pitch.

Reek came to a sudden stop in front of me, causing me to stumble into his back before I could catch myself.

The demon chuckled. "The demon pet is still too mortal. It hasn't accepted its power. Not yet. Not yet."

Darkness lightened to shades of silver around me. The room I stood in now was lit with the light of the moon beyond the large window in the corner and the faint glow of the sconces in the hall beyond. I was back in the main castle.

I looked at the crowded furniture and paintings stacked in the room. These were Aiden's mother's belongings. The last of what remained of her.

"How did we get here?" I whispered. The faint sound of Aiden's music could be heard from the next room, but not a single guard patrolled these halls.

Reek remained hidden in shadow, though I could see the stark white of his eyes and the sharp points of his too-small teeth in the dim light.

"Reek helped his friend. That is how it got here," he said as if it were obvious.

I studied the shadowed form of the strange demon barely visible in the dark. "You're not a normal demon are you, Reek?"

The demon's smile grew almost bashful. "Reek is extraordinary. Demon pet will be too if it listens to Reek's words."

"What words?" I asked, trepidation growing as the whites of his eyes studied me.

"Find the answers to Reek's game and it will know," he said, no longer smiling. "Does it know what, once given, is honored to return in death?"

My brows furrowed as the music in the next room stopped abruptly. "No?"

Reek sighed, stepping further into the shadows. "It will. Reek fears it will know when all is painted red and lying dead."

The essence signaled Aiden's approach a moment later. When I glanced toward the corner where Reek had just been standing, I wasn't entirely surprised to find it empty.

As soon as Aiden's footsteps came to a stop outside the door, I rushed to hide the vials of potion beneath the covered sofa and moved toward the window.

The door opened behind me, letting in a beam of light.

"Esme?" he said, surprised to find me. "What are you doing in here?"

I turned slowly, desperate to come up with an excuse. "Couldn't sleep?"

His expression turned to a mixture of disbelief and curiosity as he studied the room around us. "So, you snuck into my mother's room?"

I was at a loss for words. The embarrassment at being caught must've shown on my face because his expression softened. Whatever conclusion he came to about my strange appearance in this room was better than any excuse I would have come up with.

"Why were you playing my family's song?" I asked in an effort to distract him from questioning me further.

Aiden blinked, taken aback. A faint flush dusted his cheeks as he shifted his weight from foot to foot. "I thought you might like to hear something familiar."

I took a step toward him. The first time I inquired after the song, he shrugged it off like it was nothing. "So, you decided to learn our song?"

He nodded. "After...what happened, I'd hoped it would bring you some peace."

I considered this as I studied him.

"I didn't know you could play," I admitted.

He shrugged, running a hand through his shaggy hair. "I was taught as a child, and Fen made me continue lessons long after I reached adolescence."

I smiled. "And I assume you're incapable of telling Fen no, just like everyone else around here?"

Aiden smiled and it spoke to a part of me I'd previously thought to be broken. "Fen is much tougher than she looks. Don't let her fool you."

"I'll keep that in mind."

His smile faded a little as he glanced around the room. "Who were you speaking to a moment ago? I heard another voice."

"No one," I said too quickly. Guilt rattled me as I glanced toward the vials hidden beneath the sofa. I just had to do this one last thing for Ephraim, then I would be free to uncover the secrets that still surrounded my family's deaths.

I could tell he didn't believe me, but he didn't press for more information. Aiden turned, gesturing to the hall.

"May I walk you to your room?" There was an underlying hopeful gleam in his eye that warmed me.

I raised a brow. "Am I not allowed to stay here? Maybe I wanted to invade your personal space and look through your things." I nodded to the stack of paintings in the corner. "Or maybe steal some of those for myself. It's been weeks and I still haven't gotten used to your lack of decor."

Aiden's smirk returned. "Another time. It's late and we both know Tarsa won't let you off the hook if you show up late to training in the morning."

"Very well," I relented, moving past him with a dramatic sigh.

He chuckled softly, following me into the hall. The essence made it difficult to focus on anything other than his proximity as we strolled past his guards who were gaping openly at us.

"It seems we haven't been doing a very good job keeping up appearances," I muttered under my breath as we came across another set of guards who appeared surprised to see us together.

Aiden nodded to the guards before they moved away. "So my father tells me."

I studied him from the corner of my eye. "You've been speaking to your father about us?"

"Only in letters or through his messengers."

"Is he still suspicious?" With so many secrets coming to light, I hadn't thought beyond the immediate threats to consider if Ofrin believed I was still after his crown or not.

Aiden brushed invisible dirt from his shirt. "I think no matter what we do he won't trust us. His age has made him exercise caution where caution is not due."

We turned down the hall leading to our adjoining rooms. This corridor was as quiet as the others this late in the night.

"Will that happen to you too?" I asked as we came to a stop outside my own door.

His brow furrowed. "What?"

"Will you begin to doubt everything and lose your trust in your friends when you become the God of Death?" I studied his closed off expression for any hint of response.

Aiden tucked a strand of hair behind my ear. "Not if I have you there to keep me sane."

"But I am only mortal," I said, voicing what we both knew. "My lifetime will be a blink compared to yours. Especially with so many who still wish me dead."

I watched his expression falter. Not entirely, but enough that I could see a slip of the man beneath. The emotion there surprised me with its vulnerability, and its sadness.

"Do you fear it?" I asked when he didn't speak.

"Going mad?" he asked. I nodded, pulling a soft chuckle from him.

He cradled my face in his hands, his touch featherlight. My heart began to race again, pounding against my ribs like a war drum. Heat flooded my cheeks beneath his touch while his gaze burned along my skin.

When his thumb brushed across my lower lip, I lost my ability to breathe.

"What I fear most is knowing that it'll be the loss of you that drives me into madness," he whispered. "You are the source of all my strength, Esme."

Aiden leaned closer. My skin was on fire beneath his gaze. Every inch of me burned for more.

I thought he might kiss me, and I didn't fear it. I didn't even dislike the idea. My breath lodged in my throat the moment his nose brushed mine.

His voice was hoarse as he whispered, "Sleep well, Princess."

Before I could respond, he released me from his touch and disappeared into his room.

I slumped against my door, forcing breath back into my lungs. I raised a hand to my cheek, feeling the heated flush that remained. There was no use in hiding my feelings for him any longer. As much as I may have resented it before, I still loved him. And knowing that might just be what would get me killed.

TWENTY-NINE

I SLEPT RESTLESSLY THAT night. My mind tossed with my feelings for Aiden, devotion to my family, and the deal I'd made with Ephraim, all conflicting with each other and turning my emotions into a raging storm of confusion.

In the morning, Fen joined me for breakfast, as she often did. I could tell she noticed the change in my demeanor as I sat silently and nibbled on a biscuit. I could hear her telling me about the gown she was designing for me to wear to Ofrin's solstice ball, but I couldn't concentrate on her words.

What I really wanted was my mother. To sit with her and spill my feelings and seek her guidance.

I knew I didn't want to kill Aiden. Not as I once thought I did. But I still wanted to be rid of this curse, and Ephraim said he could help me. Aiden had made no such promises, nor did he even hint at wanting to help me break the curse. Yet it was all I wanted.

An hour before training with Tarsa, I dressed in the warmest clothes I could find and left Fen in my room to wander the yard. With my mind in disarray, I needed the comfort of the overgrown corner of the garden.

I hugged the cloak around my shoulders as I stepped from the warmth of the castle and out into the cold morning air. A layer of frost lingered on the grass, making it crunch beneath my boots. My breath fogged in the air as I strolled through the grounds, aware of the many sets of eyes on me.

The majority of the garden remained well kept, even in winter. A stone path was clearly visible winding through the well-groomed foliage. The flowers had all wilted and died off for the season, but the shriveled plants remained in the garden. It made it easy to imagine how beautiful it must look in spring.

I turned down the path where the stones were less visible in the ground. It would've taken years for this corner of the garden to become so overgrown that even in winter the grass covered the stones. It held a wild beauty the rest of the garden didn't; it was far more peaceful than any groomed garden could be.

A chill raced over my skin, making me pull the cloak tighter across my shoulders to keep out the cool air. I huddled further into myself as I stared at the large bent tree surrounded by the dead chaos of bushes and lifeless flowers.

My shoulders relaxed as I stopped there. A tension I hadn't realized I was holding escaped me as I leaned against the frozen bark of the tree, just taking in the beauty of this small corner of the realm.

"You know, the rest of the garden is much more appealing than this place," Aiden's voice said from behind me.

I sighed, not bothering to turn and face him. "I like it here."

"Why?" he asked, voice thoughtful.

I studied the overgrown garden. "It's peaceful."

His steps were silent as he came to stand beside me. Out of the corner of my eye I watched him scrutinize the space around us. A frown appeared as he finally looked at me.

I shrugged. "For someone who refuses to decorate the interior of his home, you care an awful lot about where I choose to sit in your garden."

It was Aiden's turn to shrug. "Hakan is responsible for the garden's upkeep. I'm only waiting for him to question why you don't think the rest of his garden is good enough for your attention, but this messy corner is."

"Hakan tends to the gardens?" I asked, disbelief plain in my voice. I couldn't picture the ever serious, burly warrior planting and trimming flowers.

"He does, and he takes it very seriously." There was a hint of a smile in his voice.

I chuckled. "That is a sight I would love to see."

Aiden's shoulders relaxed. "If he hears you say that he may force you to plant flowers with him come springtime. He'll spend the rest of winter talking your ear off about which flowers plant best at certain times of the season if you let him."

I laughed outright. "That's almost as bad as Alfie with his stories."

A wave of sadness overtook me as I stared at the wild garden, thinking of my brother. It was then that I realized why I liked this small corner of the grounds. In all its overgrown, messy glory, it reminded me of my family and the peace they brought me.

"What is it?" Concern was etched in his tone.

I twirled a loose piece of hair around a finger. "If Hakan sees me out here, he's not going to start tending to this corner of the garden, is he?"

"That's a real possibility." A line formed between his brows as he studied me.

I marveled at the overgrown grass, dull wildflowers, and crooked trees. "Could you ask him not to?"

My trepidation must've shown because Aiden turned toward me fully. I could feel his gaze sweeping over my face, analyzing every minute expression as he attempted to decipher the emotion in my words.

"I like this part of the garden as it is," I said finally. "It's real. It's peaceful. My family would've liked it."

He stayed quiet for so long I almost wasn't sure he'd heard me. When I dared a glance at him, he appeared thoughtful. His eyes surveyed me with unnerving clarity.

"I will make sure this corner of the garden remains untouched," he vowed.

I nodded. "Thank you."

A small smile pulled at the corners of his lips. It was one of his rare, delicate smiles that warmed my chest.

"Was there something you needed?" I asked. I forced myself to turn back to the garden, hoping it would provide some relief from the storm of my emotions.

Aiden sighed. "Fen mentioned you'd been unlike yourself this morning, and for once you weren't in your study."

"I'm surprised you didn't just ask one of your dozens of guards for my whereabouts. They've hardly let me out of their sight since I left my chambers."

We both glanced toward the gate where a small huddle of guards stood watch. As soon as our gaze landed on them, they quickly turned away and dispersed.

"I suppose I could ask them to be a bit more discreet," Aiden said. I nearly laughed at the reluctance in his voice.

"That would be much appreciated," I said, grinning.

"Sir," Hakan's voice sounded from the path behind us.

Aiden turned toward the immortal while I let my gaze return to the overgrown bushes. I wasn't ready to give up the little peace this corner of the garden offered for whatever trouble Hakan was bringing to us.

"There's been news," Hakan said stiffly, making my heart race with the possibilities.

When he didn't elaborate, I turned from the garden. Killian stood at his side, and although the young immortal smiled in greeting, it was fleeting; both men appeared brisk and uncertain before us.

"What sort of news?" I asked when no one spoke. Aiden continued to stare at Hakan as if they were having a silent conversation.

"We can discuss it later," Aiden said dismissively. I frowned but he ignored it. "Tarsa will be in the training room soon. We'll join you as soon as we can."

"Am I not allowed to hear the news?" I asked, hiding my hurt with frustration.

Aiden only smiled, though it was stiff; an attempt to hide something from me. He tucked a strand of hair behind my ear then immediately turned to follow the two immortals back to the castle.

My feet dragged the entire way to the training room. My thoughts circled with what they could possibly be keeping from me.

I was so wrapped up in my thoughts I didn't even realize there was more than one person in the training room. I came nose to nose with Alvize just as someone stepped up behind me and locked the door.

Alvize sneered down his nose at me. "It's about time we found you alone again, *Princess*," he crooned. "Your bodyguards have been ever diligent at keeping you under their careful watch."

I stepped back, colliding with Delvin's chest. The essence awakened instantly. "What are you doing here? Did you not learn your lesson last time?"

Delvin's hands gripped tightly onto my upper arms, keeping me in place. Two more figures wearing guard uniforms came into view; I didn't know their names, but I recognized them from my introduction to the court. I had little doubt the two strangers were meant to be the guards standing watch outside this very room.

Panic rushed through my veins a moment before the essence squelched it, hollowing me out so all that was left was its power.

Alvize gripped my chin tightly in his hands, forcing me to look at him. "You got her killed."

"That was her own doing," I snapped. "And you're a fool to think otherwise."

Alvize punched me, hard. My head swung back into Delvin's chest as the broad man held me still.

"Stupid human," Alvize cursed. "You should've been left to die in the mortal realm."

My blood burned with a fiery rage, heating every inch of me to match the rise of the essence. Power, raw and scorching, erupted from me. The veil slid over my eyes as easily as taking a breath.

I swung my foot back and up, landing a solid kick in the side of Delvin's knee. The young man grunted, releasing one of my arms to cradle his injured leg.

Alvize moved forward, ready to strike again, but one of his other minions beat him to it.

A girl I didn't recognize dove forward with a sharp knife pointed at my gut. I barely had enough time to jump out of the way before her knife sliced the air where I'd been standing.

Delvin's hold on my other arm made me stumble slightly, struggling with my footing as I dodged another attack from the girl.

She placed too much force into her next swing of the knife, causing her to lose balance. With her back slightly turned, I swept her feet out from underneath her.

As her back hit the floor, her grip on the knife slipped. I watched it arc through the air and clatter to the floor a few feet away, just out of arm's reach.

Delvin struck quickly, hobbling on one good leg. His hands moved to close around my throat, squeezing tightly. I gasped as blackness slowly crept over my vision.

That small gasp was propelled from my lungs as Delvin slammed me on my back, keeping a tight hold around my neck. As soon as my lungs began to burn, power erupted from me.

All four of my attackers were thrown backward into the air, landing harshly on the stone floor or crashing with a sickening thud into the walls.

Alvize was the first to rouse. The anger on his face was nearly enough to make me fearful, but the essence blanketed my mortal emotions.

I slowly got my feet, mirroring his movements as he yanked a knife free from his belt.

"You're going to pay for that," he said through clenched teeth.

Something surged from my chest, latching onto him. Alvize didn't seem to notice the change as he launched in my direction. But I could feel it, whatever it was.

A body slammed into my side a moment before Alvize reached me. The air I'd just regained in my lungs left in a rush as I crashed to the floor beneath the girl.

Her face was scrunched up in a snarl as she pinned me to the floor. I struggled beneath her grip, but it was no use. The little knowledge I'd gained of fighting paled in comparison to the years she'd obviously spent training.

The girl placed her knee in the center of my chest, keeping me pinned. I reached for her hair, ready to use the tail of her braid to drag her off of me.

Alvize grabbed my arm before I could, pinning it to the floor beside me.

"Do it," he barked at the girl. I could hear Delvin and the other boy moving closer now too. My panic tried to rise again but the essence smothered it.

The girl fumbled with the knife. I watched it slip from her shaky fingers and land just a hairsbreadth from my face.

Delvin cursed as he knelt at Alvize's side. I squirmed beneath them, fingers reaching desperately for the knife.

"Watch her," Alvize cautioned.

Her knee dug in harder against my ribs as we wrestled for the blade, and Alvize's grip tightened on my arm. My annoyance flared a moment before the essence surged, striking through my thoughts as I wished to be free of him.

Alvize released me a second later, as if stung by my very thoughts. He cursed, fear making his voice breathy as he glowered at me.

I grabbed the girl's wrist, trying to rip the knife away from her. Our struggle sent us toppling sideways, rolling from our momentum.

The girl gasped. Warmth spread over my hand a second later, the liquid thick and sticky.

I looked down, surprised and a little horrified to see the knife sticking out of her chest. She coughed blood, spattering it across my face. I nearly gagged as I shoved away from her and got to my feet.

Something yanked me backward as the girl's blood pooled on the floor.

"You'll pay for that too," Alvize said into my ear.

But I couldn't look away from the girl. The way her blood fanned out from her crumpled form reminded me too much of my family's final moments.

The tether between Alvize and I strengthened until I felt a jolt inside of me. He released me with a gasp.

"What did you do?" His voice came out in a panicked snarl.

Alvize raised his fist for another strike. And everything slowed.

The essence in me spread outward, casting a shadow so wide it engulfed the entire room. The tether between Alvize and I remained, but more souls were added. I could feel Delvin and the other boy there now too. Somehow, I could feel their souls at the end of the tethers.

Their souls were now tied to mine. As soon as I realized it, the essence hummed in confirmation.

The doors slammed open with such force the walls shook. An axe whirled past my face, landing in the third boy's chest. I hadn't even noticed he'd aimed a knife in my direction until it clattered onto the floor.

The tether between us snapped, shattering like glass as his lifeless body fell to the ground.

I let the veil fall, pulling the essence back inside myself and lifting the dark shadows from my eyes.

Tarsa marched into the room like a force to be reckoned with. Her tawny skin was flushed with anger as she pulled me to my feet. But for once her anger wasn't directed at me.

I watched her eyes take in the scene. I saw how she cataloged the casual stances of the two boys before settling on the dead girl at my feet.

Her gaze was scrutinizing as she caught my wide-eyed stare. My body began to ache with the aftermath of the struggle. My throat burned and my muscles protested even the slightest movement.

Daemon cursed as he came to a skidding stop behind us. "What happened?"

Tarsa and I studied each other a moment longer. Whatever she saw in my face was enough to provoke a flicker of fear in her eyes.

"We need to go to Aiden. Now." There was a subtle panic to her voice that Daemon didn't even bother to tease her for. Instead, we followed her in silence. Just me, Daemon, and my two new soul-bound companions.

THIRTY

AIDEN PACED HIS STUDY furiously. His gaze switched between murderous glares toward the two immortals standing in the corner and worried glances aimed at me. But as soon as his eyes landed on the bruises forming around my neck, that murderous glare reappeared.

"Why were there no guards at the door?" he asked as soon as Jadan and Seraphine entered the room. The latter shot me a worried glance before carefully placing herself between the attackers and myself.

"They were relieved of their post by the assailants," Jadan said, nodding toward my remaining attackers.

Aiden spun toward the pair. The air felt heavy, thick with the threat of violence. Out of the corner of my eye I saw Hakan step closer, ready to intervene on his prince's behalf.

"You told the guards to leave," Aiden stated.

Delvin nodded, there was no regret in his stare. "I did."

Aiden stepped closer, his posture threatening. "Why?"

"She needed to pay," Alvize interjected coldly.

The temperature in the room dropped. I felt more than heard Killian and Seraphine step closer, so they flanked me on either side.

"And what is it you believe my wife needs to pay for?" Aiden demanded.

Alvize turned his glare toward me. "She is the reason Drusilla is dead. We just wanted to even the score."

"You aimed to kill me?" I asked, more angry than scared.

He flashed a cold grin. "Eventually."

Aiden slammed him against the wall, his arm across the boy's throat. "I should kill you all where you stand."

I sent a confused glance toward Seraphine, but she wouldn't meet my eyes. In fact, she looked fearful as she kept her body turned so she could see me and the immortals at the same time.

"But I don't know what that would do to Esme, and it is her safety I care most about," Aiden continued. He eased his vice grip on Alvize's neck ever so slightly, shoulders slumping in something akin to defeat.

"Why would killing them do anything to me?" I asked.

"Because you bound their souls to yours," Tarsa cut in. Her cool demeanor was less noticeable now that Aiden posed the biggest threat in the room.

I gaped at her. "No I didn't."

Killian placed a calming hand on my arm. "But you did. It's why they stopped attacking you. They couldn't attack you once you bound their souls to yours."

I looked to Aiden for confirmation, but he too was reluctant to meet my eye. "What does that mean? How do we undo it?"

"We can't," Tarsa said briskly. "Only you can do that now. You, and maybe Ofrin if he finds out."

Hakan's dark gaze studied me closely. "Let's hope he doesn't."

"What happens if he does?" Seraphine asked. Everyone turned to Aiden for answers.

Daemon stepped forward, inky black hair falling into his eyes as he looked down at me. "If the God of Death finds out his Soul Collector has become so powerful that he is no longer the only person in existence able to bind a soul, then there's no saying what he might do."

A shiver raced down my spine as Aiden caught my gaze. There was a barely contained panic in his eyes, well hidden behind the anger still emanating from him.

"I didn't do it on purpose," I said hastily.

"We know," Seraphine offered. Her hand squeezed mine in gentle comfort. "But it is now an additional issue we didn't foresee."

"What can you make them do?" Daemon asked suddenly.

Aiden snarled. "They still need to be punished for trying to hurt you."

"She killed one of our own. Again," Alvize snapped. "Now we're bound to her for the rest of her life. That's punishment enough."

"Can you make them jump off the roof?" Daemon asked, and then chuckled as if he'd made a joke.

"Can't I just unbind them? Then they can be imprisoned or something." I was suddenly growing very nervous at the idea of having these immortals' souls bound to me, whatever that meant.

"Maybe she can make them dance until their feet bleed," Killian muttered to Daemon.

The demon-born laughed. "Oh, please do that, Princess."

"Will you two fools quit acting like children?" Hakan barked, silencing them with a glare. "This is not the time for jokes."

Daemon sighed, moving to stand by Jadan. The white-haired immortal was so quiet I'd almost forgotten he was there. "Fine," Daemon said begrudgingly. "But it would've been fun to see."

Jadan patted his friend on the shoulder, fighting a smile.

"For now, do not speak of this to anyone," Aiden ordered. Though he looked to everyone in the room, his threat was mostly directed at the two in the corner. "Is that clear?"

As one, they both turned to me. It took a moment before I realized they were waiting for me to give them an order. Their gazes were angry, both of them looking utterly repulsed that they had to wait for my bidding.

Sensing my unease, Aiden stepped closer, towering over me.

"What do I do?" I whispered so only he could hear.

His hand squeezed mine. "No mortal has ever bound a soul to them before, so this is new territory for us all. From the little I know of soul bonds among demons, they still have their own free will, but your word is final. It's law."

I glanced nervously toward the demons. "How do I tell them to go away?"

The corners of his lips quirked up. "The same way you would tell anyone."

"But it needs to come from the essence you carry," Tarsa added.

The essence warmed my chest as my nervousness grew. I felt the anger and unease coming from the demons sulking in the corner, and I could feel the power I held over each of them.

"Go," I said in a voice I didn't recognize. A voice that alluded to a deep well of power. "Speak of this to no one."

They responded immediately, dipping their chins in a shallow mock of a bow and leaving the room in silence.

When Jadan and Daemon turned to trail after them, I let the essence slip back to rest. My shoulders drooped with the release of the tension I'd been holding.

"We need to fix this before Ofrin finds out," Tarsa said as she pushed off of her perch on Aiden's desk. Her lithe form towered over me as she strode past, sparing me a scowl.

"What if we can't break the bonds?" Killian asked, brushing his golden curls from his eyes.

Seraphine shrugged, her hands fidgeting nervously at her sides. "At best, Ofrin might just lock her away in his castle until he can steal the bonds for his own."

"And at worst?" I asked, uncertain if I truly wanted an answer.

Aiden sighed. "At worst, he could just siphon the essence from you knowing it would kill you."

The pain in his eyes was not entirely unexpected. But seeing it before me was a confirmation I wasn't sure I could handle right now.

"It would certainly solve a lot of his problems," Hakan noted casually.

I scowled. "How so?"

"You are supposed to be serving him in the mortal realm," Tarsa said. "Instead, you are in his realm, married to his son. Your power has gotten exponentially stronger since being here. Though whether that's from your proximity to the Crossroads, or your marriage bond, we can't be sure."

"And you now have two demons with their souls bound to you," Seraphine added.

"There is a chance he already felt their bonds snap into place," Hakan said.

Aiden sighed, running a hand through his hair. "If he had, he would be here already. The fact that he hasn't noticed their bonds missing from his grasp is a blessing in disguise."

"If he finds out, then he definitely won't believe your marriage to be one of love," Tarsa said disdainfully.

"Maybe you should be seen together more," Seraphine suggested. "Jadan and Daemon have served well as spies, but we all know there are more hidden in your court. The people need to believe that you love each other. Not just Ofrin."

Aiden ran a hand over his face, his growing exasperation apparent.

"And not just among those here in the castle, but in the village too," Seraphine continued. "Let the people see you together."

"Maybe start bringing Esme to court proceedings every once in a while," Hakan suggested.

I waited for Aiden's response, but he only watched me expectantly.

"What?" I asked when he didn't speak.

"The choice is yours," he said simply. "I will not force you to attend court if you do not wish it."

I considered this as I studied him. His expression remained partially closed off, as if guarded against an inevitable rejection.

"Okay," I finally relented.

"Very well," Aiden said, nodding as he glanced at the bruises along my neck. "In the meantime, try to avoid using the essence as much as you can."

I frowned. "I can't always control when that happens."

"Well, you need to," Tarsa said. "One of these days Ofrin will feel you using the essence and he'll come to investigate."

Aiden's hand squeezed mine. "It'll be all right," he whispered softly.

I could only nod, unable to find my voice amidst my growing panic.

"None of this will matter once the ball passes," Killian said cheerily. "Once Ofrin realizes you didn't marry to steal his throne, we can go after Ephraim as planned and you'll be free."

I offered him the smile he expected, but it felt stiff.

They began to speak of ways to plan in secret, out of sight of Ofrin's spies. But my mind remained filled with my desperation to be rid of this curse.

From the corner of my gaze I felt Aiden watching me, sensing the sour tone of my thoughts. Guilt pulled at me once more. I felt it urge me to come clean about my foolish bargain with Ephraim. About Viema. About Aiden's mother.

I opened my mouth, ready to spill my secrets to the world, when Tarsa shifted into view. The light from the window caught on her axes, momentarily blinding me. Her sharp gaze watched me too clearly, effectively silencing me.

With nothing more to say, I fled the room. My cowardice pressed down on my shoulders all the way to my chambers.

I needed to complete this bargain with Ephraim. Only then, when I was freed from him, could I tell Aiden the truth.

THIRTY-ONE

IT WAS MORE DIFFICULT to sneak through the castle that night. My two new reluctant guards became my shadows, in addition to the guards already monitoring my safety.

Even when I returned to my rooms after dinner, I had to order both of them away just so they wouldn't stand in my room and watch me sleep. None of us were very happy with this new situation.

Outside, the grounds were quiet. Aiden's guards continued patrolling the wall, but no one noticed me. Somehow, I was lucky enough to remain a wraith in the night.

I clung to the shadows, forcing my ragged breath to remain quiet in the cool night air as I slipped from the garden and through the gap in the stone wall.

The forest beyond appeared the same, only now it was covered with frost and a dusting of snow. The trees appeared black in the dark night with only the frost-covered ground for contrast.

My heart pounded in my chest with growing anxiety as I raced to the same small clearing where I'd previously met Ephraim. It'd been exactly three weeks since our most recent secret encounter, and tonight would be our last.

Dove grey wings caught my eye from the shadows. Sensing my arrival, Ephraim turned, letting the moonlight reflect off his dark horns. My stomach tightened at the blatant reminder of his true power.

"I was beginning to worry you would disappoint me," he said into the quiet night. "You have not sent letters or spoken with Viema in many days. I worried you may have abandoned your promise."

I swallowed nervously, clutching the sack of vials against my chest. "We made a bargain. I get these vials for you, and in return you consider our previous agreement void."

"Yes." His voice was as clipped and closed off as his expression. I couldn't decipher what he was feeling, but from the sudden stiffness of his posture I knew he sensed something in me had changed.

I tossed the sack of vials at him. The angel caught it effortlessly, his eyes never leaving my face.

"That's what you asked for, is it not?" I asked as he began to sift through the vials of the strange potion.

"It is."

My hands fisted in my cloak nervously. "Then it's done. I fulfilled my part of the bargain."

"And now you want me to fulfill my part of the deal?" He flashed a sinister smile.

A chill snaked down my spine. "No. I gave you what you asked for, but I no longer need your help. My former request is no longer pertinent. That was the deal. I retrieve these vials for you, then I'm done."

"Do you not care for your family any longer?" he asked. Anguish burned through my chest at their memory. He took a slow, predatory step in my direction. "Are you so wrapped up in the fairytale of becoming a princess that you have relinquished your vow of revenge? Has your love for them truly faded so quickly?"

I dared a step back, matching his slow pace until my back collided with a tree. "No. But I do not wish to be further entangled with your antics."

His voice was taunting as he bent down, towering over me. "Will you abandon your family's memory just to hide away with your prince? Because that's what you're doing, isn't it?"

"No." I pushed as much force into that single word as I could muster, urging him to hear my certainty.

Ephraim laughed, the chilling sound grating along my skin. His hands grabbed my face a moment later, effectively cutting off the pretense of laughter.

His touch was cold against my skin as he held me still, forcing me to meet his icy gaze. "You love him. And you would allow that mortal emotion to blind your need for the revenge you once craved more than anything. You would damn your family's souls for this fleeting emotion."

"That's not true," I argued. "I am only refusing to be of any assistance with the revenge you've been craving for centuries. If your plan solely relied on me, then it was a weak one."

A low growl erupted from his chest as he slammed me back against the tree. "You are just like all the other mortals. Nothing but a weak coward distracted by temptation."

I continued to struggle in his grip as he held me captive. My heart began to race as my nerves awoke the essence within me.

"You truly wish to break our bargain?" he asked, glowering down at me.

I stared into the depths of his lifeless eyes. "Our former bargain became moot the moment we agreed I would retrieve these vials and you would leave me alone. I have no wish to damn the innocents here for something I took no part in."

Ephraim smiled. The gesture was more a flash of teeth than a grin. "You didn't take part in it?"

"I had nothing to do with the death of your mother," I said. His entire body stiffened at the mention of her. "I will not participate in your sinister plan when I no longer seek the revenge I once thought I needed."

"You have been told lies, then. Lies that have twisted your perception of what really happened to your family."

"I was finally told the truth," I said. "You can no longer give me what I seek."

His arms began to shake as he held me against the tree. The raw fury that now showed on his face made my heart race against my ribs.

"You no longer wish to be rid of this curse?" There was a careful absence of emotion in his voice that increased my fear.

"I no longer wish for you to help me break my family's curse," I clarified.

"I see." His hands released me a moment later, his movements slow with barely restrained fury.

Ephraim struck before the words died on his lips. The breath left my lungs in a rush of air as excruciating pain spread across my torso.

I looked down at the source of the pain. Ephraim had pulled his poisoned knife while I wasn't looking and stabbed it through my ribcage. A trickle of blood rushed over his hand as he kept the knife embedded in my side, letting the poison spread through my veins.

Fiery pain erupted through me, moving faster with my quickening pulse.

"You didn't keep your word. What makes you think I'd keep mine?" Ephraim smiled when I looked into his face. "Turns out I don't care what you want, darling. I need that essence you carry, and you're going to give it to me."

I choked on the pain as he yanked the knife free. "I won't."

Viema appeared from the shadows. There was a hint of a smile on her mouth as she stepped to Ephraim's shoulder.

"Oh, you don't get a choice," Ephraim taunted. "Because I'm going to take it from you."

Viema struck fast and hard. A smaller knife dug into the very center of my chest. I coughed up blood as Viema twisted the weapon ever so slightly through my ribs, narrowly missing my heart.

"Careful," Ephraim cautioned his companion. "You can't kill her yet."

Viema smiled, the gesture coldly beautiful. "Not until I get that essence."

Suddenly everything clicked into place. Viema's persistence, Ephraim's determination that I practice and grow stronger.

"You want the essence for yourself," I said between gasping breaths. "You don't want to destroy it. You want to use it."

Viema's grin widened. "You are not deserving of such power."

"And you are?" The essence in question began to rise, burning through my chest until I could feel it on the edge of the white blade Viema kept lodged in my chest.

The angel snarled. "I am capable of awakening its full potential. That power could flatten realms and capture every soul in existence. Yet you whine and beg for it to be taken away. You are a fool."

I glanced at Ephraim. He watched his companion closely, but there was a hunger to his gaze that told me he knew something I didn't.

"That's how you're going to get your revenge?" I asked, fighting against the rising power within me. I could feel it struggling against the pull of whatever magic lived within the small knife Viema used, but the poison from Ephraim's knife left me weak. "You're not just planning on hurting Ofrin. You're going to use the essence to destroy the entire realm?"

Ephraim only grinned. My knees began to shake as the poison continued to spread through my veins. I was going to die. They were going to take the essence and I was going to die.

My vision began to dim just as the essence flashed through my chest. I could feel it expand, welcoming the presence of the nearby souls and the two tied to it. I felt it when they awakened, sensing my pain and fear. Somehow, the essence knew to call them.

Ephraim's hand cradled the back of my head, turning me to look at him. "I had great hopes for you, Esme," he said. "But beyond being a source of weakness for Aiden, you are no longer of any use to me."

The veil of power slipped over my eyes the same moment I felt the essence pull at my guards' awareness. Something must've shown on my face because Ephraim released me a moment later. His expression turned hesitant as he looked into my eyes.

"Viema," he cautioned. "Now, Viema. Take it now."

The angel twisted the knife again. A cry tore from my mouth as the pain surged. "It's refusing the knife. It shouldn't be able to do that," she said, disbelief heavy in her tone.

Ephraim shoved her away, pulling the knife free from my chest. "It's not working," he snarled. I could hear growing voices in the distance, shouting for me.

"We can't leave without that essence," Viema snapped, quickly rising to her feet. The two angels glowered at each other, ignoring me entirely.

I slumped to my knees, limbs shaking uncontrollably with the poison flowing through my veins. The souls bound to me were still too far away; they wouldn't make it in time before I succumbed to the poison.

"You'll get the essence," Ephraim swore to his companion. When his eyes met mine, I let him see every ounce of anger I could muster through the fog of poison and pain. Desperate rage filled his face. "Nothing will keep us from it."

His hand fisted in my hair, forcing me to meet his gaze. "You had a chance to join me, Esme," he said scathingly. "You could've avenged your family like they deserved. Instead, you selfishly chose to protect yourself. And after I went through all that trouble to have Elroy capture you. You're more trouble than you're worth."

I blinked through the growing fog. "Yet when you had Elroy arrest me, you were too weak to take me."

Ephraim's arrogant grin shifted into a snarl worthy of a rabid wolf. "If it weren't for the damned protections on the essence, I would've had you weeks before Aiden showed up. But the fool just couldn't forget you."

My body went cold. Whether from the poison, blood loss, or anger, I couldn't be sure. The essence flared inside me.

"So really, I should consider you responsible for the deaths of my family. Had you not told Elroy about me, they would still live," I said through clenched teeth, fighting against the growing darkness.

Ephraim bent so we were nearly nose to nose. A smile pulled at his mouth; the gesture screamed arrogance as he forced me to keep his gaze.

"It's a shame your prince managed to interfere on your brother and sister's behalf," he said. "He should've let them die like the rest of your pathetic family."

The essence responded to my anger. Ephraim was thrown back into a nearby tree, and his wings made a satisfying crack against the bark. I collapsed onto my hands and knees, exhausted from the use of power and the spreading poison.

Voices carried through the trees, nearer now but still on the far side of the wall surrounding Aiden's castle. Through the tether binding our souls, they could feel that I was near, and hurt. But they couldn't pinpoint my location.

"Do not threaten my family." My voice was surprisingly strong, though the life was slowly slipping from me.

Viema laughed, bending over Ephraim's crumpled form. She hauled him into her arms with inhuman strength. "The rest of your family was killed easily enough, so it shouldn't be much harder to kill those that remain."

They vanished into the forest as soon as the threat left her mouth.

Pain burned through my limbs with the spreading poison. My entire body shook as I crawled over the ground, eager to escape the forest.

Frost covered my knees and hands before I finally came to the fissure in the stone. I fought the darkness the entire way, but as the voices grew closer, I felt it swallow me whole.

THIRTY-TWO

I ROUSED AS SOMEONE yanked on my wrist, dragging me through the mud. The movement pulled at my wounds, awakening the pain.

"She's here," someone yelled. The voice was strangely familiar, but I couldn't place it.

Next came the feeling of being carried. The jostling of my body brought with it a wave of nausea to add to the fire in my ribs.

Someone cursed. Killian, it was Killian.

"Give her to me," Killian demanded. The authority in his voice was unrecognizable, but whoever held me handed my limp body over without question.

I was no more than dead weight in Killian's arms. I tried to open my eyes, tell him what happened, but the darkness pulled me under again.

The next thing I felt was a rising burn through my chest, like someone stuck a white-hot poker into my ribs.

I cried out, trying desperately to get away from the growing agony.

"It's poison." Killian again. His voice was tight, pained.

"Go get him." Tarsa. That commanding voice belonged to Tarsa.

Quick footsteps sounded again, growing dimmer as they ran off into the distance. The air was warmer now, no longer the frigid cold of outside. We must be in the castle. Why couldn't I open my eyes?

"Esme?" Killian's arms tightened around me. I could feel my heart pounding in my chest as it struggled to pump the blood through my veins. Even now I could feel the warm, sticky substance soaking through my shirt. I'd lost so much of it, and whatever remained was tainted with poison.

"Esme, can you hear me?" Killian's body shifted as he raced through the castle. I could feel his heart pounding in his chest against my ear.

I tried to speak, to say anything, but I fell victim to the darkness again.

My next conscious thought was that the pain had spread so far through my body that I was numb to it.

A loud crash sounded nearby, shaking the walls. The soft surface beneath me did not stir. A bed. I was lying on a bed.

"What happened?" a deep voice, tight with fury, demanded. Aiden. Aiden was here.

A cool hand swept across my brow. "We found her like this." Seraphine.

I felt the bed shift beneath me as she stood. Aiden's hands replaced hers as they cradled my face. His touch was so gentle, like he was afraid I would shatter.

"Esme? Stay with me." Aiden's voice sounded far away, but the edge of panic was clear. "I've got you. Stay with me." I felt the tremble in his hands as he brushed them across my face. "Who?" he demanded, voice breaking.

"We don't know," Killian said from a few feet away. "I heard the commotion and found her in Alvize's arms."

Aiden's presence vanished before the words died on the air. Another crash sounded at the same time Killian cursed colorfully.

"What did you do to her?" Aiden yelled. All sense of humanity had left his voice. If I could have seen him, I would've guessed he looked every bit the Prince of Death.

"It wasn't us," Alvize said, slightly panicked. "She called us, and we found her in the garden."

"She was crawling under the crack in the wall," Delvin clarified in his deep voice. Even he sounded scared.

"What?" Aiden's voice had lost some of its edge, but there was still danger in his tone.

I needed to warn them. They needed to find Mousa and Cordelia and keep them safe. I knew Ephraim well enough to know his threat was not empty.

"Aiden." My voice was a rough, broken whisper.

The room went still. I felt Aiden kneel beside the bed a second later. His hands brushed along my cheek.

"Esme? Esme, what is it?" His voice was as gentle as I'd ever heard it.

I opened my mouth to tell him, to warn them. But the only sound I made was garbled as a bloody cough overtook me. The movement jostled my ribs, increasing the pain from my wounds.

Aiden's panicked voice rose, growing desperate. But I could no longer make out what anyone was saying as the darkness pulled me under again.

I awoke in darkness. There was no sound, no smell, no taste to the air. Everything was just dark. I looked down at myself, seeing nothing. My heart raced in my chest as my panic began to rise, but even as I placed my hands where my body should be, I felt nothing.

"What is happening?" I asked the emptiness.

Voices slowly trickled into my consciousness; panicked and angry voices that calmed me.

"There's another wound." A female's voice echoed through the darkness. Seraphine. It was Seraphine.

I spun around, desperate to find her in the shadows.

"No," a deep voice said, horror prominent in his tone. Aiden. It was Aiden again. He was still here.

I blinked through the burning in my eyes as I searched for them.

"It's poison, Aiden," Seraphine's voice said again. "She's been poisoned."

Something flew past my face in a blur. I reacted without thinking, ducking before a loud crash sounded. When I stood, the space around me slowly came into focus.

I was standing in my room. Alvize and Delvin stood cowering in the corner. A chair lay shattered on the ground at their feet.

My panicked breathing quickened as I took in my dim surroundings. It was as if I was looking through a foggy window, perceiving mostly shapes and colors. I could see enough to know what was happening, but it wasn't clear.

I froze when I caught sight of the bed.

Seraphine knelt at its side, tending to the prone figure lying on it. A large puddle of blood seeped from the figure's chest, staining the sheets and soaking the mattress.

The immortal warrior's fiery red hair was tied back from her face, letting me see the tears and panic in her eyes as she desperately wiped at the wounds.

Another figure moved into view, making my heart nearly stop. Aiden paced frantically, his eyes never straying from the bloodied figure.

"Tarsa's on her way," Hakan said, stepping into the room. The door dangled from its hinges. A crack in the wall behind it told me whoever slammed it open did so with great strength.

Aiden only nodded, refusing to stop his pacing or drop his gaze from the bed.

This couldn't be right. I shouldn't be seeing the room like this. Not when I was the body on the bed.

Tears burned my throat as I pushed forward, keeping stride with Aiden as he paced by the bedside.

"Aiden," I said, voice tight with tears. "Aiden, can you hear me?" I let my voice rise with my panic.

"Can anyone hear me? Something's wrong. I shouldn't be here like this." My voice broke with tears as I stared at my body.

Two stab wounds marked my chest. One lower, beneath my arm where Ephraim had stabbed with his poisoned blade. And one higher up, directly in the middle of my chest where Viema tried to pry the essence from me.

I placed a phantom hand against my chest, desperate to feel the essence hiding there. But I felt nothing. Not the essence. Not my breath. Not my heartbeat.

A sound behind me pulled me from my rising panic.

"I'm here," Ridha said, moving through the room at a brisk pace. Tarsa was hot on her heels, carrying a large sack I guessed contained the witch's remedies.

Aiden towered over the witch. "Fix her." His voice was cold and demanding, harsh with terror. I watched his hands shake at his sides as Ridha placed a calming hand on his arm.

"I will do my best," she promised.

Hakan tucked his arm beneath Aiden's, pulling him out of the way while the witch knelt at Seraphine's side.

"Let her work," Hakan said quietly.

Ridha quickly dug through her bag, searching for something I couldn't see clearly through the haze.

Though every eye in the room was focused on her, Ridha worked diligently. Killian pulled Seraphine away, giving her more room to work. The two immortals huddled together in the corner, tears flowing freely down both of their cheeks as they waited with bated breath.

A gasp sounded behind me. "What happened?" Fen stormed into the room. Fury filled every line in her face as she glowered at the two demons trembling in the corner.

"Ephraim," Tarsa said simply. She appeared the least affected by my physical state, opting to keep her eyes on the two souls bound to me instead of the chaos behind her.

Fen cursed loudly. "Where is he?"

"Gone," Hakan said, keeping a close eye on Aiden as the demon prince moved to kneel on the other side of the bed. "There's no sign of him anywhere in the realm."

"Well, clearly you need to look again," Fen snapped. "He obviously has no trouble sneaking past your spies. He managed to get into her room without anyone the wiser. Look again." The cool demand in her voice was a reminder of the warrior she'd once been.

"She wasn't in her room," Tarsa corrected. "These two found her half-buried beneath the wall outside."

"What was she doing out there?" Fen demanded.

Jadan and Daemon stepped into the room at that moment, the former looking uncharacteristically disgruntled.

"They're in place," Jadan said coolly. Daemon swallowed loudly, looking oddly pale as he stared, wide-eyed, at my blood-soaked form.

Hakan nodded his thanks. "No one is to go near her siblings without my say." The two demons nodded their acceptance.

My shoulders slumped. They were protecting my family, even though I had bartered with their enemy. Though whether they'd deciphered that secret or not was a mystery to me.

A hand closed over my shoulder, startling me.

I spun around, eager to discover who could see me in this state only to stop short. If my lungs had been working, I knew they would've seized at what I saw now.

On the bed beyond, Ridha still worked to heal my body and Aiden held onto my hand desperately. His whispered pleas pulled at my heart.

The aged face before me warmed into a sad grin. "My dear Esme," she said in her familiar, deep voice.

I blinked through tears. "Nonna?"

Nonna's hands came up to cup my cheeks as she wiped my eyes. I could feel her just as truly as I had in Cordovia. Her skin was as soft and warm as it always had been. And yet, I knew this couldn't be real. I had to be dreaming.

"I watched you die," I said in shock.

"You did," she said, nodding in agreement.

"How?"

She sighed deeply, letting her shoulders sag beneath the familiar shawl she always wore. "I am here before you now in the same way Kesson came to you all those weeks ago in Elroy's castle," she said simply.

"So, you're really here?" I asked.

She shrugged. "As much as I can be."

"I don't understand. Why are you here now?" I glanced toward my lifeless body on the bed. "Are you here for my soul?"

Tears rimmed Nonna's eyes as she beheld my body. I watched her glance around the room, noting the distressed looks on my friends' faces.

"I hope not," she said softly. "I only hoped to speak with you. But it seems your gift has adapted to its new environment. Its skills are beyond anything I could've imagined."

"I don't understand." Behind Nonna, Ridha said something to Aiden that made him clench his jaw so tight I was surprised his teeth didn't crack.

"I've been trying to reach you since your parents joined the stars," she said slowly. My gaze shot back to hers. "I saw the guilt you carried from their deaths, and I watched how it affected you."

My throat burned with tears as I stared at her familiar face. The same fierce determination still lived there, even in death.

"You need not feel guilty for what happened to our family, dear," she said. Her hand squeezed mine, silencing the words I was about to speak. "They do not blame you for their deaths, so you shouldn't either."

I shook my head, trying to clear the growing confusion. "You've spoken to them? How?"

Her smile turned sad as she glanced toward the scene playing out behind her. "Accept your gift, Esme. And accept all that comes with it."

"What do you mean?" I watched Ridha pour a small vial of familiar liquid into my body's throat. Aiden's head bowed as he clutched my hand tightly in both of his.

Nonna turned to me, offering a warm smile that had once provided comfort. "You already have the answers. You just need to trust your heart."

I shook my head. "I don't understand. What answers?"

Nonna took my face in her hands once more, a tear slipping free to fall down her cheek. "Live, Esme. Truly live. You will not be alone. We are always here."

Her hand pressed against my chest, just over my heart.

A warm shock jolted through me. I looked to Nonna for answers, but she was already gone.

I glanced around, growing more nervous as the room began to disappear, taking my vision with it. I only just caught a glimpse of familiar white eyes, hidden in the shadows of my room, before the darkness swallowed me whole again.

THIRTY-THREE

EVERYTHING CAME BACK TO me slowly. First the feel of the warm sheets around my shoulders. Then the sound of a fire crackling, and its residual heat. And eventually, the feel of a hand in mine.

It wasn't until the memories came flooding back that I forced my eyes open.

The room I lay in was familiar, but not my own. A large hearth provided the only light in the dim space with its roaring fire. It was peaceful despite the dark skies and powdered snow falling to the ground beyond the large window.

A deep, even breath tore my attention away from the room. I turned my head, wincing as the movement pulled at the wounds in my chest. Everything ached. I could still recall the feel of Ephraim's knife as he thrust it between my ribs, and the cool steel of Viema's knife as it bore into my chest.

My breath began to quicken as my sense of calm faltered at the memory of their attack.

The hand holding mine tightened, centering me. Finally, my gaze landed on the person at my side.

His face was relaxed in sleep, though shadows darkened the skin beneath his eyes like this was the first sleep he'd had in days. Tangled hair hung around his face in waves as he slouched in the chair.

Aiden's thumb stroked the back of my hand in a gentle sweep again, like the gesture was natural and required no conscious thought.

Emotions poured through me as I watched him sleep. All the frustration, the darkness and betrayal - it was still there in my heart, but it was no longer targeted at Aiden. Smothering the anger was the love and comfort I'd grown to accept. I still felt pain at the loss of my family, but I no longer blamed Aiden for their deaths.

Whatever Ephraim had planned next, it was a path I'd helped him along. And now I would pay the consequences—we all would—if I couldn't stop him.

Aiden's eyes flew open, likely sensing my growing discomfort. I watched him blink into the darkened room before his gaze found mine, his shoulders sagging with relief.

I offered a small smile. "Hi."

Aiden choked on a half-hearted laugh. His hand squeezed mine once more before he sat up. His free hand brushed the hair from my face as he leaned over the bed.

"How are you?" His voice was strained, tight.

I frowned, trying to force my brain past the fog of sleep. "I'm okay." I winced as I tried to sit up. "A little sore."

Aiden's frown returned. He quickly adjusted the pillows behind me to allow me to sit up with support. "You almost died. You were nearly dead already by the time you were found."

"I know," I said quietly, ashamed. The strain in his voice pulled at my heart with guilt.

"What happened?" he demanded gently.

I sighed, wincing as the movement jostled my stitches. "Ephraim," I said, trying to consider how best to reveal the secrets I'd been harboring. "He tried to take the essence from me. He wants to give it to one of his angels, Viema."

Aiden's demeanor changed, growing rigid with tension. "Viema. Did he say anything else?"

I sent him a look which only made his lips twitch. "I didn't get the chance to ask. He stabbed me with his poisoned knife, then had Viema stab me with a much smaller knife. It was doing something to the essence, but whatever it was supposed to do didn't work."

"They tried to siphon it from you," he said, nodding as his gaze turned distant. "That must be what they're planning. Or part of it, at least."

"I think he plans to use the essence against you and your father," I admitted.

Aiden frowned. "I'll send Jadan north and have him speak with my father about this. Perhaps he can provide more answers. And then he'll realize waiting until after your coronation is pointless."

I nodded, silently agreeing even though my guilt threatened to swallow me whole.

With a fortifying breath, I turned, trying to face him, but the movement brought a burning pain to my chest.

"Don't move," he said. There was a command in his tone that I'd often heard him use on his guards. "Drink this." He handed me a small vial of dark liquid he pulled from his pocket.

I lifted the vial to my nose. It smelled repulsive. "What is this?"

"It's for the pain," he explained, expression apologetic. "Ridha warned it may cause you to sleep, but she promised it'll disperse any lingering pain you might feel from your wounds or the poison."

A muscle feathered in his jaw at the mention of the poison. My hand flew to the wound along the side of my ribs. The pain was much worse than my previous encounter with Ephraim's knife.

As if he remembered it too, his eyes shot to the scar across my neck. An emotion I couldn't put a name to crossed his face for a brief moment.

"Drink," he ordered patiently. "It'll help."

I stared at the vial, untrusting. After a little encouragement, I managed to swallow the putrid liquid in one gulp.

I coughed, choking on the thick mixture. "That's disgusting."

Aiden smiled, replacing the empty vial in his pocket. "Sorry. Ridha did say she tried to add mint leaves to it."

"I think that only made it worse," I said, scrunching my face as the disgusting taste remained on my tongue.

He chuckled, returning his hand to mine. We fell into a comfortable silence. I struggled with the right words, trying to decide how best to tell him about my entanglement with Ephraim.

My faded memories sharpened, bringing a familiar face to mind.

"I saw Nonna." The words were no more than a whisper of air. I felt myself pulling our intertwined hands closer to my chest before my hazy mind caught up to the movement.

He stopped breathing. "Adine is dead." There was a nervous edge to his voice that wasn't there before.

I sighed deeply. "I know. She came when I died. At least I think I died."

The bed shifted as he leaned closer. His hand brushed along my cheek, urging me to stay awake. "You didn't die, Esme. I'm sure of it."

I offered him a sad smile that he didn't return. "I saw my body, Aiden. I saw you, and Seraphine and Killian. Fen and Tarsa. Ridha and Hakan and my soul minions. I watched everything from the corner of the room, and no one saw me standing there."

His expression became one of anguish. Aiden looked away quickly, hiding whatever he didn't want me to see in his face. My heart ached for an entirely different reason now as his former words crashed into me again. Something deep in my chest opened, something I thought I closed long ago.

I tugged on his hand. "I'm alive," I said into the silence of the room. "Ridha healed me."

"We were almost too late," he said in a broken whisper. When he turned back to me, I was surprised at the raw emotion still there. I'd half expected him to hide behind the mask he so often donned.

I reached up, cupping his cheek in my hand. Aiden stiffened for a heartbeat before relaxing into my touch.

He placed his hand over mine, gently pulling it away. "Esme," he said slowly. Aiden kept his eyes downcast, like he wasn't sure he was ready to speak whatever words formed on his tongue. "I need you to know what happened. What really happened."

My lungs seized. "Ofrin told me." Shock widened his eyes. "When he came here after the souls got loose. He told me what you did to save Mousa and Cordelia. I know you tried to save them all."

Aiden's hand tightened over mine as if desperate to keep me from pulling away. "So that's why you finally read your mother's letter."

"Yes."

He sighed, shaking his head while his eyes filled with sorrow. "I can never apologize enough for the part I played in their deaths, Esme. But I will spend the rest of my existence trying to make up for it."

"I don't want you to do that." My voice was a broken whisper as I brushed a falling tear from his cheek. The long-hidden emotion in my chest opened further, bringing with it my own need to put all the cards on the table. "I... There's something that I need to tell you."

I tried to sit up, but the pain shot through my body like a jolt of lightning. Aiden's hand came down around mine, gently pulling it from his face. I watched him place a gentle kiss first on my palm, then on the marriage mark decorating the back of my hand.

"Just rest, Esme," he said. I could see the hurt he tried to hide at what he assumed was my rejection. "Whatever it is, we can worry about it tomorrow."

I hesitated, the words ready to bubble out of me and lay my shame out for him to plainly see, but he would have none of it. Aiden gently shifted the pillows so I had no choice but to lie back and allow the drowsiness from the potion to cloud my mind.

I caught his hand in mine, studying the vines tattooed along our hands. "Stay with me?"

Aiden studied me for a moment, trying to decipher the desperation in my eyes before nodding. He crawled onto the bed beside me without a word, watching me for any sign of pain at the jostle of the mattress. There was a hesitancy from both of us that brought a flush to my cheeks as he settled beside me.

We didn't touch. His bed was large enough that we could lie side by side and still have space between us. But he lay close enough that when I placed my hand on the blanket, he took it.

I struggled against the pull of Ridha's medicine. I wasn't ready to fall back into a world of sleep when there was finally a comfortable peace between us.

Aiden squeezed my hand gently. "Sleep, Esme. I will be here when you wake."

I looked into the familiar blue-grey eyes and found only peace.

I nodded, pulling our intertwined hands closer. "You will?"

Aiden leaned in, brushing his lips across my brow. "I swear it," he whispered against my skin.

He began to hum a familiar tune. The rhythm of my family's song tangled in the air, comforting me as I let the darkness pull me under once more.

THIRTY-FOUR

"SHE'S STILL RESTING." AIDEN'S muted voice pulled me from a deep slumber.

I blinked, the brightness of the room forcing me to squint. The window was open to the winter air, letting the breeze cool the fevered sweat along my brow. Outside, the sky was light with the dawn, yet I felt far too well-rested for it to only have been a few hours since I fell asleep.

"I need to check her wounds." Ridha's voice. I turned to find Aiden's back to me. He was blocking the doorway as Ridha stood in the hall just out of view.

"She needs to rest," he said firmly.

I heard Ridha give an exasperated sigh. "She's been sleeping for two days. Not including the entire day she slept after the attack. I won't wake her. I promise."

"It's okay, Aiden. I'm awake," I called with a hoarse voice.

He turned at once, eyes bright with relief as I slowly pulled myself upright. I reached for the glass of water by the bed, but he got there first, moving like the swift immortal warrior he was.

He handed me the glass as Ridha moved into the room. I felt her eyes studying me closely as I took a deep swallow. My body felt too dry, too parched.

"Have I really been asleep for nearly three days?" I asked, handing the empty glass back to Aiden.

Ridha crossed her arms over her chest. "Yes. Nearly dying will do that to a person. Especially a mortal."

Aiden sent her a warning scowl which she ignored.

"Has anything happened since?" I asked. I ran a hand over the bandages along my ribs. The skin was still marked with stitching, but it felt far less tender than when I'd last been awake.

Aiden sighed, releasing some of his tension as he turned back to me. "No. Ephraim has not been seen or heard from since your attack."

"And Reek?" I asked, another memory coming to me.

Aiden's brows furrowed. "No. Why?"

I shrugged, wincing slightly as that movement pulled at the stitches. "I remember seeing him when I...when Nonna appeared."

"You saw your dead grandmother? Sounds like you were closer to death than I thought," Ridha said with her casual briskness. Again, she ignored the look Aiden sent her way as she moved past him to sit on the edge of the bed.

I studied the sack she placed beside me. The strong scent of mixed herbs burned my nose.

"You'll get used to it," Ridha commented unapologetically. "You need to wait outside," she said to Aiden.

His scowl deepened. "Not likely."

The witch spun to face him, hands landing on her hips in an argumentative stance. "I am going to inspect her wounds. Which means I must lift her shirt. I don't think she would like to be exposed as such, even in front of her husband. Now, leave us. I will not harm her, nor will she be harmed by any other while I am here."

Warmth filled Aiden's cheeks as he quickly glanced in my direction. I could see the concern for me battling his embarrassment as he stood firm.

Finally, Ridha groaned. "Just stand over there and turn your back then if you're so reluctant to leave her, even though no one is likely to attack her again so soon."

Aiden moved to the hearth, careful to keep his back to me as he glowered into the flames. "That is precisely when they will attack."

Ridha sent me an annoyed look before gently helping me sit upright. "You are becoming as distrustful as your father, young prince," she said. My body felt unnaturally stiff as she helped me raise the shirt above my shoulders, exposing the wounds.

Aiden grunted but made no other response.

I watched, wide-eyed, as Ridha carefully cut away the bandages wrapped around my torso. The marks beneath were ragged and deep. Small dark veins spread outward from the angry red cut between my ribs. Ephraim's poison still lingered though I did not feel it as I had before.

The wound further up my chest was much smaller. It was as red and angry as Ephraim's, but it lacked the markings of poison. It was only as big as a fingernail and firmly placed in the very center of my chest.

"These are healing well," Ridha confirmed out loud. Out of the corner of my eye I caught the release of tension from Aiden's shoulders.

Ridha worked swiftly as she cut away the stitches and covered the wounds with a floral - scented paste.

"You're lucky you were found when you were," Ridha said quietly, though I was sure Aiden could still hear.

I frowned. "I don't feel very lucky."

Her mouth curved in a small smile. "Had the poison had any more time to spread, there would've been no saving you."

"Ridha," Aiden cautioned. There was a pained strain to his voice as his fists clenched at his sides.

I glanced toward his back. "What do you mean?"

"The antidote to the angel's poison is gone," she said. There was an undercurrent of anger to her words. "Someone stole all the vials of antidote I made, apart from one."

Realization dawned as soon as she began to poke at the poisoned wound, making me wince. Panic and shame bloomed deep in my chest, stealing my breath and twisting my heart.

"Sorry," she said gently, catching my sharp inhale. Aiden shifted slightly, nearly turning to study what she'd done before catching himself.

"Can you not make more?" I asked, nervous for an entirely different reason now.

Ridha sighed. "Of course I can. But it takes weeks to make one small dose. If Ephraim decides to attack, or manages to make more of his poison, then many will die before I have another vial of antidote ready."

My stomach tightened. "Is there nothing else you can make to keep people alive until more of the antidote can be made?"

Her hands paused while wrapping me in a new bandage. "Are you expecting an attack we don't know about?"

I stiffened at her accusatory tone, though she wasn't wrong. On the other side of the room Aiden stilled as well, though whether from her tone or from the possibility of the truth of her statement I couldn't be sure.

"It's Ephraim. We can't predict his actions." I ignored the way nerves sent my heart racing.

Luckily, she didn't seem to notice my uncertainty as she returned to bandaging my freshly cleaned wounds. Her hands were sure and confident as she worked, much like my mother's used to be when patching up my siblings' many injuries.

The door burst open as soon as she tied off the bandages.

Fen stormed through the door, sparing Aiden a scowl before catching sight of me sitting up in bed. Luckily, Ridha had just let my shirt fall to cover me when she heard the door burst open.

Fen clapped her hands together, a smile spreading across her face. "I knew you'd be all right."

Seraphine and Killian were quick on her heels as they joined us in the room, each looking at me with smiling, relieved faces.

Ridha quickly packed up her concoctions while Fen took her place at my side. There were tears lining her eyes as she took my face gently in her hands.

"Don't you scare me like that again." Her voice was firm though her expression remained gentle.

The resemblance to my mother's fierce protectiveness over my family brought tears to my eyes. I nodded as she hugged me carefully.

"How are you feeling?" Seraphine asked, standing near the foot of the bed.

I sighed, pulling away from Fen. "I'm fine. Ridha said my wounds are healing well." I looked to the witch, but she was already fleeing through the door.

Killian sat at my feet, tangled curls bouncing with the movement. "I'd say so. You finally no longer look like a corpse."

Seraphine smacked the back of his head. "Don't call her a corpse, you fool."

"I didn't. I only said she *used* to look like one," he whined, rubbing the spot on his head.

I smiled. "I did look pretty bad, didn't I?"

The three of them stared at me, each wearing mixed expressions of surprise and concern.

Aiden sighed. "The three of you, out. Esme still needs her rest."

Fen scowled at him. "Careful, boy. I was there when you were born. Just because you wear a crown does not mean you can boss me around."

Killian ducked his chin to hide a grin. Sensing the young immortal's amusement, Aiden sent him a firm scowl.

"I'm all right. Really," I swore to the group.

"But you still need your rest," Aiden repeated, looking at the other three. "You're not fully healed yet."

Fen waved away his concern. "What she needs is a good meal. Come, Killian. You'll help me carry the tray."

The young immortal groaned, slowly rising to his feet. Killian waved over his shoulder before disappearing into the hall after Fen.

Seraphine sighed, taking Killian's place at my feet. "What do you remember?"

I glanced at Aiden, careful of his watchful eye. "It's all a little fuzzy."

Seraphine opened her mouth to continue, but Ridha returned.

"Take this three times a day," she said, setting several small vials of liquid on the table by the bed. "Preferably with a meal. It'll help speed your healing and prevent infection."

"And the poison?" Aiden asked. He'd moved to stand on my other side.

Ridha nodded. "I've already begun the process of creating more of the antidote, but I believe I've gotten as much of the poison out as I can for now. Whatever remains shouldn't be too bad other than some discomfort. I've contained it to the wound itself so it shouldn't spread for now."

"And?" Aiden asked, quickly returning to the serious, cold prince.

"And," she began slowly, "if there is more poison in her system than I believe there to be, then we'll know. Immediately." She turned to me, effectively dismissing the others in the room. "If you feel any burning or pain in Ephraim's wound that isn't related to the fact there was a knife stuck between your ribs, then send word to me straight away."

"If there's no antidote, then what can you even do for her if the poison spreads?" Seraphine asked.

Ridha scowled at the warrior. "My very best to keep her alive."

Seraphine seemed reluctant to accept her words as she turned back to me. The witch glanced once more in my direction, looking as though she might speak again, but thought better of it. She left without another word.

Killian and Fen returned as soon as the witch left. The former carried a large tray overflowing with various foods while Fen carried a fresh pitcher of water.

"Lurik couldn't decide what you might want to eat," he said, placing the tray on my lap.

Aiden moved to take the tray. "She's been asleep for three days. If she eats all of that she'll get sick."

I waved away his concern. "It's fine," I said, smiling at Killian. His grin grew as he sat beside me.

"Very well," Aiden relented with a sigh. His lips brushed along my brow as he tucked a loose curl behind my ear, startling me. "Just promise me you'll rest a while longer. There's no need for you to push yourself so hard just yet."

My cheeks flushed brilliantly as I nodded, unable to find my voice.

"Killian." The single word was a command from Aiden.

The immortal in question jumped to his feet, immediately following after him.

"Seraphine, I'm trusting you with her life. Do not let any harm come to her," Aiden said. His gaze caught mine as soon as the words left his mouth, stealing whatever breath remained in my lungs.

My cheeks heated further under his stare, making Seraphine smile. "She's safe with me," she vowed.

Aiden nodded, not dropping my gaze until he turned from the room, Killian going with him.

Seraphine smiled. "Don't think we won't all be incredibly protective of you now," she warned.

"I'm really okay."

"Now you might be," she said, gesturing to me as I picked at the warm biscuit covered in strawberry jam. "But three days ago you were practically dead. We had to burn your mattress because it was soaked through with so much blood."

I glanced around Aiden's room, now understanding why I'd been placed in here. "I remember." My voice was quiet as I reluctantly recalled the memory of seeing my body bleeding out.

Something flashed across her face before she carefully schooled her features. "But nothing from the attack?"

My mind whirled with Ephraim's words and Viema's determination to take the essence from me. "Just that they were desperate to get the essence from me."

Fen handed me a glass of water. "That's enough of that talk. Eat your breakfast. You need your strength."

I smiled at her appreciatively. The last thing I wanted to do was recall everything that occurred between Ephraim and me. Those secrets needed to be shared with Aiden first.

Fen handed me a vial of Ridha's medicine as soon as I finished the last of the biscuit. Like the previous one, this concoction was revolting, but it somehow carried a sweeter flavor.

Seraphine smiled at my sour look. "Just be glad she bothered to try and make it taste better. Usually, she hands off the medicine as-is. I've seen men turn green from the poor taste."

"Don't exaggerate, Sera," Fen scolded lightly. "It's not so bad."

"Clearly Ridha goes easy on you then. She probably gives you only the very best." Seraphine's smile returned as she glanced at Fen.

I felt myself mirror her smile as Fen rolled her eyes. "Has there truly been no word from Ephraim, or was Aiden just trying to spare me?"

The two women shared a private look. I took another small bite of food while they silently debated what to tell me. My stomach was already full, but Lurik's food smelled too good to let it go to waste.

"There are rumors that he has someone on the inside," Seraphine said slowly.

"A traitor." Fen's voice was crisp and cold.

I swallowed around the lump in my throat. "Do you know who?"

Fen shook her head, silver-streaked hair falling over her shoulder as she settled into Aiden's chair. "No. But whoever it is, they were able to break into Ridha's workshop without getting caught and slipped past the guards unnoticed."

"Aiden is furious about it," Seraphine added. "He ordered everyone to be questioned by Tarsa and Hakan until we find the person responsible."

My heart fluttered nervously. "No luck?"

Seraphine sighed. "No. None yet. And the guards patrolling the realm with Tarsa haven't found an entry point yet. We've no way of knowing how they were able to sneak past all of our defenses."

"But that's not for you to worry about," Fen added hastily. "You just need to focus on getting better. Court politics are no concern of yours right now."

"Aren't they though?" I questioned. Guilt at my secrecy rattled my bones. "Ephraim is planning something. And I think we can all agree that whatever he has up his sleeve won't end well for any of us. Especially without the antidote."

"Ridha is working on that," Seraphine said reassuringly.

"And how long will that take? Ephraim could attack any day. And if he does, we could all die without that antidote. We'll definitely die if we don't figure out where he's hiding or what he's planning."

"Well, Princess, how do you suggest we go about finding that out?" Fen asked. There was a level of respect and approval in her voice I hadn't heard before.

I shrugged, ignoring the pulling sensation of the movement against my wounds. "I don't know. There must be a way to find at least one of Ephraim's angels. Viema has been lingering around here for weeks. There must be others we can interrogate."

"Viema?" Fen asked, voice filled with mild horror.

I nodded, cheeks reddening. "I've seen her a few times. She was with Ephraim when they tried to take the essence."

Seraphine stared into the hearth's flames, thoughtful. "Ephraim wouldn't leave just anyone behind. If anyone remains, they must know at least a fraction of Ephraim's plan."

I sighed, relaxing into the pillows. "My thoughts exactly."

Fen squeezed my hand. "Imagine how angry it would make Ofrin to have his realm saved by a mortal girl."

Seraphine smiled, settling more onto the foot of the bed. "Oh, he'd be furious." I shook my head, heart fluttering with nerves as Ofrin's insistence at my greed for his power returned. "Rest assured, Esme. Aiden has everyone working tirelessly to figure out Ephraim's plan. He won't rest until you're safe. None of us will."

"It's not me I'm worried about," I admitted under my breath.

Her hand squeezed mine gently. "Mousa and Cordelia are under heavy watch. Our most trusted warriors were sent to look out for them. Even Elias."

I nodded, recalling hearing the command while in my half-dead state. "What do we do until then?"

Fen shrugged, leaning back into the chair and placing her feet on the edge of the bed. "We wait for you to heal. Then we prepare for war."

THIRTY-FIVE

RIDHA'S MEDICINE WORKED WONDERS. In only two days the wounds had sealed enough that I was finally allowed to leave my room. I still wasn't well enough to train with Tarsa, but I wasn't entirely upset about that.

My new minions still shadowed me through the castle—I could hear them now standing outside my study door—since Aiden had been unsuccessful in finding a way to undo the bindings I created between our souls. I'd spent most of the day searching through the books I'd collected in my study, but to no avail.

A knock sounded at my door.

"Come in," I called, slamming a book closed in my lap. My study still lacked furniture, so I'd taken to sitting on the floor beneath the glowing map to read.

Daemon's head poked into the room. "Hiding out, Princess?"

His grin widened at my scowl. "No. Not exactly."

The demon stepped into the room, pointedly looking around the mostly empty space. "I like what you've done with the place."

"I've been a little busy, Daemon."

He brushed a finger along an empty shelf, checking for dust. "Yes, I recall. We've questioned every guard in Aiden's employ and have not found any more of Ephraim's angels. There has also been no word of Ephraim's whereabouts."

I sighed, glaring at the books as if they would spill their secrets to me. "He wants the essence. That much we know."

"Yes, and we are keeping you under safeguard so he can't get to you."

I waved away his concern. "But what will he do to get it? He must know Aiden won't let me wander around alone. Especially not now."

"And he knows the way Aiden thinks, so there's little we can do that might surprise him." The sour tone of his voice echoed the dreaded feeling I carried as well. We both remembered how close Aiden and Ephraim had been earlier in Aiden's lifetime.

But only I knew just how close they truly were.

The door to my study opened again. Hakan backed into the room, a very large chair in his arms.

"What is this?" I asked, lurching out of their path.

Killian appeared behind Hakan, carrying a matching chair. "You need furniture," he said cheerily.

I glanced between the two chairs, each looking brand new with the matching violet fabrics and cushions lining them.

"There's more." Killian's grin stretched from ear to ear as he disappeared from the room.

Hakan sighed, setting his chair near the large window. "Just be glad this is all they decided to bring you for now."

My brows furrowed. "What else is there?"

Killian backed into the room, quickly followed by Aiden. There was a slender cedar table between them. When they set it down, the three of them turned to me, expressions hopeful for approval.

I chuckled. "Not a fan of my lack of décor?"

A soft smile played with the corners of Aiden's mouth. "You're worse than me."

"Now that is an insult," I said, letting my smile grow.

Daemon collapsed into one of the chairs. "Not bad. Could use a pillow or two though."

Hakan scowled at the demon. "Then go get one."

"No," Daemon sighed, leaning back until the sun warmed his face and his horns showed through his dark hair. "I think I'll take a nice nap instead."

I rolled my eyes. "I didn't realize the chairs were brought here for your use."

He smiled lazily, keeping his eyes closed. "There are two chairs, and only one of you. I claim this one."

I shook my head, tempted to have the minions throw him out just to prove a point.

"How are you?" Aiden asked, stepping closer so the others could pretend to ignore us.

"I'm fine." He'd asked me nearly every hour since I'd woken up two days ago. It seemed Ridha was still worried the lingering poison in my veins might begin to spread, and that had put everyone on high alert as they waited for me to collapse.

I assured everyone I felt fine and could not feel the poison at all. But it seemed no one was ready to believe me just yet.

He nodded, a small grin spreading across his face. "Good."

I flushed under his warm gaze. Since my bed still hadn't been replaced, I'd been sleeping in Aiden's room. It felt more intimate than I expected, even though he'd been careful to be absent every night. I never asked where he slept.

Aiden nodded toward the book I held. "What are you reading today?"

"*Histories of the Crown: An Anthology of Mythology Within the Court for the Dead*. I hoped it might tell me more about the binding I made with those two," I said, nodding toward the doorway where the minions waited outside. "But so far, it's been little help. I started reading the histories of the war, hoping it could help answer questions about Ephraim's next moves. But that hasn't been much help either. The drawings of swords and daggers are at least nice to look at though."

Aiden stared at the growing pile of books in the corner. Jester, his Keeper of Books, had been kindly offering me every book in his library to help answer all the questions I had. But so far, I was coming up blank. The uncertainty was making me lose my mind.

"Do you think I could steal you away from your books for a while?" Aiden asked softly.

I glanced at the map over my shoulder, pleased to see once again that my siblings were both safe, even though they were still apart in the desert.

"I think that would be nice," I said. When he offered his hand to me, I stared at it for a beat before placing my hand in his.

Aiden's smile was warm as he led me from the room. The minions attempted to follow, but I ordered them to remain in the castle. I'd hoped we would develop some boundaries with them, but they remained ever-attentive servants.

Stopping only to slip cloaks over our shoulders, Aiden led me outside and into the garden. Snow had fallen since my attack and now it covered the ground in a heavy powder. The sun was painfully bright as it reflected off the white ground.

The air was so cold it burned my cheeks as I followed Aiden along the path in the garden.

"I've thought about what you said," he started slowly, hesitant, "about that corner of the garden." I nodded as he gestured toward the overgrown path we turned down.

"Hakan didn't change it while I slept, did he?" I asked, growing nervous.

Aiden smiled, shaking his head. The light did wonderful things to the red tones in his hair as we walked through the snow. "No. But we did make a slight addition."

"I'm afraid to ask."

He laughed at my dry tone. "You mentioned it reminded you of your family, that it gave you a sense of home. As much as an overgrown corner of a garden can, at least."

"I did," I said, my trepidation growing.

Aiden pulled me to a stop just at the edge of the path. The tree's branches hung low, weighed down by snow, but I could still see through them to the beauty of the untamed garden beyond.

Water droplets fell from slowly melting icicles and snow decorated every remaining plant in a blanket of white. Everywhere I looked, it glistened in the light...even the stone bench.

I turned to Aiden, a question on my face.

His expression was soft, almost shy. "I wanted to give that to you. A place to honor your family, or feel like you could visit them as one might visit a grave in your realm."

I turned back to the bench. A storm of emotions erupted through me as I stared at the addition to the garden. Its dark stone features contrasted brilliantly against the white snow. It was beautiful.

Aiden hung back while I stepped closer. I ran a trembling hand over the bench, recognizing it as the same one that I'd seen in the room of Aiden's mother's things. The stone was freezing beneath my touch, cold enough to burn. It was a simple design, only large enough to fit two people side by side. The armrests were thin, decorated to look like vines while the ends of them were styled like roses wide with bloom, hanging like bells.

Tears began to burn my eyes as I caught sight of the back of the bench. Vines and thorns matching the marriage mark on my hand embellished the stone. And beside each rose was a name.

Adine. Leander. Emira. Alfie. Amara. Even Aunt Kiva, Uncle Malik and Nadira and Jac.

The name of every member of my family that had died to get me here was carved into the bench.

"I wanted to honor their memory," Aiden said from behind me. He hadn't moved from the path in the garden. "I wanted to give you a place to remember them, to feel loved by them."

"Are their souls truly gone?" My voice was thick with tears I didn't shed.

"No." His certainty was unwavering. "But they are not in a place you can visit. Any of us who serve Death cannot visit the souls in the Crossroads. It can have a dangerous effect on the souls we visit; it wouldn't be safe for them."

I nearly laughed, but it would've been a cold sound. I didn't want to taint this peaceful corner with my frustration. "Even with their deaths I am a danger to them. How poetic."

Aiden's body heat enveloped me as he joined me by the bench. He didn't speak. He didn't need to. I felt comfort from his presence alone as I battled with my emotions.

A tear trickled down my cheek as I ran my hand over the bench. The names stood out against the dark stone as the ice coating them remained in shadow, unable to melt.

Something burned through my chest as I looked out over the garden, and I knew then what I was feeling. I'd spent so long avoiding putting a name to it that I nearly forgot what it felt like.

Love.

The wildness of this corner of the garden felt so much like home that I could only feel peace in it. The wind across my face was the gentle stroke of my mother's hand. The branches groaning beneath the weight of snow were my father's whispered words of wisdom. Even in the chaos of the tangled, overgrown foliage I could see my siblings. Yet it was what I felt for the man at my side that made it truly welcoming.

I'd been so distracted by my anger for Aiden and guilt for still loving him that I didn't bother to look beyond my own problems and see what he continued to show me.

He loved me.

"I tried to protect them," he said softly, voice hesitant. "When they offered their bargain to my father, I did everything I could to keep them alive for you."

I kept my gaze focused on the bench. "I know."

"Your parents told Mousa and Cordelia before the bargain was struck and they'd no longer be able to speak of the deal," Aiden explained slowly. "Once accepted, no one is able to of speak or physically interfere with Death's bargains in any way. But I did my best to stop King Elroy."

"Ofrin mentioned something about that."

Aiden fisted his hands at his sides. "I meant what I said before, about each of our powers growing stronger with the death of every member of your family. I could not physically interfere on your family's behalf, or your behalf, but I fought against the bargain with every ounce of my soul.

"Watching him break you like that–" Aiden's voice cut off as he closed his eyes, "–that is not something I will ever forget. With every life he took, I feared you would never recover. It shattered something in me to see you in such pain."

I studied his expression with new clarity. "It pained me to see you in your true form as well."

"I know," he said, stiffening at my cold tone. "To this day I believe you should hate me for what was done, what you were forced to endure. By the time Amara died, enough of my power had returned that I was able to break into Elroy's mind, stopping him from killing Mousa and Cordelia."

"Why?" I asked, genuinely curious.

Aiden looked at me, aghast. "Because I *could* stop him. I couldn't before. But when his guard stepped behind your brother, I knew I could save them. I had to.

"Even as they ran from the room, I feared their lives wouldn't be enough for you to recover from the loss," Aiden continued. "You were so broken, so full of rage and anguish. Until you weren't. I watched you pack all your emotions away until you were no more than a shell, ready to throw yourself onto a sword for your family."

"Why didn't you tell me this earlier?" I asked.

"Part of me wanted you to keep hating me," he admitted. "Seeing you hate me so much was almost a relief after watching the shell you'd become. Even if you felt pain and anger, it was better than losing you to the hurt and nothingness."

"I don't know how I should be feeling." My hand tightened along the bench until my knuckles turned white. "I survived; Mousa and Cordelia survived. I know it wasn't your doing, but it still hurts."

"Being able to survive something doesn't make it okay, Esme." His voice had grown gentle as he studied me. "It will take time for your heart to heal."

My hand passed over the list of names again, the stone icy on the tips of my fingers.

"It was my birthday," I whispered. Aiden remained silent, watching me closely. "They were killed on my birthday."

He didn't speak again, holding his tongue as I thought through everything I'd learned in the past few weeks about my family's demise. There was still so much I wanted to know, and so much I needed to tell him.

I thought over his declaration. Everything he said filled in the gaps Ofrin's reveal had left empty. I feared the pain of their secrecy and deaths would always remain. But far beneath the depths of my pain remained a spark of love I had to let ignite.

When I finally turned to him, I wasn't surprised to see the look on his face. Because the expression Aiden wore now.... I had no words for it. Only that I knew he loved me.

I watched emotions flash through his gaze as we stood there, staring at each other. With hesitant movements, he took my face in his hands, his touch gentle. "I am not deserving of you," he whispered, leaning close so our noses nearly touched. "But I will do anything it takes to earn the honor of your affection."

My heart began to pound in my chest as we drew closer. It would only take the slightest movement for our lips to touch now. The essence awoke in my chest, humming alongside the flutters of my heart.

I sighed, pulling away. "Aiden, there's still something I need to tell you."

Someone cleared their throat nearby. I leapt back, startled.

Aiden's lips twitched toward a smile before he turned to face the intruder.

"I apologize," Hakan said, not the slightest bit embarrassed at the position we were in. "There's a situation that needs your urgent attention."

Aiden sighed, all evidence of the almost kiss slipping away as he returned to his role as the prince.

I erased my disappointment as he turned to me. There was a look in his eye I didn't understand as he took my hand in his.

"Would you like to come with me?" Aiden asked.

Surprise flashed through me before tentative excitement replaced it. "Can I?"

"Of course," Aiden said. "You are the Princess of Death after all. You have every right to protect the realm as I do."

I offered him a grin, hesitant of this change between us. Aiden returned it without hesitation before the two of us trailed after Hakan.

THIRTY-SIX

HAKAN LED US THROUGH the castle. The bare walls echoed ominously with the sound of our steps as we neared the winding stairwell.

Hushed, agitated voices could be heard arguing within Aiden's study as we approached, but their words were too soft for me to clearly discern. Hakan pushed open the door for us while my two soul-bound demons stood on either side, guarding the stairwell.

The room's inhabitants stopped speaking abruptly. Seraphine and Killian stood over the desk, frowning. I felt Tarsa's gaze narrow on me a moment before I spotted her in the corner, watching me closely.

Aiden and I paused in the doorway, glancing around the room as all eyes landed on us. Even Daemon looked put off by something.

"What?" I asked when no one spoke.

Tarsa's ever-present scowl grew angrier as she watched me. Her mouth was pressed into a thin line so tight I wasn't sure how her jaw hadn't snapped.

Hakan gestured to Tarsa, and the two left without a word, neither sparing me more than a nod in passing.

As soon as the door closed behind them, I turned to Aiden. "What's going on?"

No one spoke, they just continued to watch me warily. Aiden moved to his desk, glancing down at the map laid out before the others.

"What is this?" he asked.

Killian pointed to a place on the map I couldn't see. "This is where our last spy went missing."

Aiden ran a hand through his hair. "Another."

"That's not all," Seraphine said cautiously. I moved to Aiden's side, eager to study the map they spoke of. "Some of our guards have been hearing whispers in the village."

"Most are farther north, near your father's castle, but there are some that have begun to spread here as well," Killian added.

Again, everyone glanced at me uncertainly. "Okay? What does that mean?" I asked.

"It means," Aiden said, turning so I could see his expression clearly, "that everyone is growing nervous about your strength now. Not just my father."

I shook my head, not following.

Aiden took my hands in his, staring down at the matching marks decorating the backs of our left hands. Something akin to sorrow played out on his face a moment before he cleared his expression. He so frequently hid behind a mask.

"Princess," he began in a forced, light-hearted tone, "the more people that learn of the power you wield, the more people will begin to wish you harm."

A flicker of dread churned my stomach. "Would you rather I give up the essence?"

He shook his head. "No. It is as much a part of you as anything else."

"Then I don't understand."

"Jadan has brought word that Ofrin has begun to grow more desperate in his quest to rid himself of you," Daemon said as if that would explain everything.

"I thought he wanted me under his control. That he wanted the power I wield. Wasn't that the entire point of my family siphoning souls for him for generations?"

Aiden squeezed my hands gently, calming me. "Yes, but you are my wife now. You are the Princess of the Soul Realm. Your power is tied to mine as much as our souls are entwined. As you grow stronger, so do I. In name at least."

"So your father is concerned not only about my growing power, but that our combined strength could topple his throne?"

He nodded. "So it seems."

"And we were brought here to tell me to, what? Hide in my room until your father forgets I exist or until Ephraim attacks and kills us all?"

"Neither. That would be entirely against your nature." A knowing smile turned up the corners of his mouth.

"But you will ask me to tread with caution," I said, voicing what I knew he'd say next.

His eyes were grave. "My father's spies still linger. If they see you openly using your power, he will be sure to hear of it."

"And you have spies going missing?" I asked, nodding to the map.

"Yes," he said, turning back to the table.

I frowned, studying the burn marks in the map. "What do those points mean?"

"Those were the spies," Killian said. He pointed to a burn mark located deep in the western forest. "Like your map, their souls glow here. Like a small flame. But every spy we've sent out looking for Ephraim has been snuffed out. Their souls just evaporate somehow. There's no way to track them. All that's left of them is a burn mark on the map right where they went missing."

I ran a hand along one of the marks. The canvas beneath my fingers felt rough and brittle. Like someone truly had held a small flame to the pages.

"There looks to be nearly thirty marks." My pulse jumped in my veins.

Aiden's arm brushed mine as he pulled the map closer. "We can't figure out what is happening to them. We haven't been able to recover any of their bodies, and there has been no sign of them beyond these marks."

"Our best guess at this point is that Ephraim is somehow managing to destroy their entire existence." Seraphine's dark eyes were filled with sorrow.

"Some of the rumors are saying it's Esme," Daemon chimed in.

Aiden stared at me a moment more before turning to him. "What do you mean?"

"Some people think she's responsible for the missing demons," he said, shrugging. "She is the Soul Collector after all."

"Many still fear her power," Killian added somewhat reluctantly. He sent me an apologetic look before continuing. "After the news of your marriage, and then what she did with those loose souls, some have grown wary of her being here."

"Not to mention she is the only mortal in existence to have bound souls to her as if she were the God of Death herself," Seraphine said. Her eyes darted to the doorway where my two soul-bound waited in the stairwell.

I sighed, leaning into Aiden without thought. "Have you learned how to break the bond I created between Alvize and Delvin?"

Aiden's arms wrapped around my shoulders, tucking me against his side. The gesture was so comfortable, like we'd done it a million times, and yet it was wholly new.

"Not yet. But I will," he vowed.

I nodded, letting myself sink deeper into the comforting warmth he provided. Any hesitation I felt at our changing relationship vanished as I stood there. The feelings I'd long fought against and abhorred now felt utterly right.

"In the meantime, please try to refrain from binding any more souls to yours." There was a hint of laughter in the serious tone of his voice that made me pull away to look at his face.

The teasing gleam in his eye made me smile. "I'll do my best."

I felt his thumb trace my lower lip. "And please do not get stabbed again. My heart couldn't take it."

"Let's hope Ephraim doesn't show up any time soon then," I said breathlessly. His thumb continued tracing my lower lip as I spoke. I could feel my cheeks burning as I remained the sole focus of his attention.

Aiden sighed. "Why is it the one time I bring a wife home, everyone tries to kill her?"

Daemon whispered something to Killian which made the young immortal chuckle softly.

I ignored their teasing whispers. "Your father has only proven to be a vague and distant threat, while Ephraim could attack any moment. I know who I would bet on being the real danger to us."

"They're both a threat, Esme," he cautioned. "Do not think my father is safe simply because he doesn't outright attack. He is more skilled in political battles than Ephraim is. I don't doubt he already has plans in motion to harm you."

I shrugged, hoping to erase some of the worry I could see brewing in his eyes. "Then we'll deal with it."

My word choice brought him up short. I could almost swear I felt his heart stutter beneath my hand as he stared down at me. His eyes searched my face for confirmation of my words.

I only smiled, thrilled that I'd surprised him for once.

Aiden shook his head, an answering smile spreading across his face. "You are truly a force to be reckoned with, Princess. I pray for the fool that chooses to stand against you."

My smile slowly slipped from my face as the still healing wounds in my chest burned with the memory. Could it really have only been a couple of days since I lay on my deathbed?

Sensing the change in my thoughts, Aiden's smile fell. A muscle feathered in his cheek as those same memories resurfaced in his mind. "Is there nothing that you remember? Nothing that could help us find him before he tries to hurt you again?"

My mind raced through every conversation I'd had with the angel. And yet the only piece of information I could think of that held any importance was that of their shared mother; that was the real reason behind Ephraim's need for revenge. He blamed Ofrin, and Aiden, for the death of his mother and the strain it put on the angels.

I mulled over the thought of telling Aiden the truth, here and now. If that cramped little room full of his mother's few remaining things was any indication, I knew he'd want to know the truth about her.

Coming to a decision, I sighed, pulling away if only to spare myself the blow this would cause him. Seraphine watched me closely, sensing the change in my emotions.

"Aiden, there's something you should know," I started slowly. My heart felt as if it were trying to claw its way out of my throat. "It's about Ephraim."

"What is it?" His eyes tracked over my face as if desperate to understand the thoughts whirling in my mind.

"I've been—"

The words died on my tongue as the door burst open. I jumped, pulling away from Aiden's grip as Hakan returned.

"Apologies, but there's been an attack." His voice was void of emotion. Ever the diligent warrior.

"Where?" Aiden asked as I worked to slow my nervous heart. His hand found mine of its own accord, squeezing once in comfort.

"The village," Hakan said, eyes tracking the movement. "It was Ephraim."

"How do you know?" I asked, heart racing for an entirely different reason now.

Hakan's dark eyes met mine and there was a challenge in them I hadn't expected. "Because he's left a message. For the Princess of Death."

THIRTY-SEVEN

THE VILLAGE WAS IN an uproar. Everywhere I looked people were running in a frenzy. Soot-stained cheeks were streaked with tears and fear permeated the air. Parents carried screaming children, adolescents aided the elderly, and bodies littered the ground every few feet. The horror of the scene sent my stomach spiraling.

Where buildings once stood, only smoking piles of rubble remained. Everything in sight was charred as if scorched by unnatural means. There was hardly a building still standing upright.

"Maybe you should return to the castle." There was a hint of icy menace in Aiden's tone upon seeing the destruction of his village.

I glanced around at the mayhem. "They need help, Aiden."

A muscle feathered in his cheek. "Have the attackers been caught?" He directed his question to Hakan and Jadan.

Jadan surveyed the chaos. "No. But they couldn't have gotten far. They might still be in the area."

"What makes you say that?" Seraphine asked, standing at my shoulder.

"Because of that." Jadan nodded toward the side of one of the last standing buildings.

I kept to Aiden's side, my unease growing as the groans of the injured echoed through the village.

Whispers followed us as we moved down the street, word of our presence now spreading among the survivors. Heads turned toward us; some people scowled, while some wept in relief. Most just looked at me with uncertainty as we moved through the remains of their village.

Jadan led us through the rubble. The stucco sides of the building we aimed for were blackened from the dispersed flames, but the building itself remained standing.

Aiden took my hand, helping me over fallen debris as we moved down the alley that once separated two tall buildings. I hadn't realized my hands were shaking until he gave them a gentle squeeze.

Like his expression, Jadan's voice lacked emotion. "This was left for her."

Seraphine stiffened beside me as she read the large words painted on the only untouched side of the building. The white wall dripped with the blood painted across it.

I told you. Anything.

My knees began to shake as I stared up at those four words. Ephraim's warning, just for me.

"What makes you think this is for Esme?" Killian asked, turning so his eyes and loaded bow were focused on the forest at our backs.

"Because that's not all that was left." Hakan's voice was flat.

He turned as if to grasp something at his side, but Tarsa appeared from the shadows like a wraith. She placed something small and folded into his palm. The immortal scowled at me before turning and disappearing into the mess of the village.

Hakan handed Aiden the folded cloth. I strained my neck to see what it contained, but Aiden was careful to keep it just out of sight.

"What is it?" I asked, growing anxious as Aiden's muscles went taut.

His face had gone stony. "The desert?"

Jadan nodded, white hair brushing his forehead. His gaze darted in my direction. "Both safe and guarded."

"What is?" I asked.

"Have you confirmed this since the attack?" Aiden asked.

Jadan remained expressionless. "Daemon is headed there now."

Aiden sighed, the gesture relaxing some of the tension in his shoulders. "Make sure he gets this." He handed the folded cloth to the demon. "It needs to get to her."

Jadan sketched a shallow bow, turning on his heel without a word.

"What was on the cloth?" I asked once he was gone.

When Aiden turned to me, the unease written across his face made the essence awaken, responding to my nerves.

"It was a threat to your siblings." His eyes darted across my face, scrutinizing my emotions.

I scowled, letting my anger hide my panic. "Are they okay?"

Seraphine's hand came down on my shoulder with a comforting squeeze. "They are under heavy guard and may not even know of the threat. They're as safe as they can be."

I nodded, not really hearing her as the essence hummed in my chest erratically. I could feel it open the tethers to my soul-bound. Their response to being called upon echoed down the tether and into my own soul.

"How many lost?" Aiden asked Hakan.

The warrior shrugged, glancing down the alley to the bloodied streets beyond. "They're still counting. Witnesses say the fire started first, then the angels came."

"The angels attacked after setting the fire?" I asked. I glanced toward the wounded lying in the streets. My heart began to pound against my ribs as I counted. If any of them had the smallest drop of Ephraim's poison in their veins, there would be no antidote to save them.

"There were approximately forty of them," Hakan clarified.

Aiden stiffened. "That many?"

"That's almost a small army." Killian's voice was soft with horror.

I looked around our small group, growing more anxious with every breath. "Did they get away?"

"They did." Hakan's anger showed in his jaw.

"Ridha is on her way," Tarsa said, reappearing. "Fen is safe in her cottage and out of harm's way," she added for Seraphine's benefit.

My friend relaxed a little. I leaned into her, allowing myself to find relief knowing Fen was not among the wounded. Or worse, among the dead.

Killian's eyes continued to dart around the surrounding trees. "The forest needs to be searched."

"I have guards waiting to begin their search on your order. Some villagers have already dispersed into the trees to begin looking," Hakan said, turning to lead us back toward the market square. "If they're still out there, we'll find them."

A thought occurred to me. "I can look for them." If my brief and horrid bargain with Ephraim had taught me anything it was that the reach of my power was far stronger than I first believed.

Aiden gave me a dry look. "I will not send you into the forest alone to look for those who want you dead."

I pulled at my sleeves. "I don't mean to run out into the forest. I can use the essence to search for them."

"How so?" Tarsa asked, skeptical of my offer.

"Angels don't have souls," I said, struggling to keep up with their quick steps over the fallen debris. Aiden, sensing my struggle, offered me his hand again as I stepped over a particularly large pile of rubble. "I can use the essence to find something without a soul. It's almost easier to feel than a mortal with a soul because it's just a void. I just have to look for something that should have a soul attached to it."

"That sounds dangerous," Seraphine said, unconvinced.

"Will the God of Death be able to feel you using the essence like that?" Killian asked, opting to walk a few paces behind us should something appear from the forest.

"I'm sure he could," Aiden said, thoughtful. There was a considering look in his eye as we came to a stop at the edge of the market. But I could also see the concern for me in his face as he pondered my offer.

"I won't have to go into the forest," I said, directing my argument for only Aiden. "You can leave me with Fen at her cottage, and I'll use the essence there. When I find them, you'll know where to send the guards."

I tried to keep the nervousness off my face as Aiden studied me with unnerving clarity. The whispers of our presence carried through the fallen village, but neither of us paid them any mind as I waited for his answer.

"A decision needs to be made," Tarsa said, sounding bored. "We're drawing a crowd."

Aiden and I broke our stare to glance around us. Those that were able to move had begun to linger. The injured were laid out nearby while being tended to, but they too watched us closely.

"We can't risk it," Aiden finally said, somewhat reluctantly. "We need to be careful with how much you're using the essence. Hakan and his men will find them."

Hakan nodded his consent, disappearing into the crowd to find his guards. As his departure formed a path through the crowd, I caught a glimpse of more of the injured nearby.

"Are there no more healers?" I asked, unable to pull my eyes away from the two people moving frantically through the wounded.

One was a boy about my age. The other I guessed was his mother as she seemed to have no problem ordering him about, and they each wore matching scowls.

"Ridha is the only one we have." Sadness tightened Seraphine's voice. She twisted her red braids atop her head and out of the way like she was readying for battle.

"We could send word to your father," Hakan offered, voice hushed. "He would surely send a few more skilled healers to aid our people."

Aiden loosed a frustrated breath, scowling. "He wouldn't take the risk. In his mind, this could just be a ploy on Esme's part to weaken his defenses. If he sends his healers to us, then they won't be there when he needs them."

"So we're alone in this," I said, the essence humming in response to my anger.

Displeasure tightened the corners of his mouth. "We are."

"Well, if I can't use the essence to search for the angels, I can at least help the wounded." I began to roll up my sleeves as more injured townsfolk were carried to the far corner of the market.

"What do you know of tending wounds?" Tarsa asked. I couldn't be sure, but it almost sounded as if she was surprised I'd offered. Like maybe she expected me to turn and run to the safety of the castle at the first sight of bloodshed.

I scowled. "You learn a lot about patching up wounds when you grow up in a family who throws knives and flaming arrows for a living."

An emotion I never expected from Tarsa flashed across her face, so brief I was almost certain I imagined it. Respect.

"Sera, Killian, stay with her," Aiden ordered. His hand brushed my cheek. "Stay safe."

I offered a half-hearted smile, conscious of the many faces watching us. "You too."

Seraphine and Killian stayed close as I strode through the market. Aiden spoke to the villagers lingering nearby, but I didn't focus on the words of comfort he offered.

The ground crunched beneath my boots. The white snow was now stained black with soot and spattered red with blood. Debris contrasted sharply with the bits of untouched snow covering the ground.

"It's a wonder anything is standing," Killian noted quietly.

"They only attacked the market," Seraphine whispered back. "The houses are untouched and many of the shops on the outer edge of the village are fine."

"Why just the market?" I asked.

People began to move out of our way as we strode down the street. Those who were able moved aside large pieces of debris or helped move the injured to the makeshift hospital near the edge of the market.

Killian shrugged. "Most people mill about in the market every day. It would've offered the most casualties."

"But why target them at all?" Seraphine questioned. "What Ephraim wants is Esme, the essence. There's no need for him to attack these people."

I couldn't say the words aloud. Wouldn't dare speak the truth with so many ears listening nearby. We no longer had an antidote to his poison. One prick would kill anyone with ties to Death even if they weren't a demon.

"Is there something in this market that he would want to destroy?" I asked. The woman seemingly in charge of overseeing the wounded stood as we neared. She wore a blank expression, like she'd seen enough mangled bodies to bring nightmares and was forcing herself to ignore the horror around her.

"No," Killian said, gazing around at the destruction. "We don't have anything here. Anything important is up north in the mountains with Ofrin."

Seraphine turned slowly, eyes widening with horror. "Everything except you."

The woman stopped in front of us, a tin pail filled with bloody water dangling from her hand. "Do you have more bandages?" Her voice was sharp, curt.

"Ridha is coming," Seraphine assured her.

The woman grimaced, turning away from her patients so they wouldn't see her face. "If she doesn't get here soon, there won't be anyone left to save."

I stared past her to the horror of the bloodshed. Men and women lay propped up against fallen stones or lay flat on their backs, moaning in pain. The boy aiding her hurried about, hands stained red with blood.

A man nearby jolted into consciousness. A cut above his brow bled freely down his cheek. He cried out, lashing at invisible attackers before Seraphine knelt beside him. She had his arms pinned down by the time I knelt beside her.

"It's okay," she said calmly. "You're safe."

I took the mostly clean bandage the woman held out to me, placing it gently against the man's brow.

The man lurched like I'd struck him. His eyes opened wider, a brilliant shade of hazel against the dark soot staining his skin. He gripped my wrist tightly, jerking away from my touch.

"It's okay." I forced calm into my voice. "I just need to clean your wound before I can patch it up. Ridha, the prince's witch, will be here with more medicine soon."

The man's eyes cleared, panic receding as he took in his surroundings. I watched accusation fill his eyes as he looked at me. "You're the princess."

I nodded, surprised by his hostility. "I am."

He shoved away from me, stumbling to his feet. Blood gushed from his open brow, coating his face and dripping onto his shirt. From his lack of coordination, I wondered if the injury was more serious than I thought.

"This is your doing," he spat. Seraphine and Killian shifted nearby. "They came for you and got us instead."

"You don't know what you speak of," Seraphine said, quick to come to my defense.

The man shook his head, fury lining every hard edge of his face. "You cursed us all when you came here."

I didn't stop him as he moved away. I could feel the eyes of the villagers watching me as I knelt beside the next victim. But I couldn't bring myself to acknowledge them.

Those with smaller cuts or bruises were sent home to wait for Ridha to make her rounds after she arrived. Those who couldn't move or bled too freely were left on the street, lined up and waiting for us to help them.

"He's right." I spun on my heel, gaze searching the crowd for any familiar faces.

Seraphine moved further away, kneeling beside a young girl with tear-stained cheeks. "You didn't do this, Esme."

Guilt and horror swallowed me whole as the pieces melded together. "We have to get everyone out of here."

"What? Why?" Killian went on alert from my sharp tone. His hold on his bow tightened, readying for a battle that had yet to come.

"Because you said the only thing important here is me," I said in a rush. "If that's true, if there really is nothing in this village that Ephraim could want, then he did this to lure me here."

Killian cursed colorfully. I frantically searched the crowd for any sign of Aiden, desperate to confirm with my own eyes that he remained unharmed.

"He's helping them clear away debris," Killian said, coming to my side. Seraphine remained crouched by a young girl who cradled a broken arm.

I stared across the suddenly vast space. The villagers moved briskly, carrying the burnt remains of their market square.

Aiden was nowhere in sight, but I could still feel him nearby thanks to the growing strength of the essence.

Something frigid and dark brushed against my awareness. A shiver whispered down my spine from the cold touch.

I scanned the forest around us, nervously searching for any sign of the source.

"What is it?" Killian asked, gaze following mine.

I sucked in a sharp breath, "They never left."

The wave of coldness brushed along my awareness again. Whatever warmth I felt beneath my cloak evaporated. I stood on shaking legs in the center of the village square as a light dusting of snow began to fall around us.

"I'll check the forest," Killian offered, stance still stiff and ready for a fight.

"No. Hakan said he has people in the forest. You need to stay with the wounded. They're too vulnerable like this." Far on the other end of the tether I could sense the demons bound to me.

A quick glance around at those filling the market told me no one else felt the strange sensation in the air.

Someone's scream pierced the air, shrill and brisk.

Chaos erupted before the scream fell silent, and the hair on my neck rose. Villagers raced through the remains of the market as panic spread like wildfire again.

Seraphine was at my side in an instant. "We should get you back to the castle."

Angels poured from the trees not a moment later. Swords already encrusted with blood slashed down onto the remaining villagers. Children screamed and ran, parents fell. The fresh snow on the ground ran red with blood.

An angel bent over the child Seraphine had been treating moments earlier. I watched him place a knife at the young girl's throat.

Fear had me pulling my knife before my mind could catch up. The essence opened, sensing the cold void within the angel.

The hilt of the knife was cool in my palm as I moved in their direction.

As soon as the angel prepared to deal the fatal blow, my knife flew through the air to find its home in his eye.

"Esme!" Seraphine's shout of warning came only a moment before something hard slammed into me, tackling me to the ground.

THIRTY-EIGHT

THE BREATH RUSHED FROM my lungs as I crashed to the cold ground. My freshly healed wounds throbbed painfully as I struggled beneath the angel.

"Be still," the angel's flat voice sent a shiver down my spine.

I grappled with him as he attempted to lodge his knife into my chest.

A bright head of flaming hair appeared behind him. Seraphine yanked the angel off of me a second later, using her immortal strength to launch him across the street.

"Are you okay?" She pulled me to my feet with ease, her gaze sweeping over me for injury.

I fought to keep the pain from my face. "I'm fine. Where's Aiden?"

Seraphine looked around the chaos. "He'll be fine. Hakan and Tarsa are still with him."

All around us, angels stormed onto the street. The remaining villagers were weak from injuries or stunned from the earlier attack. But there were many who were furious at having seen their village burned, and fought with fervor.

Every time an angel was cut down, though, they rose again. No matter how many wounds they received, they wouldn't die.

"We have to get you back to the castle, Princess." Seraphine's use of my formal title was a gentle reminder that I was supposed to follow my guards' suggestions.

I scowled at the disorder around us. "We cannot leave them like this."

"More help will come from the castle," she promised.

Swords crashed together like strikes of lightning and a chorus of battle sounds echoed around us. The essence warmed in my chest, its power flowing through me. I spared one thought toward the souls bound to me before an angel launched in my direction.

Seraphine jumped in front of me, her dual knives no more than a blur of silver in the air as she fought.

I made time to pull a knife from one of the fallen angels before Seraphine cut another down. The angel collapsed to the ground, unconscious and bleeding.

"Will you let me take you back to the castle now?" she asked, face speckled with blood. "We don't have proper weapons to kill angels. The most we can do is render them immobile and burn their bodies before they wake."

I snorted. Burn them like Cordovia's witches. How ironic.

The sound of a familiar voice caught my attention and I turned to see Tarsa through the crowd. Demons and angels alike raced through the space between us. But Tarsa easily stood out among them with her fierce weapons.

Her axes dripped blood as she battled three angels at once. If she was close, then Aiden must be as well. My heart pounded nervously as I took off in her direction, eager to find Aiden among the bloodshed.

The three angels Tarsa fought were highly skilled. They carried two weapons each. Yet she met them blow for blow.

My veins burned with the strength of the essence as it searched for something to siphon. But these immortals were without souls, rendering my power useless against them.

I wasn't sure how to find a weapon that could kill an angel as easily as their poison could harm a demon.

Tarsa knocked one of her opponents aside and turned to face the other two. I struggled against the current of the crowd, dodging the blow of swords and the grapple of fists.

Blood pounded loudly in my ears as I raced onward. The half-healed wounds in my chest ached painfully, but I forced myself to ignore them.

One of Tarsa's axes fell after a strong blow from her opponent. The angel was an entire head taller than her and thick with muscles. Left with only one weapon, she spun to face the other angel, leaving her back exposed.

I shoved my way through the crowd, no longer worrying about who I might hurt as I elbowed past.

The breath caught in my throat as I watched the large angel catch both of Tarsa's wrists in his hands, leaving her unable to wield her remaining axe. Behind her, the other angel raised his knife, preparing for a strike.

The essence's power pooled in my fingertips as I forced my way toward them.

Neither angel paid me any mind, though Tarsa's eyes widened at my approach.

The handle of the knife felt solid and comfortable in my hand. My body recalled Tarsa's brutal training, recalling on its own how to stand as I leapt between them.

I blocked the angel's attack with my free arm while driving the knife into his chest, right between his ribs.

The angel's eyes widened, finally looking at me. I saw a moment of clarity flicker in his steely gaze before he collapsed to the ground.

"Shouldn't you be hiding somewhere?" Tarsa snapped, shaking free of the large angel's grip.

I ignored the churning of my stomach as I watched the angels twitch on the ground. "You're welcome."

She only grunted a response before continuing her battle with the remaining angel. It would only be moments before the angel I struck down rose again, ready to fight.

A flicker of familiar crimson hair caught my eye as I turned away from the horror.

I froze, gaping at Viema's angry stare. She stood half cloaked in shadow at the edge of the forest. Her hands were fisted at her sides as she watched her fellow angels fall at the hands of the demons.

Sensing my gaze, her eyes snapped to mine. A snarl pulled at the corners of her mouth before she spun and raced into the trees.

I didn't even think before I raced after her.

The essence hummed in my veins as my adrenaline amplified. I could feel the pull of my bound souls as they raced from the castle, eager to join us.

Viema's haunting laughter echoed through the trees as we left the sounds of the battle behind. Since I was only a mortal, I couldn't move as fast as her, and I quickly lost sight of her crimson hair in the dark of the forest as she sped away.

I skidded to a stop, crouching over my knees as I fought to catch my breath. The rapid movement of my lungs sent my ribs screaming as the wounds strained against my still-healing skin.

A feminine chuckle sounded over my shoulder. "I should've known you'd be among them. Fighting alongside the demons. Pretending to be something you're not."

"And what am I not?" I forced ice into my voice, lifting my chin with a bravado I didn't feel.

Her movements were filled with deadly grace as she strolled into view. Viema twisted her wrist, and the small sword she held glistened in the faint light, drawing attention to the blood that painted the weapon.

"Strong," she said, mocking. "Demon. Immortal. Take your pick. But you are only a human. You do not know the games demons play or wield the strength they have. You certainly don't have the strength to fight against an angel."

"I survived your attack just fine." I let the memory of the pain anchor my fear, turning it to anger.

Viema loosed a venomous laugh. "Calling your obedient dogs to aid you does not make you a survivor."

I shrugged, attempting to adopt some of Aiden's casual arrogance. The essence dampened my emotions, letting its strength fill me instead. "I lived. And I still have the essence, so I'd have to disagree."

Her mouth pressed into a thin line as fury contorted her face. "That essence will be mine."

The essence hummed mockingly in my chest. I grinned. "Then take it."

A roar of defiance left her mouth as she launched at me. The essence thrummed through me, sensing my adrenaline. I felt it center me, guiding my steps as I dodged her blows. Only the constant training with Aiden and Tarsa these last weeks kept me standing as I continued to spin out of reach.

"You wouldn't be so arrogant if I spilled your secrets to your dear husband." Viema's thinly veiled threat did little to unnerve me.

The angel landed a kick to my middle, sending me careening into a nearby tree. I gasped for air, barely maintaining enough concentration to avoid another blow.

"Fight back you coward," she snarled. "Or are you only brave when someone is there to save you?"

"I don't need someone to save me," I said, landing a blow to her knee.

She grunted, stumbling back. "That essence cannot save you from me."

Blinding, raw power vibrated through my chest. The dark veil slipped over my eyes, momentarily rendering me blind as the essence opened into an endless void within.

That moment of weakness was all she needed.

Viema attacked again, but it was the essence that answered.

The last time the essence had reacted this way, I was shrouded in darkness. But this time, I only fell to my knees. I watched a dark power erupt from my chest, throwing Viema backward and into the forest.

Her body had barely hit the ground before an arrow landed in her side.

Killian and Aiden appeared on the other side of her. Killian kept his freshly loaded bow aimed at the angel, but Aiden had eyes only for me.

His chest heaved with labored breaths as he marched to my side. Aiden pulled me to my feet, gaze searching every inch of me for injury.

Violence glittered in Viema's eyes. "This is why mortals don't belong in our realm. They're always in need of rescuing."

Aiden stared down his nose at the angel. "Actually, I believe it was us who saved you from her, Viema. I have little doubt my wife would have shown you no mercy had we left you in her hands."

Viema yanked the arrow from her side with a grunt. Blood ran freely from the wound as she slowly got to her feet.

"You took a mortal under your protection, Prince." Her words were coated in disdain. "And now your people have paid the price for that."

Aiden's body went with the promise of violence. "You will pay for what you've done to my people. And your threat toward my wife."

She bared her teeth. "Someone will pay for the actions you two have set in motion, but I guess we'll see who that is."

The angel spun on her heel, launching into the forest and quickly disappearing from view. Killian moved to chase after her.

"No." Aiden's command cut through the air. "Let her return to her master. Hakan has others."

The young immortal nodded, stopping mid stride.

"Come," Aiden said softly. His hand felt oddly warm in mine. It was then that I noticed my cloak was missing. Between the snow falling around us and the cold void of the angels' presence, I was shivering.

I let Aiden pull me toward the remains of the village. From the tree line I could see further down the road where most of the houses remained. But the market itself was officially in shambles.

More bodies lay strewn about, pools of blood soaking into the snow beneath them. Ridha worked frantically among the wounded, the mother and her son assisting where they could.

"There you are," Seraphine's frantic voice called over the rubble.

Her fiery red braids were a beacon among the destruction as she quickly made her way to me. The relief on her face was nearly enough to bring tears to my eyes as she hugged me.

"Don't you dare run into battle alone like that again," she whispered into my hair.

I offered her a small smile, pulling back. "I'm fine. Promise."

She looked to Aiden for confirmation but the two only shared a silent glance.

Shouted complaints cut through the momentary silence.

As one, the four of us turned toward the forest on the far side of the street. Alvize and Delvin appeared, bloodstained and bruised. Each of them dragged an angel with them.

"These are the prisoners?" Hakan's voice was sharp as he stepped Aiden's side. Like the others, he too had specks of blood spattered across his face. A small cut bled on his lip, but he otherwise looked unharmed.

The two demons glanced at me, awaiting orders. I felt Seraphine stiffen slightly next to me.

I noted the hatred that lined every inch of the angels' faces as they glowered at us. Their weapons, laid out at their feet, were stained with the blood of our people. The essence burned through me again, sensing the anger I harbored toward these survivors. It wanted them dead.

Before I could reign in the essence, the demons skewered their swords through the angels' necks. They dropped the angels into the snow, stepping back from the spray of blood.

I could only stare. Already the angels' bodies were slowly beginning to knit together. They remained unconscious, but they'd awaken soon.

Murmurs of unease filtered through the crowd as they pieced together my connection with the demons. The essence calmed almost as soon as each of my soul-bound turned to me expectantly.

"Very well then," Hakan said to himself.

"Did we leave any survivors?" Aiden asked him. More guards from the castle began arriving, aiding in the cleanup of battle and treating the wounded.

Hakan nodded toward a small group near the road to the castle. "They were our only prisoners. All the others were burned and destroyed."

"Or ran away," Killian added under his breath.

Aiden sighed. "She will tell Ephraim of what happened here. And he will know his attempts to slaughter my people, and harm my wife, were wasted."

"Were they?" Tarsa asked. She stood behind us, arms crossed over her chest.

"What do you mean?" Seraphine asked.

Tarsa glanced around at the remains of the village square. Those who lived were watching us closely. "Did they not learn just how thin our defenses here are? Or witness Esme tap into the essence's power? I'd say they learned a great many things from this quarrel."

I felt Aiden go still beside me. Tension rolled off of him in waves as the growing crowd began to surround us.

"Will they come back, Your Highness?" one called from somewhere in the depths of the crowd.

I placed my hand in Aiden's as we turned to face the crowd, our people. His comforting grin was fleeting but it warmed my heart to see it amidst the destruction of the day.

"I don't believe they will," Aiden said, speaking to the crowd at large.

"What are we to do?" one asked.

"What about our businesses and our homes?" another yelled from the back.

Tear-stained faces looked at us with terror in their eyes and hopelessness on their faces. My heart constricted for them. The words slipped out before I could reconsider. "Those that have seen their homes destroyed are welcome to stay at ours."

From the corner of my eye I saw Tarsa's eyes narrow before I swung my attention to Aiden.

"Is that okay?" I whispered hastily under my breath.

His smile was warm, tender. "If that is what you wish, then of course."

"Seraphine?" I said to my friend. She stepped up immediately. "Will you please help organize a list of who will need a place to stay and make sure they find comfort in the castle?"

The smile she gave me was proud. She bent at the waist, bowing lower than I thought necessary. "At once, Princess."

I nodded, waiting for another villager to object to my offer. Instead, I was only met with silence.

The nearly seventy people that stood before me watched in wonder. Not a sound beyond the faint moans of the injured could be heard in the valley.

A small figure moved through the crowd, parting a path through the people. When her face appeared at the front of the group, I nearly collapsed with relief at seeing the young girl alive. Her broken arm was freshly wrapped and hanging in a sling around her shoulder. The blood that had coated her face had been washed away, leaving her youthful smile on display.

"You fought the angels," she said, voice filled with awe. "You saved me. You saved us all, Princess."

My cheeks flushed with her respect. But that didn't prepare me for what came next.

Her words were carried in whispers through the crowd. When many turned back in my direction, their gazes were filled with mixtures of surprise and respect.

But it was the little girl falling to her knees before me that sent my heart racing and cheeks flaming. As soon as she knelt in the snow, the crowd quickly followed.

Aiden's arm wrapped around my waist as he tucked me against his side, letting me use him for support as the crowd knelt before us. This was nothing like the way Aiden had his court kneel to me. This wasn't a part of courtly proceedings. This came from the people I was responsible for. The people who, until now, I'd never thought twice about.

I felt Aiden lean closer so his lips brushed the shell of my ear. "I'm proud of you, Esme."

I felt the threat of tears as I studied the crowd. Not from the embarrassment I felt at being on display. And not from the show of loyalty from the villagers. But because I knew what I'd cost these people.

Ephraim attacked because of me. These people lost their businesses and homes because I broke my bargain with Ephraim. They lost their lives, their loved ones, because I carried the essence of Death within me.

As I stood there, staring out among the sea of bowed heads, I silently swore I would get the revenge I'd sought. The only difference was I wouldn't allow Ephraim to take anyone else under my protection. I couldn't save my family, but I wouldn't allow him to harm any more innocents to get to me.

If he wanted me, he could have me. But I would come with swords.

THIRTY-NINE

"Is that the best you can do?" Aiden drawled, smirking as I struggled in his grip.

I frowned, twisting away from him. My wooden practice sword clattered to the ground in my struggle.

We'd been training for only half an hour, yet my healing body already felt drained. The wounds in my chest were now soft pink scars against my tanned skin. Thanks to Ridha's medicine, they'd healed quickly.

My lungs burned. "You cheated."

Aiden's smirk widened into a grin. "Is that so?"

I panted, bent over my knees as I caught my breath. "You were already attacking before Killian said to."

We turned to the blond immortal leaning against the wall. From his wide grin I knew he was taking pleasure in our debate.

"Want another try?" Killian asked.

I groaned. "Can you make him wait until you say go?"

Aiden laughed. A full, unbridled laugh that brought a smile to my face. "Have you always been such a stickler for the rules?"

I nodded, picking my sword up off the ground. "Of course. It's why Mousa stopped letting me play with him and Kesson as kids. They always tried to cheat."

Daemon flashed a saccharine-sweet grin. "I think she's right. You cheated. How rude of you."

Aiden gave the demon-born a dry look. Daemon and Jadan had returned early that morning from the mortal realm and the former hadn't left my side since.

"Don't you have somewhere else to be?" Aiden asked. Though his scowl remained, his tone was lighthearted.

Daemon shrugged, moving to sit beside Killian and Seraphine. "I'm to protect the princess and report her doings to your father. So, I shall remain with the princess."

I scowled. "Is Ofrin really still demanding you spy on me?"

"Of course. You are the biggest threat to his power at the moment."

"Does he truly not consider Ephraim a threat? I hardly think I am any more dangerous than he is."

Tarsa sent Aiden a look I didn't understand before turning away, returning to the careful polishing of her axes.

"If you continue to wield your power, that could make you as strong as Ofrin even without the title he holds," Seraphine explained.

Aiden brushed a strand of hair from my face. "My father doesn't consider Ephraim a threat because he doesn't believe the angels are capable of usurping his power. He sees you as a threat because you *are* his power."

Killian dragged his hands over his face. "Can this conversation wait until later? You're supposed to be training."

"Esme is tired of losing. I think she might need a break," Aiden said, eyes glinting with amusement.

I fought the urge to roll my eyes. "Let's go again." Aiden raised his brows at the command in my voice, but I only focused on the warmth spreading through my chest.

"All right. On the count of three," Killian called. "One.... Two..." I smiled as the essence poured through me. "Three."

Aiden was advancing before the word fully left Killian's mouth. It always surprised me how fast he could move. Or how dangerous he truly was. This was a man I'd known most of my life as no more than the boy who appeared after a performance to speak with Nonna. Now, I knew him as the Prince of Death...and my husband.

His practice sword whooshed as he sliced through the air. I ducked just in time to dodge what would've normally been a beheading. The essence's power slipped over my mind as I let it engulf my very being.

"Now who's cheating?" Aiden said, dodging an attack of my own.

I stopped the blow of Aiden's sword with mine. They crashed together midair, and a large crack split down the center of my wooden blade.

"Play fair, children." Seraphine's gentle scolding cut across the room.

"She's going to kick his ass," Daemon muttered, quietly enough that I probably wasn't supposed to hear.

"No way. Aiden will win this round no problem," Killian countered.

I scowled, putting a little more strength behind my blows as I landed a kick to Aiden's ribs. His eyes widened to reveal his bewilderment before his hand tightened on his blade.

"Loser helps Lurik in the kitchens?" Daemon offered, extending a hand.

A pause. "Deal." Killian's hand clasped Daemons.

Aiden feigned an attack, causing me to lose my balance and clumsily leap away from his next jab. "That pause was very comforting, Killian," he said dryly.

My eyes narrowed as I registered the ease with which he could bat my attacks aside. "Why are you talking? We're supposed to be sparring."

His hand shot out in a blur of movement, gripping my wrist tightly enough to make me drop the sword. Aiden used his grip to pull me closer so we were nearly chest to chest.

My face heated as he looked down at me, a smile playing at the corners of his mouth. "Then fight me, Princess. Because I'm getting bored."

A soft chuckle behind me only further ignited my frustration.

Aiden continued to hold me against him. His grip eased slightly as his eyes followed the growing flush in my cheeks. I was careful to keep the scowl off my face, letting him focus on my reddening cheeks.

His eyes dipped to my mouth. I inhaled sharply as he leaned forward ever so slightly, as if he might kiss me. Here, in front of everyone.

Then I saw his other arm move ever so slightly out of the corner of my eye.

I didn't even think, just let my body react and followed my instincts from what little training my mother had imparted on me as a young girl.

I drew my knee up sharply before his sword could make contact with my side.

Every man in the room groaned as Aiden crashed to his knees. His face had gone ashen and his eyes bugged out of his head as he gasped for breath.

Seraphine broke out into laughter. "Now that was well deserved."

"What?" Aiden rasped. There was a look of mild respect in his eyes as he studied me, but mostly he looked pale from pain.

Seraphine toyed with the end of one of her braids. "Were you not about to strike her down while you had her distracted?"

I saw Aiden's answer in his eyes as he got to his feet.

"I think what I did was more than fair," I added with off-handed arrogance.

He raised a brow. "So, which of you two has to help Lurik in the kitchens now?" he asked, turning to a frowning Killian and a smug looking Daemon.

The demon-born pointed to Killian. "Oh, that's all him. I would never bet against my princess."

"Smart choice," Seraphine said, getting to her feet. "Now, if you'll excuse me, I need to visit Fen and see what needs to be done about repairing the village."

Most of the villagers who'd had their homes or businesses destroyed were currently staying in the far wing of the castle. There were just enough rooms to house those who needed it. Lurik was having the time of his life making meals for everyone. However, that meant he was busy preparing meals and doing dishes nearly every minute of the day, so Aiden decided some of the guards would rotate through the kitchens to help him as needed. Today, it seemed Killian would be among them.

"Maybe next time you'll have a little more faith in me, Killian," I teased, tossing my cracked practice sword aside.

The young immortal blushed. "I didn't know you would use the essence."

"She doesn't need the essence to be strong," Aiden said. "She's just as powerful without it."

I tried chewing on my lip to keep the blush from my face, but based on Seraphine's knowing smile I didn't succeed.

Killian shrugged off Aiden's remark. "I know, I know. But you were cheating. I figured if you were cheating then you'd make sure she wouldn't win."

It was Daemon's turn to laugh as he sauntered over to Tarsa. He placed an arm around her shoulders, ignoring the deadly scowl on her face. "You knew he was cheating but you didn't think she would retaliate in kind? She's too stubborn to let him get away with any of that crap."

Tarsa shrugged free of his grip and left the room, freshly polished axes gleaming at her hips.

Daemon smiled after her, a look of longing in his dark eyes. "Now that is a woman I would never dare to bet against."

"Yeah, Tarsa's a great fighter," Killian acknowledged, still pouting over his loss.

"That's not the only thing I was referring to." Daemon's smug grin made the young immortal blush.

Seraphine chuckled. "Stop picking on Killian. He's still young."

Killian muttered something unintelligible under his breath before stalking from the room. Whatever he said made Daemon howl with laughter before trailing after him.

Seraphine looked at me helplessly. "I do not envy Lurik having to deal with a pouting Killian all day." She sent us a halfhearted wave. "See you in the village?"

Aiden nodded. "Hakan and I will join you after lunch."

She nodded before leaving the room, leaving Aiden and I alone. I turned away, choosing to distract myself by throwing the small daggers against a distant target. I was nowhere near as good as my parents or Mousa, but it felt nice to do something familiar.

"You're going back to the village?" I asked. My knife landed in the center of the wooden target with a thwack. The second quickly followed, landing a hairsbreadth from the first.

He nodded, shoving his sweat-slicked hair from his face. "I'm helping to clear debris before the rebuilding starts."

"Can I come?" My third knife landed beside the other two. I smiled proudly to myself.

When I turned, I saw Aiden studying me with a considering look. "Of course. I think everyone would love to see you again."

I nodded, relieved. "Good. I'd like to go this afternoon. I can even bring the minions for some extra help."

"You can't keep calling them that," he chuckled. "I'm sure they'd take great offense if they heard you refer to them that way."

I shrugged. "So? They're only bound because they attacked me. Again."

"Fair point." Violence gleamed in his eyes as he recalled the incident. "Forget I said anything. Call them every crude name you can think of and maybe threaten their lives a little more too."

I laughed, following him out the door. "I think you've done that enough for the both of us."

Aiden stopped in the middle of the hall, turning to face me. His face was thoughtful as he stared down at me. I had to crane my neck to look up at him since we stood so close. I could see his thoughts playing out in his eyes as he struggled to come to some sort of decision.

"Will you have lunch with me? Just us two?" Though his voice was soft—hesitant—his gaze did not waver from mine.

My heart fluttered in my chest, the feeling echoed by the essence. "I'd love to," I said, offering a small smile.

His shoulders eased. Aiden took my hand in his as he led the way to the dining hall.

FORTY

AIDEN AND I WERE still laughing when we finally strolled into the village. Our lunch had been the most comfortable we'd ever been together. Something about that realization made my heart refuse to slow its rapid pace.

People milled about the market in a semi organized manner. My soul-bound immortals trailed after me like reluctant shadows.

"How long have they been working?" I asked, mindful of the many gazes shooting our way among the crowd.

"As far as I know, they haven't stopped," Aiden responded just as softly.

I noted the growing piles of rubble in various places throughout the market square. "We could burn the rubble," I suggested. "It'll keep those who've refused to stay in the castle warm overnight. And I'm sure Lurik could bring food here for everyone to eat together around the fire."

Aiden grinned, pride gleaming in his eyes. "That's a wonderful idea."

I stared at the sad faces as the villagers cleaned up the remains of the lives they'd built here. "They could use a little joy."

"As could we all."

He was right. So much had happened to all of us these past months. But I was glad to be with him.

"Aiden," Hakan said in greeting. His long black hair was in its usual braid down his spine, swinging beside the broadsword he carried there. "We could use you near the armory."

Aiden nodded, turning to me as Hakan walked away. "Will you be all right on your own?"

I sent a pointed look to the two pouting demons nearby. "I won't be alone. But I'll be fine. I think I'm going to check in on Fen before helping with the cleanup."

He brushed his knuckles along my cheek. "Enjoy. I'm sure she'll be happy to see you."

I smiled as he walked away. The crowd parted for him easily, recognizing their prince. Some stopped to speak with him and thank him for his efforts in rebuilding their village, but many still sent me uneasy glances.

A deep chuckle sounded behind me. "Looks like we're not the only ones who want you gone."

I leveled a scowl at Alvize before turning down the path that led to Fen's cottage. "Careful, Alvy. I'm pretty sure I can take away your ability to speak if I feel like it."

He scoffed, disbelieving. "You wouldn't."

I watched him swallow uncertainly as I surveyed him. "Keep talking and I guess we'll find out, won't we?"

Their glares burned along my back as I led the three of us to Fen's cottage.

The forest was dusted with snow. The dark bark of the trees stood out in stark contrast to the white powder on the ground. I huddled further into my cloak as I stepped up to Fen's door.

"Stay out here and keep watch," I said, growing more comfortable with ordering them around. The essence tightened around their bindings, making my command final.

Delvin snarled. "It's cold. We'll freeze out here."

"Then next time, bring an extra cloak."

I stepped through the door without another word, leaving them to mumble to themselves.

Fen's cottage was as warm and inviting as ever. The hearth was roaring with a large fire, spreading its heat easily through the small space.

"Esme," Fen said cheerily, appearing from the hallway. "I was hoping I would see you here again soon."

I smiled, stepping into her embrace. "I was in the village with Aiden and wanted to stop by before I got covered in soot."

"Yes, it's a tragic thing. I've already started making some spare cloaks for those that are choosing to camp outside instead of finding shelter with others or at the castle." Her expression sobered as she nodded to a large pile of folded cloth in the corner.

"But I do have your dress nearly finished," she added with forced cheer.

"What?" I blinked, taken aback by the sudden change in topic.

"For Ofrin's solstice ball," she said, brows furrowing at my confusion. "It's only a few days away now."

I'd nearly forgotten about the ball Ofrin planned to throw in honor of Aiden's and my marriage. That was far from my mind after the many recent tragedies.

"Would you like to see it?" she asked, pulling me from my reverie.

I nodded, mind full of an all new sense of worry.

Half an hour later, I was buttoned into the elegant dress. Fen had chosen a bright gold silk that hugged my body and layered it with shimmering gold chiffon over the top. The smallest movement made the skirts glisten like starlight. It was beautiful.

"Hold still," she cautioned, adding another pin into the bodice.

She'd designed the dress so it clung to every curve before draping to the floor below my knees. Pins and needles still stuck out at random places, but I could imagine the beauty it would become.

"There," she said, slowly getting to her feet. "Turn to the mirror and let me know what you think."

She placed her hands on my bare shoulders, turning me around gently.

I froze at what I saw. The dress was magnificent. The color complemented the golden complexion of my skin and contrasted with the dark curls hanging around my shoulders. The neckline was wide, scooping low to reveal my collar bones clear to the tops of my shoulders. Willowy sleeves hung down my arms in sheer golden chiffon, making it appear as if the sparkles came from my own skin.

"You have a real talent, Fen," I whispered in awe.

The woman smiled, her eyes crinkling. "I do, don't I?"

I could only smile at her as I turned in the mirror, wanting to admire the dress from every angle.

A dark band along my wrist caught my attention. I frowned, holding my arm in front of my face to study it.

It was one of the scars from King Elroy's chains. The dark, blotchy skin wrapped around my right wrist, and a second matching scar decorated the left.

I looked back to the mirror and suddenly I couldn't see the young princess it had just displayed; all I could see were the scars.

The harsh scars at my wrists. The small red scar at my neck. I could even feel the horrid scars at my ankles burning though they remained hidden from view. The weight of my limbs suddenly became heavy with phantom chains.

I swallowed deeply, forcing the memories from my mind and the panic in my heart to ease. "I think I should return to the village now."

Fen frowned at the sudden change in my demeanor. "Of course. I'm sure they could use your help with the cleanup."

I nodded, not trusting my voice as my shame grew, making my cheeks flame.

I dressed quickly, not accepting Fen's help as I pondered the many other scars that haunted my skin, not counting the two newest additions thanks to Ephraim and Viema.

The minions didn't speak a word as I quickly raced from the house. Whether they were angry at me for making them wait outside or somehow sensed my emotions through our bond, I couldn't be sure. But either way, I was glad they didn't speak.

The village was organized chaos when we returned. More people had shown up to aid in the repairs. A large group of men carried loads of debris and wood from fallen buildings to the many growing piles scattered throughout the market square.

Whatever snow had once dusted this bit of land was now flattened into the ground and blackened with soot.

I sighed. "We should probably find somewhere to offer help."

One of my men scoffed behind me but I didn't turn to see who. My mind was still too preoccupied to make threats.

A child appeared in my path, stopping me. He had bright red hair that stood out in loose curls above his head. The freckles dotting his cheeks vanished behind the flush that appeared on his face as we looked at each other.

"Are you the princess?" he asked in a shy voice. His wide, round eyes studied me curiously.

I nodded. "I am."

His lips twitched toward a smile. "You were a wanderer in the mortal realm too, right?"

I smiled, remembering the life I used to live. "I was."

The boy shifted his weight nervously, looking to his feet. "I've never met a wanderer before. They don't exist here."

"Is that so?" I glanced around the people nearest us, searching for this child's guardian and hoping they hadn't been lost to the attack.

"Yeah," he said, growing more confident. "My mom says you guys could do cool magic. Not like the witches or Prince Aiden. But real magic, like magic tricks and stuff with knives."

I grinned. "My parents had a knife throwing act that they would do for performances, but I don't know that there was any magic involved. Just a lot of practice."

His expression turned shy again as he stared up at me. "Would you show me?"

"What?" I asked, startled. Some of the passersby had stopped to watch our exchange now.

He reached for his boot. I was surprised when he pulled a small, very dull knife free and held it out to me. "Could you show me how to do it?"

"I've seen her do it," a familiar voice piped up. When I looked toward the sound, I recognized the young girl from the attack. Her broken arm remained in a sling around her shoulders and the bruise on her face had darkened drastically, but she still smiled widely.

"Really?" the boy asked, enraptured.

The girl nodded, puffing out her chest proudly. "That's how she saved me."

When the boy turned back to me there was an eager curiosity in his expression that made my heart ache. It was the same expression Alfie had worn when reading one of his books or questioning the immortals about their weapons.

"I wouldn't mind seeing the princess perform her family's act. Would anyone else?" a familiar deep voice called. My heart skipped as I caught Aiden's eye. He stood on the far side of the rubble-covered street, smiling widely at me.

Much of the crowd cheered their agreement.

Aiden's soot-covered face flashed a brilliant smile while the cheering grew. I fought to hide my grin as I turned back to the boy.

"Very well," I said over the noise. "But I'm going to require the prince's aid."

FORTY-ONE

"DON'T LOOK SO PANICKED," I quipped softly. I had to work to keep from laughing.

Aiden frowned, looking particularly frazzled. "When I suggested you perform, I didn't mean to offer myself as your target."

I laughed. My back was to the crowd as I positioned Aiden in the middle of the wall. There was only one building still standing in the market square, so that was what we had to work with even though it wasn't ideal. The wall we stood by was narrow. A door stood immediately to Aiden's left and there was a broken window to his right. I just had to make sure to hit somewhere in the middle, without hitting Aiden.

"Don't do that. Don't look nervous."

My smile grew. "I was only thinking of the time I nearly sliced Mousa's ear off. Or the time I nearly hit my father in the eye. Or hit Cordelia in the throat."

Aiden fought a smile. "Are you saying you're about to maim me?"

"I think you're just nervous, dear husband." I turned away from his grin, facing the crowd.

"I should warn you all, this is not my area of expertise," I called over the rumble of the crowd.

"What performance did you do?" a young girl asked. Many of the children sat or knelt at the very front of the crowd, giddy with excitement.

I held my hands outward, a dramatic gesture I'd often seen my father use in his performances. "I was their Soul Collector. I siphoned souls for the God of Death and performed soul readings through people's palms. It was my parents who drew in a crowd with their daring knife act."

"You're not going to hurt Prince Aiden, are you?" another young girl asked, wide eyes focused on the prince behind me.

Aiden chuckled as I shook my head. "I will do my best. But I do need a knife."

"Here," the redheaded boy jumped up, practically tossing me his dull blade. "You can use mine."

I studied it. I wasn't even sure this utensil could be considered a knife as I attempted to prick my finger with its edge.

I smirked at the crowd. The children held their breath as they caught sight of my expression.

Everyone let out a soft yelp as I spun, throwing the child's weapon directly at Aiden's chest.

Aiden stood still as it gently bounced off his middle and landed at his feet. When his eyes met mine, a wild grin lit up his face.

I shrugged, turning back to the crowd as they all sighed with relief. Some chuckled nervously as they realized their overreaction.

"Perhaps something with a little more of an edge," I suggested.

Hakan stepped forward, a mischievous twinkle in his eye. "Here you go, Princess."

"Thanks for your support, Hakan," Aiden deadpanned.

The immortal only offered a grin before stepping back. I gripped the two knives he'd handed me, testing their weight. I'd be lying if I said I wasn't a little nervous. I didn't have the same hours of practice as my parents or Mousa did.

"Oh, wait," Killian called, rushing forward.

The crowd laughed as he placed a half-eaten apple atop Aiden's head. The young immortal chuckled to himself as he joined Hakan off to the side.

I smiled widely at Aiden, not even bothering to hide my amusement. Here was a big, scary demon warrior standing in front of a bunch of children with a half-eaten apple on his head, waiting for his wife to throw knives at him. Prince of Death, indeed.

"Anything else?" he grumbled, getting a few giggles out of the children.

I stifled my laughter. "I think that'll do."

The crowd waited with bated breath as I stepped into position. I flexed my grip on the knives, tossing my arms around dramatically like I was preparing to throw them. I even fit in a few leg movements before the children began to chuckle and Aiden loosed a dramatic sigh.

When I looked up at Aiden, he was smiling at me. There was a sort of wonder in his eye; pride shone through too.

I winked at him, watching the way his cheeks warmed momentarily.

Forcing my heart to slow, I stared at the apple atop his head. Aiden was so much taller than me, I worried this might prove impossible. Of course there was also the chance I would hit him square in the face or miss him entirely. It really could go either way.

The crowd hushed as I drew my arm back. The knife cut through the air a second later, leaving a whisper of air behind. I threw the second knife before the first even hit.

The consecutive thumps sounded loudly in the silence. Aiden didn't even blink. He kept his gaze focused on mine as he slowly stepped away from the wall, showing the half-eaten apple pinned to the building with both knives skewering it in place.

Cheers erupted around us as children jumped to their feet. Aiden walked over to me, taking me in his arms.

"I didn't doubt you for a second," he whispered into my ear.

"Liar."

His chest rumbled with quiet laughter before drawing away. "Isn't she brilliant?" he called to the crowd, getting even more cheers in answer.

My smile was beginning to ache as I fought the flush that burned through my cheeks.

"Do it again," one of the children yelled.

Aiden smiled at the children. "Unfortunately, I must return to work. But I'm sure my wife would be more than happy to remain."

"Can you read my palm?" one girl asked. She looked to be no older than six, with brown curls that bounced around her face.

Aiden slipped away into the crowd as children began to surround me on all sides. Even the occasional adult appeared to ask me to read them. I wasn't able to read every palm placed before me; there were far too many people for that.

The souls of the immortals here were different than in the mortal realm. Some were aged, displaying their long lives both in the mortal realm and here long after they offered their souls to Death. Even those who were born to immortal parents or lived a mortal lifespan in this realm had a soul that appeared differently from the essence I carried.

It was hours later when the crowd slowly began to disperse.

A firm hand came down gently on my shoulder. "I'm sorry folks, but if it's all right with you, I would like my wife back."

My cheeks flushed as I met his gaze. Ever since Ephraim's attempt on my life, he'd grown more comfortable referring to me as his wife. And I couldn't ignore that I'd also begun to think of him as my husband. A strange thought to have when thinking of him, but a pleasant thought nonetheless.

I let Aiden whisk me away, working to ignore the way my heart stuttered as he smiled at me.

"Lurik has asked, or I should say demanded," he paused to smirk, making me grin, "that you help him prepare dinner. Apparently when he sent Killian to deliver the meals to our guests, he never returned."

We both glanced across the busy square to the young immortal as he sat with the children, showing them how to shoot with his bow.

"Can't say I'm surprised," I muttered.

Aiden chuckled, squeezing my hand. "Since this bonfire was your idea, he asked that you assist him in the kitchens for the rest of the afternoon to prepare."

I sighed, glancing around the growing piles of rubble. "I can do that. Does he want me there now?"

"He did ask that you return to the kitchens at once."

"I'm only going because Killian abandoned him," I insisted.

His eyes gleamed with humor. "I'm sure it has nothing to do with your intent to steal a bite here or there as he cooks."

I placed a hand on my chest, the portrait of innocence. "Me? I would never."

My stomach took that opportunity to growl loudly. Aiden laughed, wrapping his arms around me as easily as if we'd done this a thousand times.

The essence warmed my chest and my pulse throbbed in my veins, but I managed to pull myself away from him. This closeness was still too new between us. Even in Cordovia we'd remained distant as our duties kept a barrier between us. But it was harder to pull away than I cared to admit, harder than it had been only the day before. It seemed every moment I spent with him made it harder to leave.

And that thought lingered as I made my way back to the castle.

FORTY-TWO

THOUGH THE NIGHT AIR was sharp from the winter winds, the four large fires spilling their flames into the night sky kept me warm.

I worked in Lurik's kitchen–stealing bites of food when he wasn't looking–for nearly five hours before I was finally allowed to join the fun. Lurik even joined me once we'd brought all the food to the village. He strutted around the grounds with trays in each hand, offering his meals to anyone with empty hands.

"You should've seen her," Fen was saying, grabbing my attention. "She looked like a goddess."

I felt my cheeks warm as she fawned over the dress again. She'd spent the past several minutes telling Tarsa and Seraphine all about it. I did my best to tune her out in an effort to avoid blushing. I wasn't successful.

"I don't doubt it." The smile in Seraphine's voice was evident.

The four of us sat on a thick blanket near one of the colossal fires, its flames rising to the height of the nearby trees.

"It's just a dress," I nearly whined.

Fen scoffed. "Just a dress. This will be your introduction to Ofrin's court and your first official outing to the entirety of the realm as our princess."

I groaned, tearing off a piece of warm bread and shoving it into my mouth. "Please don't remind me."

Seraphine laughed. "You can't truly be that nervous?"

"The God of Death thinks I'm working against him. Why wouldn't I be nervous?"

Tarsa's frown deepened. "Then don't go."

Fen and Seraphine looked at her, aghast.

"What?" Seraphine exclaimed.

"She must go. She's the princess," Fen retorted.

Tarsa shrugged, uncaring as she turned away. "Just a suggestion if she's so worried about it."

I scowled, turning my gaze to the fire. I could feel the heat of the flames along my skin, but I didn't move. The cold fear of the upcoming ball had begun to haunt me more in the last few hours since I'd tried on the magnificent gown.

Not to mention the threat of Ephraim still loomed over our heads. We may not have had any more spies go missing, but I couldn't shake the feeling of being closely watched. It made the skin between my shoulders itch. Our only luck so far was that he'd refrained from using the angel's poison during their latest attack.

"I wonder why he didn't use it." Deep in thought, I hadn't meant to speak the words aloud.

"What?" Seraphine asked, setting her empty plate aside.

"Ephraim." I turned away from the flames. "He didn't use any of his poison. Why? Does he not have more than what coats his knife? Why just show up and burn the village and maim half the people?"

Tarsa considered this, gaze turning distant.

Fen shrugged. "Let's just hope he doesn't have any more."

"How does he make it? Is it like the antidote that takes several weeks?" I asked.

"We aren't entirely sure," Seraphine admitted. "It's a very rare thing to create a poison only deadly to demons or those who've tied their souls to Death. I'd imagine it isn't exactly easy to come by."

I nodded, letting my mind wander.

Someone started singing on the other side of the square. A moment later, more voices joined in, then someone began playing a stringed instrument that sounded like one my uncle had used. A song began, dancing through the night and echoing through the crowd. It was magical.

Fen and Seraphine joined in, their voices soft and melodic. It was a song unfamiliar to me, but I could hear the joy in it. People stood, taking partners as they began to dance around the flames.

Seraphine stood, taking Fen with her. I watched the two of them join in the dancing as couples twirled around in the melting snow.

Mortals and immortals alike joined hands, dancing around the flames to the strange tune. Through the firelight, the silver strands in Fen's hair seemed to glow orange. In the short time I'd been in this realm, she'd already changed, her hair forming more strands of silver, while Seraphine appeared frozen in time at her side.

"Does it bother you?" I asked Tarsa. "Seeing your sister age as a mortal when you will outlive her many lifetimes over?"

Tarsa's gaze slid over to me. Her dark eyes were clouded in a way I wouldn't have expected from her.

"Fen and I have spent centuries fighting other people's wars," she finally said. "I've seen her isolate herself time and again because of the damage we've caused, the horrors we've seen. All she's ever wanted is a family. Someone to return home to at the end of the day and curl up with at night. Somewhere to place her heart and know it will be safely guarded. She has that now. She's earned it."

"But?" I prompted, sensing the change in her emotions.

Tarsa sighed, turning her gaze toward her sister. "But I've never lived a day without her. I will lay down my life for her at the first chance if it means keeping her safe. Even if she only has one day left of her mortal life to live."

My gaze turned to the dancing around us. Couples of all ages twirled and spun, kicking up the light dusting of snow as it began to melt near the fires.

Despite the tragedy they'd experienced, they were all finding joy in this one moment. Everyone wore a smile or howled with laughter as they lingered. Young couples clung together, parents smiled with their laughing children, and all around them people danced.

I smiled, thoroughly enjoying the familiarity of the scene playing out before me. There had been so many nights like this with my family; we'd often gather with Kesson's family after a performance to eat and dance by the fire.

The longer I stayed in this realm, the more it was beginning to feel like home. Whether that was because of the number of memories it conjured or simply because I was among friends, I couldn't be sure.

But would these people be enough to stop Ephraim?

"I know how Aiden feels about you," Tarsa said suddenly, startling me.

"What?"

She scrutinized me with unwavering clarity. "He loves you. Even a blind man could see that. He would jump in front of an arrow for you. Yet you've spent your entire time here antagonizing him and hating him."

I had to look away. "Things have changed."

"You mean you grew bored with hurting him?" Her voice, though hushed, was sharp as a blade. "Or is it simply that you were too stupid to see that you loved him too?"

I scowled at her. "I thought he killed my family. I shouldn't be expected to forgive someone for that so quickly."

"And yet even when you did find out he was not responsible, you didn't accept him. You still haven't accepted him for who he is, what he is."

"And what is that?" I snapped.

"Death," she said. "Aiden is the Prince of Death, heir to the Realm of Souls, and a demon. And you can't accept that."

"I have accepted it," I retorted stubbornly.

She shook her head, scowling at me in disapproval. "You haven't and he knows it. Why do you think he continues to hide his true form around you? He hasn't shown his wings since the wedding ceremony at the white tree."

Shame soured my mood, forcing me to turn away and hide my face behind my curtain of hair. I'd acknowledged that I still loved Aiden. Even when I thought he sent my family to their deaths, I'd loved him. I hated myself for it, but I couldn't stop loving him. I hadn't realized he still thought I hated him.

"If you truly have accepted him, he deserves to know." Her voice became uncharacteristically soft. "And if you can't accept him, then tell him before he falls any further. If you wait too long, he may not recover."

Her advice surprised me. Knowing her cold side all too well, I'd never expected her to display any sense of sympathy for the prince she guarded.

"You two look too glum for a party," Killian said, plopping onto the ground between us. A boyish grin lit up his face as he took a gulp of ale from his mug.

Tarsa scowled down her nose at him. "Aren't you supposed to be guarding the grounds?"

Killian smiled lazily. "Hakan took over."

"Good thing too because the kid here has been guzzling ale all night," Daemon teased, sitting on Tarsa's other side.

"It's a party. I shouldn't have to stay in the shadows like a wraith and scowl at everything. That sounds like the perfect job for Hakan." Killian's grin was lopsided as he turned to me, seeking affirmation.

I laughed, nodding my half-hearted agreement. "Of course, Killian. How rude of Aiden to expect you to stand guard over a party and not have any fun."

The young immortal smiled wider. "Exactly. I knew I liked you."

I shook my head, fighting the laughter that bubbled out of me. Beside me, Killian lay on his back, gazing up at the night sky. I caught Daemon whispering to Tarsa out of the corner of my eye, but her serious expression gave no indication as to what he might be saying.

"You were raised to believe the souls go to the stars, right?" Killian asked.

I nodded, lying beside him. "Yes."

The sky above us was clear. Not a cloud hovered in sight. Whatever snow covered the ground would hopefully be all that we would get for a while.

"I like that thought," he whispered almost to himself.

I smiled, admiring the gleam of the stars. Even the giant flames from the fires couldn't hide their glow.

"Even though I know souls go to the Crossroads, I still like to think it's true," I admitted.

He turned to me, scrutinizing my words. "Perhaps it is. None of us know what is beyond the Crossroads."

I sighed, wistful. "I guess someday we'll know, won't we?"

"Let's hope that day doesn't come too soon," he said, sitting up and pulling me with him. "There's still a party to be had."

"And a ball," Daemon tacked on. Tarsa was walking away, disappearing into the shadows beyond the crowd.

I groaned. "Please. No talk of Ofrin's ball tonight. I'm tired of hearing of it."

"Okay," Killian said, smile mischievous. "What about your birthday?"

I scowled. "That was weeks ago." The memory of my latest birthday wasn't one I'd be able to forget any time soon, if ever.

"Yes, Aiden said as much, but we still haven't celebrated." Killian wiggled his brows, the mischievous gleam in his eye only growing.

"When was your birthday?" Daemon asked, taking Killian's mug of ale from him.

"The day my family died," I muttered dryly.

The mug paused halfway to his mouth. I saw empathy flash in his eyes a moment before he recovered his emotions.

"Sorry. Worst birthday ever." Though his voice was understanding, it held a light-hearted tone to help keep the memory of the pain away.

I shook my head. "My birthday doesn't need to be celebrated."

Killian turned wide eyes on me. "Of course it does. Get up and dance. Have some ale. Yell at a child. Just do something fun."

I frowned. "Yell at a child?"

"You did not just offer to get the princess drunk," Daemon said with false scorn.

The young immortal shrugged, tangled golden curls falling into his eyes. "They're just suggestions."

A familiar deep chuckle sounded behind me. "As much as I'm sure watching Esme try ale would be fun, how about a dance instead?"

Aiden held his hand out to me in offering. I smiled, remembering the last time we danced together.

Placing my hand in his felt like second nature now as I let him pull me to my feet.

Killian sighed dramatically. "Fine, dance with your wife. But I still think drinking ale would've been more fun."

Aiden wrapped an arm around my waist and my pulse jumped at the contact. "Why don't you two go find Sera and Fen? I believe they were headed back to the castle."

I watched the two share a look before quickly getting to their feet, smiling widely at me like there was something I didn't know.

"Of course," Daemon said, bowing with a flourish.

Killian laughed. "As you wish, Your Highness."

The two were still laughing as I watched them vanish down the wooded path.

"Are they up to something?" I asked.

Aiden shook his head. "It's nothing. I'm sure even if they stayed here they would find some sort of trouble to get into."

Before I could respond, he pulled me against him. Our chests were pressed together, his arm snaking around my waist to settle at the small of my back as the song changed. The new chords sounded a bit off, the tune sounding only vaguely familiar as the musicians struggled to find the rhythm.

Recognition slammed into me as he began to spin us around the fires. "This is a wanderer song," I said, smiling widely.

He answered my smile immediately. "It is. I asked them to play it."

I hugged him closer, letting my hand settle at the back of his neck. "Why?"

For once, his expression remained so open that I could see the contemplation in his eyes as he looked at me. I felt my cheeks heat underneath his steady gaze. Every part of me that touched him burned, wanting and needing more. And yet I held back. Tarsa's words about my acceptance of his true nature rang clearly in my mind.

"Because it is a part of you," he finally responded. "I want to make this feel like a home you can come to love, Esme. Not just a place for you to sleep and dream of the life you used to live. I hope this can become a place where you will want to build a life."

I considered his words as we spun slowly around the fires. The song was upbeat, almost peppy. The other couples spun in an unorganized manner around us.

Finally, I nodded, smiling. "Okay."

His shoulders relaxed. "Okay?" There was an air of uncertainty in his voice that made me chuckle.

"I think it could be." I didn't let him know that I'd already begun to consider this my home. That I already felt the joys of comfort here. There were still some things I needed to figure out before I could give him that hope.

There was a bit of disbelief in his expression that he quickly shielded. "We can discuss this another time," he said, pulling me closer. "For now, let's just dance."

He picked me up, spinning me around the other dancers before I could say anything more. The boyish grin on his face was enough to elicit a laugh from me.

Aiden's chest rumbled with his own laughter as we danced. My feet hardly touched the ground as he spun us around. By the time the song came to an end, my cheeks hurt from smiling.

"Where did everyone else go?" I asked, glancing around at the other dancers, noting my friends' missing faces.

Aiden's mouth turned up in a crooked smile as he took my hand, leading me from the designated dance floor between the fires. "I think I might have an idea."

I chewed on my lip as we walked through the wooded path to the castle. The occasional villager milled about, whether returning to the comfort of a bed or to the festivities, I couldn't be sure.

The night sky remained open, bright with starlight. Aiden had found a cloak somewhere at the grounds and wrapped it around both of our shoulders during the walk. Without the raging fires to keep warm it was hard to forget it was nearing the middle of winter.

I glanced over my shoulder, watching the shadows of the dancers move across the snow-covered ground.

"We're not truly going to keep waiting to find Ephraim, are we?" I asked. Aiden's spies had no word of Ephraim's whereabouts since I'd last seen him myself. Plans were still being formed, but due to my weakened state I had not been in attendance for those meetings after my attack.

Aiden sighed, his arm tightening around my shoulders. "Jadan has assured me my father has more spies than we are aware of within my court. If they see us gathering forces, or preparing for war, I fear my father's suspicions against you will cause more harm than good."

I frowned. "How so? We've already been attacked by Ephraim's angels. It would be easy for them to do it again now that we are weakened."

"It would," he agreed, "but if my father retaliates against us for believing you to be after his crown, it will cause a divide among our own people. Should Ephraim remain true to his word and attack before we're ready, we cannot afford to be at war with each other."

"We'd have no hope of surviving if we had to fight your father and Ephraim." My heart sank as I glanced one last time toward the shattered village.

"No," he sighed, somber. "But we are putting preparations in place for the days immediately following my father's solstice ball. We just have to wait until then."

"What if we wait too long?"

Aiden pulled me closer as the path curved toward the castle gates. "We can worry about battle plans tomorrow. Tonight, there is no talk of war."

I groaned. "Do I even want to know what secrets you are keeping?"

Killian came bounding into view as soon as the words left my mouth. "There you are!"

I narrowed my gaze at the young immortal as he shot Aiden a knowing look.

"Took you long enough."

"It hasn't been but a few minutes," Aiden said, serious again. I thought I even detected a hint of nervousness to his demeanor.

Killian practically bounced on the balls of his feet as he led us through the castle. Voices and laughter echoed through the bare corridors as villagers slowly began to return to the spare rooms they occupied in this wing.

"Where are we going?" I finally asked when Killian turned down the narrow stairs that led directly to Lurik's kitchens.

"There's something you need to see." Killian's voice was tight with the struggle to hold in his amusement.

I sent a questioning look to Aiden but he only smiled.

The door to the kitchen was closed, but light could still be seen from beneath the misshapen door.

Killian stepped aside, ushering me through the door first.

As soon as I pushed the door aside, I came to a stop.

"Surprise!" everyone shouted at once.

I stared at the room. Lurik had a much larger kitchen where he worked to feed the villagers and our guests, but most days he opted for this smaller kitchen. It was brown and plain. The wooden cabinets had seen better days and the table in the middle of the room had grooves from his knives.

But it was the people that filled it that had my attention now.

Tarsa leaned against the hearth to the side, trying to remain inconspicuous. Hakan and Jadan stood in the far corner, half hidden behind Seraphine, Fen, and Daemon, who sat at the table.

I blinked at the gathering, confusion still present. "What is this?"

Seraphine laughed. "It's for you."

Fen's smiling face didn't give me the answers I needed either. Killian patted me on the shoulder as he moved past, taking a seat beside Daemon. The two of them pushed a small cake forward on the table.

I felt Aiden's warmth as he moved closer. He leaned down so his lips brushed my cheek. "Happy Birthday, Esme."

FORTY-THREE

I ARCHED A BROW, shock rocketing through me. "My birthday was weeks ago."

His eyes were soft, and his smile sheepish. "I know," he said, shrugging. "But I still thought you should have at least one pleasant memory from this birthday."

I swallowed the lump in my throat. My hand reached for his without thought. His eyes widened slightly, startled by my affection.

"We baked you a cake," Killian said excitedly, wiggling in his chair as he struggled to remain patient.

I smiled. "You did?"

"No. He did not," Fen said, shooting the young immortal a halfhearted scowl. "But I did."

Killian looked unperturbed by her rejection. Seraphine stepped forward, placing something on the table before them. The cake was beautifully decorated in red frosting and read "Happy Belated Birthday Esme" on the top.

Daemon grinned. "The frosting is rather bland, but the cake beneath it is fantastic."

Fen shot him a scowl. "How would you know?"

The demon-born smirked. "You left the cake unguarded. What did you expect me to do?"

I laughed as Fen frantically searched the cake for any sign it had been tampered with. Daemon winked at me as he turned, putting Fen at his back but leaving his hands exposed so I could see them. He held a mixing bowl and a wooden spoon, each covered in chocolate batter.

Killian's mouth hung open. "How did you get that?"

"I took it," Daemon answered with a sly grin.

Fen smacked the demon on the back of the head. He feigned a wince, reluctantly handing over the mixing bowl.

Hakan shook his head as he and Jadan watched the commotion in silent amusement.

Seraphine cut the cake and passed a slice to everyone in the room.

"Can we give her our presents now?" Killian asked around a mouthful.

I had only just taken a bite when he turned excited eyes on me. The chocolate cake was rich in flavor, and the frosting was thick with cream. It was divine, not something I wanted to rush through.

Seraphine gave him an exasperated look. "We've only just cut the cake."

Killian jumped from the table, practically dancing to the closet in the corner. "I know, but I can't wait any longer."

Aiden took my plate from me, freeing my hands as Killian pranced back into the room.

He held a shiny white bow and a quiver full of arrows. The design of the bow was slender, smaller than the one he carried. It looked simple from far away, but up close I could see the elegance of the white wood used to craft it.

"It was made with wood from the white tree," he said, delighted. "Well, just one of its branches to be exact. It is said that whoever wields a weapon made from the white tree will never fall in battle. The arrows are made from the same wood so they will always hit their intended target."

The smile that lit up his face was bright enough to make even the sun seem dull.

I could only smile in return, taking the weapon into my hands. "Thank you so much, Killian. I love it."

His cheeks turned a brilliant pink as I studied the weapon. It was lightweight, perfect for someone of my stature. The feathers at the ends of the arrows were dyed a dark red that looked like blood.

"Do you know how to shoot?" he asked.

I shrugged. "A little. I'm not very good though."

"I can teach you." His answer came immediately, causing the others to chuckle at his excitement.

"Give her a moment to relax, Killian," Seraphine said. "She's only practically just walked through the door."

Killian was still smiling as he returned to his seat. Seraphine stepped forward, her own smile just as wide.

"This is from me and Fen," she said, handing me a large box.

I caught Fen's grin from across the room as I set the box on the table. Aiden watched it all in silence, though the corners of his mouth were turned up.

The present was magnificent. I pulled the clothing from the box, letting it unfold to study it further. The fabric felt thin to the touch, but it was weighty in my grip, far heavier than an ordinary shirt.

"It's armor," Seraphine said before I could offer a guess.

"It is made of a special fabric originally created by the angels," Fen added, smiling proudly at her work. "They needed armor that would protect against the struggling souls, should they attack. Of course, over time it has been used for many other things as well. But this should help protect you against violent souls, stabbings, poisoned blades, or arrows."

I studied her under raised brows. "You make it sound like I get attacked often."

She sent me a wry grin. "More than anyone I know."

"And that's really saying something," Seraphine added. "Do you like it?"

I smiled, folding the armored shirt back into the box. "I love it. Thank you."

She wrapped me in a hug so tight I was nearly certain my ribs would crack. It felt much the same as hugging my sisters in Cordovia, and another corner of my heart patched itself together. When we finally pulled apart my heart felt lighter, freer.

"After seeing your skills this afternoon, I know I picked the right gift." His usually serious voice had a lilt of humor to it as he pulled something from beneath his tunic.

My eyes went wide at the knife he held out to me.

"There hasn't been a chance to get you fitted for a proper weapon with the blacksmith, so I was only able to have one of my own knives altered to better suit you," he explained with a casual shrug.

I took the knife gently from his hands. It was large, nearly as long as my forearm, yet it felt lighter than I expected. The blade itself was dark, made of a sort of metal I didn't yet know and was probably only found in this realm. The hilt fit perfectly into my palm. The leather was smooth and soft against the hardened blisters I'd formed in my weeks of training.

"It's beautiful," I said in awe.

Hakan gave an indiscernible grunt. "It'll do the job. Just keep it sharp and clean. If you don't know how to properly clean your weapons, learn soon. Otherwise, you'll dull the blade and it'll be useless."

Aiden chuckled at his friend's bluntness. "She'll learn," he promised.

Hakan nodded, stepping back to the corner of the kitchen. Aiden took the knife from me, tucking it into the box with the armor.

"I'll have a sheath made so you don't have to worry about stabbing yourself while wearing it," he whispered into my ear.

I nodded, my smile stretching from ear to ear, enjoying this far too much.

"Well, we didn't get you anything," Daemon said with a nod toward Jadan. "But in our defense, no one told us when your birthday was, or that we would be celebrating it tonight."

"Or that we were expected to get you anything," Jadan tacked on.

I waved away their apology. "That's fine. I really didn't need any presents."

"Of course you did," Seraphine argued lightly. "Everyone needs presents on their birthday."

Fen sent a pointed look to Tarsa, who had yet to speak. The two sisters glared at each other before Tarsa finally stepped forward with a sigh.

"Well, I've been teaching you how to stay alive and not get killed in a fight. I think that can count for my present," she said simply.

Fen scowled but said nothing.

I nodded. "Thank you. I really do appreciate it."

Her earlier words seemed to return to both of our thoughts as we stared at each other a moment longer. Though her expression clouded with scrutiny, her eyes were kinder as she studied Aiden and I together.

"Okay, I think I'll take Esme to her last present if you all don't mind." Aiden stood, keeping his hand at the small of my back as he gently led me from the room.

"What did you get her?" Fen asked, a gleam to her eye that made a light flush appear on Aiden's cheeks.

"It's for Esme," Aiden said, mischief etched into his grin.

Fen sighed, tossing her braid over her shoulder. "Fine, boy. Don't tell me. I only practically raised you, but keep your secrets."

The others chuckled as Aiden led me from the room. When we finally made it to the main level of the castle, I couldn't take the silent suspense any longer.

"Where are we going?" I asked, nervousness making my heart pound while my tentative excitement had me easily keeping pace with his long strides.

Aiden sent me a sly look, the corners of his mouth quirking up. "Almost there."

"Are we going back outside?" I asked.

"No."

"Can I have a hint?"

"No."

I groaned, ignoring his answering laugh. His hand moved from my back to my hand, squeezing lightly. I felt the nervous jump of his pulse in his wrist as I wrapped my other hand around our entwined hands.

"Should I be nervous that you're nervous?" I asked.

The look on his face changed. I hadn't noticed the mask he used to cover his expression until it disappeared. His mouth was pressed into a thin line. A telltale sign that he was nervous.

I squeezed his hand in comfort. "Don't be nervous."

"I'm not," he said a little too quickly.

I laughed. "If you say so."

The halfhearted scowl he sent me only made me laugh more. His expression lightened at the sound. We turned down a familiar hall, barren of guards.

"Why are we down here?" I glanced around the empty space.

The room containing his mother's belongings was up ahead, door closed and presumably locked. I hadn't returned to it since retrieving the antidote for Ephraim.

Aiden came to a stop outside the door beside his mother's room. The brief look he gave me was uncertain, like he was almost second guessing his decision.

"I realize this might not be the best thing to offer you," he started slowly, leading us into the room. "But I thought the best gift wouldn't necessarily be something tangible, rather something to make you feel comfortable here. At home."

Realization steadied me as I glanced around the empty room. The walls were bare, matching the rest of his castle. The only light in the room came from the small hearth between the windows along the far wall, casting the dark room in a soft, orange glow.

A single chair sat in the middle of the empty space, a stringed instrument leaning against it.

Emotion stole my breath. "My family's song?"

His expression was guarded, waiting for me to reject his offer and run from the room.

I had to blink away the tears before I could speak. "Will you play it for me?"

My voice was suddenly shy. I'd heard bits of the song twice in my time here, but I hadn't heard it in its entirety since before my family's demise.

Aiden didn't say anything as he strode to the chair. I remained frozen, watching him place the large instrument on the floor between his knees. His eyes shot to mine, locking his gaze onto mine as he began to play.

The bow he moved across the strings was slender, but it drew forth the notes of the song beautifully.

As soon as the first note echoed through the room, my heart swelled. My feet carried me forward before I'd even realized I was moving.

Aiden's expression was open, eyes watching me closely as I knelt beside him, enraptured with his playing.

The song was a joyful one, something to be played at the start of the night to get folks onto the dance floor. It was a song that meant I was home, safe. One that wrapped around me tightly with its comforting embrace.

When the song came to an end, I almost asked him to play it again. That part of my heart that ached for my family finally felt whole. Poorly patched together and fragile, but whole. It swelled with love.

Aiden's thumb brushed across my cheek, catching a fallen tear. I quickly wiped it away, embarrassed.

"What is it?" His voice was soft, tender.

I shook my head, blinking away the threat of more tears. "I just never realized it before. Or at least I never wanted to see it."

His brows furrowed. "See what?"

I met his gaze, letting him see the emotion I had fought to ignore for so long.

My heart beat unevenly as guilt erased my brief moment of peace. "Aiden," I began slowly. "There's something we need to discuss, about Ephraim."

"Esme, this night is to celebrate your birthday," he said, pulling me to my feet. "We can discuss Ephraim tomorrow. Tonight, we celebrate you."

I let him pull me toward the door, willing to let him momentarily subdue my guilt.

But that comfort was far too brief. "This can't wait," I said, noting the gathering voices beyond the windows as more villagers returned to their guest rooms in the distant wing of the castle.

Aiden studied me curiously, quick to return to the matter at hand. "What is it?"

I stared into his face, seeing the way his smile fell and his expression quickly grew bleak. The secrets I bore might just tear him apart. But I couldn't keep them from him any longer.

"Ephraim told me something...about your mother." I took a steadying breath as his hand grew cold in mine. "She's not just *your* mother, Aiden."

He shook his head as if to clear it. "What do you mean?"

"She's his mother too," I said gently. His hand slipped from mine, and I felt an ache deep in my chest. "Ephraim told me about how his mother was captured by Ofrin, and eventually they bore a son—you. That's why he slipped into Ofrin's ranks, to be close to you. That's why he is so hell-bent on destroying Ofrin."

I watched the emotions play out over his face. Disbelief. Denial. Fury. Pain. Acceptance. Each was echoed by the thunderous beating of my heart.

Finally, he sighed. His chin fell, letting his dark hair fall over his eyes. "I'd always wondered why, out of everyone, he stuck by my side for so long."

"I'm so sorry," I whispered.

Aiden took my hand again and it felt like a part of myself had been returned. "You are not responsible for his choices, Esme."

"But I should have told you sooner," I argued. We'd stopped in the middle of the corridor, the voices of nearing villagers echoing off the bare stone.

"You almost died, Esme," he said, squeezing my hand. "I cannot blame you for that little detail slipping your mind."

Stars. He thought Ephraim told me this the night I was attacked. If only he knew.

"But you can tell me all about what Ephraim said tomorrow," Aiden insisted, leading me toward the stairs that would lead to our rooms. "For tonight, try not to dwell on it."

A group of villagers passed by, taking no notice of us. Out of habit, I pulled away from Aiden.

When the crowd finally dispersed, Aiden remained standing along the far wall, watching me curiously. "May I walk you to your room?" His voice had gone soft again, uncharacteristically shy.

"Don't you mean your room?" I teased, attempting to return to the lighthearted atmosphere we'd been enjoying earlier.

A grin turned up the corners of his mouth. "Yes. That is exactly what I mean."

I smiled, taking his outstretched hand. "When will I get a new mattress? I feel bad knowing you had to give up your room for me."

"I don't mind. You are my wife, and you are welcome to anything that is mine."

My cheeks flushed brilliantly, forcing me to drop his gaze as we climbed the stairs. "Where have you been sleeping? I haven't even bothered to ask."

He ran a hand through his hair. "In my study."

The smile slipped from my face, but I said nothing further. As the sight of our chamber doors came into view, a new thought occurred to me.

As soon as Ofrin had released him from the bargain, Aiden told me how he felt. He never tried to hide it even after I asked him never to speak the words again. Even though his methods were questionable, he did everything imaginable to keep me safe, just like my family had.

The storm of my feelings had finally cleared, but now I could only think of Tarsa's argument as we neared his chambers. I'd always known how I felt, but she believed Aiden thought I still hadn't accepted him. I worked so hard at convincing myself I hated him that for a while I believed it to be true. Perhaps he truly thought the same.

We paused outside the door to his bed chambers. My heart felt as if it were in my throat when I turned to him.

"Will you show them to me?" I asked, voice breathless with nerves.

His brows furrowed. "What?"

"Your wings. Can I see them?"

Aiden searched my face for any hint of what I might be feeling, but I worked to keep all emotion from my face. I couldn't be sure how I would feel after having the reminder of his true identity staring me in the face; I didn't want to risk hurting him if I couldn't handle it.

Even though I still harbored secrets that were just as painful.

I could see the moment he came to a decision. Aiden's spine straightened, the movement putting a little more space between us. With a pop of air, his wings appeared.

Two feathered, raven black wings protruded from his back. They came to peaks just above his head and stretched out wide enough to cast us in shadow, hiding the light from the sconces.

I reached out a tentative hand, pausing just a hairsbreadth away. "May I?"

Aiden only nodded, seemingly unable to find his voice as he waited for what he assumed would be inevitable repulsion.

The feathers were soft beneath my touch, each so light it felt like I was only touching the night air. They hovered above me, blocking the rest of the corridor from view. These might be the wings of the Prince of Death, but Aiden was still Aiden to me. As I was sure he always would be.

A sense of surety rang through me as I drew back. Something heavy lifted from my shoulders, easing the throb of my heart.

"Esme?" Aiden's voice was guarded and uncertain, though hope remained alight in his eyes.

My voice remained small and soft. "Tell me again."

His heart beat loudly enough that I could hear it over the pounding of my own. Tears began to blur my vision as I stared into his face, waiting to hear the words I was finally ready to accept.

Aiden pressed his forehead against mine. He took a ragged breath before he finally straightened enough so I could see his face.

"I love you." Though his voice was soft as a breath, the words he spoke were momentous. "I've always loved you."

A stray tear ran down my cheek, but my smile was so wide that my cheeks ached. And though I knew it was selfish, though I knew he deserved more of the truth than I'd given him, I gave him one more bit of truth that would change the trajectory of our lives. "I love you too."

Surprise flitted across his face for the briefest of moments before his mouth crashed into mine.

FORTY-FOUR

HOURS LATER, IN THE dark of night, Aiden lay by my side. His breathing was even and deep with sleep. The shadows in the room stretched across the floor inch by inch as the moon drifted across the sky. We'd spent hours talking. We shared stories from our past, my family's performances, and even dared the topic of my family's demise. And yet, while sleep welcomed Aiden, it evaded me as my thoughts continued to whirl with the coming war.

I slipped from his bed, careful to keep my footsteps silent as I crept back into my room. Though my hearth remained unlit, the curtains were cast aside, allowing the star-filled sky to light my path.

Alfie's notebook remained where I'd left it in the drawer beside my destroyed bed. I flipped through the pages, watching the way his letters would become stilted as his excitement with each story grew. Daggers and swords were drawn throughout the margins. Wings and crowns filled every other available space on the pages. As I came to my mother's letter, I ran a hand over the page, feeling the rough indentions of her pen on the paper.

An idea occurred to me as I reread her last, desperate goodbye. Grabbing a pen, I flipped to the last page and began to write three letters.

Aiden might've had blind faith in the success of our plan, but I had lost too many people I'd loved to allow even a glimmer of hope to distract me from protecting them.

When I was done, I tore the three letters from the notebook, placing them in separate envelopes and addressing them accordingly. For now, they would remain hidden, but when all was lost, I would have no choice but to make them known.

A soft rattling sound came from beneath my bed. I bent down, looking beneath the bloodstained frame. There, hidden in the depths of the shadows, was Ephraim's box.

I pulled it into my lap, watching it rattle and shake in my grip like a living, angry being. Slowly, with a pounding heart, I opened it. I'd nearly forgotten about the strange object, but it certainly hadn't forgotten about me. Inside was an array of letters, all addressed in Ephraim's curving scrawl.

The box shook again, making me gasp. In a blink all the letters were gone, apart from one. I opened it with trembling hands, eager to return to Aiden in the other room before he awoke.

"How many more will your secret kill before you give me what I want?"

I slammed the box closed, locking the letter away as I raced on silent feet into Aiden's room. Enough embers remained in the hearth to stoke a fire. By the time Aiden stirred with the golden dawn, the flames had grown enough to burn the contents of Ephraim's letter and erase any sign of the box from the world.

"Pay attention," Tarsa snapped.

I forced my thoughts to return to the present. My night with Aiden still echoed through my mind, my skin searing with each memory.

"I am," I groused.

Her eyes narrowed on my stance. "Clearly not," she said, sweeping my feet out from under me in a move so simple I should've seen it coming.

The air left my lungs in a rush as I collapsed onto the hard ground. The sound of Daemon's soft chuckle from across the room made my already flushed cheeks brighten.

"If you were paying attention, you would've heard my instructions regarding your footwork." Tarsa paced around me slowly, like a cat who'd cornered its prey.

My jaw tightened. "Then consider me distracted."

"Thinking of anything in particular, Princess?" Daemon called, an amused lilt to his voice.

"Not at all."

His knowing smirk made my flush deepen.

"Distraction will get you killed," Tarsa said, flipping the axe in her grip. Since I'd walked into the training room this morning, she had acted as if our conversation at the bonfire the night before hadn't happened. Something I was perfectly fine with as I'd since discovered that I truly could accept Aiden for who and what he was.

"Then I'm glad you're not actually trying to kill me." I wiped the sweat from my brow as I got to my feet. We'd been training for nearly two hours. Soon we would stop for the day, and I would return to the village to aid with the rest of the cleanup. Aiden was already there now.

Thoughts of him made my pulse jump. I shook my head, struggling to clear my mind. From Daemon's grin I knew he guessed where my mind wandered so often this morning.

"Not now," Tarsa said, bringing me back to the present.

"You intend to kill me someday then?"

She shrugged, admiring the sharp gleam of her axe. "If you hurt the prince, then yes."

"Well, that's rude," Daemon drawled. His shaggy hair hung in his eyes as he slid down the wall to stretch out on the floor.

Tarsa turned to him. "Aiden is under my protection. If he gets hurt, by anyone, then it is my responsibility to kill them. No matter who they are."

When she turned back to me, I could see the sincerity in her eyes. I knew, without a doubt, that if she ever learned of the bargain I once had with Ephraim, she would kill me. Or worse.

"I have no intention of ever hurting Aiden," I swore.

Tarsa didn't say anything more, instead choosing to launch into another attack.

We parried well together. Though my skills were far from those of any of the immortals, I was no longer floundering around like a clumsy child.

Tarsa's arm came down on my wrist, hard. The jolt of the blow caused my hand to spasm, dropping the practice sword onto the ground with a loud clatter. Tarsa had her axe at my throat in the next breath.

"Dead." Her voice was soft, threatening.

"Ok, wonderful. You've killed the princess. Now what do you do when Aiden tries to kill you?" Daemon's eyes remained closed as he sprawled on his back, resting his head on his arms, feigning sleep.

"He will understand it was for the best," she said. But even I could hear the hint of uncertainty in her words.

Daemon only smiled at the ceiling.

"Let's just get back to training," I said, stepping out of her grip.

"Why don't you ever train with the essence?" Daemon asked.

Tarsa's sigh came out a hiss of breath. "The essence is something that could be taken from her or returned to Death. She must learn to fight without it so she doesn't begin to rely on it for survival. It might not always be there when she needs it," Tarsa explained slowly, like she was speaking to a petulant child.

"I understand that," Daemon said, slowly sitting up so he leaned on his elbows. "But wouldn't it make sense for her to train with it while she has the power it could give her? It could help her in a time when she needs it most."

Tarsa returned her axes to their places at her sides, dangling from her belt. "All right then. You can train her."

Daemon looked aghast. "What?"

"If you're so keen on wanting her to be trained with her essence, then you train her," Tarsa said, shrugging.

"Why me?"

Tarsa strode toward the door. "You know more about raw power like that than I do. That makes you the perfect teacher."

As soon as she disappeared into the hall, Daemon cursed colorfully.

"What did she mean?" I asked, studying the demon-born.

Daemon pulled himself clumsily to his feet, very unlike the normally graceful immortals.

The demon sighed, brushing his dark hair from his eyes so I could see his horns. "Some of us that are born to demon parents possess magic, of a sort."

I felt my brows rise toward my hairline. "You have magic? Like a witch?"

He gave me an insulted look. "No. Nothing like a witch."

It was my turn to be annoyed. "Then why did she say you have to train me?"

Daemon sighed again, seeming to collect himself before strolling over to stand before me. There was a weight to his shoulders that wasn't there before. His expression was one of exhaustion as he finally looked at me.

"The demon-born and the angels have more in common than you might believe," he started slowly. "As you know, the angels were created to guard the Crossroads. Because of that, they were given power by Death so they could fight the souls. Over the last few hundred years since their rebellion, it has become popular opinion that they no longer possess that power."

"So what sort of magic do they have?"

He shrugged. "We don't know. Maybe none? Maybe something even stronger."

"But you still have magic?" I asked.

"A little," he said, brows furrowing like he was trying to find the right words. "What I do is sense magic in others. That's pretty much all any demon-born can do anymore. That's how I know when you're using the essence and when you're just relying on your poor mortal reflexes."

I let the insult go, choosing to ignore it. "How will that let you help me practice with the essence?" I thought back to my nights with Ephraim.

Perhaps he still possessed some of that power if he was so keen on teaching me to awaken it.

"I don't know," he admitted with a laugh. "But I'm all you've got, Princess."

My gaze landed on the door. "Maybe you should ask Tarsa to come back."

"Why me?" he whined.

I levied a pointed glance. "Because you're the reason she left."

"I think she left because she doesn't like you."

"She doesn't like you either," I retorted.

That made him chuckle. "I'm working on that."

I brushed my hair over my shoulder. "Fine. You can teach me. What do you want me to do?"

His gaze swept over me, evaluating. "Just call the essence forward and we'll go from there I guess."

I fought against a frustrated sigh as I opened up the essence within myself. It responded in kind, as if it had been waiting to be called.

My blood turned molten in my veins, burning like I held every star in the night sky within me. Daemon drew in a sharp inhale as I let the essence expand until the familiar veil of power slipped over my eyes.

His brows furrowed, hiding the surprise in his eyes. "What can you normally do with it?"

I shrugged. "I can sense when a soul is nearby. Sometimes I can call that soul to me, but after binding Alvize and Delvin I don't think I should try that."

He nodded slowly, still staring at me with a bewildered expression. "What about using it as a weapon?"

"I've never been able to do that on purpose," I said, thinking back to Ephraim's attempt to take the essence.

"Aiden did say it responds to your emotions," he muttered, thinking to himself.

I thought that through as I remembered every instance where it had lashed out at an attacker. Each time I was scared and hurt. But surely there must be some way to get it to act on my command instead of at random interludes.

Daemon attacked before my thought was finished. His movements were a blur before he launched me through the air.

I grunted as my back collided with the wall. My vision swam as I slowly got to my feet, legs shaking and ground wobbling beneath me.

Daemon's hand steadied me at the elbow. "Sorry. I'd hoped that would make it react."

Nausea clawed its way up my throat. "Let's maybe try something different."

"What are you two doing in here?" Seraphine's voice cut through the room like a knife.

She marched over to me, gently pulling me from Daemon's grip as the demon stepped back, giving us room.

"We were training," Daemon explained casually.

"You threw her across the room." Seraphine's voice was harsh as she glowered at him.

Daemon's tone remained bland. "I was testing a theory."

"What theory?" Killian asked, striding in behind Seraphine.

"Probably something entirely idiotic," Seraphine scolded. I leaned into her, letting her take the brunt of my weight as the room finally stopped spinning.

"I thought, maybe, that the essence would react to her emotions if she was placed in a dangerous position." Daemon spoke nonchalantly, like he hadn't just casually tossed me across the room.

"Did it work?" Killian asked, face lit with curious excitement as he looked me over.

I grimaced. "No. And I'll have the bruises to prove it."

Daemon ran a hand through his hair. "It was a solid theory."

"A stupid theory," Seraphine muttered under her breath. "Are you all right? Should I send for Ridha?"

I shook my head, stepping free from her grip. "No. I'm fine. Just a little sore."

"Are you sure? You're still not fully healed from Ephraim's attack." Seraphine sent a pointed scowl to Daemon as she spoke. The demon quickly lowered his gaze to his feet, but not before I caught the slight widening of his eyes as he remembered my near demise.

"I'm fine. Really," I said, waving away her concern.

Seraphine visibly relaxed. "Okay. Then we should get you cleaned up before we return to the village. Fen asked to see you before we get covered in soot again. Something about your dress I believe."

My stomach somersaulted.

She turned, striding for the door as Killian picked up a practice sword to begin training with Daemon.

"Where is Jadan?" I asked, surprised the white-haired demon wasn't popping up to join his friends as he often did.

Daemon's expression soured. "Ofrin called him back to the north."

I frowned, not understanding. "Why?"

His expression clouded. "We don't know. But it can't be good."

"Why do you say that?" I asked, noting the apprehension in his eyes.

Daemon wouldn't meet my gaze as he moved to join Killian on the far side of the room. "It never is."

And with that newfound worry running through me, I fled from the room.

Seraphine waited while I quickly bathed and changed. I took the opportunity to wear my new armored shirt—it was cool against my skin and surprisingly heavy along my shoulders. I knew there really was no point in bathing now when I would only need to do it again after helping with the village cleanup, but I despised the idea of trying on Fen's dress while salty with sweat.

Once dressed, we made our way out of the castle and down the wooded path that would lead us directly past Fen's cottage.

"Aiden seemed in good spirits this morning," Seraphine noted as we walked.

I avoided her gaze. "Did he?"

She nodded, sending me a knowing look. "Did something happen after you two left the kitchen?"

I shrugged, fighting to keep the heat out of my cheeks. "He played a song for me."

"He did?" Her shock was a surprise to me.

"Did you not know he could play? He's been practicing my family's song and played it for me last night."

She shook her head, a little bewildered. "Fen once told me that Aiden's mother wanted him to have something peaceful to do, like learning to play an instrument or paint. But I guess I never realized he did it."

"He's very good," I said. Even I could hear the daze in my voice as I thought back to the night before.

Seraphine snorted. "I didn't need to know that."

My cheeks blazed. "No. No, that's not what I meant."

She only laughed, wrapping her arm over my shoulder. "Are you sure? Because I don't think I've ever seen you so red."

"I was referring to the song he played," I said firmly. The winter air did little to fight the heat in my cheeks.

Seraphine's laughter grew, echoing off the snow-covered woods around us. I could only laugh with her, foregoing my embarrassment. After everything we'd been through these last few weeks, it felt nice to just have a moment to laugh together.

As with Aiden, I'd pushed away from Seraphine's friendship. I'd isolated myself with only my misery for companionship, then fell into a bargain with the one person who was capable of destroying the whole realm and everyone I cared about along with it.

Her laughter cut off abruptly, drawing me from my thoughts.

I felt her body go rigid beside me as she froze in the middle of the path. My breath fogged on the cold air before me as I followed her gaze.

Fen's cottage stood settled between the trees. The windows were dark, no sign of life lingering beyond them. But what truly made my panic surge was the broken door hanging off its hinges and the spatter of blood dripping from the wood.

FORTY-FIVE

Seraphine burst through the door before I could fully understand what I was seeing.

"Fen?" Seraphine's brown eyes were wide, all color leached from her face.

I joined her in the small cottage, taking in the destruction. Just beyond the broken door, the kitchen sat in disarray. Cabinets were broken, and dishes were shattered on the floor.

Her voice became shrill with panic. "Stars, Fen, are you okay?"

I followed her into the sitting room, noting the unlit hearth and overturned furniture. But once I caught sight of Fen, unconscious and bleeding on the floor, my chest seized.

Fen's greying hair was stained with blood that poured from a cut on her temple. Bruises had already begun to form over her eye and chin. Her body lay at an odd angle, like there might be something broken.

"Stay with her." Seraphine's command was that of a warrior, sharp and cold.

I took Seraphine's place at Fen's side. Fen's blood soaked through the knees of my pants as I knelt to tend to her head wound. I pressed the hem of my cloak against it, trying desperately to stop the flow of blood.

Seraphine moved through the house, silent as a wraith and just as deadly. Her eyes were narrowed with focus as she searched the rest of the cottage for the attacker.

Fen groaned, making me jump.

"Fen? Can you hear me?" I asked, silently begging her to open her eyes.

"Is she all right? Esme, tell me she's all right," Seraphine called as she returned from the back rooms.

I nodded, relief flooding my chest. "I think so. She's alive, but she's badly hurt. Is Ridha still in the village helping the wounded?"

Her eyes were wide as she studied Fen's injuries. "I don't know. I think so?"

"Go. Get her and bring her here."

A shadow appeared in the doorway, startling us both. Seraphine had her knives up before I could blink.

Tarsa stepped forward, letting the light illuminate her face. "What happened?" Her voice was accusatory as she glowered at me.

"We just found her," Seraphine said. I could see the panic threatening to overthrow her warrior's calm.

Tarsa didn't respond, only turning on her heel to disappear through the door.

"Where is she going?" I asked. The hem of my cloak had soaked through with blood, the warm, sticky liquid coating my hands as I applied pressure to the gash.

"She's getting Ridha." Seraphine moved closer, kneeling on Fen's other side. "Help me get her to the bed. Tarsa is fast; she'll be back soon."

I trailed after her as she delicately carried Fen down the hall to the bedroom in the back of the small cottage. The wound at her temple continued to bleed freely as she lay, too still, on the small cot.

"Nothing is worse than this," Seraphine muttered, kneeling by the edge of the bed.

I forced the panic away. "She'll be fine, Seraphine. It's Fen. She'll get through this."

She shook her head, slowly, sadly. "Nothing is worse than watching the person you've spent decades loving age and grow closer to the end of their life while you can do nothing to help them. Or even join them in death."

I studied her, watching the way tears spilled down her cheeks as she gently stroked Fen's hair. "How long were you together before she regained her mortality?"

"Long enough that I didn't think she would ask for her mortality back."

There was nothing to say as I stood awkwardly in the doorway. I could only think of what Fen's death would do to Seraphine. The pain it would cause.

Then I thought of Aiden. I too was only a mortal. My lifespan would be a mere blink compared to his own. What would my death do to him?

I shook my head, refusing to think on it anymore.

"I'll grab a rag to start cleaning the blood away," I said, only earning a small nod in response.

The house was destroyed, as though Fen had struggled against the attacker. My heart swelled with pride for the mortal warrior.

I grabbed the first rag I could find. The stained cloth was half hidden in the destruction of the kitchen.

As soon as I gripped the cloth, the essence opened. I didn't think I'd called on it, but I felt it pulse through my veins.

The two souls belonging to Fen and Seraphine were where I left them in the bedroom. But there was something else nearby, too close. A void that made my skin cold and the hair on my neck rise.

I spun around just as the angel struck. The knife whizzed past my face so close I felt the brush of air across my cheek.

Dark eyes met mine beneath a curtain of crimson hair. "You will give me that essence," she snarled.

The essence hummed dangerously in my chest. "Did Ephraim send you?"

Viema's laugh was cold and bitter. "That bastard is too busy with his own agenda to keep track of my movements."

I jumped back as she made to stab me again. My back collided with the cabinets as I struggled to avoid her attack. Viema had always been a good fighter, fast and strong as she was. But there was a new desperation to her movements that hadn't been there before. And they made her clumsy.

I yanked my new knife free from its hiding place beneath my sleeve as I raced from the cottage, away from Fen's vulnerable position.

Viema followed me, a rage-filled cry erupting from her throat as I sped through the trees.

She was faster than I was and caught up to me in no time. The breath rushed from my lungs as she tackled me from behind, using her strength to pin me to the snow-covered ground.

A maniacal laugh spilled from her mouth. "Got you now, Soul Collector. And nobody can save you. Not Ephraim, not the Dark Angel, and not your precious essence."

I struggled under her. She dug her knees into my hips, pinning them to the earth. I tried to maneuver my other hand to block the blow I knew would come.

Her hand wrapped around my wrist, squeezing just enough to pull a cry from my lips. My bones felt as if they were on the verge of shattering.

"I see being married to Aiden hasn't made you any stronger," she said, digging her nails into the skin at my wrist.

"I see following Ephraim hasn't made you any smarter," I snapped.

Her lip curled in a sneer just before I moved. My free hand brushed against the hilt of a knife in the grass. I winced as her hold on my other wrist tightened, twisting it at an odd angle. Before she could completely shatter my wrist, I wrapped my hand around the knife's hilt, and dug it into her gut, right where I suspected a still-healing wound from Killian's arrow remained.

She screeched, launching off of me. Her blood dripped onto my clothes as I held the knife aloft. Viema clutched a hand to her side as she stumbled on her feet.

I stood slowly, aware of the gathering souls nearby.

"Give me the essence, or I will take it from your cold, dead body." Though her voice was steady with anger, I could see the slight shaking in her hands as her body recognized the pain I'd caused.

The essence burned. "No."

Viema shouted a cry of war before launching herself at me again.

Even injured, she was faster than me, and my mortal body still wasn't quick enough to avoid all of her blows.

I felt her fist collide with my chin a moment before something collided with the tender spot on my chest.

The world paused. Viema stood before me, a wild look of triumph on her face as she stared down at her hand gripping the small knife.

I took a steadying breath, waiting for the pain to hit. But it never came. I smiled, watching the uncertainty and fear spread across her face.

Viema pulled the knife away, staring at the spot with wide eyes. "I don't understand," she said. We both glanced at my unmarked chest.

I noticed the nearby souls before Viema did.

I leapt back as Aiden crashed into her, sending her flying into a nearby tree. My husband crouched before me, raven black wings outstretched in a shield before me.

Viema slowly got to her feet, blood dripping from her wound. Tarsa and Hakan appeared behind her, weapons glinting in the light.

The angel cursed. I watched her hateful gaze narrow on me as she studied the armored shirt I wore.

"That's impossible," she said between gasping breaths.

Aiden straightened from his crouch. "Why are you here?"

Tarsa roughly yanked Viema to her feet, making the angel cry out. "I will not speak to you," she spat between her teeth.

I stepped forward, pausing at Aiden's outstretched wing. Though his eyes never left the angel, I felt his concentration slip to me. Something passed through his eyes a moment before he tucked his wings along his back, leaving me room to step out from behind their protection.

"You said Ephraim doesn't know you are here," I started slowly, forcing my breathing to return to an even rhythm as my adrenaline subsided. "Is that true?"

She spat at my feet. Her pointed face was scrunched up in a look of absolute hatred. "You are not deserving of it. You are but a filthy mortal."

Aiden's hands fisted at his sides as he trembled with restraint.

"Why did you come here?" Hakan asked, keeping his sword in his hand in case he needed to cut her down quickly.

A smirk graced the corners of Viema's mouth as her eyes met mine. "Keeping secrets can be a deadly game," she said. "I'm willing to pay the price. Are you?"

Fear slammed into me. I could feel Tarsa's watchful gaze deciphering my emotions. If Viema told Aiden of the deal I'd made with Ephraim, would he believe her? Or would Tarsa strike me down before I could explain?

"If you keep threatening my wife, you will find a fate far worse than death," Aiden drawled, sounding bored beneath his princely mask.

The angel's mouth curled in a snarl of rage before she launched herself at me.

Viema's hands gripped the front of my armored shirt.

"He will learn," she whispered, pulling me close enough that I could feel her cold breath on my face. "He will learn. And when he does, you will be in chains, and it will be you who never knows peace."

The true possibility of her threat stalled my breath. Despite my desire to be released from these secrets, the fear of my punishment held my tongue.

Sensing my inner turmoil, she laughed, the sound cold and shrill in the silence of the forest. "I wonder if your family will survive. Perhaps they're already dead. Mousa is quite the fighter, you know. And that sister of yours." She yanked me closer, pulling me off balance. "She's a skilled fighter too, but she's too arrogant with her skills and too trusting with her heart. It will get her killed."

I drove my knee upward, hitting the wound in her gut. She gagged, doubling over as the pain made her limbs spasm.

"Do not threaten my family again," I said vehemently. The power poured through my veins until it burned as bright as the stars.

Hakan stepped forward, yanking Viema to her feet. The angel slumped in his arms, either giving up or in too much pain to fight back.

"I'll take her to the dungeons," he said, the ever-dutiful soldier.

I met his gaze and realized he was speaking to me. Hidden in the well of his dark eyes was a budding respect I wasn't sure had been there before.

I nodded, watching him practically drag Viema through the snow until they disappeared down the path.

Tarsa lingered a moment, her jaw set and her knuckles white as she kept a tight grip on her axe. I watched her eyes flicker between Aiden and I before she finally turned to trail after Hakan.

Familiar warmth settled along my back as Aiden leaned into me, his wings still visible.

"Are you harmed?" he asked, voice tight.

I brushed the hair from my face. "I'm fine. Fen is hurt though."

"I know. We left Ridha at the cottage when we heard you fighting."

"I wonder why she came here without Ephraim knowing," I said, lost in thought. Aiden's hands wrapped around my waist, forcing more of his warmth into my cold limbs.

"Do you want to question her now?"

I shook my head. Something flickered in the corner of my vision, catching my attention. Pulling free of Aiden's grip, I moved toward it.

A small white blade was half buried in the snow a few feet away, right where Viema would've dropped it when Aiden knocked her away from me. The essence rattled in my chest, uneasy at the proximity to this weapon.

The knife was heavy for such a small thing. I held it in the light, studying the designs inscribed along the metal. The entire weapon was pure white, blinding in the sun, but the designs were etched with a dark ink in a language I didn't understand.

"What is it?" Aiden asked, coming to look over my shoulder.

I straightened just as recognition hit. "I think I've seen this before."

Aiden frowned. "Is this the knife she used to try and take the essence from you?"

"It is," I said, handing it to him. "But I've seen it another time too. I think it's in Alfie's notebook. I don't know where he would've come across this, but it looks just like one of his sketches."

He handed it back to me. "Take care with it. I don't want you accidentally pricking a finger and removing the essence yourself."

I rolled my eyes which made him smile. He took my face in his hands, keeping my head tilted so I had to look at him.

"Are you sure you are unharmed?" His voice was soft.

"I'm sure," I promised.

He kissed me. The kiss was tender, speaking all the words he couldn't say aloud about how much he feared for me.

We walked hand in hand down the winding path. His expression was calm, nearly blank, but I could see the lingering violence in his eyes as we headed toward where our newest prisoner was waiting.

My mind was determined to linger on Viema's words. The threat she made against my family. The threat she made against me. She'd seen my brother and sister, of that I was certain. But she would not see them again. I was sure Alfie had written about this knife; I just needed to find some answers.

FORTY-SIX

I WAS RIGHT. MIXED in with Alfie's endless scribbles was a poorly drawn replica of the knife Viema used in her attempt to take the essence.

The knife in question sat on the small table between the two chairs in my study. Daemon hadn't stopped staring at it since he joined me. But, like the essence, he seemed hesitant to get near it.

"It was created by the first recorded God of Death," I noted out loud.

Daemon grunted noncommittally, leaning over to study the blade from a distance.

"Death used it to create the first angels," I said, continuing to read from Alfie's scribbles.

Daemon shivered. "That explains the feeling."

"What feeling?" I asked, finally looking up from my brother's notebook.

"I don't know. But it has a pulling sensation about it, like it's trying to get me to touch it." He continued to stare quizzically as he leaned back in his chair. "But when I get too close it feels cold, like frostbite along my skin. And empty. It feels like the angels."

I frowned at the knife, willing it to explain its importance to me. "I wonder what the angels used it for."

"Does it not say in that battered notebook?" he asked.

"No," I sighed, setting Alfie's journal aside delicately. "Only a reference to a history book I don't remember reading."

Daemon pivoted in his chair toward the bookcases lining the wall. His hand shot outward, pointing toward a familiar title. "What about that one? *Histories of the Crown*? You've read that one, haven't you?"

I pulled the book from the shelf. "I've already read this multiple times. I don't think there's any mention of this knife."

"Maybe there is but you just didn't realize that's what you were reading about," he mused.

I sighed, settling into the other chair. The late afternoon sun beat down on our backs through the large window. Snow had begun to melt, but solstice was only a few days away. There was still more winter to come.

I flipped through the pages, skimming frantically for any sign of this knife. With Ofrin's ball looming on the horizon, Viema in our dungeons, and her vague threat against my family, my nerves were ricocheting off of each other in a storm of panic.

"Does it siphon the way you can siphon souls?" Daemon asked.

I shrugged. "Maybe? I'm not sure what creating the first angels would entail."

An idea occurred to me, and I flipped quickly to the beginning of the book.

"Aha!" I jumped up from my seat with excitement.

"What did you find?"

"You were right; the knife originally siphoned the souls of demons to create the first angels." I began to pace the small room as I read. "But it was stolen by the angels during the rebellion."

Daemon's brows furrowed as he watched me pace. "But they don't have souls. Why would they need something that was made to siphon souls?"

I kept skimming through the pages, pulling bits of information from them. "I don't know. There's very little written about it once it was taken. Only that they believed it was passed down the line of the Angels of Life until Ephraim's mother had it, then it was passed to him when she was taken by Death."

Daemon's eyes turned distant, recalling a past I could only guess at. "I bet they used dark magic on it."

My feet were moving before my mind could catch up with my thoughts.

"Where are you going?" he called, opting to remain with the knife instead of trailing after me.

I tucked the book under my arm. "I think I know who to ask about this."

The cold winter air whipping against me did little to slow me as I raced to the witch's office. Guards stepped out of my way as I passed, and visitors from the village waved as I raced by.

I skidded to a stop at Ridha's door.

"Ridha?" I called, knocking on the door as I pushed it open.

Ridha turned toward me as I strode into the crowded room. "Princess. I hadn't expected to see you again so soon. If you're here about your friend, she should be fine. I left Fen in the care of her sister."

I nodded, glad to hear the news. "That's not why I'm here."

Her brows rose as she returned to her work. "Oh? Then to what do I owe this intrusion?"

I let her remark slide, stepping further into the room. "What do you know of the knife created by Death to make the angels?"

Her entire body went rigid. Ridha carefully set down the herbs she'd been mixing. The expression she wore was carefully void of emotion; the kind of expression someone only wore if they were hiding something.

"Only what is taught in history." Even her voice was bland as she spoke.

"And what would that be?" I asked, watching her hands knit together in her lap.

"Why are you asking?"

I frowned, setting the book on the table before her. "Because Viema has attempted to use it on me twice now. She, like Ephraim, believes it can be used to harness the essence and take it for herself. I want to know if this is true."

"There is much you do not know," she said quietly. Her eyes were wide as they stared at the pages of the history book, open upon her table.

"If I had a coin for every time one of you immortals said that to me, I'd have enough to buy half of Cordovia."

Her expression hardened at my sour tone.

I chewed my lip as she flipped through the pages, reading what I'd just learned.

"A witch did something to it, didn't they?" I asked when she finally shoved the book aside.

Ridha was silent for a moment. Her usually stern expression was closed off, blank. But her eyes were wide when she finally turned to me.

"Ephraim's mother needed to find a way to create more angels," she started slowly. "They were being hunted by Ofrin's spies and their birth rate was too low to keep their population up."

"So they asked you for help." My tone was accusatory, making her flinch.

Ridha steeled herself, spine straightening as she finally met my eyes. "Ephraim tortured me for weeks before I finally agreed to help them," she said hotly. "They needed to create more angels. A way to steal the souls of mortals and bring them to their realm. I gave them that."

I pointed to the illustration in the book. "You used magic on the knife, giving the angels the ability to siphon souls because they couldn't do what Ofrin could. They didn't have that power."

"No, they didn't." She fixed me with a glare. "Siphoning the souls of mortals is a feat only Death can achieve. Angels were created to guard souls, not rip them from mortal bodies."

"So what can this knife do now?"

Her face had gone stony. "It can still siphon souls, but it was adapted to steal more than that."

"Ridha, what can it steal?" Nerves made my heart race in my chest, seizing my lungs.

I watched her swallow, bracing herself to say the words I already suspected.

"It steals Death," she finally said. "When wielded by an angel, it can steal the essence of Death itself, leaving this entire world without a God of Death to aid the souls at the end of their mortal lives."

"And should that happen, what would that mean for our realm? Or the mortal realm?" I asked.

"If souls were left to roam the realms without passing through the Crossroads, they could destroy everything."

I frowned, thinking of the souls that escaped from the Crossroads weeks earlier. "Would another God of Death not be created if Ofrin died?"

"If he simply died and there was another capable of wielding his power, yes," she said. "But if the essence of his power was ripped from him, then I don't think so. I don't know of a way to create a God of Death without using the essence from the former."

I blanched with horror. "Why would Ephraim want this? Why would his mother want to end Death's reign?"

Memories slammed into me as soon as the words left my mouth. I stumbled back, gripping onto the edge of the table for support as I recalled the words spoken only hours before my family was murdered.

"Is this knife only capable of siphoning the essence? Would there be no way to put it into someone else?" I asked. My voice sounded distant to my own ears, but I forced myself to remain focused on the matter at hand.

Ridha watched me curiously. "Yes. But only someone very powerful could do that."

"Viema believed she could use the knife to steal my essence and wield it for herself," I noted.

The witch shrugged, turning back to her work. "I doubt the angel is that strong, but Ephraim might be."

A familiar head of curly blond hair poked into the room. "What are you doing out here?" Killian asked, eyeing the witch warily as he stepped to my side.

"I needed to ask some questions about the knife," I said, noting the way he positioned himself as if to protect me from Ridha. The witch had turned back to her work, ignoring his arrival.

Killian kept his eyes on her. "Come." He looped his arm through mine. "It's cold and you don't have your cloak. You can't catch a mortal illness before the ball."

I tucked the book under my free arm. "Thank you for answering my questions," I said to the witch. Ridha only waved me away with her hand, not bothering to turn around.

Killian quickly led me back to the castle and the warmth it provided.

"Why did you go to the witch?" he asked, leading me toward my study.

I noted his stiff posture. "Because she had the answers I needed."

"What did she have to say?" My study was empty when we returned, Daemon nowhere to be found. But the dagger remained untouched.

I kicked the door closed behind us. "She only confirmed my suspicions about the knife."

Killian leaned against the window, staring into the garden beyond. I knew what he was looking at; the window offered a perfect view of the bench Aiden had gifted me.

"It's a thing of dark magic, Esme." His voice had turned hollow. "I thought Ephraim's poison was bad, but even I can feel the power radiating from that thing. And I don't have magic."

I joined him at the window, thinking through everything I'd just learned. As far as we knew, this was the only knife that could siphon the essence from me. But if such a knife existed, why didn't Ofrin attempt to retrieve it, or have a new one created for himself if he was so desperate to have the essence back? What was stopping him?

My gaze landed on the bench. I hadn't had a chance to finish talking with Aiden. He'd unexpectedly taken the news of his mother quite well. But I knew he still had many questions. And I had many other secrets he deserved to know.

"I did try to protect her." Killian's whisper broke the silence.

"Who?" I asked. When I turned to him, he was already watching me with sad, regretful eyes.

"Cordelia. Before Aiden sent me to the white tree, I promised her she'd be safe. I'm just sorry I wasn't there to protect the rest of your family."

I hugged him, surprising both of us. "There was nothing you could've done, Killian. Ephraim already had his claws in King Elroy's mind, as did Ofrin. No one could've saved them."

Someone cleared their throat behind us. Killian and I pulled apart, startled that someone could've entered my study without one of us noticing. I hadn't felt anyone nearby through the essence.

"Pardon the interruption," the portly man said, though his expression looked anything but sorry. He was stout and his hair was beginning to grey near his temples. I'd never seen him before, but there was an air of confidence about him that told me he wasn't of this court.

"Who are you?" I asked. Killian had grown inhumanly still at my side, stepping away just enough to draw his weapons if needed.

The man dipped his chin in the shadow of a bow. "I am a representative on behalf of the God of Death. I was sent from his court to speak with the Prince and Princess about yesterday's attack."

I nodded, pinching the ends of my sleeves in my hands nervously. "Fine. Follow me and I will take you to my husband's study."

The man continued to watch Killian as I strode past, practically ignoring me. Why a stranger was walking around our castle without anyone's knowledge was beyond me. Especially considering the number of guards we had watching the premises.

I knocked at Aiden's study, sensing his presence through our marriage bond.

"Yes?" he called through the thick cedar door.

I pushed it open, letting myself in. "Someone from your father's court is here to speak with us."

Aiden looked up from the papers he was reading immediately. What looked like worry passed over his face so quickly I was almost sure I imagined it. But his wings shifted, tucking in across his back, revealing his emotions.

He nodded, quickly setting his work aside. "Very well. Come, send him in."

I pushed the door open further, letting the man into the room. Killian followed closely on his heels with Hakan after him.

I closed the door after the two warriors and leaned against it, opting to remain as far from the strange man as I could in the crowded space.

Aiden shifted, drawing my gaze. Though he continued to sit on the far side of the room, he held his hand out to me, beckoning.

I glanced once at the man, noting the watchful look on his face as I moved to join Aiden. He stood, gently placing me in his seat as he stood at my shoulder, his position mirroring Hakan's on my other side.

"What can I do for you?" Aiden's voice was cold. It was the tone of the Prince of Death.

The man glanced between the two of us, letting his eyes land on Killian once before turning back to us.

"Your father has asked that you report every detail of yesterday's attack. I am here to collect that report." A blast of recognition hit me as I focused on the stranger's voice. But I had no idea where I would have met him before—his face remained unfamiliar.

Aiden sighed, annoyed. "Why doesn't he just ask one of the many spies he insists on keeping in my court? I noticed he recalled Jadan to his territory, but Daemon still lingers. Why not call on him to provide a thorough overview of the events?"

The man glanced at me briefly and I felt Aiden shift closer in response. "He also wished to get another look into your personal affairs."

"Of course," Aiden drawled. The smile that turned up his mouth was anything but warm. "You are here to check on my wife. Tell me, is she as pleasing as you expected her to be?"

There was a threatening edge to Aiden's voice as the man's eyes returned to mine. I waited for the silent acknowledgement of a previous introduction to register in his eyes. But it never came. I narrowed my gaze at him, forcing my mind to search for any memory of the oddly familiar demon.

"I expected," he enunciated the words carefully, "to find your wife as enthralled with you as you claim to be with her. Instead, I found her in the arms of another."

Killian's cheeks flushed bright red as the man turned his glare on him. I scowled, disliking the man more and more.

"He is a friend," I said, letting my anger show in my voice. "Nothing more."

"Is that so?" he asked, turning his gaze to me. His manner became threatening; not in the way he spoke or glowered at me like he wished me dead, but in the way he carried himself. Every movement he made screamed of danger.

"Whatever you think you saw, I can assure you that you are wrong." Aiden's voice was cutting as he pierced the man with his stare.

The stranger shrugged. "It should not matter what I think. Only that your father will be most interested to learn of this development."

Hakan moved to open the door for the strange demon. "I will be sure to send Daemon with word of the attack then, since you only seem interested in my wife," Aiden said as the man began to leave.

When he turned, he only had eyes for me. "Good luck, Princess. I have a feeling you will need it." And with that, he disappeared through the doorway.

"Hakan." Aiden spoke his name like a command.

The immortal warrior nodded, disappearing after the stranger. Killian began to move too, practically fleeing from the room.

"Wait," Aiden said in a soft voice laced with power, stopping Killian in his tracks.

Killian turned to face him, unable to look at me entirely. "Yes, Your Highness?"

"What was he talking about?" he asked slowly.

I rolled my eyes. "I just hugged him. We were talking about Cordelia, and my family."

Aiden didn't look at me. "No matter how innocent, as I have no doubt it was, it won't appear that way to my father."

"I expect this messenger of his will be delighted to embellish the situation also," Killian muttered.

I sighed. "Fine. Then what is there to do about it?"

Aiden shrugged, keeping his arm around my waist. "Nothing."

"Then why bring it up at all?" I argued stubbornly.

"Because my father's ball is only days away. Whatever he learns between now and then will dictate his behavior during our stay," Aiden explained simply.

"And Ephraim? Are we just supposed to ignore the threat hanging over our heads while we put on a show for your father?"

"We're watching for him," Killian vowed. "Some of us will go with you. But many will stay here to watch the castle and the villagers. We'll see him coming."

"But we didn't last time," I complained. "Surely there must be a way to find him, or any angel in this realm."

"We are being cautious," Aiden assured me. "Plus, we are still planning on drawing him out after the ball. Once we have done that, we can prevent him from causing any further damage to this realm, or any realm."

I sighed. Our plan to capture Ephraim was faulty at best, and as far as I was concerned, it felt less like a plan and more like a desperate hope for peace.

"Has Viema awoken yet?" Aiden asked Killian.

The demon shook his head. "She's been unconscious since Hakan left her in the dungeons. There are guards standing watch at all hours. If she wakes, we'll know."

Tarsa barged into the room then; her eyes were a wild storm of anger as she slammed the door closed behind her.

My shoulders curved inward as I sensed the full force of her anger targeted at me. Aiden stepped closer, watching her warily.

She leaned over the desk so we were eye to eye, slamming her hands on the wood so hard I flinched.

Her voice was as sharp as the axes glinting at her waist. "When were you going to tell us you were working with Ephraim?"

FORTY-SEVEN

My insides turned frigid. No one spoke. No one dared to breathe. I could feel their eyes on me like arrows in my back, but I couldn't bring myself to meet their gazes.

Tarsa scrutinized every miniscule expression flitting across my face. My heart pounded away in my chest as guilt reared its ugly head.

"That's not possible," Killian said, quickly coming to my defense. "Whoever told you that is lying. Esme would never work with Ephraim."

My cheeks burned as his voice slowly drifted off. When I dared to glance in his direction, the disbelief and hurt were easy to read.

"You've been working with him this whole time," Tarsa snapped. "You are his spy."

I shook my head, desperate for them to understand the truth. "No. I'm not."

"You are," she continued. "You were so distraught, believing Aiden to be the cause of your family's demise, that you ran to the first person who hated us as much as you do. And he waited for you with open arms. You told him every secret of ours. No wonder our spies never returned, because you told him where they were searching. You're probably why Ridha's stash of the antidote went missing."

Panic rose like burning bile in my throat. Aiden was already backing away when I turned to him, anguish present in his eyes until he wiped his expression clean.

"I swear I'm not, Aiden," I pleaded. I rose from the chair, taking a step toward him only for him to back away again. My heart splintered. "I'm not anymore. I was, at one time. But as soon as I learned the truth, I stopped working for him. That's why he tried to kill me and take the essence. Because I refused him."

Tarsa slammed her hands on the desk again, making me jump. "Stop lying! Our entire realm may be doomed because of your stupidity."

My eyes burned, but I couldn't tear my gaze away from Aiden's blank stare. "I'm not lying. After the first time you tried to tell me of my parents' bargain, I did go to him. I was hurt and he offered to help me get the revenge I thought I wanted. But as soon as I learned the truth, I tried to break it off with him."

Tarsa scoffed but quieted her retort as Aiden held up a hand, silencing her.

"Tell me everything," he said in a dead voice.

So I did. I told them every emotion and every thought that crossed my mind after my family died. And I told them how I came to find Ephraim in the woods and what he told me of Aiden's mother. Only Killian showed any sign of surprise at that news. I told them everything I believed Ephraim knew and everything I'd guessed about his plans. Anything I could think of that involved Ephraim and the angels, I told them.

When I told them about how I first tried to sever the bargain I'd made, Tarsa snorted.

"So, you were the one who stole the antidote," she exclaimed.

"I didn't know what it was. He just said he needed one of Ridha's potions."

Killian stepped forward. "And what did you think it was? Whatever you might've suspected, you must have known he didn't want it for good reasons."

"I couldn't find any other way to end the deal I'd made with him."

"So that's why he nearly killed you." Aiden's voice was soft, distant, as he spoke for the first time since I began the story.

"Yes."

"Because you told him you had no interest in spying for him any longer."

I nodded. "Yes."

Aiden sighed, the portrait of exasperation as he ran a hand over his face. When his eyes returned to mine, they were burning with the aftermath of my secrets. "Why didn't you tell me right away? There's much more we could have done had we known sooner."

"Like add more protection around the village," Tarsa muttered.

I dropped my head. All those innocents dead, their homes and businesses destroyed, because of me.

I felt his hand beneath my chin before I realized he'd stepped closer. Aiden tilted my head so I had to look at him. His gaze searched my face.

"I do not fault you for partnering with him," Aiden said slowly. Tarsa muttered her disagreement, but he ignored it. "But I do fault you for keeping your mistakes hidden when we needed to know the truth."

His hand fell from my chin. "After everything," hurt filled his gaze, "I would have thought you believed I deserved to know the truth."

My eyes burned. "I'm sorry. I was so ashamed of what I'd done. I wasn't sure how I could tell you."

"How about 'Hey friends. So I did this really stupid thing and got caught up in our enemy's dirty tricks, and now he knows more about our defenses than you first thought. I'm real sorry though,'" Killian added dryly.

"I am sorry," I admitted in a small voice.

Aiden watched me sadly, emotions slowly bleeding back onto his face. Tarsa, however, would not be swayed.

Tarsa studied me with unnerving clarity, her gaze steely. "You put all of our lives at risk."

Aiden held up a placating hand. "Will you two give us a moment please?"

Killian obliged, immediately heading for the door. But Tarsa remained. The glower she sent my way nearly made me tremble in my boots.

"Please, Tarsa. It'll be fine," Aiden added. "And speak of this to no one. Not yet. Just tell Hakan and Daemon to keep an extra eye out."

Reluctantly, Tarsa nodded, relenting to his command. The two left in silence, softly closing the door behind them.

I didn't know what to say. Didn't know how to explain why I didn't immediately tell them what I'd been doing. There were no words to describe the guilt that was slowly eating me up inside.

"Look at me, Esme." Aiden's voice was a soft plea.

There was pain in his eyes, the aftereffects of my betrayal. But there was also a deep-rooted understanding that cut me far deeper.

"Don't look at me like that," I said hoarsely.

He stepped closer. "It's going to be okay," he said, the words searing.

A knot corded in my throat. "I should've said something sooner. I should have tried harder to tell you instead of giving in when we got interrupted."

"Yes," he agreed. "You should have. But you didn't. And now we have to work with the consequences."

He took my hands in his, running his thumb over the vines tattooed on the back of my hand. Our marriage bond.

"I'm sorry," I said again.

Aiden squeezed my hands. "I know. And I am sorry I could not tell you the truth about your family's deaths sooner. Had I been able to, maybe we could've avoided this entirely."

I choked on a laugh. "Maybe."

He pulled me closer, enveloping me in his arms as if trying to erase the pain both of our secrets had caused us.

"We'll get through this," he promised. "There's still time to stop Ephraim. We just can't waste any time once the solstice passes."

I sighed, wrapping my arms around his waist. "He doesn't know that we intend to capture him. I think he assumes that because we don't have access to his realm we don't have plans beyond basic defenses."

"It'll be all right."

Hakan knocked once before entering, looking disgruntled.

"Hakan? What is it?" Aiden asked, stepping away from me sooner than I would've liked.

Hakan spared me a glance. "Viema is awake."

"And? Is she saying anything?" The panic that rocked through me was only increased by the scowl he sent my way.

"She isn't speaking." His voice was curt.

Aiden frowned. "What do you mean? Is she injured?"

Hakan shook his head. "No. She will speak to no one." He turned to me, and his gaze was piercing. "Except for you."

FORTY-EIGHT

THE DUNGEONS WERE DARK and frosty with winter air. The only sound beyond our echoing footsteps was the steady drip of moisture onto cold stone. As we walked down the uneven stairs, I could see my breath begin to fog as we crept lower into the depths of the castle.

At the bottom of the stairs, Hakan led us through a narrow hall. Sconces were placed every few steps, their light making the shadows dance across the frost coated walls.

"How many people are down here?" Though I spoke quietly, my voice carried eerily in the empty hall of the dungeon.

"In this part of the dungeon? Not enough," Hakan said quietly.

When we turned a blind corner, I nearly came to a stop. Large steel doors lined the walls on either side, each with no more than a barred opening just above eye level.

"If this isn't the only dungeon in your castle, then who exactly do you keep down here?" My heart began to pound against my ribs, as eager to escape my chest as I was to escape the prison.

Aiden stepped closer as we passed the nearest doors. From inside I could hear various grunts of pain and the moaning of madness.

"Just because one sells their soul to my father doesn't mean they are exempt from his laws." Aiden kept his gaze straight ahead. "There are dungeons in his mountains as well. That is where he prefers to keep those who do not heed his bargains."

Something slammed into one of the steel doors, making me lurch into Aiden. Cold that had nothing to do with the winter air bit into my skin.

Aiden settled his hands on my shoulders, guiding me past the cell. "Sometimes, if a soul will not pass through the veil after my father or I visit the Crossroads, he has them locked away in these cells."

I frowned at the steel doors lining the walls. "Can't they get out? The souls that got loose had no problem getting past locked doors."

"These cells are enchanted, thanks to Ofrin and Ridha's magic." Hakan's voice was low and calculating as he glowered at the doors. "There is no escaping once the door has been locked."

As we turned another corner, four guards came into view. Until now, the corridors had remained mostly empty. But the cell we approached had two guards standing on either side of the door, each dressed in black with helmets over their heads so I could only see their eyes.

"She's here," Hakan said, nodding to the cell.

I glanced back the way we came. "Why are there guards outside of only her cell?"

"Like all the doors in the dungeon, this one was spelled by Ridha, so it's impenetrable without the specific key," Aiden explained. "But because of who she is... We didn't want to take any risks. We've never held an angel here before."

I could only nod, suddenly feeling my nerves spasm.

"Are you sure you want to do this?" Though his voice was calm, I could see the tightness around his eyes as he studied my expression.

Forcing a deep breath into my lungs, I nodded. "She'll only talk to me. It may be the only way to get the answers we still need."

Hakan didn't wait for Aiden to object. He pulled a key from his pocket and unlocked the door.

Hakan entered first, letting his torch light the room.

The cell was dark and cold. I could hear a steady drip of melting frost as I stepped into the small space. There was no window or candle, leaving the room in complete darkness.

"I was wondering when you'd show up." The words ended on a harsh cough.

"I was told you would only speak to me," I said, pushing steadiness into my voice. I felt Aiden step closer as Hakan used his torch to light a small sconce on the wall.

The light from the flame brightened the room, casting it in an orange glow. The cell was small, barely wide enough for someone of my height to lay flat on the floor without touching the opposite wall. There was no bed, no bale of hay, no sign of any comfort at all.

Only a bucket in the corner, and a hunched figure along the far wall.

Viema turned slowly, like the movement hurt. Her hands were pressed against the wound I'd reopened in her stomach. Blood continued to stain her shirt, flowing freely. I was surprised she hadn't already healed like most immortals would have. She appeared to be healing as slowly as a mortal.

"You're not healing?" I asked.

Her laugh was harsh, hoarse. "Why postpone the inevitable? Your dear husband wouldn't dare let me live after what I've done to you."

Aiden grunted his confirmation.

The noise seemed to remind her of his presence. Viema turned her attention to Hakan, scowling, though she looked too pale and weak to do anything more threatening. "I told you I only wanted the princess."

"Well, you got me," Aiden said sharply.

The angel glowered at him.

"Only the princess. I will speak to no one else." Her voice was as cold as the dungeon.

My jaw set. "He already knows. Might as well say what you have to say in front of him."

The look the angel sent me was scathing. Whatever leverage she thought she had was officially gone.

Her lips curled into a snarl. "So, you told him how you planned to kill him."

"Actually, she tried to kill me already," Aiden chimed in nonchalantly, "before she ever made a deal with your king."

"Don't you mean your brother?"

Aiden's head snapped in her direction, eyes blazing. Whatever cool exterior he'd displayed before vanished as the reminder of his connection to Ephraim was thrown in his face.

"Careful, Viema," Aiden cautioned, his voice oozing venom. "I've managed to refrain from killing you so far. Don't think I won't slip and find my knife lodged in your throat."

She coughed a sardonic laugh. "Petty threats are beneath you."

When her eyes met mine, all I saw was anger. A need for revenge overshadowed all the pain she must have felt. She looked at me as if my death, or my pain, would be the only thing to make her feel joy again.

"Why did you want to speak with me?" I asked, growing frustrated and ready to be out of the dungeon.

"The deal you made with Ephraim," she said in a clear and resolute voice. "The one where he helps you get rid of your curse, and you get to kill Aiden as revenge for what he did to your family, and in exchange you help him get his own revenge? Remember that?"

Hakan didn't take his gaze off of the angel, but I felt his concentration center on me. "Yes," I said through gritted teeth.

She flashed her teeth in a feral grin. "Good. Because he does too. And he intends to follow through with your bargain."

"I will not help Ephraim destroy this realm. Or any realm."

"Then your family will die," she said simply.

Anger ignited within me, awakening the essence.

Sensing my distress, Aiden put a placating hand on my arm.

"Did you learn nothing about threatening my family?" I asked, jaw tight with anger. The essence, the raw power of Death, seared every inch of my skin. Though my veins were scorched by its strength, it made me feel alive.

Her expression changed. A flicker of fear lit her eyes as she studied me, like she hadn't truly seen me before. In a blink the fear vanished. Viema's arrogant smile filled her face once more, the perfect depiction of control. "The last time anyone did anything to your family, you married him. Now, I have no interest in marrying you, but I seriously doubt you'll have me killed for a mere threat."

I knelt before her, letting her see the strength of the essence she'd helped Ephraim awaken. "Aiden did not kill my family. King Elroy did.

At the behest of your angel, and a deal made with Death. If anyone is going to pay for what was done to my family, it is your king."

She had the audacity to smirk. "With what is coming for you, you won't have time to hunt Ephraim."

"And just what is coming?" I asked.

Viema's teeth were stained with blood as she grinned. I watched her body shudder in pain as she shifted, turning so the light revealed the true cruelty of her wound.

"All that power you think you possess, all the whispers and talk of planning you think will be enough—it will be your downfall."

The essence pulsed unsteadily, darkening my vision as the deep well of power opened wider until I could see the cavernous pit of strength it possessed.

Aiden gently pulled me to my feet. His whispered words of comfort were too muddled for me to decipher.

Viema studied the two of us together. "You still have the witch that blessed the knife, don't you?"

"What do you know about Ridha?" Aiden asked sharply.

Viema grinned. "Oh, I remember her. She screamed like a pig being butchered. It was fun having her as our prisoner."

A rivulet of icy sweat trickled down my spine. "*You* tortured her?"

"Me. Ephraim. We took turns." There was a smile in her voice as she recalled the memories.

Hakan's hands turned into white-knuckled fists at his sides.

"We were all very annoyed when she escaped," Viema continued. She studied her nails absentmindedly. "Luckily she is not the only witch in existence."

Hakan's jaw unclenched. "No witch would willingly work with cursed filth such as you."

Viema smiled, eyes alight with simmering violence. "Oh, you're wrong about that."

"Who is the witch working with Ephraim?" I asked, trying to distract Hakan from his barely contained anger.

"Just one witch?" Viema mused.

I frowned at the angel. "He has more than one witch?"

Viema shrugged, seeming suddenly at complete ease. "He could have one. Or, he could have an entire clan. But, of course, that would mean Ephraim would be unstoppable. There would be nothing to protect you from him then."

"I still have the essence."

The angel smiled, eyes glistening in the faint firelight. "For now."

I scowled. "It does not matter. I have Ephraim's siphoning knife. He can't get the essence."

"And that is the only knife?" Viema asked, studying me closely as her cryptic words severed my surety. Her smile grew as my anger flared.

Aiden was suddenly there, a steady presence at my side. His glower settled on the angel. I knew he could sense the power rumbling in my veins.

"That's enough. Let's get you out of here," he said to me, though his eyes never left the enemy.

Viema smiled at him. "It's getting stronger, isn't it? You can feel it. I can too. So can Ephraim."

"What is she talking about?" I whispered. Aiden only shook his head.

"I wonder how it makes your father feel? I'd bet his fragile ego is quite threatened." Viema didn't even blink as she spoke to Aiden, a mischievous gleam in her eyes. "And we both know what happens when someone like your father feels threatened."

Aiden's gaze shot to me, a muscle feathering in his jaw. "It's not like that."

"No?" Viema asked before a sharp hiss escaped her teeth. Her hand applied pressure to the oozing wound in her side in a poor effort to staunch the flow of blood. "I can see what it does, how it reacts. It's growing. And it won't stop growing until all of her humanity is gone and there's nothing left but an empty shell. It's not made for mortals."

"What isn't?" I asked, glancing between the two of them.

Viema met my gaze, and in that moment I knew I wouldn't like her answer. "The essence. If you keep it, you will lose your humanity. And your soul."

I froze. Memories came flooding back of Nonna's cautionary words to me about the curse. I'd always assumed it was just the God of Death I had to worry about.

"That won't happen," Aiden cut in.

"It won't?" Viema asked, arching a brow. "You mean she hasn't already been acting differently? Like maybe there is something else making decisions for her when her emotions run out of control?"

I watched the muscle tighten in Aiden's jaw. My stomach clenched.

Viema's cracked lips turned up in an enigmatic grin. "That's what I thought. It's a shame there's only one way to stop that."

"What is it?" My heart beat unevenly against my ribs as the essence continued to pulse through my veins.

"That's enough," Aiden said forcefully. His arm wrapped around my waist, gently guiding me from the room.

"I wonder what will come first," Viema called as we left her cell. "Ephraim's plan, your father's threat, or the loss of your wife's humanity? I await the answer, young Prince."

Aiden and Hakan shared a look that I didn't know how to interpret.

The door slammed shut, cutting off her maniacal laughter. Aiden didn't stop, didn't wait to see if Hakan followed. He just led me from the dungeon as quickly as possible, as if to outrun Viema's vague threat. But no matter how fast we moved, we couldn't escape the sound of her haunting laughter echoing through the halls behind us.

FORTY-NINE

WE WERE ONLY IN our chambers for a moment before dinner arrived. I could feel Aiden's eyes on me as I pushed food around my plate. Viema had managed to tell us nothing and everything in the span of a few minutes, and now my mind was whirling with information.

Ephraim was planning something drastic, that much we'd already surmised. But, according to Viema, the more I used the essence, the closer I was to losing my humanity.

"What she said may not come to pass. I won't let it," Aiden said, sensing the direction of my thoughts. He placed his hand over both of mine, squeezing gently.

I sighed, looking into the blazing hearth before us. "It's already begun," I said, stating what we both already knew.

Aiden's hand pulled mine closer, urging me to look at him. "I won't let anything like that happen."

"How?" I asked, not bothering to hide the panic in my voice. "How can you stop this? I've seen the way Seraphine and the others look at me when I use the essence. I know they understand what's happening."

He pulled me closer, determined to make me listen. "No, Esme. We can stop it."

"It didn't sound like something that could be stopped."

Aiden sighed, dropping my gaze to stare at our intertwined fingers. "In order to keep from losing your humanity, you'd have to become immortal. Sell your soul to my father and swear fealty to him until he decides you've served long enough."

"That doesn't sound much like keeping my humanity," I mumbled, frowning. "Aren't I already doing that as his Soul Collector?"

"Normally, I would say yes," he said slowly. "But you've been in this realm for a while now. You've grown stronger than any Soul Collector has before, and you also no longer collect souls for him from the mortal realm."

A thought occurred to me. "Nonna explained that my family served Death because there hadn't been a war in centuries and your father needed more souls to gain power."

Aiden shot me with an uncertain look. "I remember what she told you."

"There's more to that story, isn't there?"

"A little." He stared into the flames, thoughtful. "There's some truth to what you were told. But the debt originally began because of Ephraim's influence over me. I was young and naive. I thought it would help my father see me as a responsible heir." He ran a hand through his hair. "I was wrong."

"And yet, several generations later, the curse on my bloodline remains," I noted.

He nodded. "As far as I know, there are only a few ways to remove it."

"End the God of Death's reign, have him remove it, or kill the demon who offered it."

His brows shot upward. "Oh? When did you learn this?"

"Nadira told me," I said, thinking back to my cousin's words just before everything changed. "I guess Nonna told her. Actually, my entire family knew long before they finally told me."

Aiden pulled me closer so my head rested on his shoulder. One of his wings wrapped around us. "I'm sure they just wanted to protect you."

Mourning slumped my shoulders. "I know. That's all they ever did."

"I'm surprised my mentioning you becoming immortal didn't frighten you." Though he hid his worry behind a smile, I could still detect it.

"It does." My mind filled with every interaction I'd had with Fen and Seraphine. Listening to them talk about their years together. Watching Seraphine caring for Fen as she lay fragile and bleeding.

"But?" he prompted.

I sighed. "I don't know. I've never thought about giving up my mortality to serve Death. I don't know that I ever could."

Aiden leaned away so I had to look up at him. "We don't have to make a decision now. There's still time."

"If we survive whatever Ephraim has planned, then we can discuss it?"

He sent me an unamused look at my sarcastic tone. "We'll survive Ephraim. And my father. Once the threats are gone, then we'll figure out what to do with forever."

"One problem at a time," I mused, leaning into him.

His chest shook with silent laughter. "Exactly. For now, we have your ball to worry about."

I groaned. "I think it's incredibly foolish to ignore Ephraim for the sake of your father's suspicions."

"I agree," Aiden said simply. "Nonetheless, we must play the part my father demands. If we step on his toes now, he'll keep us in his castle, entirely unable to stop Ephraim before it's too late."

"But Viema did say Ephraim had witches with him," I said thoughtfully.

Aiden stiffened. "No matter how many witches he has, they cannot provide him with enough power to claim the entire realm."

"Even if they make more siphoning knives for him?"

Aiden was silent for a moment, thoughtful. The threat of Ephraim's attack hung over our heads every day, and we were forced to sit and do nothing. Luckily, Aiden didn't listen. Our guards remained throughout the castle and in the village. Many even remained in Cordovia to look after my siblings and Prince Elias. If angels attacked, we would be as ready as we could be, even if our forces were divided. We just had to hope that we could get to Ephraim before he came here.

"I'll speak with Hakan in the morning and get a plan together," he said, coming to a decision. Aiden held me against him, wrapping his arms around my waist. "We'll have to leave the next morning if we want to make it to my father's in time for your ball."

I frowned. "It's not my ball. Stop calling it that."

He placed a delicate kiss on my brow. "It is. All the demons my father has deemed important in his realm will be there to honor their new princess. It is a celebration for you."

"Don't remind me," I groaned.

Aiden laughed, kissing me again. It was in our brief moments like this when I allowed myself to forget the threats looming over our heads. My family still wasn't safe. I had no idea what Elias was up to. Ofrin remained skeptical of everything I said or did. And Ephraim was ready to enact the vengeance he'd been planning for centuries.

I stared into my husband's face, recounting all the times our secrets had threatened to tear us apart. But now I feared this next threat might be the final blow.

He shook his head, sensing the direction of my thoughts and silenced me with a kiss. "Tomorrow. We'll worry about it all tomorrow."

Morning came too quickly, and with it, several inches of snowfall.

Aiden woke before me, returning to his study at the first sign of dawn to work with Hakan. I left them to finalize plans to draw out Ephraim and capture him before he could attack. With the essence growing stronger, we all agreed it would be best if I didn't actively seek out the angels. My control over it remained questionable at best.

Instead, I walked to Fen's. Seraphine was staying with her, helping her heal. The path to Fen's cottage was buried beneath the excess snowfall. My trousers were soaked up to my knees by the time I walked through Fen's door.

"Esme, I'm so glad you made it. With the snowfall I was worried you wouldn't be able to come," Fen called. She was sitting in her armchair before the roaring fire. Several blankets were tucked around her shoulders, pinning her in place.

I smiled, happy to see she was awake. "I'm surprised you noticed the snow at all. I can imagine it's quite easy to ignore the cold outside when stuffed under so many blankets."

She laughed delicately as I sat on the sofa. A bruise darkened the side of her face, from temple to jaw. There was a bandage wrapped around the top of her head, covering part of the bruise and, I suspected, the stitching Ridha had to put in.

"If she had it her way, she'd be in the village helping with the cleanup," Seraphine said, appearing from the back hall. She hugged me, sitting at my side.

"Why does that not surprise me?" I teased, eyeing the injured woman.

Fen looked affronted. "Now why would I ignore the very stern commands of my healer?"

The look Seraphine sent her was full of teasing scorn. "We both know if I wasn't here to keep you inside, then you would still be out there or working upstairs."

Fen brightened at that, turning to me. "Which reminds me, your dress is ready, Esme."

Seraphine leaned in. "She refused to stop working on it, even after Ridha told her not to."

"I couldn't very well let the princess show up to her own ball in one of the gowns from her wardrobe. It is a *ball* after all."

"That really wasn't necessary. I would have been fine in something else. You should rest," I said. Their civility made me wonder if they had yet to hear of my betrayal.

She waved away my concern. "Don't be silly, it was no trouble. I did make a few adjustments though. Nothing too big."

"But you are okay?" I asked, noting the stiffness with which she held herself.

She nodded, waving away my concern. "I am. Ridha took good care of me."

I sighed, feeling a sense of relief. "I'm glad."

"So, when do you leave for the north?" Seraphine asked.

"In the morning," I said. "Aiden wants to get there a day early to speak with his father about Ephraim."

"Tarsa mentioned you spoke with Viema." Fen said it simply, like she held no ill will toward the angel, or me.

My brows furrowed. "Yes. She spoke with me and Aiden."

"And?" Seraphine said quickly, pulling my attention away from Fen.

I glanced between the two of them. "She said a few things about Ephraim and what he might be planning, but it was pretty vague. Aiden and Hakan are going over their planned protections for while we're gone."

Seraphine nodded, eyes distant. "And you'll have Tarsa, Hakan, and Killian with you in the north. I don't think Ephraim will attack while you're away."

"What makes you say that?"

She shrugged, watching Fen adjust her blankets. "Ephraim is arrogant. If he is going to attack, he's going to do it when he knows he'll have an audience. If you're not here, he won't come."

"Let's just hope we can get to him before he even realizes we're back from the ball," I said with a sigh.

Fen chuckled, the sound barely more than a rasp. "That is assuming Ofrin doesn't decide to lock you away thinking you're still out to get his crown."

Seraphine's brown eyes were thoughtful as she studied me. "Let's hope Ofrin believes you. If he did hold you captive, that might drive Ephraim to act sooner rather than later."

My throat tightened with apprehension. "How so?"

"Ephraim is arrogant enough and desperate enough to do anything if it means a chance at getting the essence." A flicker of concern showed in her eyes as she spoke.

"And once he gets it, there's no limit to the destruction he will surely cause," Fen added.

I left Fen's cottage with a full stomach and a worried heart. On my way out the door, Seraphine stopped me to explain Fen's lack of fear of Viema. Evidentially Fen wasn't able to remember her attack at all, something that worried Seraphine more than she dared to admit.

Fresh snow had fallen in the few hours I'd been at the cottage. I struggled through the heavy snowfall, quickly losing feeling in my toes as I trudged through the powdery covering on the forest floor.

Something caught my eye up ahead. In the distance I could just see the castle gates, but on the ground, only a few paces in front of me, sat a letter.

I spun around, searching for any sign of someone in the forest around me. The snow remained fresh, untouched. The only footprints denting the snow were my own. Just to be sure, I opened myself to the essence, forgoing Viema's previous warning.

Apart from the guards at the gates, there were no souls nearby.

I studied the letter on the ground. The snow hadn't soaked through it yet, meaning it hadn't been there long.

The hair on my neck stood on end, the way it would if I was being watched.

I quickly scooped it up, noting the lingering warmth of its previous carrier on the parchment. With one final, sweeping glance of the forest around me, I raced for the gate. My fear propelled my feet through the thick snow. Only after I was safely inside the warm castle did I look at the envelope clutched tightly in my grasp.

My name was written across the front in a slanted scrawl I didn't recognize. Whoever left this letter for me...it wasn't Ephraim. I tore it open, nervously eager to read its contents.

Remember, a burden to one is a weapon to another.
Every life bound can be wielded in earnest.
Each one who offers can be returned.
Kill the one who seeks only Death.

I frowned. I read the letter over and over, and every time, it still didn't make sense. But one thing I did know: whoever left this letter had been close by. And they didn't have a soul.

FIFTY

AIDEN WOKE ME AT dawn the following day. The snow was still coming down in large flakes as we rode his obsidian horses.

I burrowed further into him, tightening the cloak around my shoulders. "Shouldn't we have taken a carriage at least?" I complained, not for the first time.

I felt Aiden's chest rumble with soft laughter. "This is faster."

Tarsa rode ahead of us. I'd forgotten how large these horses were. They were unlike any I'd seen in the mortal realm, each large and built like small houses, and black as the night sky.

"It doesn't feel very fast," I muttered sourly.

Killian laughed, moving to ride at our side. "It's not so bad," he said cheerily. "Ridha made some sort of potion that these cloaks were washed in, so they repel water and snow. They'll keep us warm the entire journey."

I studied the cloak I huddled beneath. "She did?"

"You think I would let you freeze while we ride north?" Aiden whispered in my ear.

I shivered at his proximity. Killian and Daemon hadn't let their thoughts on our now-evident romance go ignored. They seized every opportunity to offer jabs at our closeness during our travels.

"We're nearly there," Tarsa called from up ahead. Unlike the others, she remained wary of me. After she'd revealed my bargain with Ephraim, my friends had gradually come to terms with my betrayal. Since they knew I'd thought them responsible for my family's deaths, they didn't hold my choices against me. Only Tarsa remained reluctant to move past the terrible error of my ways.

"Do you think there will be a feast tonight?" Killian asked, elated by the idea.

Daemon gave a disgruntled shake of his head. "Doubtful. We'll be lucky if Ofrin's cook has anything available for us to eat tonight. Everything is being prepared for the ball tomorrow."

"No food?" Killian turned wide eyes to Aiden. "What are we supposed to eat?"

Hakan tossed a small sack at the young immortal. "I had Lurik make you a sandwich before we left. Should tide you over for now."

Killian flashed a thankful grin before tearing into the sack. The aroma of the sandwich set my stomach rumbling. It had only been a few hours since breakfast, but I was already starving.

"Just a while longer," Aiden said softly. "I can send Hakan into the nearby village for food if my father truly has nothing to spare."

I leaned my head back against his chest, turning so he could see my thankful grin. "Thank you."

He kissed me, and it was answered with whistles from our friends around us. Tarsa didn't bother to turn around at the commotion, instead keeping her scowl on the road ahead.

We traveled the remainder of the distance in silence. Snow began to fall around us in heavy sheets until Tarsa was but a mere shadow ahead.

Even through the spelled cloak I could feel the drop in temperature as we grew closer to the mountains. The air was thinner, and the sky was dark as the clouds drew closer to our heads with every step up the mountain path.

Finally, when my lungs felt unable to bear the cold air any longer, large black gates came into view.

The gates were tall enough that a fall from the top would kill a mortal, and armed enough that anyone would be foolish to consider forcing their way through.

Tarsa stopped at the entrance to the castle, frowning at the guards standing high above on the trusses. The stone was unlike any I'd seen. The wall was black as night, like it was encased with Death's power, and it rippled with shadows as if it was sentient and could sense our presence.

The gate was made of steel and looked like its own weapon. Embellishments of roaring monsters and swords twisted through the metal.

Before anyone could speak, the gates swung inward. I felt my heart pound against my ribs in nervous beats as we moved through the entrance.

Guards appeared from hidden places along the wall, coming to stand on either side of us; the path they created forced us forward.

The castle that loomed before us now was nothing like I'd expected. It was lavish; several times larger than the one Aiden lived in. Turrets jutted up to the sky from every corner. Like the surrounding wall, the castle was made from obsidian stone. There was no light to this place, only darkness. Only Death.

We came to a stop at the bottom of a wide staircase. Our friends dismounted first, handing their horses to the waiting stable hands before more rushed over to take the reins from Aiden.

When we were both safely on the ground, Aiden led me up the stairs. I could feel the eyes of every guard watching us closely. My skin itched between my shoulder blades for the entire journey up the stairway until the door finally closed behind us.

Aiden barely spared the pageboy a glance as we were ushered through the door. "Where is my father?"

The young boy looked no older than Alfie had been. "Busy, Your Highness."

"Too busy to welcome his son and his wife to his home?" Aiden's tone had returned to that of the Prince of Death.

The pageboy's face brightened, a mix of nerves and embarrassment. "I-I'm sorry, Your Highnesses. He said he would be down as soon as he could."

"Typical," Hakan muttered under his breath, though I don't think the page heard him.

"Where is he?" Aiden's voice remained cool.

The boy nodded toward the stairs. "In his study."

Aiden grabbed my hand, pulling me along. The page scurried off as soon as Aiden's back was turned.

Guards kept watchful eyes on us as we moved silently through the castle. The itching along my spine increased under their scrutiny. Though that could've been the strange pulse the essence released with each step further into the castle.

I couldn't help but compare this castle to Aiden's. Though it was larger in size, the sheer amount of artwork decorating the walls and the sculptures at the end of every hall made it feel smaller.

Like the exterior, everything inside was dark. We passed dozens of closed doors and half a dozen stairwells before finally continuing to the higher level of the castle. The one commonality that I noticed was the black stone on every surface.

The hall Aiden led us down was surprisingly plain. There were still half a dozen paintings on the walls, but they were small. I didn't take the time to study them before Aiden pulled me to a stop.

A pair of soldiers stood guard on either side of the closed door, staring over our heads at the wall opposite them.

I don't know what Aiden expected of them, but when they continued to ignore our arrival, he scoffed and opened the door himself.

The space beyond was nearly as large as my bed chamber. Two large windows sat on either side of a large oak desk, filling the room with the grey light from outside.

"Father," Aiden said in a voice that was anything but pleasant.

Ofrin looked up with wide eyes, feigning surprise. "Oh, Aiden. I wasn't expecting you so soon. And you've brought Esme, how wonderful."

I scowled, annoyed by his antics. But Aiden seemed to expect them. I stayed at his side as the five of us entered the large study. Ofrin didn't even stand as we stopped on the other side of his desk.

"Did your lackey tell you about Ephraim's latest attack?" Though Aiden's voice was soft, it was filled with carefully blanketed fury.

Ofrin loosed an exasperated sigh. "Do not torture yourself with your friend's betrayal, Aiden. He is too cowardly to attack."

"You're still not worried he poses a threat?" I asked.

"No." Ofrin did his best to look unconcerned, but I could see the hint of fear in his eye.

"You're just worried about me and the threat you think I pose, then?" My skin had grown hot with anger.

Aiden's hand tightened around mine in warning. Ofrin finally met my eyes. There was no longer fear on his face, just a belligerent rage. He looked at me like one might look at muck on the bottom of their boot.

"I think I will speak to your new bride in private, Aiden." Ofrin didn't take his glowering gaze off of me as he spoke to his son. This felt strangely similar to the last time I'd spoken with Ofrin. I wondered what his arrogance would reveal this time.

"Whatever you have to say to her you can say in front of me." Aiden's voice was steely, determined.

Finally, Ofrin turned to his son, standing slowly with a deadly grace. "You will leave us."

The two stared at each other, having a silent battle of wills. I could feel Aiden's thumb stroke across my knuckles. Whatever thoughts were whirling through his mind left him unwilling to part from me.

Aiden dipped his chin in a mock bow and turned to me. His hand brushed across my cheek briefly before he let me go. Only when our four companions left the room with him did Ofrin finally speak.

"You think me a fool for ignoring your increasing power." Ofrin's voice was much more clipped and cold than it had been when Aiden stood at my side. It was enough to elicit a flicker of fear in me.

"No. I think you're a fool for refusing to acknowledge Ephraim as a threat," I replied, forcing calm into my thin voice.

He gave me a disbelieving look. "Ephraim is weak and cowardly. He will not allow his ego to be shattered from an attempted attack."

"So, you are not concerned that the village outside our home has been burned to ash and many of our people were left wounded or killed? Or that he has successfully been sneaking into your realm for centuries without anyone the wiser?"

He gave me a scathing look before turning to gaze out the window. "If Aiden is incapable of looking after those he is responsible for, then that is not a concern of mine. Apparently I should have created another heir to replace him."

"You think him weak." I scrutinized the demon as he remained the portrait of calm before the window.

"Yes." When he turned, he remained in the light of the window, no more than a black silhouette against the bright grey sky. I had to squint just to keep my vision. "Aiden was always weak. Too emotional. Too rash. And then he had to go and claim you as his bride."

"If you think he's so weak, then why bother keeping him as your heir?" I asked, genuinely curious.

He sighed, eyes blazing with anger. "He is my son. Whether he can survive the role placed before him, I do not know. But he is still my son."

"Yet you speak as if you'd rather replace him." I tried to keep the frustration from my voice and failed. Ofrin's brows furrowed as he took a step toward me.

"Once, I thought Ephraim would make a better heir than Aiden. If Ephraim hadn't betrayed me, I would have considered naming him and stripping Aiden of his power."

I gaped at him. "Why? Aiden has done nothing wrong."

His hand came down on his desk, hard enough to make me jump. "He brought you *here*. He lets you grow stronger, more powerful. And now you have your own soul-bound and it threatens everything I have done to keep this realm and your precious mortal realm safe."

The essence pulsed again, shivering down my spine. "How so?"

"I accepted Aiden's offer to your family generations ago as a way to humor him. Nothing more," he said, stepping around the desk so he stood directly before me. My flicker of fear ignited to something more. "Your family was supposed to die out long ago. Yet you've managed to survive. Even though I accepted your parents' foolish offer of claiming their souls in exchange for keeping you alive, members of your family still live. Tell me, how are they liking the desert? I hear their queen can be quite bloodthirsty."

I scowled. "Why accept my parents' offer at all if you just wanted us to die?"

"Aiden was supposed to leave you with Elroy. I knew what his captivity did to you. I knew what you were ready to do to avoid being in chains. Had Aiden simply left you alone, you wouldn't be standing here now."

My wrists burned with the memory of Elroy's chains. A feeling I'd nearly let myself forget these recent months.

"And you've almost managed to awaken the essence fully," he continued, stalking toward me. "You, a mere mortal girl, have somehow managed to strengthen a power so ancient that it should shatter your humanity in a blink. Yet here you stand."

"Here I stand," I said, echoing his words with a scowl. "Why don't you tell me what you want? Clearly there is something you seek, or else Aiden would have been able to remain."

The crooked smile that turned up the corners of his mouth was laced with menace. "I require the essence. The part of my power that lives in you must be returned to me. Then I might consider letting you remain with my son."

"You want it back?" I asked, hesitation growing as the essence stirred in my chest. "Then my family's debt will no longer exist? My siblings will be safe?"

He shrugged indifferently. "I care little for the fate of your family. Only that of my power."

I shook my head. "Not until you promise that my family will be safe."

Ofrin looked at me, aghast. "How long have you begged for this power to be torn from your bloodline? And now you dare to make a bargain *with me*? You are not in a position to strike a bargain, girl."

"All I've ever wanted is for my family to be safe," I said slowly, carefully hiding the anger in my voice. "If you cannot promise me that, then perhaps I can protect them better than you. I will not risk the lives of my family to feed your ego with a false sense of power."

His dark power wrapped its phantom hands around my throat. "You dare insult me? I could have your soul expunged from existence with a mere thought. You would cease to exist in any realm. Do not think my power false, I am not your mortal king."

My lungs burned in my chest, desperate for air as the grip of his power tightened around my throat. When he released me, it was with such force that I stumbled back, gasping for breath.

"You want the essence? Then why not just take it?" I asked when I had control of my breathing again.

Pure death loomed in his eyes. "The protections placed on the essence in your bloodline are too great to penetrate."

"So even you are not powerful enough to take it," I said, laughing.

He snarled at my mockery. My laughing ceased immediately as a dark gleam lit his eyes, bright with whatever thought just occurred to him. "If you returned the essence, my son would live and remain my heir. But," he said, flashing an evil grin, "should you refuse to give me what is rightfully mine, then I would no longer consider him my heir or offer him the protections worthy of the title."

I scowled, not understanding. "You are so concerned with this power that has not been yours for generations, yet Ephraim is out there now posing a real threat to this realm, and you ignore it? Ephraim will follow through on his threat, but you say you would not give your son the aid needed to defend *your* realm?"

Ofrin's eyes bled black as his power swelled. I could feel it cut through the air like a blade. My essence awakened, sensing its call.

"Your obsession with Ephraim is laughable." Ofrin's voice trembled with hatred. "You are letting his words blind you, as is my son. Perhaps you should have died with your family after all."

I was fighting a losing battle with my frustration. Ofrin's petty refusal to see Ephraim as the danger he was would get him killed; it would get us all killed.

"And what about his mother?" I dared ask.

Ofrin stilled. The touch of his power vanished from the room. "What?"

"Aiden's mother," I said, white rage nearly blinding me. "Did you think her weak, too? Is that why you captured her and kept her alive long enough to bear you a son? Because you thought her as weak as Aiden, or Ephraim, and then killed her as soon as you got the chance."

The God of Death stared at me with wide, disbelieving eyes that revealed the depth of his emotions. "What do you know of her?"

"That she was the Angel of Life." I rolled my shoulders back with a bravado I didn't feel. "And that she was also Ephraim's mother."

Though his eyes remained focused on me, his gaze turned distant, as if he wasn't really seeing me anymore.

"Do not speak of her again," Ofrin warned in a pained voice. His eyes hollowed out, suddenly making him appear human and frail. "You do not know of what you speak."

He turned his back, dismissing me. I spun on my heel, moving toward the door before the essence could explode with my growing anger.

"If Ephraim comes before we can stop him," I said, pausing at the door, "he will leave no one alive, and nothing standing. The pain you caused him has haunted his mind for centuries. It is with you he seeks to exact his revenge. Not me. But I have stood in his way often enough that killing me would satisfy him. So, while you sit in your obsidian castle and play at being a false god, we will fight him for you."

Ofrin's sneer snapped into place. "You stupid girl. I *am* a god."

I smiled; the same cold, mocking smile I'd learned from Aiden. "You are nothing but a coward who hides behind the power of his title. I just hope that when Ephraim comes, and we die, you decide to use your power for something other than inflating your ego."

His mouth hung open as I left the room.

FIFTY-ONE

THE MAIDS PULLED AND twisted my hair back from my face so sharply my scalp stung. From the corner of my eye, I saw Tarsa's lips twitch toward a smile with every wince.

"Apologies, Your Highness. We're nearly finished," one of the maids said.

Ofrin had sent two of his servants at the first sign of dawn to begin preparing me for tonight's solstice ball. Aiden left after breakfast to commune with Hakan and Killian about preparations for Ephraim's capture. Since the ball had finally arrived, Aiden was feeling confident that our plan would work.

The day was nearly gone now. It amazed me how one could spend an entire day being bathed, groomed, and fawned over.

"Is there any word from Aiden?" I asked, glancing at Tarsa's reflection in the mirror. While one maid pinned my hair back, the other painted my face with cosmetics. I'd been sitting still for so long I couldn't feel my legs.

"No," she said briskly. Tarsa had disappeared for an hour to bathe and dress but returned as soon as she was ready. Unlike me, she was able to wear a simple, yet elegant, emerald gown with no extravagant jewels or powders on her face. I was certain she even had knives strapped to her legs beneath the gown and along her wrists.

I wouldn't be allowed the luxury of weapons. According to Ofrin, it wouldn't be proper to allow the princess to be armed during her coronation. It was due to his stubbornness that my new weapons were to remain stored with our belongings and not hidden beneath my skirts. But I did have that mysterious letter that had been left for me in the snow. I could feel it burning a hole in my pocket now.

When the maids stepped back I sighed, eager to be done. The young girl who had tended to my hair helped me to my feet, aware of the lack of blood flow.

I let her escort me to the small pedestal placed in the middle of the room. They'd given me a simple black robe to wear after my bath. She began to untie it, pulling it from my shoulders as the other maid returned to the room with my gown in tow.

Tarsa dropped her eyes, allowing me a sense of privacy as the girls lifted the gown over my head.

It fit as I remembered, snug across the bust and flowing to my feet. The gold silk hugged my form beneath a layer of chiffon. The simple design of the gown looked dazzling in the candlelight, shining at every angle.

But there was a new addition I hadn't expected.

The sheer veil of shining gold remained, hanging loose from my shoulders down to my wrists, but beneath those original sleeves was a tighter fabric, butter-soft along my skin.

I fiddled with the ends of the new sleeves, noting how they covered my wrists, hiding the scars that marred my skin.

Strong emotion tightened my chest as I recalled the last time I wore this dress. Fen was far more observant than I gave her credit for.

"Anything else, Your Highness?" the young maid asked. They both stood back now, closer to the door.

I shook my head. "No, thank you."

They left before I'd finished speaking, leaving me alone with Tarsa.

I stared at the reflection in the full-length mirror propped against the wall. Though they'd spent hours on my face and hair, I could still see the person beneath. The bits that were my mother and the parts from my father were all there.

"Here," Tarsa said, stepping into view. "You'll need this too."

When I turned to her, I froze. In her hands was my crown, the golden band embellished with wings and rubies that glimmered in the evening light.

I bent, letting her place it delicately upon my freshly styled hair. It fit perfectly, sitting atop the intricate braids and curls.

The reflection I saw now was worthy of the title Aiden had bestowed upon me.

"Everything is in place," Tarsa said, interrupting my thoughts. "Aiden has everything prepared so we can leave swiftly as soon as this night is over."

I sighed. "We're as ready as we can be, I suppose."

"If Ephraim tries to take you, Aiden will throw himself before you. He'd let himself get killed to protect you. You know that." Her voice held the same sting it usually did. This was exactly why I wouldn't be going with them to hunt Ephraim tomorrow. Ephraim's biggest concern remained acquiring the essence, and Aiden feared what the angel might do to get it.

"You don't approve?" When I turned to her, she kept her expression carefully blank. But there was fire in her eyes as she studied me.

Her lips drew into a fine line. "I swore to Aiden's mother, on her deathbed, that I would do everything to keep him safe."

I held her gaze. "And I jeopardize that."

"You are his weakness," she said. "Threatening you is the best way for an enemy to weaken him."

"That works both ways," I said, stepping down from the pedestal. "If anyone threatened Aiden, I would offer myself in exchange for his life."

Tarsa stepped closer, spearing me with a threatening glare. "And that is where we have a problem. Ephraim knows how you feel about Aiden, about your family. They are your weaknesses. And they will get you killed, or worse, they will get Aiden killed."

"I don't want Aiden harmed," I answered honestly.

"I see that now." Her eyes scrutinized every emotion flitting across my face. "But that doesn't mean your relationship with him doesn't pose a threat."

A knock sounded at the door, pausing our discussion. Killian poked his head in a moment later, eyes squeezed closed.

"Is everyone dressed?" he called loudly into the room.

"If not, we're still coming in!" Daemon's voice came from the other side of the door. He chuckled at his own joke a moment later.

"We're dressed," I said, turning to them.

The two demons entered, stopping in their tracks as they looked at us. Killian's eyes went wide, glancing from me to Tarsa in quick succession.

But Daemon only had eyes for the warrior. I watched the perusal of his gaze, his eyes widening with appreciation. When his gaze landed on her face, it was filled with heated desire.

"Wow," Killian said, wide eyes staring admiringly. "You look...."

"Devastatingly beautiful." Daemon's voice was low and soft with awe.

"Yeah, that," Killian said.

I smiled. "You all right there, Daemon?"

The demon straightened, swallowing deeply as he forced his eyes away from the warrior. "You look good too."

"Thank you," I said, laughing. Out of the corner of my eye, I noticed Tarsa still hadn't taken her eyes off of the demon-born. I cleared my throat, pulling her from her stupor. "You two look nice."

Both demons smiled, finding something to fidget with on their jackets. They were dressed simply but still far more elegantly than their usual attire. Daemon wore a dark green jacket that nearly matched the exact shade of Tarsa's gown, whereas Killian wore a simple black suit.

The young immortal blushed, smiling widely at the compliment. "They're ready for you if you're ready to head down."

I sighed, feeling the arrival of the nerves I'd been working to hide all day. Tonight, I would be paraded before the entirety of the God of Death's court. Aiden had already warned me that there would be far more demons today than he'd allowed at my formal introduction to his court. Not to mention, many of the demons here would be far more hesitant in their acceptance of me.

Daemon offered his arm to Tarsa as he grinned from ear to ear, desire still heating his gaze. She rolled her eyes, striding past without a backward glance.

He chuckled, finally turning to me. "Making progress," he said, striding after her.

Killian smiled at me, offering me his arm. "Milady."

I returned his smile easily, momentarily forgetting the nerves shooting through me. Killian remained a calming presence as he led me from the room. The hall was lined with guards, though none acknowledged us as we strode past. With every step my pulse quickened, my nerves returning immediately.

Daemon and Tarsa waited ahead, just at the top of the large staircase. Voices floated up to us. An indiscernible chorus of noise hinted at the number of guests waiting to meet their prince's new bride.

My heart was in my throat as we rounded the corner, coming to a stop beside Tarsa and Daemon.

"You'll be great," Killian whispered, smiling warmly. I could only offer a shaky smile in response before he squeezed my hand reassuringly and released me.

I watched him trail after Daemon, the two strutting down the stairs and dispersing into the crowd below.

As I followed them down the stairs, I prayed to the stars that I wouldn't trip.

The stairs wound around the wall. Paintings depicting the God of Death in various battles lined the wall above my head. In every painting, he was posed in a way that highlighted his importance, while his own forces appeared far beneath him.

The crowd fell silent as soon as I came to the bend in the stairs, pulling my focus away from the paintings. Killian and Daemon were lost to the crowd, but Tarsa remained a few steps ahead, waiting.

Blood pounded in my ears as I searched the now-silent room for the familiar eyes I knew would bring me comfort.

Every face was turned to me, studying and judging me as I remained frozen. I scanned the crowd for those blue-grey eyes, unable to move any further as my nerves rooted me to the spot.

Finally, he appeared. Aiden left his position along the wall, slowly making his way through the crowd. His hair was groomed, the sides tied back from his face, and like Killian, he wore all black.

He smiled, and there was such love in that smile I could've wept. Aiden came to a stop at the last step, holding his hand out to me.

My feet were finally able to move again. Tarsa stepped aside, letting me pass. When my skin touched his, the tightness in my chest eased.

Aiden pulled me close, letting his other arm wrap around my waist as he bent to whisper in my ear. "You are exquisite."

I flushed, turning just enough so my lips brushed his. "As are you, dear husband."

His smile widened. Aiden gently led me through the crowd, paying no mind to the dozens of eyes watching us closely.

The crown felt heavy on my head as the weight of their stares settled on me.

The doors to the ballroom were propped open, allowing us to enter the vast chamber. Flowers of every kind hung from rafters and tapestries along the walls, giving off an intoxicating aroma. I wondered where all the greenery had come from in the dead of winter. The room itself soared three stories high, seeming to touch the heavens with its vaulted ceiling.

I gaped openly at the space, making Aiden's smile grow. The crowd of people parted easily, and I took note of the silence trailing in our wake.

Demons watched us like wolves ready to devour their prey. Women, men, and children all stood by, each eager to see what their king made of us.

The king in question sat on a throne so large it resembled a carriage. Like the stone that made up his castle, it was pure obsidian. The high back came to sharp points above Ofrin's head.

As the gathered crowd turned to his dais, we came to a stop before him. I could feel the tension radiating from Aiden. When I left Ofrin's study the night before, I'd immediately told him what was offered to me. Aiden was not pleased, and though he wouldn't admit it, I knew he was worried.

"Welcome," Ofrin said in a voice that easily carried through the room. "It is with great pleasure that I formally introduce my son's new bride to my court."

He was met with wild applause. Aiden squeezed my hand, offering me a comforting smile.

"Esme has served me valiantly for years, as has her entire bloodline," Ofrin continued, sending a sly grin my way. "Now, she shall serve me as the wife of my son and heir. For when my time as Death has ended, she will aid in his reign."

The crowd cheered again. Cheers of my name and Aiden's sounded over the applause.

"Come," Ofrin said, holding his arms outward. "Let us celebrate this happy union with a celebration in their honor."

As the applause continued, I caught Ofrin's eye. There was no kindness in his gaze now. Only hatred.

Aiden gently pulled me toward the dance floor, putting his father at our backs.

"Are we leaving already?" I asked in a hushed whisper.

He smirked though his eyes revealed the worry he hid. "No, they want to see us dance."

"What?" I asked, growing more nervous as the crowd parted to reveal a painted dance floor in the middle of the room. Aiden took me in his arms, holding me close like he once had in Cordovia. But the dancing of wanderers was not the same as royalty. There was no structure to our dancing. "Aiden, I can't dance like this."

His hand moved along my spine, inching down as the music slowly began. My eyes widened as he leaned forward, and our cheeks settled side by side as he whispered in my ear.

"Follow my lead, Princess."

Aiden spun us around in elegant circles and loops as the music played. It was a song I'd never heard and yet I felt it in my bones as the essence thrummed along with it.

As the music grew, Aiden released my waist, spinning me around him. The crowd cheered as I curled back against his chest.

The smile that spread across his face was dazzling. I gasped as he leaned me back, dipping me low enough that I was sure I would fall.

He leaned in to press a delicate kiss against my lips. I was vaguely aware of the crowd's cheers as Aiden straightened, bringing me with him.

When the music came to a stop we were met with momentary silence before applause split the air.

Aiden still held me in his arms, even long after a new song began.

"Do we leave now?" I asked, breathless under his stare.

His eyes darkened with an emotion that made my toes curl. "If you keep looking at me like that, we're going to have to."

I smiled, moving to kiss him again.

Someone coughed, interrupting us. With a frustrated sigh Aiden pulled back, turning to face the demon.

"Yes?" Aiden asked the man. I frowned, recognizing him as the one sent by Ofrin after Viema attacked the village. I still couldn't recall where I'd heard his voice before.

"I was wondering if I might steal your bride for a dance." Though his voice was kind, his eyes conveyed a danger that made me uncertain. The essence pulsed in my chest, unable to detect any sign of a soul from this strange demon.

"Of course," Aiden said, reluctantly. He turned to me with guarded eyes. "One dance. You won't be out of my sight for a moment. We will return home immediately after, okay?"

I nodded, forcing a smile at the man.

Aiden turned to the demon. "Be careful with her."

"I will guard her with my life," he vowed.

He took my hand, holding me at arm's length as Aiden disappeared into the crowd.

"Royalty suits you," he said, spinning us slowly around the dance floor. This was nothing like dancing with Aiden. Where Aiden was all fluidity and warmth, this demon moved in a stiff, staccato style that made it difficult to anticipate his next move.

"Thank you," I said politely. "I'm sorry, but I don't believe I ever caught your name."

"My friends call me Gavriel." His eyes were critical as he studied me. Almost like he was desperate to read my thoughts.

"And we are friends?"

He shrugged, pulling us further from the center of the dance floor. "That has yet to be decided."

"And why is that?" I asked, desperately trying to recall where I'd heard his voice.

"Your fate is not yet determined, young Princess," he said, leaning in close so as not to be overheard. "And once it is, that will determine the manner of our friendship."

I frowned. "I don't understand."

"We have a friend in common," he said slowly, careful to keep his voice low. "He thinks you will play an important role in the events to come. I have learned to trust his judgment. No matter how far-fetched it may seem."

A sliver of recognition settled over me. "And who is this friend?"

The smile he gave me was as threatening as any sword. "He lingers in shadows and plays deadly games. I believe you owe him a favor now as well."

The strange letter burned in my pocket. Reek. This was Reek's handler. My heart began to race against my ribs, tightening my lungs and shortening my breath.

I scanned the surrounding crowd, desperate to find Aiden. But we had moved to the far corner of the dance floor, farthest from the dais.

"You were with Drusilla as well," I said, memories flooding back to me as my panic rose. "I heard you speaking with her and Alvize in the castle."

He nodded, smiling like a proud teacher. "Very good. You are perhaps smarter than your bloodline suggests."

"Why are you working with them?" I asked.

"Drusilla had hoped to join Ofrin's court," he said with a dismissive sigh. "Her men only planned to follow her. They all thought themselves worthy of serving the God of Death, and offered themselves as spies."

The song came to a close, but Gavriel didn't release me. "And did they spy on me?"

"Of course," he said. "At least until you had Drusilla killed and bound her men to you like dogs. Once they became compromised, I left them at your mercy. I'd hoped your bloodthirsty husband would kill them, but alas, he trusted you to keep them under control."

"They are under my control," I argued.

Gavriel's grin was edged with condescension. "Are they? Tell me, do you know how a soul-bond works?"

"I know enough."

"So, no." His smile only grew at my frown. "They are bound to you now. They must obey your every command. But do not mistake that for loyalty."

"You're saying they're working with you to kill me?" My anger was quickly rising as we remained half-hidden in shadow.

He shrugged. "I think you should figure out if it's them you have to worry about, or who they serve."

"They serve me."

"Do they?" he asked, smiling wickedly. His eyes landed on something over my head, and whatever he saw made his smile grow. "I think you should pay more attention to the people around you, young Princess.

You'll find your biggest threats are not always the ones who flaunt an army."

The tension in the room changed. I could feel it like a tangible sting along my skin as Gavriel finally released me.

"Good luck, Esme," he said, backing away. "I do hope we meet again. Reek would be so disappointed if his newest friend was killed so soon."

I watched him vanish into shadow, magic unlike any I'd seen before.

A hand gripped onto my upper arm, pulling me away from the crowd. I spun around, ready to strike, when a familiar voice hissed in my ear.

"It's me," Tarsa snapped. "We have to get you out of here. Something is happening."

"What?" I asked in a panicked whisper. "Is it Ephraim?"

She yanked me closer to the exit. "No. Hakan is getting Aiden now."

The crowd had gone deathly silent. Everyone stood so still they looked like statues as they stared, wide-eyed, at the dais.

I couldn't help it—I had to look. But what I saw sent my stomach spiraling.

"Wait," I said, tugging against Tarsa's hold. "It's Jadan."

The warrior paused, glancing over her shoulder. The white-haired demon was bound, beaten and bleeding on the dais. There was a gag over his mouth to keep him from speaking, though he barely looked conscious enough to do so.

Ofrin stood behind him, eyes on me as if he'd known where I was in the crowd the entire time.

This felt all too familiar. The essence fluttered in my chest, sensing my rising panic as I stared at the scene before me.

Killian joined us at the back of the room. "We have to get out of here, now," he whispered harshly.

"Aiden?" I asked, letting my gaze sweep the room in a desperate attempt to find him. Whatever was about to happen, it wouldn't end well.

"He's—"

His words cut off with the booming of Ofrin's voice.

"While tonight was supposed to be a time of celebration," he said, eyes never straying from my face, "it seems we have some unfortunate business to attend to as well."

Hushed whispers ran through the crowd. As parents began to turn their children away from the dais, my stomach dropped.

"One of my most trusted spies has betrayed me, and this court," Ofrin continued. "He has joined forces with my son in hopes of using his young bride's newfound power to overthrow me. They want this realm for their own. The princess even admitted to me last night that they planned to form a defensive army."

The crowd cursed loudly, shouting angry words into the air.

"That is not what I said," I whispered anxiously.

Killian scoffed. "Well clearly he only heard what he wanted to."

"But this doesn't make sense," I whispered to my companions. "Aiden is still his heir. Does he not understand that he will rule this realm some day?"

"Ofrin has always thought of himself as a true immortal," Tarsa explained quietly, watchful eyes on the crowd for any sign of a threat.

"He thinks he will never die and Aiden will never take the throne," Killian added.

I scowled at the God of Death. "Then he is a fool." Ofrin's threat to expel Aiden as his heir filtered through my mind as I scanned the crowd for my husband. If Ofrin truly thought he would never die, then there would be no reason to keep Aiden alive. Especially if I refused to give him the essence.

Daemon joined us along the wall. "What is going on?"

Killian shook his head as we slowly backed toward the exit.

"I've since learned that my son and his bride doubt the strength in my veins." Ofrin's voice echoed through the room. "They think me weak for not calling arms to attack the angels. They think me weak for wanting my essence returned. And they think me weak for distrusting their sham of a marriage."

Daemon took a step forward, catching sight of the bloodied and bound demon kneeling before the god.

Tarsa stopped him with a white-knuckled grip on his arm. "You can't interfere. If you do, you will die."

"That's my friend. I am not leaving him up there like that," he argued, voice pained.

Tarsa pulled him further from the crowd. "If you try to interfere, you will fail. There is one of you, and hundreds of them. You will die for nothing. And you will get the princess killed."

Daemon's focus returned to the dais, his gaze full of turmoil. Jadan's head hung over his chest. If he was conscious, we couldn't tell.

As we took another step toward the exit, Ofrin called out to us.

"Esme," Ofrin exclaimed, freezing us in place. "Do join me, dear."

I remained cemented in place, aware of everyone's eyes turning toward me. Aiden was nowhere in sight.

Ofrin's guards moved, gripping tightly onto my upper arms so I was forced through the crowd. When I was only steps from the dais, they released me. I stumbled, nearly crashing to my knees. But Aiden was there.

His hand settled at my elbow, steadying me. Though his expression was the carefully blank mask I recognized, I could still see the worry in his eyes. Whatever was about to happen, he hadn't expected it. Knowing he was as surprised by this turn of events as I was only made my nerves worse.

Ofrin smiled, cold and threatening. "Wonderful. It would be a shame if you left now and missed the finale."

"What is this, Father?" Aiden called over the growing rumble of the crowd. "Esme and I have not worked against you. In fact, we've done the very opposite."

"So, you haven't been meeting in private with Ephraim, or forming your own army to steal my throne?" Ofrin asked in a voice that suggested he knew the answer.

Aiden's brows furrowed. "Of course not."

"Can you say the same for your wife?" The voice that spoke now sent my heart racing.

Ephraim stepped from the crowd, grinning like a boy who'd won a prize. "Miss me?"

FIFTY-TWO

My stomach plummeted. "Ephraim?"

Aiden's gaze bounced between his father and the angel. "Father, what is this?"

The crowd behind us had grown uncertain. Nervous whispers began as they shifted back, hoping to avoid potential bloodshed.

"I offered him a deal," Ofrin said with arrogance dripping from every word.

Ephraim continued to stare at me like he'd just gotten everything he'd ever wished for. I scowled at him, refusing to let him see my fear.

"A deal?" Aiden seethed. Anger radiated from him in a deadly pulse as he fought against the violence raging within.

Ofrin clasped his hands behind his back, completely at ease. "Ephraim wants to take the essence from Esme."

"I'm aware," I muttered dryly. The angel smirked at me.

"And you're just going to let him take it?" Aiden spat.

Ofrin flashed an unamused grimace. "Of course not. I only need the knife his witches created to take the essence from her."

Ephraim's confident smirk slipped, revealing his confusion.

Viema had spoken true. Ephraim did have more than one siphoning knife. We just had to hope he also didn't have more of his deadly poison.

"Guards." Ofrin barked the word like a command.

Three of his guards moved forward, surrounding Ephraim. The angel scowled as two pinned him between them, the third searching his pockets.

"What is this?" He thrashed in their unyielding grip. "The deal was I take the essence."

"Yes," Ofrin said simply. "You would help me *take* the essence, but you would not get to *keep* the essence. You are only my spy, after all. You did your duty. You lured the princess away and proved she'd rather destroy my reign and take the power for herself than simply return the essence and leave this place."

Ephraim struggled against the guards' hold, only stilling when they found his knife. Something flashed in his eyes as he glanced toward the God of Death, but he made no further attempt to break free.

Aiden stepped closer to me, shielding me with his body as the guard handed the weapon to Ofrin.

The God of Death met my gaze, and there was no humanity left in his eyes. "That essence is mine. And I intend to have it returned."

I felt it awaken at his words, responding to my rising anger and fear. It wrapped around my heart in a deadly caress. If he tried to take it, it wouldn't go willingly. And it would cost me my life.

"So, you lied about the protections on the essence," I said, recalling his claim the night before.

Ofrin chuckled coldly. "No. It cannot be removed by force alone. But the angels have been so kind as to create a device that siphons the essence for me." A wicked gleam shone in his eyes. "You just won't survive the process. Though based on your last experience you might have already assumed as much. And as it turns out, I don't really care if you live."

"A loophole," Ephraim smirked. He appeared unconcernedly at ease, though he remained surrounded by Ofrin's guards.

More demons appeared, surrounding us. The crowd continued to hastily move toward the exits.

Hakan and Killian appeared on either side of Aiden and I, close enough to interfere should things get bloody. I felt Killian turn and put his back to mine, protecting me from behind.

Hakan drew his sword, holding it in front of him as he took his place at Aiden's side.

"Move aside, Aiden, and I'll consider letting her soul remain bound here," Ofrin said sternly. He moved down the dais steps, forgetting Jadan's slumped form altogether.

"You're lying. You won't let her exist in any way after claiming such a scandal against us," Aiden spat. I could feel fear and anger tightening his muscles, preparing for battle.

Ofrin stood face to face with his son. The two were nearly matched in height, but where Ofrin hid behind the intimidation of his title, Aiden shuddered with real power behind his rage.

"You have created an army, have you not?" Ofrin demanded.

Aiden's jaw clenched with restraint. "Not against you. I've explained our plans against the angels. Plans which you have dutifully ignored, along with their threat."

Ofrin's face scrunched with disgust. "What threat? It was easy enough to lure their king into my own domain. All it took was a promise of a gift and he came running. Just like the fool I know him to be." He smiled dangerously. "You shouldn't have doubted me, son."

Laughter cut off the demon's words; it was laughter befitting a madman. A chill winnowed through me. "Wait," Ephraim said, fighting his maniacal giggles.

The guards previously holding him were slumped on the ground, bleeding. Two unfamiliar faces stood in their place, one with wings a shade darker than Ephraim's, and the other with a scowl so deadly he looked as if he didn't need the bloody weapon in his hands.

The essence pulsed through me, responding to the swarming presence of angels and my rising panic. I hadn't been able to feel them in the crowd; there were too many demons here blocking the essence's strength.

Ofrin glared at his guards. "What is this?"

Half of the guards turned toward Ofrin, swords raised toward his throat. The other half glanced around uncertainly, just as confused as the rest of us.

"What the hell?" Killian breathed.

"Did you really think I would trust your word?" Ephraim crooned. His wings were tucked in tight down his spine, ready for battle.

"You expect me to hand over my own essence?" Ofrin scoffed with arrogance, apparently not registering the danger in front of him. "It is mine, boy. Go back to the detestable realm you crawled out of."

The angel turned his eyes toward me, icy gaze piercing. I fought a shiver as he stepped toward me, ignoring Aiden entirely.

"I have fought for this essence for centuries," he said to no one in particular. "I intend to take it."

"It does not belong to you," Ofrin snapped. Aiden shifted, drawing a knife from its hidden place at his waist.

"It does not belong to you either, Ofrin," Ephraim mocked. That same maddening laughter glinted in his eyes. "You gave it up when you accepted the offer your son extended. You have no further use for it."

The God of Death's expression darkened. I felt the rumble of his awakening power, shaking the floor as Death walked forward. "I am power, boy. I am a god. You are but a runt in a species doomed for destruction. Do not think yourself worthy of something that I created."

Ephraim raised a brow. "Oh? And I suppose you'll say my mother was also a runt?"

Ofrin stilled. I watched his eyes shoot toward Aiden in a brief glance before he turned back to the angel. "She was not cowardly like you."

"Do not speak of her!" Ephraim shouted. His rage rattled the walls with the sudden swell of power.

I jumped, gripping tightly to Aiden's jacket. My heart continued to race in my chest, awaiting the inevitable.

"You do not deserve to even have memories of her." Ephraim spat at Death's feet. "Have you even told your son the truth of who and what his mother was? Why he could never truly rule this realm? Why it is about to be reduced to ash?"

Ofrin's voice was like ancient, splintering ice. "That's what this is? You have brought your kind here, under the pretense of war, because of *her*?"

"What is he talking about?" Aiden demanded, looking to his father for any sort of explanation.

Ofrin didn't spare him a glance, instead keeping his gaze on the angel. But Ephraim turned. He didn't look at Aiden though; he looked directly at me.

His smirk returned, knowing and arrogant. "Ask your wife. She's known since you first brought her here."

I was already shaking my head adamantly when Aiden turned to me. "I told you all I know. I don't know what else he's speaking of."

Ephraim's chuckle crawled along my skin like prickling spiders. "Really? You mean even after you found out who our mother was, you never once realized what that meant for your husband?" Aiden and I studied him curiously, neither of us understanding. Finally, the angel sighed. "Are the two of you always this daft or have you just become adept at playing it?"

Ofrin's gaze cut to Aiden for a brief moment, but that was all the confirmation Aiden needed. I felt his limbs slacken with disbelief as the claim Ephraim spoke rang true. Aiden would never be able to wear his father's crown; not with his angel's blood.

"And now you are without an antidote, thanks to you," Ephraim continued, bringing us back to the present. His gaze cut in my direction. "I have an army of angels ready to avenge their people, and a plan that's been centuries in the making to get retribution for my mother's fate." Ephraim began to strut around us, enjoying this far too much.

Ofrin sneered in my direction. "You are the worst of fools."

"And you let an angel and his soldiers into your very home believing you were enough to dissuade any pretense of their threat, Father," Aiden snapped. "Do not compare her discrepancies to the chaos you have created."

Cool steel settled along my throat. "Can I kill her yet?"

My blood cooled. Viema.

Aiden spun toward me, eyes widening as the angel stepped forward. Killian cursed, his surprise that the angel had slipped past his defenses obvious.

"Aren't you supposed to be in a cell?" I asked, forcing calm into my voice. The essence hummed, growing stronger with my rising emotions until I could feel nothing at all beyond its immeasurable power.

Viema laughed, digging the knife in. I felt its sharp sting as a drop of blood trickled down my neck. "I was. Until help arrived."

My eyes met Aiden's. They had attacked our home. But if Viema got out...

"Just be glad this particular blade isn't poisoned," Viema whispered in my ear.

"Without that antidote, only Death can save you now," Ephraim teased, grinning at the god. "Well, he's strong enough to probably save one of you at least."

Ofrin puffed out his chest, insulted. But he wasn't fooling me. If we didn't have Ridha's antidote, we were all dead.

"I'm surprised you let your lackey live, Ephraim," Aiden said, pulling Ephraim's attention from me, "since she did intend to betray you by taking the essence for herself."

Ephraim smiled coolly, but it was Viema who spoke. "I have seen the error of my ways."

"It's a shame there weren't any survivors," Ephraim added, keeping his gaze locked on my husband. "Your warriors fought bravely for such a weak bunch. But we cut through them easily."

Aiden's fists shook with barely controlled rage as he glowered at his brother.

"Did you let her believe she could keep the essence?" I asked, drawing Ephraim's attention. Viema's knife tightened against my throat. "You let her believe that before, but we both know you have no intention of letting anyone other than yourself keep it."

Ephraim smiled approvingly. "You are smart for a mortal, aren't you?"

Viema's grip loosened. "I am worthy of it," she claimed proudly. "I will prove as much."

I watched the considering look Ephraim gave her. Blood trickled down my throat, her knife leaving a mark that mirrored the one he'd given me the year prior.

His eyes brightened with a deadly idea. "Go to Cordovia," he said suddenly, smiling wickedly. "Bring me her siblings." My stomach dropped to my feet. "Only when their bodies lie at my feet will your greedy betrayal be fully forgiven."

I felt Viema nod behind me as his command rang through the air. My heart pounded against my ribs, panic growing. The essence hummed violently, begging to be set free.

"Well, now that's settled," Ephraim said casually.

Half the guards in the room removed their helmets, dropping them to the stone floor with a loud clang. It was these guards that held swords against the demons, who thirsted for the blood Ephraim would allow them to shed.

This was his army.

"Well, then," Ephraim called. The attention turned to him, and he soaked it up. His gaze swept the room before first settling on Aiden, then me. "Let's get what we came here for."

FIFTY-THREE

VIEMA YANKED ON MY hair, pulling me flush against her chest. "Come any closer, Prince, and she dies."

Aiden paused mid-step, gaze hardening as if he could sense the stirring power of the essence within me.

When his eyes met mine, I was ready.

I struck hard, letting my elbow hit her where I knew it would hurt most. Viema grunted, loosening her grip enough for me to wriggle free. Blood dripped down her freshly stitched wound and onto the floor.

Aiden struck before she could take another breath, driving his knife through her heart.

He took me in his arms, cupping the nape of my neck before her body hit the floor. I gazed up at him, seeing the same fear in his eyes that I felt in me.

I nodded, pulling away as he placed the hilt of the knife into my palm. He turned his back on me, fighting the onslaught of angels moving in our direction.

Killian stayed by my side, striking quick and true with the small sword he carried, his bow useless in the chaos.

An angel rushed at me. I barely dodged the blow of her knife before mine found its home in her chest.

As she fell to the floor, I caught sight of the dais. Tarsa and Daemon stood there, holding Jadan between them as they carried his unconscious body to safety.

Everywhere I looked, we were surrounded. For every demon, there were three angels. Children screamed; parents were cut down. It was mayhem.

I saw one young demon backed into a corner, trapped by two angels. I moved closer, ready to interfere on the young demon's behalf, when a blinding light split the room.

I covered my face, blinking against the harsh light as the room slowly dimmed. The angels cheered, moving toward the dais and the rift that had opened beyond it. I stared, dumbfounded, as angels began carrying demons through the portal, taking them prisoner.

Aiden was at my side in a moment. "Get to Tarsa and Daemon, they'll get you out of here."

"We can't run from this," I argued. An angel aimed a knife at my heart, but Aiden pulled me out of the way before they could strike. The blade had nothing to cut through but air.

"If you stay, they will kill you to get that essence." His touch was gentle as he lifted my chin, forcing me to meet his gaze. "Whether it be my father or Ephraim, someone will get to you."

I started to argue, but he kissed me. The kiss was brief but contained all the emotions he couldn't put into words. I pulled him closer, not wanting to let him go.

"Go," he said, pulling away. Tarsa was at my side in the next moment, cutting down two angels at once.

People fought all around us. Demons fell, angels fell. It wasn't just a vengeful bloodbath, it was an all-out war.

Angels swarmed us, attacking from all sides. Tarsa defended us well, though she couldn't fight for both of us.

I struck and spun and went through the movements I'd been taught, but my skills were no match for these angels. Especially not in a gown which tangled around my ankles with every stride.

Ofrin appeared, thrusting his power outward to strike down ten angels at once. It cost him, though; I could see the lines forming around his eyes as exhaustion settled in. Something was wrong with his power. Death should not be so weak. This knowledge unsettled me as Ephraim caught my eye, a devilish grin turning up the corners of his mouth.

With Tarsa otherwise occupied and Aiden fighting elsewhere, Ofrin made his move.

"You really are stupid if you do not run," Ofrin said, getting closer.

I smiled, but it was the essence staring back at him through my eyes. "I don't run from cowards."

He snarled, lunging. He held Ephraim's siphoning knife in his hand, aiming for my heart.

I tightened my grip on my knife, preparing for the blow.

Something slammed into Ofrin, sending him crashing to the floor. The knife skittered away, lost to the frenzy.

Ephraim smiled at Ofrin's unconscious body. "For someone who thinks himself a god, he is possibly the weakest demon I've ever met."

I bared my teeth in a snarl. "You're not getting the essence."

He raised his brows, mocking. I watched the guards carry Ofrin out of the ballroom, likely taking him somewhere to hide.

"You think so little of me, Esme," he said, stalking forward. "It wounds me."

"Then this is really going to hurt." I lunged, sinking my knife into his waist, clear to the hilt. The air rushed from his lungs as he stumbled.

"You just don't learn, do you?" he said with surprising ease.

His hand wrapped around my wrist, pulling himself free from my knife. My eyes went wide as I watched the wound close before my eyes.

"You will never be strong enough to fight me," he said, leaning close so I could hear him over the chaos. "You are a mortal. A girl. You will never be enough to defeat me."

A sword sliced Ephraim from shoulder to hip, making the angel lurch back with a cry as his wing dangled at an odd angle.

Aiden was there, sword dripping with blood as he moved to stand beside me. "But I am."

Ephraim laughed, coughing up blood as his wound slowly knit itself together. "Our mother would not be pleased to see her sons fighting."

I felt Aiden grow taut at the mention of his mother.

The essence widened in my chest, filling every part of me as I glowered. "You will not take the essence from me."

Both turned to look at me. My voice was unrecognizable, a raw power that rattled the ground and shattered the windows. The angels staggered against the rumbling as they continued to drag demons through their portal.

Ephraim's eyes glimmered with arrogance. "We'll see." And then he lunged.

Aiden appeared first, sword raised. But Ephraim easily predicted his move.

The angel held a knife in each hand, and my cry of warning wasn't enough to stop what happened next.

My heart faltered as Aiden fell, a poisoned knife sticking out between his ribs. Ephraim stood over him, smiling at me as he roughly yanked the knife free. The groan that escaped Aiden's throat tore at something deep inside me, unleashing the darkness hidden there.

I screamed, letting the essence spill outward. Every angel moving toward me exploded into shadow, ceasing to exist. The essence pounded in rhythm with my pulse, filling my ears so all I could hear was its steady drum.

Ephraim's eyes went wide with fear. "What have you done?"

Aiden didn't get back up. He lay face-down in a growing pool of blood, black veins spider-webbed outward from his wound.

My heart hammered in my chest, threatening to break free of my ribs. "You'll pay for that."

Ephraim heard the change in my voice. His eyes scanned the chaos around him, noting the number of his angels that had died at the hands of the demons. At the hand of my fully awakened power.

"Retreat," he called into the room. "Retreat."

I smiled. "You do that," I said, voice low and cold. "You're good at running. But know that no matter where you run, I will find you. You hurt my husband. You threatened my family. You will pay."

He spun on his heel, trailing after the angels retreating into his portal. I followed, ignoring the blood weighing down the hem of my gown as I walked through the destruction.

I picked up a fallen knife, flipping it in my palm to test its weight. When Ephraim paused at the mouth of the portal like I knew he would, I threw the blade.

He wailed as it pinned his wing to the wall just beyond the portal's reach. Those that remained of his army yanked it free, tossing the knife to the ground as the wing hung limp.

"You'll regret ever crossing me, Princess," Ephraim swore.

I flashed a razor-sharp smile. "No. But you will."

As soon as Ephraim disappeared through the portal, it vanished.

There was a moment of silence in the ballroom after the remaining angels were slain. I forced a deep breath into my lungs, struggling not to choke on the stench of blood.

"Esme!" Killian's panicked cry echoed through the silent room. He crashed to his knees at Aiden's side, eyes wide and panicked.

I raced through the room, fear only enraging the essence further as its power continued to stir inside me.

I knelt in a pool of blood, ignoring the warmth as it soaked through my gown. Aiden's skin was too pale, the grey of death. "Is he alive?" I asked, voice croaking with the onslaught of my emotions.

Killian nodded, keeping a hand pressed to the bleeding wound. "He is."

"Why isn't he healing?" I asked in a shrill, panicked voice. "He's supposed to be healing. He doesn't protect my family anymore. He should be at his full strength."

"It's the poison," Hakan said, kneeling at my side. "He needs the antidote."

"But we don't have any." Panic was muddling my mind.

Tarsa stood near Aiden's head. "And who do we have to thank for that?"

"Not now, Tarsa," Killian snapped. She looked taken aback by his uncharacteristic outburst but recovered quickly.

"He needs Ofrin," Hakan said, bending to scoop Aiden's long form into his arms. "You heard Ephraim. Only Death can save him now."

I nodded, panic slowly receding as the essence took over. A plan formed in my mind as Hakan began to carry Aiden away.

"Killian," I called. The young immortal turned, horrified expression buried beneath the spatter of blood. "In the pack with my weapons, you'll find three letters. Deliver them accordingly. Return as soon as you can."

Hakan paused at my tone, glancing over his shoulder. Killian remained rooted to the spot, glancing between Aiden's prone figure in Hakan's arms and whatever he saw on my face.

"At once, Princess," he finally said, bowing deeply before retreating through the doorway.

Hakan led us from the room, past the bloodshed. Ofrin's remaining guards stood nearby, uncertain about what to do now that the battle was over and their god had been taken away.

A thought occurred to me, stemming from the essence still filling my veins.

I turned, racing in the direction I'd seen Ofrin's guards carrying him to safety. Hakan yelled after me, but it was Tarsa's predatory steps I heard following me.

My heart pounded in my chest as I followed the path the essence steered me toward, letting it take me to Ofrin.

"What do you think you're doing?" Tarsa snapped, stepping in front of me.

I looked at her with hostile eyes. "I am going to save Aiden. And then I am going to hunt Ephraim."

She stared at me for a moment, dissecting whatever she saw on my face. Finally, she nodded, stepping aside.

"I am with you," she vowed.

I only nodded, returning to the path the essence carried me down. Tarsa remained at my back, a steady beacon of strength as I let the essence take a little more of my humanity. Until all that was left was a shell with my old memories and a power so raw and potent it shook the realm.

Ofrin was in a small library at the end of the wing. He only had two guards with him, but they looked as if they'd been expecting us.

"Ah, Esme," Ofrin said, the picture of health. "I was wondering how long it would take for you to come see me."

"You look relatively unharmed," I noted, moving to stand above him. Ofrin didn't even bother to stand from his chair as I moved closer. Like Ephraim, he didn't think of me as a threat. He was wrong.

"I am Death," he said as if that explained everything. "I am the most powerful person in existence. Of course, I would be stronger if my essence was returned. Then I could return to the hall and end this battle easily."

"The fight is over," Tarsa cut in. "Ephraim has fled with his men."

Ofrin chuckled, its malicious sound slithered along my skin. "As I suspected he would. Such a coward."

"Aiden is hurt." My voice broke, revealing the extent of my remaining emotions.

"Pity." Ofrin sighed, leaning back in the chair as if to get comfortable. "You could save him."

Wry amusement haunted his silken timbre. "Why would I do that?"

"Because he is your son." The essence rumbled in my chest, a beast readying to pounce.

"Give me the essence and I'll consider it," he said, smiling like he'd won. Like I was desperate enough to consider his offer my only option.

It was my turn to smile. The essence warmed, sensing the familiarity of the god before me and the darkness within.

"Actually," I said, leaning closer so he had to crane his neck to look at me. "I think I'll keep my essence and take yours."

He had a mere second to look afraid before I attacked.

Tarsa cut down his guards easily, leaving me to focus on the task at hand.

The essence within me spread outward in a wave, crashing into Ofrin. He cried, head tilted back and mouth open in a scream. The same tether that existed between me and my soul-bound extended from him, and I saw it reach toward me in slow-motion.

I leaned over the God of Death, getting close enough to whisper in his ear.

"Your soul will remain mine," I said, letting the essence blanket my mind as I pulled more power from him. "As long as I live, your soul is mine. You will not know peace until I allow it. You have caused too much pain, too much destruction to know peace. You took my family, and you refuse to help your son. You will pay for the blood you've shed."

Then I ripped his essence from his body.

FIFTY-FOUR

Tarsa dropped her axes in time to catch me as I stumbled back.

"Are you all right?" Her gaze darted between me and the former god's slumped form.

My lungs worked in overdrive as I forced air into my body.

I felt whole, new. My limbs felt stronger as I righted myself. I didn't shake, didn't ache from battle, and my wounds healed instantly. Yet there was a humming along my skin as my newfound power transformed my body into something more.

As soon as I began to answer, the ground shook. A quake so strong the windows shattered, and the stones began to fall from the ceiling.

We stumbled to the doorway, clinging to any stable surface we could find.

"What's happening?" I yelled over the noise. The essence snuffed out my concern a second later. Few emotions remained beyond my concern for Aiden. All I could feel was the overwhelming strength of my power.

Tarsa's eyes widened as she looked at me. I felt her grip my arms, forcing me to look at her. "What did you do?" There was a panic to her voice I didn't understand.

More of the ceiling began to fall around us. Guards raced down the hall, seeking safety. Those who'd attended the ball screamed and ran from the destruction. Each gown left a bloody trail in its wake.

"Esme," Tarsa snapped, forcing my attention back to her. "What did you do?"

The essence within me vibrated with the newfound strength it held. I felt the two entities meld into one, braiding together in a thread of vast power.

There was no end to it. For as long as I searched, I couldn't find a limit to the power I now contained.

Within it I felt every soul once tied to Death now tied to me. Tethers stretched out from my soul in every direction. Hundreds, thousands. I could feel every soul in this realm, and many in Cordovia as well.

Tarsa took my hand, yanking me into the fleeing crowd. "We have to get to Aiden. Maybe we can get him back to Ridha and she can find some way to save him until more of the antidote can be made."

The power calmed my growing panic. Somehow, the essence recognized the root of my concern and offered me a solution.

"He doesn't need Ridha," I said, pushing past Tarsa.

"She's the only one who can make the antidote."

I paused, turning to face her amidst the chaos around us. Her eyes remained on my face, ever watchful of my emotions.

The essence hummed in my veins, burning steadily. I reached into it, seeking the power I needed.

Everything stopped. The ground stopped shaking; the castle stopped falling. Even the people stopped screaming as they looked at me. I felt my tethers to their souls open up, allowing them to see me for what I was.

Tarsa gasped. "You took it."

I nodded, letting the true strength of the essence filter out of me, burning across my back as the power transformed me.

Gasps filtered through the hall as the demons openly gaped. Tarsa stepped back, hands falling limp at her sides.

She knelt a moment later, dipping her chin in reverence. Slowly, everyone in the hallway followed her lead, kneeling before me.

And as the power of Death consumed me, as I felt it filling my veins and replacing my mortal strength with its own, I felt my husband die.

ACKNOWLEDGEMENTS

Another book and even more people to thank for helping me transform this book from a pile of sand into a glorious sand castle.

To Bucky—people say you can't read, but since you hear me talk about storylines at all hours, I like to think you can read by now. Forever my emotional support pup!

To my extraordinary beta readers—you guys helped me transform early drafts of this story into something resembling a book. I am so thankful for your feedback!

My editors, Melissa and Kelsey—your invaluable notes gave me confidence in the things that deserved it, and solutions to things that desperately needed it. I cannot thank you two enough for helping me work through this book. You're phenomenal!

Whimsy Book Cover Graphics—once again you have designed a fantastic cover! You are a dream to work with, and an absolute creative mastermind. Thank you for designing a beautiful cover! I'm sad to see you closing your metaphorical business doors, but I can't wait to watch your publishing career flourish.

Melissa Nash—your gift for cartography is endlessly impressive. Thank you for once again creating a beautiful map for Esme's new adventures!

Lastly, to my readers—your love for Esme and her journey has been so fun to experience. From your sweet comments and messages, to your beautiful artwork, I truly am eternally grateful for your support and love! Thank you!

About the Author

Audrey Steves is a fantasy author located in the Midwest. When not writing, or reading, she often spends her time with her dog or horse. You can connect with Audrey on her social media pages or her website.

Follow Audrey Steves online.
@audreysteves on TikTok
@author.audreysteves on Instagram